THE
ORE MONGER

THE ORE MONGER

THE SPRITE SAGA — BOOK ONE

ZAID HASAN

Cover Art and Design Copyright © 2024 by Ciara Hartford
Author Photographs Copyright © 2024 by Daniel Tilley

ISBN 979-8-9914467-0-9 (Paperback)

First Edition: November 2024

Published by Zaid Hasan
www.hasanfantasy.com
contact@hasanfantasy.com
Instagram: @hasanfantasy

To my wife and my parents,

It is no easy task to have extraordinary love for an ordinary man. Your unconditional, limitless support for my art is more than I deserve. Though I fail, I aim to be a better husband and a better son everyday.

And to Samia,

Forgive me for every way in which I've failed you.
Rejoice with me for every way in which I haven't.

I miss you in every single moment I draw breath.

Poetry of Samia Siddiqi
1965 - 1996

I wish I was all cured
I wouldn't want anything more
I would do all the things I ever wanted to do
I would not worry about getting through
I'd work, play, and have a child
Go out in the world and just be wild
There wouldn't be any limits or restrictions
There would be hard work with conviction
My baby and I would find a place of our own
Just live together in peace
All alone

A Note to the Reader

Dearest Reader,

Injustice is a powerful theme in the novel you're about to read, but there would be no greater injustice than beginning this note with anything but my undying, boundless gratitude for your interest in my art. Without your wide eyes and open hearts, there'd be little power in my drive to publish this work. What good is a storyteller without those who sit and listen to the tale? Truly, thank you.

I must admit, though, that the above show of gratitude wasn't among the original purposes of this note. One of those purposes is to relay to you the Trigger/Content Warnings of the novel. There's quite a few, listed below my signature at the end of this note, and I do urge you to read them. My aim in including graphic content is never to upset or offend anyone, particularly not those of you who picked up my book.

The other original purpose of this note was to prepare you for the unexpected, genre-bending elements you might encounter in the novel. It took me three years to write this book, and throughout that time, I was often asked, "In what genre does your book fall?"

To this day, I fail to answer the question without a blank stare. I don't want to sound pretentious, but the genre does feel unique in some ways. The closest category I've found is Science Fantasy. The book includes typical fantasy elements, like monarchies and swords and magical creatures, but it also mentions hover vehicles and sophisticated lighting panels and the biochemistry and genetics of creating life.

That's all. I just wanted you to understand this information before walking into the Prologue. It's not true High Fantasy, and it's not true Science Fiction. Perhaps the real purpose of this note, I'm realizing now as I write it, is more selfish in nature than I'd like to admit. After three years, I finally got to answer the question.

Thank you again, and I truly hope you enjoy the journey.

Yours,
Zaid Hasan

TW/CW: graphic violence, murder (including one child), loss, manipulation and coercion, cults and organizations/institutions of control, non-graphic discussion of sexual abuse and grooming, mild sexual content, frequent nudity in non-sexual contexts, war, genocide, pregnancy loss due to medical complications

AERTHOMNI

LIBRARY
DOCKS
X

THE LIBRARY

BROTHEL
DOCKS

Smith
Courtesan X

**Dissolved
Nations**

Cobbler

Red-La River

CereCenters
4 to 22

Ona'

Bard

Merchant

Northern
Hills

ADERA

Luila

CereCenters
1 to 3

Soil
King

**Gerontocratic
Villages**

CereCenters
41 to 44

SunSidian
Settlement

Evic

Lahu

SunSidian
Settlement

MoonSide

Peak Haven Mountain

Ward
Fall

PEAKHAVEN

LARSO

Salta

Kinara
CereCenters
23 to 40

SunSidian
Settlement

ARLUN

Guardleaf
Grove

Deepweed

West
Wine

WEST
DOCKS
X

**Agrarian
Townlets**

The
HearthBark

INNKEEPER'S
RANCH

EVEREMBER
DOCKS
X

Meradil

SunSidian
Settlement

Pyari

PeakHaven Pass

DORUH
DOCKS

EVEREMBER

X SOUTH DOCKS

Balyan Ocean

Bibi
Sands

THE KNOWN
CONTINENTS
OF
THE ALL-SPHERE
1628 DG

Eloa

BEAUTY'S
X DOCKS

Small
Beauty

River

SunSide

Anairda
Village

CereCenters
45 to 56

X OLD
SUNSIDE
DOCKS

Lily
Beach

FlatHat
Empire

Ardev
Ocean

FeatherKnife
Mts.

Nivyan
Hollow

Nysabaan
Desert

X NEW
SUNSIDE
DOCKS

PANAERTH
DOCKS
X

SEABED

The Canopy

PANAERTH

Lily
Beach

FlatHat
Empire

Ardev
Ocean

FeatherKnife
Mts.

Nysabaan
Desert

The Canopy

PANAERTH

THE MEGAMOTHER

Theocratic-Monarchy *SunSide*
Date *50th Day of Month 10, Year 767 DG*

THERE IS NO PART OF a pixie's body that is harder to cut through than the neck. Over thousands of years, their cervical vertebrae have hardened more than those of nymphs and faeries. General Drof-Fa recalls this fact from her training as she eyes her sword carefully and considers her options.

Beyond cutting through the neck, Drof-Fa can elect to tear the ruling monarch apart using her connection to the Radiance. With a wave of her hand, she can leave the MegaMother's body shredded. A far more effortless option, yet lacking intimacy.

The faerie General does not shy away from intimacy in battle. Particularly not when victory is so close at hand.

"Surely, General," the MegaMother moans, sitting on her knees, "this isn't the hardest decision you've had to make today."

The MegaMother's sienna skin glistens against silver armor and crimson bloodstains. The faerie Lieutenant, Hay-Ro, stands over her, his puce hands outstretched, moving in a steady, circular motion. The movement keeps his connection to the Radiance intact, holding the monarch restrained. Any lapse in focus, and she'll have her fingers around his neck before he can blink.

Drof-Fa continues to eye her blade as she speaks. "Your age has made you impatient."

A soft smile loosens the MegaMother's expression. "I am only impatient for retribution. But there cannot be justice without transgression. Get on with it."

The faerie General turns to the pixie monarch with fire in her eyes. "This *is* an act of justice." She takes three heavy steps toward the captive queen, lifting her muscular legs over a guard's bloody corpse. "Justice for my clan."

"I have eradicated inequity, Drof-Fa," the MegaMother responds assuredly. "For all citizens, including the faeries."

"You have chosen the *animals* over your own kind," Drof-Fa spits the slur.

The MegaMother releases a tense breath. "You know they are called the Doruh."

"I know naming your pets does not make them family."

The queen lowers her gaze from the towering General. "It is that ideation that proves your clan to be a stain on the entire Mega species."

"The nymphs *and* the pixies would still be crawling in the mud without faerie contributions. We are thrice as populous as—"

"Numbers do not garner the faeries special treatment, General. The quality of your character does. You have proven that quality today. Tell your lover that these were my last words, once he's usurped my throne."

"I will tell him when I bring him your head." A wicked smile appears on Drof-Fa's face.

The MegaMother's body relaxes. "You've made your decision, then?"

"I have." The faerie General steps forward until she is standing next to the MegaMother, looking down at her.

The queen looks up at Drof-Fa. Her tone softens. "After you marry Red-Lo, you'll be the MegaMother. Do not rule harshly. We've worked hard to get to where we are. I know you cherish SunSide as much as I do."

"Save your sentiments. I'll be the MegaMother only in name. My duties will remain those of the General."

The monarch raises an eyebrow. "And why is that?"

Drof-Fa's sword rises, voice throbbing with pride. "Because I don't rule. I conquer."

She grasps the MegaMother's hair tightly in one hand and in a swift, calculated motion, forces the blade into the back of the ruler's neck. The MegaMother gags on the blood and tissue expelled from her mouth, and a soft, anguished cry escapes her. The pixie's hardened vertebrae survived the blow.

Drof-Fa tugs hard and dislodges the sword from the now gaping flesh before slashing down again.

Success. The MegaMother's mangled body drops to the ground. Drof-Fa lifts the head up until it is at eye level, examining it with a smile. "SunSide is ours, Hay-Ro." She awaits his response, but when she hears only silence, she turns to the Lieutenant.

Hay-Ro scans the room. The royal guards lay scattered and mutilated. Most of the faerie resistance drown in pools of their own innards. Drof-Fa sheathes her sword and places her magenta fingers on his shoulder, breaking him from the trance.

"I have taken oaths, Drof-Fa." His voice wavers as he raises his bloodstained hands between them. "To save the lives I've taken today."

Drof-Fa nods. "I understand it is difficult for a salver to see the value in bloodshed, but I promise, it is necessary." She turns and guides his gaze out of the grand throne room windows, to the star-speckled sky. "When the Four rise tomorrow, you'll be Head Salver to the Red-Lo Royal Dynasty. Your counsel will save lives all throughout the kingdom. And the blood you drew today is the reason for that."

A clearly forced smile spreads across the healer's lips.

"Come," she says, raising the severed head again. "Let's deliver this prize to SunSide's new MegaFather."

They enter the chamber known as the Forum, tightly grasping the MegaMother's head, and every eye in the room turns to the doorway. Audible gasps and screams of crippling terror bounce off the walls, joined soon thereafter by devastated sobs. One teal-skinned Mega even falls to his knees and begs the Four to give rest to their fallen queen.

The General finds her lover standing at the far end of the chamber, at the foot of a magnificent stage. His skin shimmers turquoise, and long hair flows down over his shoulders and chest. Pointed ears besiege gray eyes, void of pupils and irises—common traits amongst all Mega. He sees the prize in her arms and his expression lights up.

Drof-Fa takes long strides toward him over a polished stone floor embedded with gems. Moonlight spills in through tall windows and strikes the gems, bringing them to life like waves of glitter. With every step, escalating sobs rise from a rotund wooden table occupied by the Members of the Assembly of the Radiance.

It satisfies her to no end.

She then passes three animals, standing before the windows at sharp, focused attention: a goat, an ostrich, and a ewe. She's careful not to acknowledge their inferior presence, even as their heads tilt downward in respect.

Drof-Fa hands the severed head to Red-Lo. He cradles it on his palms and lifts it up to look into the MegaMother's dead eyes.

"You are responsible for this outcome," he states plainly. "I told you we would not sit idle and allow a pixie to cleanse SunSide of faerie footprints. This is the result you begot." He lowers the head and holds it carefully in one arm as his fingers settle softly on Drof-Fa's cheek.

"How many of our warriors remain, my love?"

Her gaze falls. "Not many, darling."

"And how many of theirs?"

Her eyes rise again and she smiles. "Not any."

He smiles in turn and wraps his arm around her waist, pulling her toward him until their lips collide. When they part, Red-Lo carries the head over to the wooden table and sets it down in the center. The Assembly Members standing nearby take a wide step back. One turns around and vomits onto the floor. Red-Lo faces the three animals on the other side of the room.

"Change," he commands. They remain still, unflinching. His volume erupts and startles everyone in the room. "Change!"

At this order, the ewe's silvery fleece shifts to an enchanting olive tone, and her wool melts into flesh. Her front two legs become thin arms, and her face shrinks into the features of a woman. Flowing dark hair cascades out of her scalp, down her back and over her shoulders.

The ostrich's neck turns into smooth, stunning bronze skin, and its beak shrinks into full lips and a nose. The goat's horns descend into its head, and its hooves become fingers.

The three Doruh shapeshifters stand nude before the room. While the two males—formerly the ostrich and the goat—avert their eyes from the MegaMother's head, the female keeps her chin level, meeting Red-Lo's gaze with fiery defiance.

One of the Assembly Members falls back into her seat and speaks. Her voice emerges strained, no louder than a whisper. "What have you done, Red-Lo?"

Red-Lo turns to her confidently. "I have saved SunSide. I have preserved the legacy of the master clan."

"This is treason!" exclaims another Member.

Red-Lo grits his teeth. "Treason? No. Treason is this legislation you all planned to pass tomorrow."

Realization dawns on their expressions and they exchange glances before a third speaks.

"That is why you chose today." Member Shersa says. He turns his head to look at the three shapeshifters still standing along the wall. "To stop Doruh Liberation."

Red-Lo smiles. "Correct. The theocracy will recognize me as SunSide's MegaFather, and then you will discontinue the Liberation. My reign dawns tomorrow with the new year."

"We will do no such thing, Red-Lo," the first Member says, drying her cheeks on the sleeve of her robe. "Mother's final legislation will be fulfilled."

Red-Lo's tone hardens. "*That* title is no longer hers. From this day forth, you will call me, 'Father.' I don't want to hear that word uttered in this kingdom unless it refers to Drof-Fa. *We* are now SunSide's Mother and Father."

Drof-Fa fails to contain her smile at Red-Lo's conviction.

"Why do you care if the Doruh are liberated?" another Member inquires, his tone defeated.

"Because faerie blood was shed to put the shackles on their wrists. And I will not let the work of my forefathers be erased in the name of your misguided 'equity.' The faeries will not be replaced by"—he lifts an accusatory finger toward the shapeshifters—"these *beasts*."

He turns back to the table. "Humans!"

Drof-Fa realizes she hadn't noticed the three humans seated at the table when she first entered the room. They are recognizable by their clans' unique anatomy: one with wings, another with an exoskeleton, and a third with fins and piscine nares.

Red-Lo continues. "You and the *animals* share a common evolutionary line. Do you believe they should be freed?"

The three human leaders silently convene and then the one with wings nods and stands. "We absolutely do not condone enslavement. We were invited here this week to celebrate the Liberation by both limbs of SunSide's government: the theocracy and the monarchy."

The human turns from Red-Lo to face the Assembly Members. "However, all three human clans possess a strict desire to avoid involvement in the affairs of other governments. It is now evident that the theocracy and the new monarch are no longer in agreement. We decline to comment."

Red-Lo's smile returns. "Excellent. A silent bystander is preferred to a vocal ally."

Member Shersa rises to his feet and leans over the table, toward the humans. "This heathen is not our new monarch. And we will never recognize him as such."

He turns and speaks to Red-Lo directly. "How can you *possibly* think that we would call you 'Father,' after what you've done? SunSide has never had a violent transition of power before, and it certainly will not for you."

He scans Red-Lo from forehead to boots and back up again, then snickers condescendingly. "The faeries have spent centuries as SunSide's ruling class. Mother and her predecessors spent decades ensuring that one's clan is not the deciding factor on their social status. They brought a balance to SunSide that didn't favor the faeries simply because of their greater population."

He turns again, this time to face the Doruh servants in the room. He gives them a reassuring smile. "And as of tomorrow's decree, they will have abolished bondage in SunSide forever."

His smile fades and he turns back to Red-Lo. "The Doruh were born of our mistakes. They deserve autonomy, amends, and above all, our apologetic support. And *you*"—he spits the word with venom—"will not get in the way of that."

Red-Lo steps toward the Member until he can feel Shersa's breath on his face. He speaks softly, but confidently. "It is sentiments like those that invigorate my resistance. You are fortunate I know the value of the theocracy—that so many of my clan and my followers practice your primitive religion. Otherwise, your head would be sitting on that table next to hers."

He steps back and speaks loudly again. "I have a proposition for the Assembly."

Member Shersa laughs. "There is nothing you can offer us that would incline us to authorize this madness." Other Members around the table nod and join his laughter.

"Not even the Temple Complex?" The laughter stops, and Red-Lo continues. "My first act as MegaFather will be to raze over half of our commercial district and build the largest compound of shrines to the Four you've ever seen. The Complex will serve thousands of devotees at a time, and will be structurally indestructible. Over a hundred warriors will act as security."

Drof-Fa steps up beside Red-Lo. "Generations of MegaParents have denied the theocracy's request. But your new MegaFather will not. His plans are feasible."

Member Shersa scoffs, but when he turns to his colleagues, his expression dissolves. The theocrats slowly give him short nods and then lower their heads in shame.

His jaw hangs slack. "You can't be serious."

"Do it, Shersa," an elderly Member instructs.

"But he murdered—"

"Do it. It is the will of the Four that the Temple Complex be constructed to worship them."

Member Shersa turns to the three Doruh servants, hours from freedom, standing across the room. "I'm so sorry," he says, his voice trembling.

All three servants burst into sobs. The ostrich drops to his knees and buries his face in his hands.

Member Shersa looks down at his feet. His voice is little more than a mutter. "The Assembly of the Radiance hereby recognizes Red-Lo as

MegaFather of the queendo—" He pauses. "—kingdom of SunSide, by the power granted to this theocracy when anointed by the Four. May they illuminate his life and his reign."

He forms a circle with his fingers and places it on his forehead, a salute of fealty and admiration for the reigning monarch. "Glory to Red-Lo, the MegaFather! Glory to the Four!" The remaining Members follow his lead.

Red-Lo holds up four fingers and places them over his own forehead, a reciprocal gesture showing respect to the theocracy. "Glory to SunSide!"

His words echo throughout the vast chamber, over the gut-wrenching sobs of the enslaved Doruh.

CHAPTER 1

THE TWINS

Occupied Territory *MoonSide*
Date *16th Day of Month 6, Year 1628 DG - 861 Years Later*

THERE'S STILL ONE PATRON IN Sultana's Chai Palace well
after the suns have retired. Salessa, the chaitender, keeps her light
brown eyes on him as she washes and dries white teacups with deep
blue floral designs. They complement her outfit—a light blue shalwar
kameez with a white dupatta tied at her hip.

The patron, clad in a hooded cloak, sits cross-legged on a soft red
pillow at a short wooden table, one of many around the room. He pulls
a teacup of ginger chai to his lips and sips softly. With his hood up,
Salessa only sees the bottom half of his face. She makes out a beard,
pink skin, and nothing more.

He's a Mega.

Salessa wonders if he is a nymph, pixie, or faerie, and breathes
deeply to still the anxious hum of her heartbeat. *So many ways to dis-
tinguish them,* she laments, *but all beneath the skin. The universe is either
poetic or sadistic.*

There's no comfort in closing the chai house alone, but Sultana left urgently about an hour earlier on a personal matter. The patron entered half an hour later, minutes from closing time. Towering over her, a blade on his hip and a voice deep enough to rattle the countertops, she didn't feel particularly secure to refuse him service.

As if her inner debate touches his pointed ears, the customer waves his hand toward a stack of napkins on another table. A single napkin delicately dances through the air and lands on his table, where he gently sets his teacup on top of it.

Salessa's racing heart slows a bit, but not entirely. He can connect to the Radiance, so he isn't a faerie, but he's still a solitary stranger in close proximity late at night. She continues to breathe deeply until he finishes his chai and approaches the counter. She finally sees his gray, pupil-less eyes under the hood.

"I'm sorry for coming in so late, Salessa," he apologizes. Her hand subconsciously moves to her name tag and she pointlessly removes it. "I've been traveling and was in dire need of some chai. I'll be sure to come earlier next time."

"I hope you enjoyed it," Salessa responds, forcing an uneasy smile onto her lips.

The Mega places two round, polished stones on the counter to pay for the chai. "Best I've had in quite some time."

She nods and continues smiling until he exits and disappears into the night. A long exhale releases the tension holding her body hostage. She marches to the door, locks it, and turns the sign to "Closed," then takes a moment to survey the area around the chai house for any potential threats.

She can see the gates to the village. Evic is a speckle on the farthest edge of MoonSide. The Red-Lo River is just beyond the gates, which marks MoonSide's border. The entire village is a narrow strip—a string inhabited by little more than broken-down homes, destitute clay huts, and the warming fires of the hungry and impoverished.

Salessa watches as the flames light the towering walls that separate the Doruh residents from the prosperous faerie settlements on the other side. Had the walls been built of glass, Evic would feel less like a village and more like a zoo, where occupying faerie citizens watch from their balconies, eating handsome meals as Doruh children search for scraps to survive.

The walls' opacity is all that keeps the villagers' dignity intact.

Behind the counter again, she quickly continues her closing procedure but stops when she hears a knock on the door. She groans, louder than intended.

"We're closed!" She keeps her eyes on her tasks.

"Open up, Lessi," a familiar voice, muffled by the glass, calls.

Salessa turns to see a young woman in a kurti that was once white, but has now been painted deep red from absorbing her blood. There's a long gash along her forehead and bite marks all over her throat. The entire right side of her face is bruised and swollen.

She bears a striking resemblance to Salessa, the only difference being their hair; while Salessa's is mid-length and as black as the night sky, the woman's is dyed auburn and cut just above her shoulders.

Salessa sighs and unlocks the door, allowing the woman to enter and sit on a stool at the counter. Trying to hold her frustration at bay, Salessa asks, "Why aren't you resting at home, Naina?"

"I need chai, Lessi," Naina growls. "Badly."

"You need rest and medication. Go home. I'll bring something on my way back to numb your pain."

Naina gestures broadly at the teacups behind the counter. "That's the only medication we can afford."

Salessa rolls her eyes. "One cup, then we go home."

Naina nods. "Deal."

"Masala chai, cardamom, gulabi, doodh patti?"

"Cardamom," Naina replies, and Salessa puts some water on to boil and drops a small spoonful of cardamom seeds into an empty teacup.

"I hope Sultana's not here," Naina remarks.

Salessa turns back to the counter and faces Naina. "Would I make you free chai if she were?"

She watches as blood drips from Naina's hand onto the counter. Pulling a roll of bandages from a low cabinet, she takes Naina's hand and wraps the wound on her sister's palm.

"Even if you lost your job, you still have another one." Naina chuckles, then winces when Salessa ties the bandage tight.

"I'm serious, Naina. How much did you make tonight?" She turns back to the boiling water and pours it into the teacup with the cardamom seeds.

"Sixteen hundred," Naina announces, beaming.

Salessa moves the cup to the sink and strains the seeds out of it, pouring it directly into another teacup. "You made sixteen hundred and you can't afford medication?"

"Every stone goes to the fund."

Salessa pours a little milk and two spoonfuls of sugar into the chai and stirs. She places the cup onto a small saucer and sets it down in front of Naina, whose eyes fixate on it like a starved wolf's.

She releases an exasperated sigh. "I'm exhausted, Naina, worrying about you night after night."

"Don't worry about me." She blows on the chai before sipping it. "I'm fine."

"Your blood is on the counter." Salessa grabs a nearby rag and runs it along the wood, wiping the drying blood away.

"Sorry," Naina responds. "But I promise you, I'm fine. I can't just walk away when they keep betting on the other fighters. I get massive payouts."

"Why do they keep betting on the other fighters when you keep winning?"

Naina smiles. "Because the other fighters walk into the Pit with something between their legs that they're confident will secure their victory. They don't realize they'll be exiting without it." She winks and gulps the chai in a single sip. "And neither do the ones betting."

Salessa knows how much Naina loves her job. The money may be *part* of the reason she continues to do it, but it's certainly not the entire reason.

"Sultana paid you today?" Naina asks, gesturing to a sack hanging from her sister's hip. She extends her hand out for the pouch.

"You'll get blood on it." Salessa hesitates.

"I'll wash it," Naina counters, her tone unwavering.

Salessa reaches into the pouch, pulls some stones out, and hands them to Naina to count.

"Why is she paying you so little?" Naina's eyebrows furrow and a growl grows in her chest.

"Maybe things have been slow here," Salessa lies.

"That's not your problem. I'll talk to her."

"No," Salessa says quickly, heart drumming against her chest. She takes the pouch off of her hip and releases the remaining stones onto the counter. "I was planning on separating out two hundred for…"

Naina's eyes expand as the truth dawns on her. "No, Lessi. No, no, no. Not again." Her volume rises. "We talked about this. You promised."

"They need me, Naina." Salessa keeps her voice low and steady. Firm.

"I need you!" Naina reaches a new decibel. Salessa puts her fingers to her lips as if her sister is one of her students, and Naina brings her volume back down. "I'm getting torn apart every night, near-death at least once a week, and you're *still* taking money out of our hands for other people?"

"They're not 'other people.' They're my students and most are orphans."

"You didn't take their parents from them, the Bravers did."

Salessa draws in a deep breath to temper her mounting frustration. "I'm all they have and—"

Naina's volume returns. "You're all *I* fucking have. You are so quick to show up when someone needs saving, but not when that someone is me."

Thick silence dwells in the air as Salessa realizes Naina is right. Her responsibilities should lie with her sister before anyone else.

Naina takes a deep breath and steadies herself, then places her hand gently on Salessa's. "All we have is the fund and each other. I'm tired of being stuck in Evic because we can't afford to leave."

"There's more keeping us in Evic than money," Salessa says plainly.

Naina pulls her hand back. "What do you mean?"

"We can't leave until we agree. What are we leaving Evic for?"

"Blood," Naina responds with cold, calculated conviction. "If I'm headed out of MoonSide, I'm out for blood."

Salessa shakes her head. "We can't keep doing this, Naina. Without experienced help, your plan is suicide."

"You know I have help."

Salessa rolls her eyes. "Fifty of your friends from the Pit won't make it through battle with thousands of Bravers. I was talking about the Revolution."

"The Revolution is dead," Naina asserts.

Salessa takes a deep breath, steeling herself to speak the truth aloud. "And our chances of justice with it. They're the only ones with enough experience to face the MegaFather and the Facilitator."

The wound in Naina's eyes looks deeper than any on her skin. "I won't let them get away with it."

Salessa pauses as her throat tightens. Her voice enters the air, strained. "They already have. It's time we start fresh, Naina. I know you want to go to SunSide, but when we raise enough money to leave, we should head west."

She slides the stones toward Naina. "Go home and put it all in the fund. I'll stop trying to help everyone."

Naina rolls her eyes. "You've said that before." She gathers the stones and pockets them before heading for the door.

"I love you!" Salessa calls out.

"I know you do…" Naina's voice trails off as the door shuts behind her and she disappears into the night.

Salessa closes up the chai house and tucks the key into one of her pockets, hoping she doesn't forget to return it to Sultana in the morning on her way to the school. Her typical walk home is extended when she deviates toward the local salver's apartment.

Journeying through dim streets, Salessa becomes a quiet shell of a person, the default stature of the Doruh in any setting where they might encounter a Braver. The warriors are funded by SunSide—dedicated by duty to the MegaFather, the kingdom, and, by extension, the faerie settlements in occupied MoonSide.

She clutches the dupatta by her cheek. It's pulled over her head to provide some coverage from patrolling faerie eyes, and holding it stable around her face makes her feel safer.

It's cloth, but it's something.

Keeping her pace steady, Salessa doesn't gaze into the streets where the Bravers roam. She turns, instead, to the settlements' towering walls, covered in artwork created by Doruh youth. The walls provide them with a canvas to express their resistance to the SunSide-sanctioned violence that comes with the occupation. Littered across the walls are slogans like "Free MoonSide," "A New Alphocracy Will Rise," and "May the Twins Protect Us."

Each of the sentiments breaks her heart, but the idea of a second Alphocracy coming into power seems particularly hopeless. The first iteration—twenty Alphas who governed MoonSide—rose to power after the Uprisings that achieved Doruh Liberation. After six hundred years of freedom, SunSide invaded and began the occupation. All twenty Alphas, and all remnants of the Uprisings, were decimated.

Walking briskly past the slogans, Salessa spies a grand mural painted on the wall. It depicts the MegaFather with blood dripping from his gray eyes, holding a large stone in each hand, as legions of Bravers prostrate at his feet. The words above his head read, "The Ore Monger."

The nickname started as a joke, one that Salessa found to be rather clever. The MegaFather discovered the substance known as ore seven years prior. Likely a mineral of some kind, to this day, no one knows its true origins, and the MegaFather refuses to disclose them.

Like wildfire, the "Ore Monger" title spread ravenously across Aerthomni. Soon, the amusing nature melted away, leaving a tone of odium. It became a slur—a volley against everything the MegaFather and his familial dynasty had done to the Doruh and to the other Mega clans. It even found its way to SunSide, where dissidents chanted it to his face.

He took it as a sign of treason, even when simply overheard in passing conversation. There'd been hundreds of arrests over it, including some of Naina and Salessa's friends, who were never seen again.

Salessa reaches the local salver's apartment, embarrassed to knock on her door so late at night. She is a kind older woman who knows how much time and money Salessa has put into the school and the students.

"I can pay you tomorrow on my way to the school," Salessa offers.

The woman shakes her head with a warm smile. "Don't be silly. After all you've done for the community, it's my pleasure."

The small vial of liquid nestled in her pocket, Salessa heads home to find Naina lying on her back on a straw cot. She appears bathed, her injuries cleaned, and she uses a small stick of sharpened wood to pick her opponent's flesh out of her teeth.

Salessa drops the vial of medication onto Naina's cot.

Naina opens her eyes and sits up. "I told you I didn't need it," she growls.

"I didn't spend any money. She gave it to me." Salessa takes a seat next to her on the cot.

"We don't take charity."

"It's not charity. It's called being part of a community. We help each other. This is something we could have more openly if we start a fresh life away from MoonSide. Somewhere safe."

Naina doesn't seem to be listening. She pops the top of the vial and throws her head back as she pours the blue liquid down her throat.

"I'm sorry about the money," Salessa says sincerely.

Naina pauses before she responds, eyebrows raised, surprised by the apology. "I know you want to help them, but once we're out of MoonSide, we're on our own. No more community, no more help. We can't trust anyone but each other."

"So you *were* listening to me," Salessa says with a half-smile.

"I'm serious, Lessi. I need to be able to trust you."

"Of course you can, Naina. Nothing is more important to me than our safety."

Naina nods. "SunSide or not, we can't stay here with the Bravers hovering. He'll find us again."

Salessa stands. "Get some rest. We can start planning tomorrow."

She walks over to her side of the hut and changes from her shalwar kameez into an old, loose nightgown. She is exhausted from teaching during the day and then working the double shift at Sultana's.

Slumber grasps her instantly. Horrific visions plague her; the image of two small girls hiding in the brush outside of a home appears in her mind. She sweats as a caravan of Bravers arrives at the dwelling and a green-skinned Mega with one arm enters the front door.

Light flashes through the windows, clothes tear, and angry wolves bark and growl. Her face contorts as she remembers the smell of burning flesh. The green Mega strides back out of the home and speaks, his voice so cool it sends chills down Salessa's spine.

"Find the girls," he says. "Do *not* kill them. I need them alive. They're special."

She wakes, confused. There are typically more images and sensations before her slumber is interrupted. Something woke her early.

Rather, *someone.*

There's a knock on the hut's door. It's the middle of the night. The twins live privately; the only visitors they would expect at this time are Bravers, who are known to perform random interrogations in the middle of the night that don't end well for the Doruh residents.

Salessa gets up and approaches the door, her heart slamming the inside of her chest.

Naina has awoken as well. "If it's them, stand back and give me room." She sits up, ready to shift at any moment. A low, vicious growl escapes her throat. Her teeth begin to sharpen and elongate, and a lupine muzzle forms on her face.

Salessa reaches the door and slowly cracks it open. She gasps, which agitates Naina further. Saliva drips out of the wolf's mouth as she growls louder and harder. Her glowing bronze skin grows gray fur.

"I know you." Salessa recognizes the pink-skinned Mega outside. "From Sultana's."

Her customer from earlier in the night faces her. She can see more of his face now, and takes notice of his scars, and the grief in his pupil-less gray eyes.

"Yes, we met earlier," he says. "I need your help."

CHAPTER 2

COMMUNITY

Occupied Territory MoonSide
Date 17th Day of Month 6, Year 1628 DG

BEFORE SALESSA CAN RESPOND, A brutal bark and the sound of tearing clothes erupt into the air. Naina's wolf form lands on all fours between her cot and the doorway. She snarls, her teeth bared viciously, her muscular body hunched forward in an offensive position. Saliva drips onto the floor, and her confident eyes fixate on her target.

Salessa knows Naina will not hesitate to turn this pink Mega into her second dinner. The chaitender turns her body and places herself steadily between the visitor and her lupine sister.

"Naina, please," she pleads. "Calm down."

Naina inches closer still, so focused on the Mega, Salessa may as well be pleading to a wall.

"I'll defend myself if I have to," the Mega announces.

"It won't come to that," Salessa responds.

Naina barks loudly and her voice enter's Salessa's mind. *The sun worshiper's dead, Lessi. Step away.*

"No, you have to calm down." Salessa winces, realizing she should've responded telepathically.

"You can understand her?" the Mega asks.

Lie, Naina instructs.

Salessa responds in haste. "It's a...a twin thing."

Lie better! comes Naina's fiery tone.

Salessa continues to diffuse as Naina inches further forward. "I've seen him connect to the Radiance at Sultana's. He's not a faerie."

Another bark comes from deep within Naina's throat and then a low growl. *Move aside, Lessi. We can't trust them.*

"I won't. I'm going to stand right here until you calm down and shift back."

Naina paces from side to side for a few moments, telepathically mumbling obscenities in Salessa's mind, until she comes to a decision and shifts back into her human form. She stands naked with her arms folded across her chest.

The tension evaporates and Salessa releases a heavy sigh. "Thank you. Now please put some clothes on."

"I'm not taking my eyes off of him."

"Watch him while getting dressed."

Naina stands defiantly, but relents when she catches Salessa's pleading expression. Her gaze remains fixed on the Mega as she backs up to a large trunk and finds new clothes.

Salessa faces the visitor, keeping her fingers secured on the door in case it needs to be closed quickly. "What do you need?"

The Mega tosses his gaze over his shoulder at the darkness outside the hut. "May I come in and explain?"

Salessa's grip on the door instinctually tightens, before she consciously relaxes it and breathes deeply. Something about the nervous, jittery expression in the Mega's pupil-less eyes informs her willingness to allow him entry.

She invites the Mega to take a seat on her cot, and he seems grateful for the invitation, bowing his head respectfully. The chaitender pulls Naina's cot closer and sits down, leaving a few feet of distance between them. Awkward silence permeates the humble dwelling until Naina joins them.

"My name is Symin," the Mega introduces himself.

"What the fuck do you want?" Naina responds quickly.

Salessa is inclined to give her sister an angry look, but acknowledges the answer is more important than how the question was phrased.

Symin rubs his hands together nervously. "All three of us want the same things."

"Respectfully, Symin," Salessa begins, "you don't know anything about us."

"I know enough. The village's elders told me about the two young girls who spent years in the forests of MoonSide, surviving on scraps and hiding in the shadows. The ones who came to them with a tale of how the green-skinned, one-armed Mega—the Facilitator—killed their parents."

A growl forms in Naina's chest. Salessa places her hand on her sister's wrist, calming her. Symin has somehow whittled their truth from the tongues of those who promised to safeguard it.

"We were children," Salessa responds, "who turned to storytelling to deal with the grief of losing their parents. It was fantasy."

"No, it wasn't," Symin insists. "It's as real a story as mine. The Facilitator took my only child from me."

A pang of empathy bubbles into Salessa's heart. Symin's grief-ridden grays betray all of his pain, and mirror her own.

"I don't believe you," Naina replies, shaking Salessa out of her compassion. "And even if it's true, it has nothing to do with us."

"It most certainly does," Symin counters. "He's still looking for you. Twelve years later and both the MegaFather and the Facilitator are on the hunt."

Salessa and Naina exchange glances.

"How do you know that?" Salessa asks.

"I've infiltrated the Bravers before. It didn't take me long to connect their stories to the ones I heard here about you two. The only reason they haven't found you is because they've assumed that, if you were here, at the edge of MoonSide, you would've fled by now. But if they ever do come here…"

"It doesn't matter if they come to Evic," Salessa bluffs. "We're not eight anymore, and they have no idea what we look like now."

"How long will that keep you safe? How many twenty-year-old twins live in this village?"

"It's kept us safe so far," Salessa reminds him.

"No matter how many minutes a cup of milk stands, it will eventually sour. I don't know why, but I know you're valuable to them. They won't stop looking."

Naina scoffs. "Are you going to keep blathering cryptically or is there a suggestion coming?"

Symin breathes deeply. "A simple plan: we cut the MegaFather off from the ore."

Salessa shakes her head. "That's not simple. It's dangerous. We aren't warriors."

"Speak for yourself, Lessi," Naina objects.

"Salessa, you can only put this behind you if they stop hunting you. It's time for you to hunt them. Warrior or not, you *are* part of the war."

"Violence is not the only solution, Symin."

"Justice is."

Salessa considers for a moment. "The line between justice and vengeance is too thin to tread. I won't put Naina's life in jeopardy unless I know which one drives you."

"Does it truly matter? I could have a steak and you could have a stew. Either way, we've killed the cow."

For the first time since Symin knocked on the door, the edge of Naina's lips perk into a half-smile.

While the pink Mega has a point, Salessa hesitates to trust him. "How do you know you can successfully cut him off from the ore?"

There's a long pause as Symin steadies himself. "Seven years ago, my team and I were part of the Revolution in SunSide before it was snuffed out. For the first time in eight hundred years, since this dynasty began, we had help from within SunSide's government. Telling us where, when and how to strike. We nearly had the monarchy on its knees."

"What happened?" Naina asks.

Symin reaches into his pocket and pulls out a small fragment of black stone. "The ore happened."

Naina holds her hand out and Symin places it into her palm.

He continues as she examines it. "The night of the Siege of the Castrum, seven years ago, he revealed it. That's when it all ended. The Revolution. Hope."

"Because it blocks your connection to the Radiance," Naina says. "I've heard about that. The nymphs and pixies that come through the chai house talk about it."

"Only their connection?" Salessa asks. "What about ours?"

"Yours?" Symin asks, raising an eyebrow. "Doruh can connect to the Radiance?"

Naina shakes her head. "Not the way you do. When we shift into our animal forms, our essences use Radiant energy. We can't actively harness it."

"The ore must not affect you then," Symin confirms. "I've seen Doruh shift without issue in SunSide's capital."

Naina hands the ore back to Symin. "Salessa's seen you access the Radiance in the chai house. How is that possible with the ore in your pocket?"

Symin tucks the stone back into his cloak. "It's a small fragment. The amount of ore, the distance from it, and the strength of the Mega's connection to the Radiance all play a role in how we're affected by it."

"And the night of the Siege, they brought out all of it," Salessa assumes.

Symin's gaze falls. "Yes. Weapons, armor, projectiles, vehicles. All constructed out of it. It decimated our connection to the Radiance. We were left with nothing, neither the numbers nor the military advantage. Now he's built it into the kingdom's infrastructure, and he uses it to buy alliances with other governments. It's everything to him. My team is ready to take it all away."

Naina leans in. "How?"

"There's a processing plant on Panaerth where the ore is refined. We can raze it. The problem is, we lose our connection to the Radiance when we get close. That's why I came looking for help—Doruh help. And I found you."

Symin's story fails to mitigate Salessa's hesitance. "Symin, it's too dangerous. You want help leveling a structure that is likely as guarded and fortified as the Castrum itself. Not to mention, on an unfamiliar continent. All we know of Panaerth is its dense forests, stone wastelands, unforgiving deserts, and sharp mountains."

"Safety is *not* an issue. Infiltration is our expertise, in any terrain. We need help from someone who can get out before it explodes. We aren't fast or agile enough without the Radiance. But Doruh wolves are."

"And what happens after?" Naina asks.

"My team will head back to SunSide and regroup with the Revolution's General. You're free to join us."

Salessa's muscles tense at the idea of Naina facing Bravers in battle. She's spent a decade protecting her sister, something she'd never be able to do on a battlefield.

As if he hears her thoughts, Symin responds to put her at ease, the way he did in the chai house. "Or you can settle elsewhere safely, knowing you helped bring the Revolution back to life."

Naina falls quiet, brows furrowed, eyes narrow, the face she makes when confronted with a difficult decision.

Salessa questions Symin further while Naina teeters between options. "Why are you telling us your plan? How can you trust us?"

Symin looks down at the floor, takes a deep breath, and then meets their gazes again. "Because we're the same. Weary from hiding and running and fighting. We all have a stake in this and we have to give each other a sense of…" He pauses, struggling to find the right word.

Salessa smiles and offers him the term he's looking for. "Community." It's what she's been looking for.

He nods and returns her smile.

"There's an old Doruh saying that comes to mind," Naina interjects. "Never trust a Mega until you've seen through their windows."

Symin raises an eyebrow. "What does it mean?"

Salessa explains. "You can establish a sense of trust with humans or Doruh when you view their essences through their windows." She points up to her eyes. "The pupils. Without pupils, it's hard to trust Mega until you've spent time getting to know them."

"I'm sorry," Symin says, "but we don't have time for you to figure out whether or not you can trust me." He stands. "I'll be in MoonSide for two more days. On the morning of the Nineteenth, I'll be heading back to rendezvous with my team, with or without you." He pauses.

"But I do hope you'll join me. PeakHaven Pass, on the Nineteenth. I'll wait until midday."

He turns and exits, leaving a haze of silence and eerie indecision behind.

Salessa slowly sits back down next to Naina. "This is what you wanted, right? To join the fight?"

Naina keeps her gaze on her feet and shakes her head. "Not with sun worshipers."

Salessa scoffs. "He's not a faerie, Naina."

"He's Mega. I don't trust them, Lessi."

"You can't misplace your anger because he walked in here with gray eyes and pointed ears. He's not our enemy."

Naina stands and paces. "How do you know that, Lessi?"

"Because we're alive. If he wanted to hurt us, he didn't have to knock on the door. He didn't have to sit here and tell us his entire plan."

Naina stops pacing. "And how do you know he wasn't lying?"

Salessa pauses. She doesn't know how to articulate what she saw in his eyes before he even walked in. "I've seen through his windows."

Naina growls. "Oh, *come on*, Lessi. You cannot be this naive. When I asked you to go to SunSide, you said it was suicide."

"I said I would go if we had experienced warriors with us. Symin was part of the Revolution. I don't think it's a coincidence he showed up at our door."

"And what happens when Symin and his team find out why the Facilitator is after us? You just let him believe we're both wolves; it won't take long before he figures out only one of us actually is."

Salessa reaches up and takes Naina's hand. "Naina, we've been telling people we're both wolves for over a decade now. No one has figured out the truth." She gives Naina's hand a slight tug to encourage her to take a seat on the cot again.

"You know me, Naina. I have reservations about this. It's obviously dangerous."

"Just get to the 'but.' I can feel it coming."

Salessa smiles. "I can't explain it, but it feels like Symin's journey led him to our doorstep for a reason."

"And what reason is that?"

Salessa turns to the door of the hut, where the Mega stood a few moments prior. "For community."

CHAPTER 3

WELCOME TO THE LIBRARY

Sovereign City-State *The Library*
Date *17th Day of Month 6, Year 1628 DG*

FROM AFAR, THE FEATHERS ON adult human wings resemble steel. They aren't, of course, but from the silver color to the polished texture, it isn't uncommon for an unwitting passerby to stop and wonder how heavy their wings must be.

Unisa sees these wings in her dreams, walking away from her. A pair of them, belonging to individuals she must've once called "Mommy" and "Daddy."

A gentle voice speaks to her as soft, celadon fingers wipe the wetness off her cheeks. "Stop crying, my love." Through the hazy vision, Unisa sees a Mega in a purple, full-sleeve tunic. "This is your home now. Welcome to the Library."

Unisa jolts awake. She's in bed, in her apartment.

She's home.

Her heart races, sweat trickling down her temple. She wipes it away and laughs at her absurd reaction to such a pleasant dream.

A gentle voice welcoming me home. The absolute horror!

She peers over the edge of her bed and sees a book lying on the floor. The title stares up at her, *The Fully Bonded You*. She must have fallen asleep reading again.

She picks the book up, returning it to her bookshelf. It's crowded with texts, so she squeezes the book between two others as best as she can. The name "Alvaro, the Prime Librarian" is etched into the spine of most of them, including the one she fell asleep reading the night before.

Unisa turns to face the window and looks up at the sky to check the time. She notes the positions of Ona and Lona, but Throna and Frona have yet to make their appearances over the horizon. A smile spreads across her face as she realizes she has plenty of time to get ready before work.

After her morning stretches, she sits before the mirror on her dresser and unwraps the scarf tied around her head to release her box braids. The protective style allows her to fly without worrying about wind or humidity. It took hours to braid them the day before, but it was well worth the effort. She applies a buttery oil to them as her rich brown skin shines in the light of the early morning suns.

Having been separated from her culture at a young age, Unisa had to learn most of what she now knows on her own. Her adoptive mother, Ora, helped as best as she could, but there's only so much a pixie can teach about human angi culture.

Unisa finishes oiling and pulls her braids up. She wraps the scarf around them again to keep them away from the water in her cramped shower. *Just one more promotion, and I can afford a bigger place.* She squeezes her wings tight against her back so she can turn around and wash her feathers.

A row of gold, cotton tunics and loose, light brown pants crowd her closet. She grabs the nearest uniform and gets dressed, then heads to the apartment three doors down the hall, entering without knocking.

Having grown up in this apartment with Ora, there's a warm sense of familiarity and nostalgia in the air as she prepares two sausages and eggs for breakfast.

"You're going to be late," comes Ora's voice from behind her.

Unisa smiles and speaks without turning. "I have plenty of time."

She can hear Ora's cane clacking to the dining table. "I can make my own breakfast. I'm retired, not dead."

"It's your first week as a retiree. This is a big deal, let me dote on you a little."

"You had the dream again," Ora says abruptly. "It's been months since the last time."

Unisa's smile fades momentarily, but she forces it back up. "How can you tell?"

"I'm your mother."

Unisa plates Ora's breakfast and gently sets it down on the table in front of the pixie. "That's a typical Mom thing to say."

Ora reaches her celadon fingers out and holds Unisa's hand. "I'm sorry."

"Sorry about what?" Unisa asks, her smile fading.

"About the way you feel after I appear in your dreams."

Unisa rolls her eyes and lovingly pats Ora's hand. "Don't be silly, Mom. You know it's not you. In fact, I think hearing your voice is the only comforting part of the dream. I don't even know why it makes me feel anxious, it's not like it's violent or intense."

Ora smiles, then raises Unisa's hand to her lips and kisses it. "I love you, Uni."

"I love you, too. But now I have to go, or I'll actually be late." She turns and heads for the door. "Don't wait for me, I'll be late tonight. I'm meeting Rafa for dinner."

She shuts Ora's door behind her quickly, hoping to silence any comments Ora might make about her and Rafael.

A long queue of Doruh valets stand outside the stout, claystone apartment building. Horses, rhinos, bears, sheep, camels—all standing on the side of the road, waiting for customers to approach and request a ride to another part of the city.

They gaze hopefully in Unisa's direction when she exits the building, but then turn away, disappointed when they see her wings and realize she's from the angi clan. There is, however, a familiar face which breaks the queue and approaches her.

"Good morning, Unisa!" A young Doruh man waves at her excitedly. He's naked, as many Doruh elect to be when in human form.

Unisa sighs and walks past him. "Morning, Chiragh." She speaks lazily as he follows behind her.

"Beautiful day for a ride!" he says, trying to keep up her pace.

"Even better for a soar." In a fluid motion, she turns around, smiles and winks at him, and then continues walking.

"Come on, Uni, I have the best prices in the Library."

"That's not the point, Chiragh. I'm taking the Loops. It's free. Why would I spend money on a ride?"

Chiragh stops following and calls out to her, "Don't be cheap, Uni! I know Librarians get paid well!"

"Have a good day!" Unisa yells back before disappearing into a crowd.

Two blocks down the street, she finds a uniformed attendant ushering a line of individuals onto a red circle marked on the ground. Next to the circle is a sign reading, "Library Loop Network - Entrance PA1035." Unisa joins the back of the line.

Above their heads is a framework of multicolored hoops that direct and manage the airborne traffic throughout the Library. A series of green hoops forms a lane of traffic in the direction in which Unisa will be traveling, while a series of blue hoops forms another lane for traffic moving in the opposite direction. Hovering red hoops indicate the entrances and exits in and out of the Loop Network.

At the front of the line is another angi human. His wings are outstretched as he stands in the red circle, waiting for the attendant to allow him entry. Behind him is a Mega woman with a blue complexion, and behind her are three Doruh waiting to take flight in their animal forms.

The line shrinks quickly as those in front enter the Loops. The attendant gives the Doruh woman before Unisa the affirmative signal to enter, and the woman shifts into a hummingbird to float delicately through the hoops and into traffic.

Unisa steps forward into the red circle. At the attendant's signal, she bends her knees and pushes forcefully upward with a strong flap of her wings. She's airborne now, and with some additional quick-paced fluttering, she enters the Loops. Her subconscious commands her wings to beat rhythmically every few minutes.

All four suns are now visible in the sky. Unisa's gaze falls on the city below as the rays glint off the Library's magnificent infrastructure.

Busy morning activity animates the Stream Network: interconnected canals, intricately woven under bridges, around buildings, and through tunnels for those who wish to travel by water, like the human mari clan.

Unisa's exit approaches and she pulls her shoulders back, stretching out her wings until her body is vertical. Descending with intention, she lands in a red circle on the street, then stands still for a moment, taking time to recover her balance.

Folding her wings, she enters a bustling marketplace and heads straight for Kura's Kitchen. It's little more than a four-post stall with a wooden counter between the customers and the scorching equipment. Torn fabric covers the top to form a shabby tent, and at the head of each post sits a rusty speaker.

Unisa's excitement flourishes when she sees Kura cooking and greeting customers with a warm smile. The heat from her equipment radiates out over the counter, so customers remain a step back. Only a human of the igni clan, with their stone exoskeletons, can work in such a small, blistering space without getting burned.

Kura sees Unisa and smiles. "Morning, Uni! Would you like your usual?"

"Yes, Kura!" Unisa shouts to her, hoping Kura can hear her over the sizzling and popping. "Actually, make it two today!"

"Two? Quite an appetite this morning."

Unisa laughs. "It's not for me, I'm picking up for a friend." Kura nods and prepares Unisa's usual breakfast order: a toasted corn bowl with vegetable stew.

The rusty speakers are common amongst every stall in the market. Unisa listens closely to the words emitted from them as she waits for her meal. It's the Prime Librarian's voice, reading from one of his own books, a book that Unisa has on her shelf and has nearly memorized, cover-to-cover.

"*The Fully Bonded individual has completely abandoned the notion of victimhood. They are responsible for the things that happen to them, and the way in which they react to those things. The Fully Bonded is able to introspectively assign blame solely where it belongs: upon themselves. When we believe we are victims, we move away from being Fully Bonded and toward being Fully Broken.*"

Unisa closes her eyes and allows the Prime's familiar, silken timbre to inspire her devotion to his teachings. She repeats one of the tenets: *The Fully Bonded believe. The Fully Bonded believe.*

"Uni," Kura interrupts from behind the wooden counter, sliding a sack with two packaged meals toward Unisa. "Lost in his words again?"

"The Fully Bonded always listen and learn," Unisa responds, "especially from the Prime." She withdraws two stones from her pouch, one blue and one green, and hands them to Kura. The blue stone is circular, while the glossy green stone is carved into a triangle. Both have the MegaFather's portrait etched into them, a feat that only faerie technology can mass produce.

"Yes, yes. No one is as Bonded as you are, Uni."

Unisa rolls her eyes and picks up the sack with the meals, keeping her ears open as she continues through the marketplace.

"The radical Doruh of MoonSide have become Fully Broken. Refusing to acknowledge their historical misdoings, the Doruh believe themselves victims. SunSide's occupation of their kingdom, and the magnanimous guardianship of the Bravers, will rid the region of savagery and rebellion, and save the civilized from the scourge."

The Prime's words fortify Unisa's resolve as both a citizen and a government official of the Library.

A metal archway with a string of blue lights sits nestled between two stone buildings, an entrance to the Catacombs beneath the city. A sign outside the archway reads "Catacomb Section 27L: *Witness.*"

Unisa steps onto a slightly elevated, circular platform under the archway, hearing it click into the ground as her weight pushes against it. A familiar voice erupts from a speaker at the top.

"Good morning! Welcome to the Library Catacomb Network. Do you have authorization to enter *Witness*?"

"Good morning, Maksi," Unisa responds loudly. "It's me."

"Morning, Uni."

The blue light surrounding the archway turns red, indicating that the security measures have been temporarily disabled, allowing Unisa to pass through. When she steps off of the platform, it pops back up out of the ground and the red light turns blue again.

Another platform, this one rectangular, descends through a shaft and carries her out of the suns' light, into the Catacombs below. A thrill pumps through her as the smell of old, worn texts and documents effervesces into the air.

The shaft opens up to a long hallway with a desk at the other end of it. Behind the desk is a massive chamber with a vaulted ceiling, garnished with illuminated square panels. There are swirling, golden designs etched into the floors that shimmer as the brilliant lights strike them.

Artwork depicting significant moments in history adorns the room, splashing the walls with splendid colors, bringing them to life. A hanging clock with four lit circles, indicating the positions of the suns, stares at her from near the desk. Just under it rests a calendar; fifty squares squeeze onto each of ten pages, accounting for all five hundred days, and ten months, of the year.

Rows upon rows of shelves and cabinets inundate the chamber behind the desk, brimming with books and documents. Morning after morning, the magnificence takes Unisa's breath away.

A wide doorway stands at the very back of the room, leading to a labyrinth of underground tunnels that connect every section of the Library's Catacomb Network. The city was built with the sole purpose of housing and cataloging the entirety of Aerthomni's written history. The records and documents held within the Catacombs are the most valuable artifacts in existence.

Librarians devote their lives to the history held herein. The various ranks dutifully collect, preserve, defend, or manage the information, but their focus remains the same regardless of where in the Library's hierarchy they fall: protect the history, protect the Catacombs, protect the city.

Even if they must do so with their lives.

Unisa places the meals gently down on her side of the metal desk and finds Maksi, also in a gold cotton tunic, focused on writing.

"Splendid morning, isn't it? Perfect for poetry." His carrot-colored hand moves feverishly as he writes, and the points of his ears jiggle back and forth from the motion. He uses the Radiance to transmit his thoughts from his mind to the page, employing the tip of his finger as a writing utensil.

Unisa removes one of the breakfast stews from the bag and slides it to Maksi's side of the desk. She watches with a wry smile, waiting for him to turn his head. Pupil-less Mega eyes aren't conclusive indicators of where they're looking.

His gaze finally leaves the paper and he turns to Unisa. "No," he says. "This is bribery."

"It's breakfast. Your *favorite*," she sings.

Maksi releases a frustrated sigh. "Uni, I cannot believe you. You know how I feel about violating policy."

"I've never been caught, Maksi. If I take something tonight, I'll bring it back to *Witness* in the morning. No one will know."

"You can *legally* check any text out of here when they give you the green linen."

Unisa shakes her head. "You know how much *Witness* means to me. I'm not waiting until they make me a Vice Ambassador before I experience what's held here. That could be years."

There's a long pause as Maksi raises an eyebrow. "You always say *Witness* means so much to you, but you've never told me why. The gold cotton will get you into most other sections, why is this one so important to you?"

The question catches her defenseless, uncomfortable.

By the age of two, Unisa had taught herself to read, and before her fourth birthday, she knew more about Aerthomni's history than most adults. Recognizing her limitless memory, and her constant, burning desire to seek knowledge, her birth parents relinquished her to Ora and the Library—to immerse her in the history she was born to consume.

The primary historical testimonies held in *Witness* are the very reason her parents abandoned her here. For Unisa, it's sacred. Holy.

She reinstates her faded smile and conjures an excuse. "A big part of the Fully Bonded individual is a thirst for history. No history is more accurate and detailed than eyewitness testimonies."

"For someone who's constantly working toward being Fully Bonded, you're oddly comfortable with rule-breaking. If they realize I turned a blind eye to your tampering, for some vegetable stew, they'll consider both of us Fully Broken."

Unisa rolls her eyes. "*Tampering*? Do you hear yourself? I don't draw on them. I know how fragile these texts are."

Maksi sighs, takes in her pleading expression, and nods in defeat.

"Thank you, Maksi!" she says, excitedly. "I promise, I won't ask again."

"I hear that at least twice a month."

The day progresses slowly. One Vice Ambassador comes in to read, while a pair of yellow tunic-clad Ambassador Librarians check out some documents. Around midday, Maksi volunteers to venture to the street market for lunch, and shortly thereafter, the intercom system notifies Unisa that someone is waiting on the entrance platform.

Unisa clears her throat and leans down to the microphone. "Good afternoon. Welcome to *Witness*. Are you authorized for entry?"

"Y-Yes, I have a letter from an Ambassador," replies a high-pitched, shaky voice on the other end.

A letter? Perhaps he meant an Official Document Request?

Unisa allows the visitor to enter, and moments later, she sees him step off the descending platform at the end of the hall. His white cotton tunic, the uniform of Librarians in training, alarms her. Students are certainly not authorized for entry in *Witness*.

His burgundy hands and pointed ears quiver as he clutches a piece of paper and slowly steps up to the desk. Unisa holds her hand out and he presents the document to her. She realizes what's happening as soon as she sees it.

"You're here to check a text out of *Witness*?" She feigns curiosity to hide her amusement.

"Yes, please." The teenager points to the paper. "An Ambassador gave me permission." The document is quite obviously written by someone who has never seen an official authorization. Unisa's grin breaks out and she tears the paper in half.

"Cute, but I'm sure you knew that wasn't going to work. Mega students use the Radiance all the time to try to sneak things out of here."

"I can't use the Radiance." The boy's gray eyes dim.

Guilt grows in Unisa's chest. "Oh, you're a faerie."

The boy nods. "Am I in trouble?"

Unisa smiles. "No, you're not."

His shoulders visibly relax.

"What did you need from *Witness*?"

"Information on the War for Bibi Sands."

"You're not in the right section, *mohuway*." She addresses the boy using a term of endearment for children in the ancient Nysabaani language. "Head south three blocks and you'll see the entrance to *Recent History*."

The teenager shakes his head. "I went there first. Everything on Bibi Sands has been checked out."

Unisa sighs and reaches into her desk drawer to withdraw paper and a writing utensil. "Write this down."

He nods and eagerly awaits her dictation.

"The War for Bibi Sands started in 1603 and ended in 1622."

He looks up from the paper. "It only ended six years ago?"

Unisa smiles. "Yes, *mohuway*, that's why it's cataloged in *Recent History*."

The boy returns her smile and hunches over the paper again.

"The igni and mari clans engaged in a territorial dispute over the island Bibi Sands. The war ended when an igni official, Courtman Tomohiro, discovered a more desirable island and claimed it. They no longer needed Bibi Sands, so they relinquished it to the mari. The new island was named Lily Beach and construction began on the settlements there."

The teenager thanks her and departs.

"Anything exciting happen while I was gone?" Maksi asks upon his return, as he hands Unisa a platter of lamb roast with rice and takes his place next to her.

Unisa hesitates to tell Maksi about the student. Her colleague is friendly, but he's also a prisoner to policy; the boy would be reported to the Academy. It took Unisa months to feel even slightly comfortable asking him to forgo his strong sense of protocol for Kura's stew.

The remainder of the day passes as painfully slow as the morning did, but when the end of their shift finally arrives, Maksi turns to Unisa. "You have ten minutes. Please hurry, Uni."

"I promise," she responds. "I'll be back in under ten."

Her heart slams against her chest as she walks through the rows of bookshelves. Although her wings are tight against her back, Unisa feels as if she is floating around *Witness*. A smile touches both ears.

She passes the first row of bookshelves, on the extinct human clan called the teri, predecessors of the angi, igni, mari, and Doruh. The second row is Mega history. Texts on the royal dynasties of SunSide are nestled toward the end of the self.

Her fingers find a thick book called *The Everlasting Journey*. She cradles the fragile text in her hands as she opens it. The name of the author, Red-Lo the MegaFather, gleams across the cover page. The book is an autobiography, penned on his deathbed and revered nearly as much as the author himself.

History remembers Red-Lo as a pacifist, something to which Unisa can relate.

The text catalogs the most intimate parts of the MegaFather's life: his marriage to Drof-Fa, the violent usurper who robbed SunSide's throne and then passed off her responsibilities when she grew tired of ruling; the perilous journey Drof-Fa coerced him into taking, in a mad search for immortality, which took her life; and Red-Lo's devotion to SunSide's scientific and technological revolution, using his work as a balm for his grief.

That grief is the reason SunSide is the most advanced society in all of Aerthomni, and why Red-Lo is rightfully venerated as the brilliant, honorable leader he always proved to be. Drof-Fa, in contrast, etched her infamy into eternity, ironically attaining the immortality she sought in darkness rather than light.

Unisa carefully cradles the delicate text to her chest, her arms crossed around it, and walks back toward the front desk.

As she exits the rows of bookshelves, Maksi approaches her briskly.

"There you are, Uni," he says, standing uncomfortably close to her. "You took so long in the bathroom."

Unisa reads his expression; sweat dots his forehead, stress lines reach out like fingers from the corners of his eyes, and his lips curl downward at the edges.

She tilts her head slightly to look past him, and her heart stops. Rustling through paperwork on the front desk is a tall nymph in a purple tunic.

Koal, Unisa and Maksi's direct supervisor. In the year that Unisa has been a Gatekeeper, this is only the second time he has visited after closing.

Unisa turns back up to Maksi's face. His growing anxiety mangles his expression further. She forces a smile in the hopes of comforting him, but the attempt falls flat.

"Sorry, Maksi," she says, "I didn't mean to *disappear*." On the last word, she gestures down to the book with her eyes. Maksi nods subtly and grasps the book firmly in one hand, keeping it in front of his body to block Koal's view. He closes his eyes.

The book disappears. At least, it appears that way until Maksi hands it back to Unisa and she realizes he's just turned it invisible. Careful not to drop it, she takes the book in one hand and lets her arms drop to the side, as if she isn't holding anything.

Together, they turn and walk back to the front desk.

"What're you doing here, Koal?" Unisa asks casually. She places the invisible book down gently and silently on her side of the desk.

"I came to collect the checkout logs and restoration reports," Koal says, absentmindedly flicking through pages on a clipboard.

"Now? I was going to bring them to you in the morning." She maintains a cool indifference in her tone, a casual wondering, not a tense inquiry.

Koal finishes and holds the clipboard at his side. "I have to take the day off tomorrow. Family emergency."

Unisa nods. "Understood."

"I'll see you both in a couple of days."

He turns to exit through the doorway behind the bookshelves, disappearing into the Catacombs. Once he is out of view, Maksi turns to Unisa, smoke practically coming out of his ears.

"I told you it was risky! We almost got fired. Or worse. Who knows?" His speed increases and his words jumble together. "Icantbelieveltrustedyouandyoualmostgotmefired..."

"Maksi!" Unisa stops him. "Take a breath."

Maksi inhales deeply and then exhales. "You have to put it back, Uni. We can't take risks like this anymore."

Unisa nods. Koal almost caught her walking out of *Witness* with a confidential text. They were lucky, but it could've gone far worse.

"I'll put it back, Maksi," she says, softly.

"Thank you," he responds. He walks over to the desk, and runs his fingertips along the cover of the invisible book, causing it to reappear.

"Good night," he says, before he makes his way down the hallway to the exit platform.

Unisa watches it ascend until he's out of view, still embarrassed at the situation she caused. She reaches for the book to return it to the shelves, when something unusual catches her eye. She squints, confused, as soft light pours out of the pages.

Her fingers move slowly, subconsciously to the back of the book, from where the light flows. The *formerly* empty pages now host a thick paragraph of new writing. The words appear before her eyes, as if they're being written at that moment. Unisa lifts her head and looks around. Perhaps Maksi, or Koal, is playing a trick on her. Trying to teach her a lesson.

But it's abundantly plain that she's alone. Her gaze falls to the book Maksi brought back to visibility, the book he revealed with the Radiance. She watches the glowing letters appear.

What more has he unintentionally revealed?

CHAPTER 4

REDEMPTION

Sovereign City-State *The Library*
Date *17th Day of Month 6, Year 1628 DG*

THE WRITING STOPS AND THE light dies. Unisa's gaze locks on a long letter now sitting on the page. A signature rests at the bottom, above a title in small print.

"Hay-Ro," Unisa whispers. "Head Salver to the Red-Lo Royal Dynasty." She lifts the fragile text, as if bringing it closer to her face will make it easier to understand.

Or easier to believe.

Hay-Ro's letter has no salutation. Unisa wonders who the intended reader is. She feels an inexplicable connection to the words, as if he is standing in front of her, pouring his heart out.

The only honest words in this text are the ones you are now reading. If you can see this, you've revealed the truth of "the Everlasting Journey." Everything written before this page has been toiled over and labored upon for weeks and months. It is manufactured to tell a story that will live on for ages, though it drips with everlasting deceit.

Red-Lo's duplicity knows no limit. Chapter by chapter, page by page, word by word, he sullies the good name of the most wonderful faerie I have ever known. My greatest regret is, and forever shall be, my silence. I watched idly as he inscribed these filthy fabrications. I beg the Four for forgiveness. One day, when the time is right, all will be revealed. On that day, my atonement shall be complete.

Here are the truths that Red-Lo has draped with deceit: Drof-Fa's campaign for the throne was not out of a penchant for violence, but a command from Red-Lo. Drof-Fa did not shirk her responsibility as MegaMother, rather she assumed every duty of the throne as Red-Lo chose his mad search for immortality over his kingdom and his marriage. Drof-Fa had no desire for it, yet Red-Lo demanded she accompany him on the Everlasting Journey.

And here, dear Discoverer, is the most heartbreaking fabrication of the entire tale: Red-Lo did not return from the journey in anguish over the loss of his wife. He was bewildered, out of his wits. He could barely stand and labored to take a single breath. His clothes were torn to shreds and much of his skin was tattered with deep burns. He was covered in soot and ash. He whispered to himself about how they took the MegaMother from him. Once he became lucid again, I asked him over and over, "Who are they? Who took the MegaMother's life?"

He denied ever having said any of it. He continued to insist that the MegaMother lost her life after falling from the top of a mountain. Only a handful of us heard the truth upon his return. I am the only one left and I'm afraid I'm not sure how much longer I have. If he senses even the slightest bit of disloyalty in me, if he finds this entry before you do, my life will be over.

If you've found this, if you've revealed the truth, tell everyone. The Mega-Mother of SunSide was not a violent usurper. She was not a lazy queen. She was not a mad faerie.

She was murdered. And she deserved better than the husband who soiled her image to guard his own. Who defiled SunSide's history to save his own face.

Find out who did it. Avenge the MegaMother. End the lies.

Hay-Ro
Head Salver of the Red-Lo Royal Dynasty

Unisa steps backward as if the letter has pushed her. Sweat collects on her brow as her breath catches in her throat. Frantically, her eyes dart across the page, hoping for the words to change, or a disclaimer to appear at the end stating that it was all a joke. A prank.

It can't be. This is the Library. Nothing is fabricated. It's history, as it happened. As it was recorded.

Unisa drops heavily into a seat. The integrity of the Library's record-keeping is more than just an oath of employment. Day in and day out, the Librarians devote their lives to it.

A haze blankets her mind as the scope of Hay-Ro's allegation dawns on her. SunSide's history, as described in this text, has been taught to generations of children around the continent. For centuries. The Everlasting Journey is a pivotal moment that set the kingdom on a course for technological and scientific revolution.

Could it be a lie?

"It can't be," she says softly, trying to reason with herself. As if the words will stop the world from spinning around her, she buries her face in her hands and whispers, "The Fully Bonded believe. The Fully Bonded believe."

They believe in the history guarded within the Catacombs, as written. Accepting Hay-Ro's claims isn't merely disapproved—it's sacrilege. It's criminal.

Unable to breathe, she tries to inhale, but the room continues to spin and the vegetable stew and grilled lamb bubble back up her throat.

A chime steals her attention and allows her to focus on something other than the impending return of her meals. The clock on the wall with the four lit circles cries out. It's late. Unisa reaches for the delicate text and closes it. She grabs a small hide bag from under the desk and places the book into it, carrying it down the hallway to the platform, and out of *Witness* with her.

Sorry, Maksi, she thinks as the platform ascends. *I can't let it out of my sight anymore.*

She exits onto the street, still in a daze until a hand falls on her shoulder and wrenches her out of it.

"There you are," Rafael says. "I was starting to worry, Uni."

Unisa had completely forgotten about her plans to meet Rafael for dinner. He's wearing his gold Gatekeeper tunic with the sleeves rolled up to his elbows, revealing his forearm fins. An empty quiver sits on his back.

"I'm so sorry, Rafa," she responds sincerely. "I just got caught up in something."

Her wavering tone betrays her distress. Rafael takes her hand gently and holds it in both of his. "Is everything alright?"

"Yes, it's fine." She forces a smile, then lifts her face toward his to initiate their usual greeting. He smiles back and leans down, placing his left cheek against Unisa's and giving her a gentle kiss. He then repeats this with the right.

She wraps her hands around his bicep, holding his arm as they walk to their usual dinner destination. "How was your archery course?" She attempts to feign a normal conversation to disguise the panic setting in.

Rafael laughs. "It's not a course, Uni. They just asked for help with their aim. Just a little practice, that's all."

"Mm-hmm," Unisa responds, taking in little of Rafael's reply as the gravity of Hay-Ro's letter continues to weigh on her.

He stops and turns to her. "Uni, if you're not well, we can reschedule. Let me take you to Ora's so she can look after you."

"No, Rafa, I'm fine. Truly." She can think of nothing less appealing than showing up with him on Ora's doorstep, for her mother to question the nature of their friendship. They continue forth as she resolves to shove Hay-Ro's letter to the back of her mind.

At least, as much as she is able to.

Not far from Kura's, their usual dinner spot is a larger restaurant with seating around the stall. Rafael, a human of the mari clan, asks to eat here frequently, as it specializes in cuisine from SeaBed. Unisa agrees every time because she enjoys participating in any mari tradition, like their greeting, that helps him feel anchored to home.

Seated at a familiar table, Rafael continues talking about his archery session. Unisa loses herself in the discussion, particularly in Rafael's excitement. Pushing Hay-Ro's letter away becomes easier when Rafael's passion lights up the conversation. He's had a knack for melting away her concerns since they met, eight years earlier, only days after his arrival at the Library. His vibrant smile remains until he hears footsteps and turns to see the waiter approaching their table.

"I didn't know he was working today," he says to Unisa.

"It doesn't matter, Rafa," Unisa says. A cloud of tension envelops them as Rafael's smile drops and he goes quiet. The igni waiter welcomes them and pours water into their glasses. He asks them if they'd like to place an order.

"We'll have our usual tapas, thank you," Unisa says. "Is that alright, Rafa?" She and the waiter turn to Rafael, who is sitting silently, his eyes transfixed on the exoskeleton of the waiter's fingers. Unisa reaches forward and places her hand gently on Rafael's, shaking him from the trance.

Rafael's eyes widen and his cheeks go red when he sees the waiter's confusion. "Sorry. Yes, that's fine. And mosto, please."

"Mosto?" Unisa questions, hoping to pull his attention from the waiter's exoskeleton. "What about sangría?"

Rafael shakes his head. "Sangría is for summer, Uni."

The waiter smiles politely and walks back to the restaurant. Rafael runs his fingers over the bracelet on his left wrist. It's silver with blue gemstones set into the links. Unisa waits until the waiter's out of earshot before she speaks.

"You still see it?" she asks. "It's been a long time since I've seen you lost like that. I thought maybe you'd gotten past it."

Rafael doesn't speak, keeping his eyes lowered.

"Rafa, it's been eight years now. It's time to get some help. There's no shame in it."

Rafael raises his gaze. "I don't need help. I just need to keep a distance from *them*." There's venom in his tone.

"There are igni all over the Library, Rafa. You can't avoid them forever."

Rafael takes one of the bracelet links between two fingers and holds it tightly. "You know I'm not going to make peace with them."

Unisa sighs. "The war is over, Rafa. It's been over six yea—"

"So I should just forget?" he interrupts her. "I see blood, Uni. On their hands. On their exoskeletons. Coming out of their eyes." His voice cracks. "*Her* blood." He takes a deep breath to steady himself. "I don't care if six centuries have passed. It isn't over. Not for me. I won't forget."

"You don't have to forget. But you do have to try to move forward. You deserve peace and happiness and love. You deserve a future where you aren't stuck with this hatred in your heart." Unisa looks into his eyes, pinpointing the loss deep within. Even in their happiest moments together, it lingers.

Rafael exhales deeply. "There isn't a future for everyone, Uni. There's nothing after exile."

"There's redemption." She leans forward and lovingly runs her fingers over the bracelet on his wrist. "Isn't that what Joaquina would have wanted for you?"

Rafael jerks his hand backward so Unisa's no longer touching Joaquina's bracelet. The angi realizes she's crossed a boundary and regrets what she said. "I think we should stop the conversation here," Rafael says sternly.

Unisa nods apologetically and they both sit in tense silence for a few minutes, until their meals and drinks arrive. Rafael's smile doesn't return until lighter conversations resume and his piscine nares take in the nostalgic aromas of the mixed olives, cheeses, and seafood.

After dinner, she holds Rafael's arm again and walks with him to his entrance to the Stream Network. "I hope you're feeling better," he says.

Unisa had completely forgotten about Hay-Ro's letter. The worry invades her heart again, but she carefully tucks it away.

"Much better," she responds with a smile. Rafael dives into the Stream and departs. The entire flight back to her apartment, Unisa's mind is abuzz with questions about the letter and what it could mean for her...and for the Library.

If the details of the Everlasting Journey are false, anything else in the Catacombs can be. This letter opens up the possibility of lies within the Library. A city built on history and truth, peddling centuries of fabrication around the continent.

There is no redemption from that.

CHAPTER 5

THE AMBASSADORS

Sovereign City-State *The Library*
Date *17th Day of Month 6, Year 1628 DG*

NEARLY IMPENETRABLE FOREST, DENSE WITH towering
conifers, surrounds the Library's golden gates. The mighty trees barricade the Library in, save for a few narrow pathways that lead to stout stone walls. Thick and wide, the walls outline the borders of the city.

Starlight strikes the gold tunic of a Gatekeeper traversing the parapets atop the walls. The Librarian passes by another in yellow silk, nodding to the Ambassador in acknowledgement. Their uniforms denote a breadth of ranks between them, but the duty on the walls homogenizes all Librarians; they all receive combat and weapons training, and are qualified for the duties this station entails.

The suns have descended past the horizon. The dark of the thicket gives birth to a caravan of travelers making their way along the narrow path toward the gates. Like a beacon in the dark night, moonlight gleams off the metal barriers.

Two moose lead the caravan, followed by an elephant and then a mule at the rear. One moose carries an Ambassador, while her Vice Ambassador, in green linen, rides the other. On elephant-back are three Recorder Librarians, with a fourth following on the mule, and a fifth flying above. The angi Recorder casts deep purple shadows over her fellow travelers.

They reach the gate and the guards recognize the Ambassador. With a respectful bow, they move aside to allow the entire caravan to enter. Just beyond the gates, the group passes by a sign that reads "Welcome to the Library." In small print underneath, it says, "*Nusta. Ista. Hosta*," a motto in Nysabaani meaning, "Knowledge. History. Truth."

The caravan reaches their drop-off location at the Center, the Library's hub for government and administration, where the Librarians dismount. The Doruh shift back into their human forms and then get dressed in the clothing they brought along.

Alba, the mari Ambassador, approaches the group of subordinates. "I need your reports on my desk in two days. The MegaFather's expecting his next ore shipment in a little over a month, so we may be going back out sooner than you'd expect."

The subordinates nod in agreement.

Alba locks eyes with one pixie Recorder in particular. "No extensions this time."

The young Librarian blushes and nods.

Alba turns back to the rest of the group and smiles. "You all did very well on this trip and have earned a spot in the promotional trials next week. I'll forward my recommendations to the promotions team, and you'll be notified about the date and time of your trials. There are only three Educator positions open currently, but earning a spot in the trials is an honor in itself. Go home and celebrate; you deserve it."

The excited Recorders journey home, elated to have gained Alba's approval. She finds Kyoko, her igni Vice Ambassador, in a discussion with the Doruh chauffeurs' manager. When he sees Alba, he speaks directly to her over Kyoko's shoulder.

"This isn't enough, Ambassador," he grunts, holding a number of colorful stones in his hand.

Alba furrows her eyebrows. "It's twelve hundred, Uzair. That's the amount in your contract. Six hundred to SunSide and six hundred back."

"Please, Ambassador," Uzair says, "the terrain was very rough."

"My hooves are killing me," one of the moose adds, and the mule standing behind her nods in agreement.

Alba frowns. "I'm sorry, but that's not our responsibility. It was your route, so you determined the terrain."

Uzair and his chauffeurs exchange glances, then he nods dejectedly before the Doruh shift and depart.

Kyoko sits on the stone ledge of a Stream Network canal and releases a heavy sigh. Alba settles next to her and presents an encouraging smile.

"I know what you're going to say," Kyoko starts. "'Don't take it personally.' Right?"

Alba nods. "Correct. The yellow silk just holds a different weight, it's not you."

"It is me," Kyoko insists. "Once you leave next week, everyone is going to expect me to be the next Alba. Full Bonded, perfect Alba."

"Please stop." Alba cringes. "I'm not perfect. And you don't have to be either. Being Kyoko is enough."

"It isn't for *him*," Kyoko counters. "He still blames me for what happened. After you leave..."

Alba wraps an arm around Kyoko's shoulders and pulls her closer. "After I leave, you'll be fine. The Prime will respect you as an Ambassador once you pass the trials next week."

Kyoko's eyes widen. "Next week! I forgot to ask!"

"Ask what?"

The igni smiles sheepishly. "For a few days off. My family just moved into the igni settlements on Lily Beach and are throwing a gathering."

Alba frowns. "You'd have to travel through the night and stay for, at most, a day, if you want to visit Lily Beach and make it back for your trials."

"That's my plan. I'll be back in time, Alba, I promise."

Alba's hesitation remains, but she knows how hard Kyoko has worked for the Ambassadorship. She trusts the igni's judgment. "Alright. Let's go to the Prime tomorrow morning and have him authorize your leave."

Kyoko's smile widens. "Thank you." She looks up at the moons' positions. "It's late. I'm sorry I kept you here so long. Ana must be waiting for you."

Alba scoffs. "You know my sister is not one to wait up for me. She likely missed me for a day then buried herself in work."

They embrace and bid farewell, knowing their next interaction will be before the Prime.

CHAPTER 6

THE THEOCRAT
AND THE MONARCH

Theocratic-Monarchy *SunSide*
Date *18th Day of Month 6, Year 1628 DG*

THERE IS NO GREATER SYMBOL of SunSide's devotion to its theocracy than the Temple Complex. Tall buildings house chapels, feast halls, council chambers, and classrooms. Towering statues, monuments, and shrines to the Four are featured in designated areas all around the vast compound. The outer rim is guarded by gates and pylons, and an ablution river runs around the center courtyard.

Once a generous gift from the conqueror to the Assembly of the Radiance, the Complex now stands as a long-enduring token of partnership between the two halves of the government. Gifts between the dynasty and the Members have been plenty, but none quite like this.

A stage constructed of ore has been erected in the courtyard overnight. It blends in with the Complex around it. What was once made of solid gold, shimmering in the light of the Four, now absorbs their radiant glow. The black hue of the ore casts an eerie aura around the place of worship.

The Complex is packed with citizens, every eager eye on the stage. A Doruh woman stands naked with her arms tied behind her and her chin held high. Her long, dark tresses fall in blissful curls, dancing down the front of her shoulders and covering her breasts. Her honey-brown eyes shine outward, beacons of hope soon to be extinguished. Her bronze skin glows against the sunlight in a way the Complex once did.

Bravers flank her on each side, carrying ore blades sheathed and strapped to their hips. There's a stillness on the stage, while the fervor in the crowd mounts with each passing second. The heavy strides of the MegaFather's boots rising on the stairs capture the attention of those on stage. The woman turns her head and smiles while the Bravers remain at attention.

Zar-Lo, the MegaFather, appears on stage and the crowd erupts into deafening cheers and applause. Many of them raise one hand, form a circle with their fingers, and place it over their foreheads, saluting the monarch. There are mostly faeries here, with some nymphs, pixies, and Doruh watching from the back, frowns littering their expressions.

Zar-Lo doesn't acknowledge the cheering crowd, projecting a stoic professionalism from his demeanor. Thick cloth embedded with fragments of ore cover his massive frame; it's similar to the Braver uniform, save for the long cape and red color. An ore blade, wider than those of the Bravers, is strapped to his waist.

He feels most regal in his ceremonial armor.

The woman's smile is unwavering as he approaches the center of the stage. With a wave of his hand, he instructs the Bravers to break formation and take a few steps backward. They do, providing him minimal privacy with the bare woman. She turns her head back toward the crowd and keeps her chin raised.

Zar-Lo approaches the woman and whispers as he speaks. The entire crowd falls silent in an attempt to hear the conversation, but their efforts are useless. "This is your last chance, Sonali. I'll only ask once more—"

"I don't require a trial," she interrupts him, still smiling. "First in a cell, now on a stage, I'm freely confessing to the crime. A trial will only waste the Assembly's time."

"Very well," Zar-Lo responds. "And you chose the Complex as the site of your execution?"

The woman glances at the statues and structures surrounding them. "I wish to die amongst the shrines of the Four, in the hopes that their light will carry me to a blissful eternity."

"Hm," Zar-Lo responds, quizzically. "Your devotion to Mega gods still strikes me as bizarre. Considering you're both Doruh and a traitor, I would think you'd reject the faith of your"—he switches to a tone of mockery—"*oppressors.*"

"I do not question the means by which the Four have brought me to their light. It is my desire, and my duty, to submit to their will."

Zar-Lo scoffs. "Don't talk to me about duty after what you've done, Sonali. If your radical comrades had succeeded, the monarchy would've fallen." He runs his fingers along the hilt of his ore blade. "If it weren't for my discovery, they would still be biting at my ankles."

"Your discovery is meaningless, Zar-Lo. Justice will be served one day. My execution is but a single step in a far longer process to attaining it."

The MegaFather chuckles. "That's the kind of delusion that drove you to treason and conspiracy. I'd forsake it now, in your final moments, or there will be no bliss to your eternity."

"I'll leave that up to the Four, not the king who comes overdressed to an execution. This isn't a battle, you don't need armor."

The MegaFather lets his gaze travel from Sonali's head to her feet, front and back. "Aren't you a bit underdressed?"

"No. I desire to leave this world just as I came into it. Proudly Doruh. This is our natural state."

"And you wonder why we consider you the lesser species," Zar-Lo remarks.

This time, Sonali laughs. "You are about to behead me in front of thousands of your subjects, as well as my followers. And yet, you have the nerve to accuse my kind of barbarism. Careful, or they might start calling you a hypocrite, Ore Monger."

The words wound him, abolishing his smile. Venom spews from him as he speaks to her. "I was going to make this quick and painless, but perhaps I'll reconsider."

"As you wish, Ore Monger," Sonali replies. She turns to the crowd, who is still silently waiting for the execution to begin. She chants, loud enough for her words to reverberate off the shrines and strike every ear in the Complex. "Ore Monger! Ore Monger!"

Zar-Lo steps back and withdraws his sword with his left hand, then gestures to two of the Bravers on stage, who flank Sonali and push her down to her knees.

She winces, but continues. "Ore Monger!"

"No," Zar-Lo says to the Bravers. "On her feet."

Immediate beheading would indeed be too quick and painless for the traitor.

The Bravers do as commanded and bring Sonali back up to her feet, as her chants bounce from shrine to shrine.

"Ore Monger! Ore Monger!"

Zar-Lo applies all of the force in his body to drive the ore blade through Sonali's back, until the cross-guard touches skin. The blade protrudes above Sonali's navel, dripping crimson, and she cries out in pain. Blood bursts from her mouth.

The MegaFather stands close behind her, the fingers of one hand wrapped around the hilt of his blade, the other hand tightly clutching Sonali's hip. He takes a moment, as the sound of her choking on her own blood enters the air, to place his nose and lips against the side of her head. He breathes deeply and allows the arousing scent of blood, fear, and justice to penetrate his nostrils.

Once he feels the life drain from her sufficiently, he steps back quickly and pulls the blade from her back. The Doruh drops to her knees and with a quick horizontal slice, the MegaFather separates her at the neck.

The crowd erupts into congratulatory celebration. Those below weep tears of joy as they embrace each other.

The two Bravers step forward to clean the site, but Zar-Lo stops them, and they return to their places. He wants her to remain there as he addresses the kingdom. He raises his hands, palms facing the crowd. It falls silent and awaits the MegaFather's words.

"This!" he says, pointing to the remains. The word is stated so powerfully that the entire audience around the Complex can hear him as if he is standing beside them. "This is their gratitude! This is what we get for granting them a seat at our table."

The crowd erupts again, this time into jeers of disappointment and ridicule. The few Doruh, nymphs, and pixies in the crowd dissolve into sobs.

"Citizens of SunSide, peace is always possible. In fact, it is a vital pillar of the kingdom we hope to be." He turns around to face the audience on the opposite side of the stage. "And yet, *they* continue to asphyxiate that hope with violence and hatred."

More jeers from Mega SunSidians to their Doruh countrymen. A small skirmish breaks out as a group of faeries attack an elderly Doruh man attempting to leave the Complex. He shifts into an armadillo to protect himself until others come to his aid to escort him out.

"Unrealistic Doruh demands have stalled progress for centuries. We granted them Liberation, and when they wanted equal representation in government, we benevolently gave it. And now these termites eat away at the work of our faerie ancestors; the same ancestors who gave them their genesis at the dawn of this era."

He turns to the third side of the stage and addresses a new audience again. "What next? Regicide? Faerie subjugation? Warfare?" He shakes his head and looks down at his feet, a show of his profound disappointment and sadness. The crowd cheers for him to convey their sympathies.

He gestures again to the remains. "This agent of their so-called *revolution* was working from within our government to dethrone my family, a dynasty that has done nothing but expand the circle of peace and extend a hand of tolerance and support for over eight hundred years."

He makes one final turn and faces the remaining unaddressed side of the stage. "I urge the Doruh to select leaders who will work with the Assembly, and work with me, as I continue to foster a long-lasting peace in both SunSide and MoonSide." He lifts his fist into the air. "The Future is Peace! The Future is Forever!"

Hearing the kingdom's official motto, the entire Complex erupts into cheers again. The stage itself rattles from the joy and excitement of those in attendance. Circled fingers fly up to faerie foreheads all around. Zar-Lo turns quickly on his heels and walks across the stage to the stairs.

The Bravers stay close behind him, flanking him on either side at the bottom of the stairs. They are joined by twelve more, who escort the MegaFather through the crowd and out of the Complex gates.

A hover chariot waits for him there, an oval vehicle with two rows of seats. The bottom half is metal, painted white, and the top is made of treated, protective glass. It hovers over the ground as a magnetized ore plate affixed to the bottom pushes against the ore embedded in the roads.

Waiting attentively outside of the chariot are the Braver General and the Facilitator. The former is a slender faerie dressed in a Braver uniform without a face mask, revealing a long mustache and puce skin. The other is a green-skinned pixie wearing black-and-red robes, with one sleeve removed and stitched at the shoulder.

Zar-Lo climbs into the front row of the vehicle, and his two underlings silently enter the back. The Facilitator runs his fingertips on the inside of the glass dome, using the Radiance to activate the chariot's locomotive mechanism. The journey to the Castrum begins.

"How was the speech, Saith?" Zar-Lo asks the Facilitator.

The pixie smiles. "Perfection, Father. As rehearsed."

"Excellent." He turns to the Braver General. "Vy-Ro, have the Librarians departed?"

"They have, Father. Alba and Kyoko were on their way back before the allegations came to light. They have no knowledge of Member Sonali's treason."

"I'd like to keep it that way. We have a month to decide how we're going to feed this to them for the Catacombs."

"I can meet with the Prime again," Saith suggests.

Zar-Lo releases a heavy sigh. "I'm out of bargaining chips. The Prime no longer finds benefit in our relationship. He refuses to bring ore anywhere near the Library, and I have little else he desires."

Saith shakes his head. "Accepting ore would tarnish his precious image. Not to worry, Father. I'll think of something to keep the treason out of the records."

"Thank you, Saith," Zar-Lo replies. "What's next on the schedule?"

Saith peers out the window to check the time. "We'll need to spend the remainder of the day rehearsing."

Zar-Lo furrows his brows. "For what?"

"The reading of Member Sonali's Final Act."

Zar-Lo grows tense and Vy-Ro's gray eyes widen.

"Absolutely not," Vy-Ro says. "She committed treachery against the throne. She doesn't get a Final Act."

Zar-Lo nods. "I agree with Vy-Ro. I recognize her right to a Final Act as a Member of the Assembly, but they can't possibly be considering this animal's wishes."

"I understand," Saith replies. "I haven't spoken with the Assembly yet, but I assure you, the reading must simply be a matter of formality. The law strictly nullifies the Final Act of any Assembly Member who has committed a crime. Treason and conspiracy both fall under that qualification."

"Then why must we even attend?" Zar-Lo questions, frustration mounting.

Saith clears his throat. "It's the right thing to do, Father. Politically speaking."

"I stopped caring about politics a long time ago," Zar-Lo grumbles.

"Kings rarely have an option. It comes with being a ruler."

"Kings aren't rulers, Saith. And we certainly aren't politicians." He turns and looks out of the glass windows at his kingdom's streets. "We're illusionists."

Sparkling starlight showers the Temple Complex. The compound is empty save for a few worshippers and the Bravers on patrol. Soothing tranquility replaces the morning's activity.

Two Bravers stand guard in the entryway of the Shrine of Ona, the oldest and strongest of the Four. The night has been calm, uneventful. They jest and laugh and spend time keeping one another awake as they guard the undecorated casket within the shrine.

A chariot enters the Complex gates and steadily moves through the ore paths, closer and closer to the shrine. The warriors watch as it approaches and comes to a halt at the front steps. A familiar figure emerges from the front row.

Member Saila of the Assembly moves to the back door, opens it, and reaches a hand forward to assist the elderly Doruh occupant onto her feet.

"Thank you, *mohuway*," the old shapeshifter says, affectionately. Saila smiles and begins leading her up the stone steps.

There are stark differences in their appearances. The Member, a pixie with jade skin, stands at nearly six feet in the colorful, embellished robes of the theocracy. Her companion is hunched, leaning heavily on Saila's arm, making her appear smaller than she must've been in her youth. She's wearing the traditional Doruh outfit: shalwar kameez with a dupatta loosely draped over her head. Her clothes are entirely pristine white.

They reach the top of the steps and the Bravers stand firm, shoulder-to-shoulder, in the doorway.

Saila sighs heavily. "Move aside, Director."

"Unfortunately, I cannot," the Legion Director responds. "Orders came from the MegaFather himself. No one is to enter until morning, when they come to dispose of the traitor's corpse."

At the word "traitor," the elderly woman winces and releases a soft whimper. Saila steadies her grip on the woman's hand, then turns to face the Braver again.

"You may report to the MegaFather and his"—she searches for a word to use instead of the insult that comes to mind—"associates, but the Assembly of the Radiance is beyond the commands of the monarchy. As an officer of law enforcement, you must recognize this. I'll repeat myself only once: move aside, Director."

The Legion Director turns to the other Braver, who nods. The two warriors separate, clearing a path for Saila and the woman. The casket sits in the center of the shrine on stone tiles. The woman's hands begin to tremble when she sees it.

The illumination of the lighting panels around the chamber has been lowered, making it difficult to see. Saila closes her eyes and uses the Radiance to raise the brightness on the panels. When she opens them, the woman is looking around and smiling.

"Amazes me that you and your father are still capable of accessing the Radiance amongst all of this ore," she says.

"His connection to the Radiance is probably the only useful thing he's ever given me," Saila responds.

"Will he be unhappy with you, if he finds out we've come here tonight?"

Saila smiles. "It doesn't matter. The Facilitator's ears are too far up Zar-Lo's backside for him to even hear about our visit."

The woman lightly taps Saila's wrist. "You know I am no admirer of his, but he is still your father. Do not speak of him that way."

Saila nods. "Sorry, Aunty." She searches the wide shrine. "There must be a chair for you somewhere."

"Oh, no, don't worry about that." She looks down at the casket a few feet away. Her voice quivers as she speaks. "My daughter rests on the ground. So shall I. Help me sit."

Saila helps her sit gently down in front of the casket, then kneels next to her. Both of them lean forward and kiss the untreated wood. Saila takes deep breaths to steady her emotions, trying not to focus on the memories running through her mind. It cuts too deep to remember the smiles she and Sonali shared.

The woman cannot control herself the same way and loses herself in loud sobs. Saila embraces her shoulders and comforts her. It takes a few minutes for the elderly woman to regain her composure.

When she does, she speaks in a whisper. "Thank you, *mohuway*, for telling me the truth."

Saila whispers back, "I couldn't let you believe that your daughter was a traitor." She runs her fingers lovingly over the casket. "She was a hero. The Revolution nearly triumphed because of her. And now, it has a second chance, thanks to her sacrifice. This is only the first step in our plan."

The elderly woman nods and leans down to whisper to the casket. "My brave girl. You will change everything."

"The last time I spoke with Sonali, I had asked her to clarify some things with you. Did she?"

Sonali's mother nods. "We spoke last night. Everything will be passed on to her son when he comes of age. And she wanted to be buried in the Northern Hills of MoonSide with her father."

Saila smiles. "It will be done."

The woman takes Saila's hand and kisses it. "Thank you for all you've done for us."

"Please, don't thank me, Aunty," she responds, shaking her head. "You were always more of a parent to me than Saith was. This is the very least I can do." She turns to the casket again as moisture develops in her eyes. "For my sister."

"Let's pray for her before we leave," the woman suggests. Saila nods and waits for the woman to begin, but Sonali's mother hesitates. "This is the holiest shrine of the Four, and I'm sitting next to a theocrat. It feels disrespectful. Perhaps I should make my prayers for her later."

Saila shakes her head. "Worship is worship. The Four teach us to respect all faiths and their prayers. Sonali and I both believed that. Please, pray for your daughter without hesitation."

The woman nods and begins. She folds her hands and lowers her gaze, while Saila raises her arms into the air toward the Four. "I call out to the Twins, holy brother and sister, to cast out the evil around my daughter's grave. Let her rest soundly, let her await my arrival in the arms of her father, and let us all be united once again in the world beyond. Come, divine siblings, and rid us of the plague on the throne. Let her sacrifice not be in vain."

She gives the casket one final kiss and Saila does the same, whispering, "Goodbye, Sona. I love you. Watch over me." She helps the woman stand and they exit the shrine. Once Sonali's mother is seated in the chariot again, Saila closes the door, turns around, and marches back up the steps until she's face-to-face with the Legion Director.

She speaks as clearly and severely as she can. "I can have you tried for disobeying a direct order from a Member of the theocracy. Don't let it happen again."

"Deepest apologies," the Braver responds with an insincere half-smirk.

Saila takes a deep breath to temper her frustration. "I'm warning you, Director."

The Braver sighs. "Let's be plain with one another, Member Saila. You can have me tried and convicted for a hundred counts of disobedience. By the end of it, you'll have wasted the kingdom's resources for me to get a month of paid leave and a slap on the wrist."

Nothing he's said is inaccurate. One thought races through Saila's mind as she returns to the chariot and drives away.

Not for long. You'll all get what's coming to you.

CHAPTER 7

THE CENTER

Sovereign City-State *The Library*
Date *18th Day of Month 6, Year 1628 DG*

THE MOONS INCH PEACEFULLY ALONG their celestial arcs, lighting up the sky like two glowing eyes. Unisa passes the night unable to sleep, cradling the delicate text she surreptitiously removed from *Witness*.

She spends hours staring at it in her lap before deciding to occupy herself with things less consequential. A stemless plant with thick, fleshy leaves grows in Ora's apartment and, from it, Unisa has extracted some oil, which she uses on her braids before tying them up.

Her bookshelf provides some refuge, offering myriad texts possessing the Prime's philosophical brilliance and explaining the tenets that hold up his framework of success: the Fully Bonded.

The Fully Bonded possess a constant thirst for knowledge, and have eliminated all prideful behaviors; fear, vulnerability, and victimhood are alien to them. They are responsible and accountable for all that happens to them and how they respond. They are honest with themselves, with one another, and with the Prime. Above all, they believe—in the history held under the city, and in the Prime, who safeguards all.

The words echo from her subconscious, up into her conscious mind, and bounce off of her tongue.

"They are honest with the Prime. They believe in the Prime's mercy."

Unisa's heart drums against her chest. The path forward hits her in a wave of clarity. The Prime must be informed about her transgressions, and about what Hay-Ro's letter insinuates. She must be honest with the Prime to make amends. To balm the wounds that Hay-Ro's words opened. No matter the consequences.

She must believe in the Prime's mercy and wisdom.

Unisa remains focused on the path ahead, as she soars through the loops on her way to work. The Prime's office is in the Center, so she'll need an excuse to get there. Maksi isn't aware of the letter. She decides against telling him and further involving him in the matter. When she presents it before the Prime, she can hide Maksi's involvement.

Before the Prime.

Her feathers tremble at the thought of confessing to her crimes before the most powerful man in the city. What will happen to her? What is she going to say to him?

The four-thousand-year-old structures you've helped to preserve, that have been standing on a bedrock of truth, have fractures in them, and I am the only one who knows.

She shudders at the thought that this ridiculous statement could be her first to an individual she's idolized for as long as she can remember.

After exiting the Loops, Unisa heads straight through the marketplace, skipping Kura's, to the metal archway. Once Maksi lets her in and she descends into the section, she keeps the bag with *The Everlasting Journey* tight against her side and away from his view.

The Mega Gatekeeper is preparing fresh visitor logs for the day. Unisa sets the bag down on the floor.

"Are you alright?" Maksi questions.

Unisa turns quickly to him. "Fine. Why?"

Maksi raises an eyebrow. "You don't have any breakfast with you, you look like you haven't slept all night, and you jump every time I look in your direction." Maksi lowers his volume, although they're the only two there. "Is this about last night?"

Unisa inhales sharply. "What about last night?"

"You know. Koal." He smiles warmly at her. "Relax. We've learned from our mistakes and we're moving forward. Everything's fine now."

Guilt tears through her. Speaking falsehoods isn't the only form of dishonesty. Omission may be worse.

She musters up a smile as best as she can. "Thanks, Maksi. You're right. I'll try to relax."

"Good. It should be an easy day, anyway, with Koal out."

Unisa's eyes widen as clarity hits her again. "Koal is off today."

Maksi nods. "Yes, he told us last night, remember? Family emergency."

Unisa continues smiling and nodding, while Maksi returns to the morning procedures. Fate has opened a doorway to the Center. With Koal off, his supervisory duties are delegated to an Educator Librarian named Roxie. A nymph who was once one of Unisa's instructors in the Academy.

Roxie teaches in the Center, only a few floors below the Prime's office.

Without alarming her colleague, Unisa searches for an excuse to visit Roxie. At first, it appears Maksi's diligence has left little room for her to manufacture a justification for leaving her station. But when her eyes wander casually around to Maksi's side of the desk, she finds his fingers cradling a recently returned document in poor condition.

"It needs a slab," she says, alluding to the process by which fragile papers are encased in a transparent, protective coating for their preservation.

Maski turns to her, lines appearing on his forehead. "What?"

"This document"—she points to it—"needs to be slabbed. The handwritten ratification of MoonSide's original Alphocracy, 784 DG. It's over eight hundred years old. I'm going to take it to Roxie to get it approved for slabbing."

Maksi hesitates to hand the document over. "Perhaps we can wait until the end of the day to see if Roxie comes by. That'll avoid leaving one of us here alone for too long."

"If we wait until the end of the day"—she thinks quickly—"it won't be sent out until tomorrow and it could be days until we get it back. If it gets approved now and I send it out before midday, it should be back by closing tomorrow. It's more secure that way."

Maksi's uncertainty permeates the air. Unisa points to the document and continues, "Do you truly want this document floating around unslabbed?" She looks down at the paper and feigns sorrow. "Such a shame that it's in such poor condition now. We have to save it."

Maksi's hesitation evaporates in an instant. He nods forcefully. "You're right, it really is a shame." He picks it up slowly and hands it to Unisa, who carefully places it into a blue envelope and then into her bag. She slings the bag over her shoulder and heads to the back of the section, behind the shelves, and through the Catacomb entrance in the back wall.

The Center is a half-hour walk through the underground tunnels. It would be longer on the street level, but the passages under the city exit directly into the building's lobby. To any new Librarian, the brightly-lit, tiled Catacombs would feel like a maze. But Unisa is more comfortable here than she is in her own apartment.

She enters into a long hallway that inclines, forming a ramp to the street level. At the end of it, Unisa finds herself in a vast atrium: the Center's lobby. It's packed with humans, Mega, and Doruh, with and without tunics. There are tables, chairs, and benches scattered around the chamber, some occupied with civilians.

There are also a number of Student Librarians walking around in their white tunics. The Academy comprises the first three floors of the Center above the atrium. Roxie's classroom is on the first level, as most of the courses she teaches are introductory.

Unisa spots the atrium's front desk. To avoid the crowd, she flaps her wings and launches up into the air, flying over the bustling masses and landing directly in front of the two Gatekeepers sitting behind the desk. The first is a Mega woman who is organizing some paperwork into a cabinet, while the other, an igni man, appears lost in translating a document from Nysabaani.

The breeze from Unisa's wings when she lands alerts the Mega Gatekeeper, who turns around.

"How can I help you?" she asks with disinterested monotony.

"I'm here to see Roxie."

"She's teaching, you'll have to come back later." She begins to turn back around to the cabinet, but Unisa stops her.

"This is important. Please let her know I'm here."

The Mega Gatekeeper rolls her eyes. "Purpose of your visit?"

"Authorization for slabbing."

"Name?"

"Unisa."

The Gatekeeper sighs, then bends forward to a microphone and speaks.

"Roxie, Unisa is here to get your authorization for slabbing." There's a momentary pause where Unisa and the Gatekeeper awkwardly stare at one another, until a familiar voice crackles over the speaker.

"Wonderful!" Roxie says cheerfully. "Send her up!"

The Gatekeeper gestures to an archway leading to stone staircases and turns back to her filing.

Long lines head into and out of the staircase. Unisa flies up into the air again and travels through the staircase above everyone else. This is considered poor manners, but the silent scrutiny she's undoubtedly receiving from the passersby is of little concern, relative to her task.

Roxie's classroom is all the way at the end of the hallway. Before Unisa can pull the door open, it swings toward her and Roxie's arms wrap around the angi. Although surprised, she happily embraces Roxie back.

"It's been too long, Uni," Roxie says, stepping back into the classroom and making space for Unisa to enter. "Come in."

The room is smaller than she remembers, as are the desks and the students. She can't help but think, *Was I that small at fourteen?*

Roxie seems older, as well. Or perhaps, just more experienced. It's been nine years since Unisa sat in this classroom, learning from the azure-skinned nymph. And now she's two promotions away from donning the same red linen tunic.

If the Prime truly is merciful.

Unisa reaches into the bag on her shoulder and pulls out the blue envelope. "I needed your authorization to have this sla—"

"In a minute," Roxie interrupts her. "Neha was just finishing up her presentation. After she's done, I'll dismiss the class and sign whatever you need."

Unisa can't come up with an excuse for urgency quickly enough. A Doruh student standing at the front of the classroom presents and Roxie turns to listen to her.

"As the War of New Clans concluded, a new era arose: Doruh Genesis," the young shapeshifter explains. "The year was dubbed 1 DG to signify the end of the Teri Age. SunSide's warriors attempted to turn the remaining humans, the teri clan, into animals and failed, creating shapeshifters and giving birth to the Doruh species."

"Excellent!" Roxie exclaims, spawning a smile on the student's face. "Very well researched, Neha." She turns to the remaining students. "Any questions?" The students remain quiet, save for one in the back row, whose snores can be heard in the atrium below.

Roxie shakes her head. "Alright, you're free to go." The students rush out, leaving the Librarians alone in the classroom. Unisa hands her the blue envelope and Roxie removes the document carefully.

"Good eye, Uni, this definitely needs a slab." She reaches into her desk and removes a blank authorization form that she begins to fill out.

Unisa nods quietly, but she's barely listening. Her attention wanders anxiously to the double doors leading to the staircases: one that goes up to the top floor, and the other that goes back down to the atrium.

"Alright," Roxie says, completing the form and placing it into the envelope with the document. "Hand this to the front desk on your way back to *Witness* and they'll send it out today."

Unisa thanks her and places the envelope in her bag. Moments later, she finds herself back in the hallway, facing the two doorways.

The doorway on the right leads to the descending stairs. To the lobby, to the Catacombs, and to *Witness*. To the safety and familiarity of the life she knows.

The doorway on the left opens to the ascending stairs. To the top floor, to the Prime's office. To consequences far greater than Unisa is certain she can handle. She wonders if her plan was made in haste. The Library could be opened to scrutiny. She could be exiled for removing a text from *Witness*.

She hesitates, but, in the end, the choice is clear. Wrongs must be made right. *The Fully Bonded believe.* She opens the doorway to the left and flies up to the top floor.

CHAPTER 8

THE EXILE

Sovereign City-State *The Library*
Date *18th Day of Month 6, Year 1628 DG*

THE TOP FLOOR OF THE Center is a wide, open chamber filled
with sturdy metal desks between flimsy wooden partitions. The room
has a constant, fluid flow, a river of Librarians. They pay no mind to
Unisa when she emerges from the staircase.

The angi Gatekeeper can see tunics of every color here, as ranks
are irrelevant. On the top floor, the hierarchy is simplified: all Librarians report directly to the Prime. Top floor positions of any rank are
coveted. Even the pink-clad Scribe Librarians that work here are more
financially secure than the Ambassadors on mission.

The Prime's Gatekeeper has historically been the highest-paid position in the Library, second only to the leader himself, of course. Those
who've held this station in the past have had no reservations about
flaunting their wealth. The current keeper of the position, however, is
simply grateful to be here at all, though he makes half of what other
Gatekeepers do.

In the eight years Unisa has known him, Rafael has never once expressed the slightest dissatisfaction with his diminished earnings. He's always made one thing clear: exile breeds humility.

The first exile to be accepted into the Library in over fifty years, Rafael's citizenship is contingent on his success under the Prime's tutelage. Rumors flourished throughout the city for months after Rafael's arrival; most speculated that their shared mari culture softened the Prime's heart to the teenager.

Unisa steps forth through the chamber. The first row of desks belong to the Scribes and Recorders, beyond which are the Educators in the middle. The final rows, which mainly sit empty, belong to Ambassadors, and their appointed Vice Ambassadors, on active missions.

Unisa counts seven doors on the back wall, one in the middle, and three huddled together on either side. The middle door leads to the Prime's office, while the six others belong to those of the Supreme Librarians. These six doors are painted blue, while the Prime's is painted black, to signify the colors of their tunics.

As the distance between Unisa and the doors dwindles, a thought occurs to her: this will be the first time she's ever asked Rafael to use his position for her benefit. It's a massive violation of their friendship, a substantial transgression of boundaries.

Rafael walks on shaky ground as it is. Hyper-aware of his actions and choices, he ensures that his permission to remain in the Library is never jeopardized. But this situation is dire. It goes far beyond either of them. She must ask him for an audience with the Prime.

This is for the good of the Library.

She reaches the black door and raises her fist to knock. Her hand trembles, and beads of sweat break onto her forehead. There's a long moment of hesitation and a deep breath…and then she knocks. The air around her thickens as she reaches a point from which return is impossible.

Rafael opens the door wearing his gold tunic and a smile. "Uni! What are you doing here?" He leans down and kisses each of her cheeks, greeting her traditionally.

"I have something important to talk to you about," she responds.

Rafael's smile fades. "Here? Now? Is everything alright?" He looks at her head and arms and legs, searching for some injury or ailment.

Unisa can't hold back a smile at his concern for her. She takes his hands in her own and refocuses him to her eyes.

"I'm fine. But can we talk in your office?"

Rafael nods, anxious lines etched onto his face. He steps to the side, allowing Unisa to enter. The room is smaller and emptier than she expected. The Prime's office door is only a few feet in front of her on the back wall. Rafael's desk is to her left, and to her right sit inexpensive wooden chairs for those waiting to meet with the Prime.

In the corner of the room, behind Rafael's desk, is a fountain with flowing water and a stack of thin paper cups.

"A gift from the Prime," Rafael says, looking at it as if it were made of gold. He drags a chair to the opposite side of his desk for Unisa to sit, then takes his place across from her.

"We'll have to keep our voices down," he informs her. "The Prime is in a meeting." Unisa nods in acknowledgment. "You've never come to my office before, this must be important."

"It is," she responds. "But before I begin, I have to ask you to trust me."

Rafael's face contorts, worry mounting. He reaches across the desk and takes Unisa's hand. "Of course, I trust you."

Unisa takes a deep breath and begins. "Last night, at dinner, you sensed my distress."

He nods. "Yes, I remember."

"I discovered something unimaginable. In *Witness*."

She hesitantly reaches into her bag and pulls out the text, placing it onto the desk. Before it even makes contact with the metal, Rafael is on his feet, backing away as if Unisa has produced a live cobra.

"Please tell me that's a copy."

Unisa shakes her head slowly, guilt driving her gaze down. "It's the original. I pulled it from *Witness*."

Rafael plummets back into his seat, his legs failing him. When he speaks, his volume is low, but his tone is harsh. "And you brought it *here*? Ten feet from the Prime? Have you lost your mind?"

"Rafa, I asked you to trust me."

Rafael shakes his head. "No. Get it out of here. Take it back and we can forget this happened." His tone switches from anger to supplication. "I'm an exile, Uni. This is the only home I have now. I can't believe you would bring this here knowing what it could do to me. Please, take it back."

"You haven't done anything wrong. I pulled it, but I promise you, I have a good reason."

"I don't want to hear it. I'm begging you, take it back."

"There are lies in the Catacombs, Rafa."

Rafael stares at her blankly. He looks at the black door, then at Unisa. "Thirty seconds."

She flips the book open to Hay-Ro's letter and pushes it across the desk to Rafael. "This letter appeared in the back of the book after an interaction with the Radiance. Red-Lo's Head Salver wrote it. He claims that everything Red-Lo wrote about the MegaMother is a lie: from seizing the throne for herself to coercing Red-Lo into the Everlasting Journey to how she died. Her whole legacy is tarnished, likely unjustly."

Rafael looks down at the letter for a moment, then back up at Unisa. "Did the MegaParents ever find the immortality they sought during the Everlasting Journey?"

Unisa stares at Rafael, dumbfounded. "No, Rafa, you know they didn't."

"Then none of this matters." He closes the book and slides it forcefully back at Unisa. "They're both long dead. Nothing has changed. Now take it back."

"Rafa, please," Unisa pleads. "You know as well as I do, this isn't just about the outcome. The facts matter; the truth matters."

"Don't lecture me about facts and truth," he hisses. "*Nusta. Ista. Hosta.* Knowledge, history, and truth. The first time I saw those words, I was in shackles. A fifteen-year-old boy. Frightened, thinking I would be hung or flayed if the Prime didn't take me in. And when he did, I promised him I would live every day of my life for the facts and the truth."

He points to the text. "But not like this. We cannot violate some tenets to protect other ones. Being this close to something illegal is going to end us both."

"You are not in danger here—I am. And I'm willing to face that danger because the facts and the truth are the only reason I'm here." Her eyes begin to burn as she speaks her next words, the vision of angi wings walking away from her growing in her mind. "It's why they left me here, Rafa. To be a Librarian and protect the history. But if the history is a lie, what was the point of it?"

Rafael takes Unisa's hand again. "Uni, if you get banished from this city, you can go back to PeakHaven. Back to your parents. There's no third chance for me. I have nowhere else to go. This is the only place I belong; I matter."

He is near tears. His frantic tone and blatant distress fall on her like a hailstorm. She's asking too much of him. "I understand. I can take it back and find another way. You always matter, Rafa."

She reaches for the text, but before she can grab it, another hand falls on it. An older hand, connected to a forearm with fins going up to the elbow, leading to a black tunic sleeve.

Neither Rafael nor Unisa had realized that the Prime's door had clicked open moments earlier. Unisa has never seen the Prime this close before. She was once at the back of a crowd during one of his speeches, but that was it.

He looks older up close. She knows he's in his late fifties, but he always carries himself with such stoic grace that she had forgotten his age until this moment, when the jagged lines of elderhood run around his cheeks, eyes, and forehead.

He holds the typical mari traits: long, dark hair, webbed fingers, fins, and the piscine nare slits where other humans have a nose. The Prime's most unique feature is his eyes; they are somehow warm and cold at the same time.

The Prime lifts the text off of Rafael's desk, as both Gatekeepers take to their feet. He examines the book quietly in his hands. Unisa looks over to Rafael and notices him trembling.

She's never seen him so frightened before.

"Red-Lo's handwriting," the Prime finally says. "The original text, out of *Witness*. How unfortunate."

"Great Prime, I can expl—" Rafael begins to say. He falls silent when the Prime quickly raises his eyes from the text.

"I'm disappointed, Rafael. After all I've done for you."

"It is not his fault, Great Prime," Unisa interjects, mustering every ounce of courage. The Prime offers her the same look, and she understands why Rafael fell silent. It's the look a butcher gives to a lamb wandering into the slaughterhouse.

The Prime squints, as if trying to recall an ancient memory. "Unisa. Gatekeeper of *Witness*."

Unisa sways between being impressed and terrified.

The Prime smiles. "I know every name that comes and goes from this city. You grew up here, and yet you violated your own ethics. You've moved off the path of the Fully Bonded, after we bestowed the honor of *Witness* upon you."

"Forgive me, Great Prime. I assure you I have good reason."

The Prime nods. "I do hope so. Please, join me. Both of you." He turns around and walks back into his office. Rafael and Unisa stare at the open doorway, frozen. Unisa turns slowly toward Rafael and tries to say something, but he ignores her and trudges after the Prime.

Unisa takes a deep breath and follows.

CHAPTER 9

THE PRIME

Sovereign City-State *The Library*
Date *18th Day of Month 6, Year 1628 DG*

"HE WON'T APPROVE MY LEAVE," Kyoko whispers to Alba, breaking the Ambassador's focus from the Prime's doorway. "One sound from outside and he just walked away, in the middle of a conversation. What makes you think he'll respect my request?"

Footfalls rescue Alba from having to respond. The Prime saunters back to his desk, holding a book with tattered edges.

"I hope what you heard at the door was worth the lapse in professionalism," Alba bitingly comments.

The Prime keeps his gaze on the book while gesturing over Alba's shoulder. "It was."

She hadn't realized two young Gatekeepers had followed the Prime into the room: Rafael and another she doesn't recognize until she gets close.

"You're Ora's daughter," she blurts out. "Unisa, right?" The Gatekeeper nods quietly and doesn't shift her gaze from the Prime.

Alba realizes she's misread the charged tone of the room, and her smile fades. The two young Librarians stand huddled together, as if protecting one another. Rafael hangs his head and, for the first time in the years she's known him, dark fear dims his usually bright eyes.

The Prime places the book gently down on the desk in front of Alba and motions for her to take it.

She does so, holding it delicately and reading the title. *"The Everlasting Journey."* The air thickens around her. Red-Lo's handwriting stares back at her. She turns to the Gatekeepers. "Did an Ambassador give this to you?"

They both hesitate, then Unisa slowly shakes her head. Alba's heart drops. Bright, sharp young people with such potential. Why would they do this?

She turns back to the Prime. "What are you going to do?"

"What does the law dictate should happen to them?" the Prime asks her. As always, it's a test. An exercise in feeding his ego and proving how well he's trained her.

"A trial. Potential banishment, for citizens." Anguish bubbles in her chest for Rafael, as she takes his hand and squeezes gently. "Worse for exiles."

His body remains still, but he lightly squeezes back.

Unisa clears her throat and raises her head. "Rafael is innocent. The crime is mine alone. Punishing him would be unjust."

"Unjust." The Prime allows the word to simmer on his tongue as he returns to the chair behind his desk and visually appraises the young Librarians. "The problem, Unisa, is that the principles of punishment and justice are subjective. Even if I followed the law and held trials, some would find the sentences mild, while others, merciless. Rafael cannot be exempt from consequence simply because you claim he wasn't involved. Many would find *that* to be unjust."

"And yet," Alba adds, hoping to intercede in some way, "if anyone can make exceptions, it would be you."

The Prime raises a finger and strokes his chin. "Indeed, Alba. I am in the unique position to empower Librarians. Rehabilitate them. Provide second" —he pauses, focusing his gaze on Rafael— "or third, chances."

His eyes shift to Unisa. "Alright, young Gatekeeper. Tell me, what is the 'good reason' you claim for breaking our laws?"

Unisa coddles her right fist in her left hand. She rubs her knuckles nervously and breathes deeply. The Prime's eyebrows narrow a little more with each passing moment.

Finally, Unisa speaks in a frantic tone, as if the words are engulfed in flames and burning her all the way out. "I believe there to be fabrications in the Library."

Alba turns to the Prime to gauge his reaction, but his expression hasn't changed in the slightest.

How did she find out? Alba wonders.

"Continue," the Prime responds.

Unisa reaches a hand out to Alba, requesting the text, and the Ambassador gives it to her. As she flips to the final pages, Alba acknowledges the young Librarian's composure when facing potential banishment.

A younger version of herself exists in Unisa.

The Gatekeeper places the book between Alba and the Prime. They each lean forward to read from it. It appears to be a letter, written by Red-Lo's Head Salver, implying falsification in the entire text regarding the MegaMother.

Alba sits in stunned silence as she realizes that Unisa jeopardized her entire career, and more, over this inconsequential allegation. *Perhaps she isn't as much like me as I thought.*

"Where did this letter come from?" the Prime asks Unisa. "How did you uncover it?"

"The book was unintentionally exposed to the Radiance, revealing the letter."

The Prime nods. "I see. And this revelation prompted you to remove the text from *Witness* and bring it to me?"

Unisa nods.

The Prime's gaze moves to Alba, and a menacing smile creeps onto his face. The tide shifts in a sinister, yet familiar way.

"I see now," he says, turning back to Unisa. "The letter does not absolve you of your transgression, but I can understand the compulsion to bring it to me."

Alba's palms sweat and she pulls her hand away from Rafael's. That familiar, menacing smile betrays the Prime's intention: he's brewing something nefarious.

The Prime rises to his feet. "The claims in the letter must be investigated."

A glint of hope shines in Unisa's eyes as a faint smile plays on her lips. She's a cod in his net. Alba watches the catastrophe unfold, unable to stop it. She thinks as quickly as she can, trying to figure out his scheme here, his plot.

The Prime continues. "Does anyone else, beyond the five of us in this room, know about this?" Unisa shakes her head. "Excellent. Then we must resolve it quietly and unconventionally."

Unisa's smile fades. "Unconventionally?"

The Prime nods emphatically. "Yes, an unusual solution." In two strides he's in front of her with his hands on her shoulders. Unisa goes rigid under the uninvited contact. "What are you willing to do to return to the path of the Fully Bonded? To continue your growth?"

Don't say it, Alba thinks, as the Prime looks over Unisa's shoulder at Rafael.

"What are you willing to do for the community that took you in? For me?"

Please, don't say it, her mind repeats.

Almost in unison, Rafael and Unisa respond. "Anything."

Alba grows nauseous. She can't save them unless she knows what the Prime is thinking. She can't save them if she doesn't know what to save them from.

The Prime removes his hands from Unisa's shoulders. "By committing a crime, you both have displayed a breach of your character. An impulsiveness that goes against your morality. Now, you have the opportunity to commit to the consequences and mend that breach."

Alba's tongue moves before she can stop it. "What consequences?"

"Unisa will go to SunSide. She will question the MegaFather and the Braver General about what their ancestors wrote. It is their history, perhaps they have some idea of the letter's legitimacy."

Alba turns to Unisa. The color has drained from the Gatekeeper's face. She clearly understands the danger that such a journey poses to a Librarian who hasn't been trained to venture beyond the walls.

"Unisa isn't permitted out of the city gates," Alba inserts, attempting to save her. "She has trained neither as a Recorder, nor as an Ambassador."

"And yet"—the Prime throws Alba's words back at her—"if anyone can make exceptions, it would be me."

Alba's stomach twists. He knows the danger this poses. *Why is he doing this?*

The Prime turns to Unisa and frowns. "You look frightened. The emotional stamp of the Fully Broken. What are you afraid of?"

Unisa hesitates. "The unknown."

The Prime moves close to her and places his hands on her shoulders again, this time running them up and down her arms. "Your body is capable of things you've never done before. You have to decide what you're willing to do to realize those things. So much is possible, simply when you *believe* you can achieve it."

"The Fully Bonded believe," Unisa states, a smile on her lips replacing the fear in her eyes.

The Prime nods. His malicious plot is wrapped in golden foil. "Not just in me, but in yourself. Conquering difficult tasks will bring you back to the right path and earn your redemption."

The question is unwilling to sit in Alba's mind any longer. It bursts from her throat. "Why are you doing this? It's dangerous."

The Prime turns quickly to her and warm fury flares from him. "I'm not *doing* anything." He erases the rage and turns back to Unisa, holding deep, tense eye contact. "I would never imperil those I love."

Unisa takes a step back and whispers, "Love?"

Alba's jaw clenches. *He has her.*

"Of course." He places his hand gently on her cheek, and this time, the touch appears more wanted, accepted. "I love all citizens. And because I love you, I wish for your success." He turns to Rafael. "This community loves you. But to be part of it, you have to decide how much you're willing to fight for it. What you're willing to do for it."

Rafael swallows hard. "I will commit to any mission you give me, Great Prime."

"Good. Go to Tusa. The TreeKeeper resides there. She's the only living being who was alive at the time of the Everlasting Journey. She may have insight."

Alba scoffs. "The TreeKeeper is a children's story. You can't possibly send them—"

The Prime cuts her sentence off. "I can and I will." He turns back to Rafael. "Do you have any questions?"

Rafael nods softly. "Where's Tusa?"

"South," Kyoko responds, drawing the attention of the room. "The southernmost island of EverEmber."

Rafael's eyes widen. "I ca-can't," he stammers.

The Prime places a hand on Rafael's chest. "Shh, shh, shh. Be calm. I understand you worry about walking into the igni homeland with fins. But you will be safe when they see you with one of their own." He raises a finger and points to Kyoko. "You. You will escort him."

Alba's anger drives into her feet and raises her. "No. She has nothing to do with this."

The fury returns to the Prime's eyes. "Her request for leave is denied until she returns from this mission."

"You cannot send them out into a world they know nothing about."

"They'll have maps," the Prime responds, facetiously, returning to the chair behind his desk.

"I'm not talking about geography. There are valid grounds to the laws that prohibit Gatekeepers from leaving the city."

The Prime's scowl hardens further. "Fine. They won't leave as Gatekeepers, then. Rafael, Unisa, and Kyoko will each be given yellow, silk tunics." He turns to each of them. "Congratulations, you're all Ambassadors now."

The heat inside Alba's chest rises. He's toying with her. And he's winning. "Promoting them three ranks won't teach them how to survive."

"I can do this," Unisa interjects. The Prime smiles and she reciprocates. "I'll do anything to return to the path. To earn redemption. To be worthy of the yellow silk."

Worry lines cover Rafael's forehead. He looks from Unisa to Alba, then to Kyoko, and finally to the Prime. "I commit to the mission." He repeats the sentiment defeatedly and mechanically.

They all turn to Kyoko. She lowers her eyes to the floor and gives a short nod.

"You leave in the morning," the Prime says. "Go home. Prepare."

"Thank you for the magnanimous opportunity, Great Prime," Unisa says, before she turns and exits behind Rafael and Kyoko.

Alba and the Prime, alone in the room, bathe in the tense silence. She slowly sinks back into the seat and attempts to draw an answer to her question again, this time with a new tactic.

"What point are you trying to make, Uncle?"

The Prime leans back in his seat and chuckles. "You were a small child the last time you called me that. To what do I owe this sudden respect?"

"Perhaps in my final days here, I can speak to what little humanity is left in your heart."

The Prime rolls his eyes. "Alba, you're not going anywhere unless I allow it. You would've left a long time ago if you thought you could hide from me. You're still here, and that means you comprehend my reach. The others must learn it, as well."

"You want them to venture out so you can teach them about your reach?"

"No, I want you to accept your fate. *They* are simply a means for me to achieve that." He leans forward, holding strong eye contact. "We're going to make a wager, do some gambling. Unisa will leave the Library tomorrow and enter into the world. I believe, regardless of what she sees out there, she will remain loyal to me, and to our teachings, and to our history. If she does, you have to accept the black tunic you've been insolently rejecting." He runs his hands down his own uniform.

"I'll die before I wear that."

"No, you won't. If you die, you know I'll come for Ana. I've always wanted it to be you, but if not, I'll settle for her."

Alba sinks back in her seat, exhausted. "Why me, Uncle? Why this obsession?"

The Prime points to the city beyond his windows. "Because to them, you embody the Fully Bonded. They know how devoted you are, and that's why you have to wear this tunic after me. You give me credibility. When they doubt me, you give me an example of what I can create. I know Unisa will return Fully Bonded. Because she aspires to be you. They all do."

"What if she recognizes the truth? That the history in the Catacombs is manufactured."

The Prime sighs. "If she returns Fully Broken, you and Ana can leave. And I will not send anyone after you. You have my word."

Alba considers. He knows the offer is exactly what she wants. "Unisa and Rafael are not tools. I'm not your trophy just because I'm your brother's daughter. And Kyoko can't be your toy to play with.

You've pulled her into this situation for no reason other than your unwarranted blame."

His fist slams down on the desk. "It is *not* unwarranted. She is responsible for everything that happened."

"Why?" Alba challenges, choosing her next words carefully. "Because she wouldn't let you take her to bed?"

The Prime grits his teeth. "You have no right to speak about things you don't understand."

Alba straightens in her seat as her volume rises. "I understand better than anyone. It's why I left your house. Why I kept Ana and Kyoko away from you. I wasn't able to do the same for Kanako, and you ruined her life."

"I was her mentor. Nothing more."

Alba fails to suppress her disgust. "You don't expect me to believe that, do you?"

He pauses. "Nothing happened until she was old enough to make those decisions for herself."

Alba unleashes the fire she's been holding in her chest for years. "Someone that young couldn't possibly make that decision. From the time she got here, you dug your claws into her. You isolated her from me, and from Kyoko. She adored you, idolized you. When the time came, those decisions were no longer sound."

"Keep your voice down, Alba," the Prime growls.

Alba takes deep breaths to steady herself.

He maintains the silence until both Librarians have calmed. "The past is over, but we can still plan for the future. Perhaps this wager can be elevated: if Unisa returns Fully Bonded, loyalty intact, you will take your place in line for succession, *but* I will allow Ana to leave freely."

Alba opens her mouth to respond, but he lifts a finger to silence her.

"If not, you and Ana are still free to go. Either way, your sister is free. You just have to play the game."

Alba considers his words carefully. Agreeing to his manipulation makes her feel filthy. She tries to reason with him one last time. "Unisa will die out there alone, Uncle."

The Prime shakes his head. "Don't be dramatic. She has her diplomatic immunity to protect her."

"What good is immunity if she's stripped of her tunic and left to rot? The yellow silk is as despised as pointed ears and gray eyes."

"Feared," the Prime corrects her. "Not despised. Feared and respected."

"Different names for the same beast."

He sighs, exasperated. "Do we have a deal or not?"

Alba hesitates. "On one condition."

She looks out of the windows at the city gates and the world beyond them. He's pulled her in again, but it could mean legitimate freedom for her and for Ana. She turns back to him. "I'm going with her."

There's a long pause in which The Prime raises an eyebrow and takes the Ambassador in. Then he stands and speaks a word soaked in ego, in hubris. "Agreed."

CHAPTER 10

PeakHaven Pass

Occupied Territory *MoonSide*
Date *19th Day of Month 6, Year 1628 DG*

STOP REACHING FOR IT, YOU'RE drawing attention to us.

Naina growls her words into Salessa's mind as they walk steadily with the crowd. The chaitender removes her hands from the sack strapped to her back and puts them in her pockets, resisting the agonizing urge to periodically check on the many pouches of stones stuffed into it.

Sorry. I'm just—she sighs—*nervous.*

Naina's eyes soften. *Change champions, Lessi.*

Her sister's words provide a modicum of ease. It was their father's saying: *Change champions when fists fail.* Anytime the twins found themselves nervous or fearful, he would remind them that physical strength is not the root of success—the ability to change and adapt is. The quote never impacted Salessa the way it did Naina, who now lives by it.

The crowd walks slowly, but with certainty, toward their communal destination: the gates to PeakHaven Pass. Towering ahead of them, the vast mountain range rises into the clouds, creating a formidable natural barrier between SunSide and its occupied state. Somewhere atop the tallest mountain is the city of PeakHaven, home to the angi humans.

The Pass was built through the narrowest part of the mountain range. It connects Arlun and Larso, the respective capital cities of MoonSide and SunSide. The twins hadn't returned to Arlun since the day they escaped the Facilitator.

Bravers in white uniforms, glittering from tiny pieces of ore embedded in the fabric, hover around the gates to PeakHaven Pass. The design creates a tight-fitting armor, with white hoods and a strip of colorful cloth wrapped around the mouth and nose. The color of the cloth denotes the Bravers' rank and leaves only gray, pupil-less eyes visible.

Crowds funnel into lines that lead to the Pass's many gates. There's a blatant correlation between the length of each line and the species of those standing in it. Bravers herd the Doruh into long, slow-moving rows to be interrogated and, often, rejected from migration. The Mega and the humans, however, wait in shorter lines, waved through the gates with far less inspection.

Salessa's eyes dart from one Mega line to the next, searching for Symin.

"He's not here," Naina says. "I told you we can't trust—"

"Me?" Symin appears from behind. Salessa turns and smiles, while Naina, startled, growls at him and bares her elongated canines.

"Don't sneak up on me unless you're willing to lose your pointy ears," she barks at him.

Symin smiles. "You truly are the nastiest and most voracious wolf I've ever met."

She rolls her eyes. "Flattery does nothing for me."

The line whittles down considerably over the next few hours. Salessa listens as the Doruh man at the front begs the Bravers to allow him and his three small children entry. His pleas continue, even as they refuse and thrash him, until he agrees to leave and return to a world where his sobbing children's safety and security is not assured.

Salessa turns away from the scene helplessly. Behind her, Naina and Symin exchange tales of how they received their various scars. "I'm not calling you a liar," Symin says, looking down at jagged lines adorning Naina's calf, "but it's hard to believe there are sharks in the Pit."

Naina releases the pant leg, and it falls back down to her ankle. "Not in the Pit. It was in a tank."

Symin raises an eyebrow. "You fought a shark in water? *That* I definitely don't believe."

Naina nods. "I understand. His widow didn't either, until I brought her the bones." Symin takes an involuntary step backward, and Naina's smile widens. "Your turn."

Symin examines his body. "I think I've told you about all of them."

"Not this one." Naina points to a scar that begins on Symin's wrist and travels up his forearm to his elbow.

Symin looks around nervously. "Another time." He tilts his head toward the Bravers and Naina nods.

They continue to converse as Salessa watches the line diminish ahead of them. Her heart thrums against her chest. With every step forward, they move further from the familiar life they've known for twelve years.

The soft sniffles of a crying child tear her from her thoughts. A young girl, perhaps eleven or twelve years old, stands behind Naina and Symin. Her clothes are covered in grimy patches, as is the sack she clutches to her chest.

Salessa walks around her companions and kneels in front of the child.

"Where are your parents?" She speaks softly, hoping not to draw any undue attention.

The girl clutches her belongings tighter and nervously eyes the swarms of uniformed warriors. "They're dead."

Salessa's heart shatters and memories of her own childhood come alive. She, at least, had Naina. This child has no one.

"You're going to SunSide alone?"

The girl nods. "My aunt lives there. I sent her a letter asking her to wait at the other side of the Pass for me today, but I don't know if she got it."

Salessa smiles gently, hoping to soothe the girl. "You can come through the Pass with us. We'll make sure you find your aunt."

"What if she's not there?" the girl asks.

"We'll find someone to look after you. My sister and I will protect you." She points to Naina. "My *twin* sister."

Lessi, wait, Naina's voice springs into Salessa's mind until the chaitender glares at her.

The girl smiles and exhales with relief. She joins Salessa ahead of Naina and Symin.

Symin leans over and whispers to Naina, "Why did mentioning that you're twins put this child at ease?"

"How much do you know about Doruh mythology?" Naina whispers back to him.

"Not a thing," Symin admits, pink cheeks glowing hotter.

Naina explains. "The Doruh deities are two siblings: a brother and a sister called 'The Twins.' They're prophesied to be resurrected one day, so all twins are revered."

"Is that why you've been getting stares all day from the Doruh passing by?"

"That's not why *I* get stares," she says with a wink.

"It's our turn," Salessa alerts them. She moves forward, holding the young girl's hand tightly. Naina and Symin follow her.

"Fare," the Braver at the gate says listlessly, holding out his hand for the funds to pass through the gate. Naina and Salessa produce the stones, emptying three of the pouches they have with them. It's a significant portion of what they've saved.

The Braver questions the girl next and she places her own pouch in his hands. He tosses it loosely in his palm.

"This isn't enough." He attempts to hand it back to her.

"But I-I..." Her voice cracks as her eyes swell and her fingers shake.

The Braver sighs and his eyes move to an officer of a higher rank standing nearby, who's watching the scene. "There's nothing I can do." He shoves the pouch more forcefully toward her, but she doesn't take it, frozen in panic.

Salessa steps forward and places her arm gently around the girl's shoulders. With her other hand, she reaches into her sack and empties another pouch of stones into the Braver's palms. "This should cover her."

The Braver turns to the higher-ranked officer, who nods, then waves the girl through with Naina and Salessa. The child wraps her arms around Salessa's waist and thanks her through tears. Salessa avoids meeting Naina's eyes; the wolf's mind overflows with fury.

Finally, the Braver turns to Symin.

"Were you waiting in *this* line?" he asks, an inflection of surprise in his voice.

"I was," Symin responds.

The Braver points to the nearest line of Mega at another gate. "We have lines for us over there." He leans closer to Symin and lowers his voice. "You don't have to wait with the *animals*."

Salessa hears the slur, but the child doesn't. She turns her face to hide her humiliation.

"Do *not* call them that," Symin responds loudly and forcefully.

Salessa and Naina exchange surprised glances. Never has a Mega defended them.

The Braver places a hand on the hilt of his blade. "Relax."

The twins are grateful, but they shake their heads to instruct Symin to remain calm.

He breathes deeply. "I'm relaxed."

The Braver eases his hand, brow still scrunched. Regardless, he waves the pink Mega through without payment.

As they walk through PeakHaven Pass, the twins hold hands. Fog settles between the two mountains that stand tall on either side of them, but they can see clearly enough to recognize the path ahead.

Change champions, Naina repeats in Salessa's mind.

With Symin at their back and the child by their side, they march on and leave MoonSide for the first time, into an uncertain future.

CHAPTER 11

LARSO

Theocratic-Monarchy SunSide
Date 19th Day of Month 6, Year 1628 DG

THE SEA OF FOG GIVES way to a shore of ore.

Symin, the twins, and their young companion reach the end of the Pass, marked by a large sign on SunSide's border. A painted image of the MegaFather, with mountains of ore surrounding him, and the words "The Future is Forever" underneath.

A vast field welcomes the travelers, swarmed with Bravers, tents, and ore vehicles on ore roads. The tents house salvers, food, and other potential necessities, along with areas for additional interrogation.

The field diverges into two paths: a dirt track winding into the forest to the south, and the ore road to the north. The road leads to something dark towering in the distance.

Salessa squints and makes out a metal wall. "Is that a settlement?"

Symin shakes his head. "That's the capital, Larso. The MegaFather's true kingdom. There's no loyalty or love for him beyond the city walls. He stays holed up in there. Protected by the ore, the Bravers, and the Facilitator."

"Coward," Naina responds with a growl.

They reach an area of the field where a crowd of Doruh have gathered. As they pass by the herd, the young girl breaks free from Salessa's hand and runs toward it. An older woman shoves through the crowd and meets the girl halfway, wrapping her up in her arms.

Salessa's heart warms, feeling fortunate to have played a small role in bringing the girl to her loved one. The young traveler waves goodbye as she departs. Salessa waves back and, when she notices Naina standing with her arms crossed at her chest, elbows her sister to join. Naina rolls her eyes and lazily waves until the girl is lost to the crowd.

Is the aunt going to pay us back? Naina questions, irritated.

Her smile paid us back.

Naina feigns vomiting.

"We have to keep moving," Symin says quietly behind them. "If we get too close to Larso, the Facilitator may be able to use the Radiance to track you. The Radiant energy of the forest is impenetrable. It'll shield you."

Salessa's eyes narrow. "The Radiance? I thought nymphs and pixies couldn't access the Radiance in Larso because of the ore?"

"The Facilitator, his daughter, and the Head Salver are exceptions to that rule. Their connection to the Radiance is so powerful, the ore can't weaken it."

"And they're all family, so it must be something in their genes," adds a fourth voice nearby.

Symin and the twins turn toward the dirt path, where an old, rickety wooden cart stands. A Mega with his cornflower-blue chest bare and a fabric skirt wrapped around his waist, climbs out of it. Two small, sheathed daggers hang from a string of twine around his waist.

His fascinating piercings grasp Salessa's attention. There's one ring in each nostril, three on each eyebrow, one on each nipple, five on each side of his body along his ribs, and those are just the ones she can count with a quick glance. The Mega appears to be the same height as the twins, close to five-and-a-half feet tall.

He opens his arms and Symin leans down to embrace him.

"This is Ray-Mi," Symin introduces him. "He's going to be helping us navigate the first leg of the journey."

Ray-Mi bows, an unusual gesture.

"Wonderful to meet you," Salessa says.

"You, as well, love," the Mega responds. He turns to Naina, expectantly.

Naina stands silently, awkwardly, for a moment. "Let's go. We're wasting daylight." She steps forward, past Ray-Mi and Symin, and climbs into the back row of the cart.

"I like her," Ray-Mi mutters to Symin, before they all join Naina. Symin places his hand on the cart and it rolls forward over the bumpy dirt path and disappears into the forest.

"This is entirely unnecessary," Zar-Lo groans, leaning on his ore desk, completely naked. The desk sits on a circular platform in the middle of the Theater. His arms are crossed and he taps his foot impatiently as he waits for the three servants across the room to finish pressing and folding his most extravagant robes.

"I disagree," Saith responds, seated on a chair near the base of the five steps that lead up the circular platform.

"Straighten your back," Saimiza, the Head Salver, instructs Saith. Her wrinkled, bony fingers run along the green skin of Saith's shoulder, using the Radiance to remove excess energy that attempts to burn its way through what remains of Saith's lost arm.

Without this treatment, he would face incredible suffering. "I will not sacrifice the remaining hours we have before the reading."

"I apologize on his behalf, Saimiza," Zar-Lo states to the old pixie. He descends from the platform and walks across the room. Every muscular striation is visible on his physique, his turquoise complexion lending a cool tone to the room's aura. "There was no reason to have your session moved here today."

The Theater rests at the top of the highest tower in the Castrum. It is the MegaFather's favorite room, and the one in which he spends most of his time. Similar to that of the Forum on the main level, the floor is polished stone, with shimmering gems embedded into it. Along the south wall, near where the servants press his robes, is a line of portraits. It begins with Red-Lo and concludes with Zar-Lo's mother, Cor-Lo the MegaMother.

Directly across from the portraits of the Red-Lo Royal Dynasty is a wall made entirely of treated, protective glass, floor to ceiling. The Facilitator and the MegaFather often stand at the window wall, gazing upon the citizens, monitoring the city.

"No apologies required, Father," Saimiza responds. A warm golden glow emanates from her palms, and with every surge of energy ripped from the stump on his shoulder, Saith breathes a sigh of relief. "I've traveled across the continent to heal strangers. I can cross the Castrum to treat my own flesh and blood."

"I'm grateful, Aunty," Saith replies, releasing another sigh. He turns to Zar-Lo. "Shall we continue the rehearsal?"

Zar-Lo grunts with irritation as he reaches the window wall and gazes down at his kingdom. Warm light from the suns drifts softly into the room and twinkles against every part of his bare anatomy.

"Be calm, Saith. I have a response to any question they could ask me. I don't think this meeting will be as interrogative as you're assuming."

"We must be prepared, Father," Saith insists. "Not *every* Member of the Assembly will be satisfied with the execution, treason or no treason."

Zar-Lo turns around to face Saith. "I'm not afraid of Saila. I'm well aware that she" — he speaks conservatively — "dislikes me."

Saimiza shakes her head. "Saila has become such a disappointment to our family. How proud we were when she was elected to the Assembly. Her father" — she gestures to Saith — "and I have spent our lives in service of the throne. Yet, this child insists on acting as a thorn in the MegaFather's side. She's no better than her mother."

"Thirty-five is hardly a child, Aunty," Saith remarks. "She's old enough to know —"

He stops speaking and rises to his feet. His eyes widen and transfix on the city beyond the window wall as he takes slow steps forward.

"What's wrong, Saith?" Zar-Lo asks, alarmed by the abrupt behavior.

Saith continues walking toward the window wall. "Everyone out. Now." He says it firmly, yet doesn't raise his volume. The servants look at one another with furrowed brows. Saimiza shares their confusion.

"Get out!" the MegaFather jumps in. The servants drop the robes and scurry from the room. Saimiza grabs her cane and hobbles out as quickly as she can. The two Bravers at the door exit and close it behind them.

"It's been twelve years," Saith whispers.

Zar-Lo's heart pounds with excitement when he realizes what Saith feels. "The twins?"

Saith nods and faces the MegaFather. "It's faint, so they must be far, perhaps by the Pass."

Zar-Lo's lips part to reveal a toothy grin. "Get them."

Saith places his hand flat onto the glass and emits a pulse of Radiant energy from his palm. The burst ripples outward, like a stone striking water. As the energy extends, the glass beneath it shatters into tiny fragments, showering onto the ground below.

Saith steps out onto the ledge beyond the window wall, then leaps. As he descends, he flips around and sends another pulse of Radiant energy skyward. The energy reaches the window wall and reassembles the shattered glass, as if it had never broken at all.

Zar-Lo watches from the Theater as Saith enters a hover chariot and uses the Radiance to launch it into the air and over the city, heading for the Pass.

The chariot lands in the field just outside of PeakHaven Pass. Saith jumps out of it before it even comes to a complete stop.

He closes his eyes to focus through the activity in his surroundings. A pulse of Radiant energy leaves his body and spreads parallel to the ground. Every organic signature around him is bland, faint, save for the oceans of energy bursting from the forest.

They're not here. He sniffs. *But they were.*

A caravan of chariots arrives, releasing Vy-Ro and more Bravers into the field.

"Where are they?" he asks the Facilitator.

Saith raises a finger to the dirt path leading into the forest. "Cloaked. The forest's energy is too strong to penetrate."

"What do we do?"

Saith takes a deep breath to keep his frustration at bay. *This is your job, imbecile.*

"Two teams: one searching the forest, the other distributing flyers in the city. Have an artist draw up an image of them."

"What do they look like?" one of the Bravers wonders.

Heat rises in Saith's chest. "They're *animals*. They all look the same. Two girls, around nineteen or twenty. I want a flyer in every hand in Larso by the end of the day."

Vy-Ro points to two blue-masked Bravers and instructs them to each lead a team: one for flyers, one for the forest. He reminds the Braver leading the forest team that the twins shouldn't be harmed. They are needed alive.

The Bravers peel away to strategize their missions, leaving Saith and Vy-Ro alone by the dirt path.

"After all these years," Vy-Ro says, "they're finally here."

Saith remains silent, focusing on the faint sense of the twins he felt earlier. It feels like trying to find a specific grain of sand in a desert.

Vy-Ro continues. "Are you going to remain here to oversee their capture?"

"Believe me," Saith finally speaks, "I want nothing more. I am the only one who can be trusted to complete this successfully."

Vy-Ro's expression contorts, but he remains silent.

Saith tries to restrain his smile. "However, it would be a personal affront to the theocracy if I weren't in attendance at the reading of the Final Act."

"The Bravers will find them," Vy-Ro reassures him.

Saith growls. "They'd better."

He turns to leave when Vy-Ro speaks again, stepping closer to Saith and lowering his volume to a whisper. "In twelve years, I have questioned neither the hunt for the twins, nor the abductions around the city. I've followed every order loyally, but I remain in the dark. I deserve to know why."

Saith locks eyes with the Braver General. "Do *not* mistake the MegaFather's soft spot for you for some kind of invincibility."

He raises a finger and points to the dirt path again. "Keep your eyes and ears in the forest, before you lose them."

CHAPTER 12

THE JOURNEY BEGINS

Sovereign City-State *The Library*
Date *19th Day of Month 6, Year 1628 DG*

THE CATACOMBS ARE CONCENTRATED IN the core of
the Library. Packed marketplaces and dense populations evaporate in
the outer neighborhoods, where open plots of greenery and farmland
take root.

The Stream and the Loop do reach the outer neighborhoods. The
last exit of each is only a few minutes walk from the Library's southern
gates. Unisa sits on the ledge of one of the Stream's canals, where Rafael said he would meet her.

The four suns strike her new, yellow silk tunic and ignite her like a
beacon. The bag sitting at her feet contains five more, along with three
casual outfits, some creams to moisturize her chestnut skin, and a few
vials of rice water and natural oils for her hair.

It's in a single braid, wrapped tightly on top of her head. The bun
gets a little heavy, particularly when she's flying, but it's a small price
to pay for being able to protect her coiled, natural hair.

A splash catches her attention. Rafael stands in the exit bay of the canal, dripping from head to toe with a waterproof bag and a bow strapped to his back. He's naked, save for his sister's bracelet, so he rummages through his bag for an outfit and gets dressed.

There's a moment of hesitation when he approaches Unisa, but then he leans forward and greets her traditionally. She can't remember the last time it wasn't done naturally, easily.

Rafael sits down next to her on the canal's ledge. Neither of them says anything and Unisa senses how tense he is. A pang of guilt ignites. The cold distance between them is a scar of her sins.

"Are you scared?" Rafael asks her, finally breaking the silence.

Unisa looks up to meet his eyes. "A little. You?"

He nods slowly. "Does that mean I'm Fully Broken?"

She pauses, then recites, "Fear is your heart's recognition that you're doing something important."

Rafael smiles. "Where did you hear that?"

"Ora," Unisa admits, then brings the conversation back. "You've been out in the world before. What are you afraid of?"

"I haven't truly. Fifteen years in SeaBed and then"—he hesitates—"eight in exile."

The light in his eyes dims and Unisa can't keep herself at a distance anymore. She wraps her arms tightly around him, but he doesn't return the embrace.

"I'm sorry, Rafa," Unisa says, as the guilt forces its way through her heart and burns her eyes.

"Don't apologize."

Unisa releases him and leans back, surprised. "It's my actions that brought us here."

"That doesn't matter now. All that matters is making it back in one piece."

"How," Unisa begins, as her eyes moisten, "can you forgive me so easily? You should be angry with me."

Rafael's gaze stays affixed to the ground. "I was. Maybe I still am. But after Joaquina died, I remembered all of the unfinished conversations we never had the chance to complete." He looks into her eyes. "Uni, we're about to go on a journey that could be dangerous. And if anything happens, I don't want our conversations left unfinished because I was angry. No one can ever replace Joaquina, but, in my exile, you've allowed me to feel like I have a sister again."

She embraces him once more, and this time, he does reciprocate. "I love you, Rafa."

"I love you, too."

They sit huddled together for another few minutes, quietly taking in one another's company, until Unisa breaks the silence. "Where's your quiver?"

Rafael laughs and reaches into his pocket to withdraw a narrow, metal cylinder. He holds it out in front of him and presses down on the center. There's a light pop and both sides of the cylinder extend outward rapidly. A sharp pyramid unfolds at one end, while a nocking point and fletchings appear at the other.

"A collapsible arrow," Unisa comments.

Rafael nods. "I have tons of them. A nymph in my building makes them. She said it's the latest design upgrade the Bravers had before the ore."

"I'm glad you'll have some protection. Hopefully you won't need to use it." She looks up at the positions of the suns. "It's time to meet Kyoko and Alba."

"Ana must have been devastated," Kyoko says, running her fingers along the cold stone beneath her.

"We both are," Alba replies, leaning against the boulder upon which Kyoko sits. Both Librarians' travel bags lie at her feet. "She accepted it after a couple of hours, though. By the morning, she was actually relieved that she has a few extra days to pack."

Kyoko smiles. "Ana the optimist. I hope she never loses that."

"She won't," Alba says with a laugh. She turns to face her Vice. "Kyoko, I'm sorry you're being forced onto this journey."

Kyoko raises an eyebrow. "Why are you apologizing? You're also being pulled into it."

"I volunteered," Alba clarifies.

"You didn't have a choice. The Prime loves his games, but he doesn't know who he's playing with."

Alba smiles. "I appreciate the confidence you have in me. I hope you have some in yourself."

Kyoko lightly brushes the yellow silk tunic she's wearing. "I haven't earned this."

Alba places her hand on Kyoko's knee. "You have. I've been so fortunate these past six years, watching you grow. You're going to make a fine Ambassador, and this journey will prove it."

Kyoko forces a smile to hide what she's truly feeling, as she looks up at the path leading through the forest and out of the Library's bounds.

"What's wrong?" Alba asks.

Kyoko hesitates. "It was right there." She lifts a finger to the edge of the forest. "Six years ago. Kanako and I were standing right there when she said it."

Alba frowns. "People say things they don't mean when they're angry. That doesn't justify her words, but if you see her, things might be different."

Kyoko groans. "I don't want to see her."

"You don't mean that."

"I do. I hope she's happy now, truly. I'm not going to spring back into her life and remind her of the terrible sister she once had."

Alba taps Kyoko's knee in reproach. "Don't say that. Those are the Prime's words."

Kyoko's eyes remain steady on the spot where her sister last spoke to her. "And Kanako's. I'm going to avoid her if I can." She turns to Alba. "I hope your journey goes smoothly. And safely."

"Thank you. I've sent word to Saila that I'm returning sooner than expected. Perhaps Unisa and I can stay with her this time."

Kyoko's stomach wraps into a thick knot. "Unisa. She has no idea what's about to happen. It's going to exhaust her."

"It's not the physical journey that concerns me. It's the philosophical one. The existential one. She's going to think her life has been wasted on a lie. The weight of that realization will crush her unless I can bring her to it piecemeal."

Kyoko smiles and puts her hand on Alba's. "She's in capable hands."

The ground vibrates as the enormous golden gates creak open. The patrolling Librarians escort Unisa and Rafael out of the city limits, then wave goodbye before heading back in.

When Kyoko sees Rafael, it occurs to her that she'll be traveling with a stranger. Aside from the occasional salutation, the most they've ever spoken was once a few weeks prior, when she saw him having lunch and asked what seafood he liked, something their cultural cuisines share.

Shrimp? Or was it salmon? No, I like salmon. Maybe we both like salmon.

The former Gatekeepers, also clad in yellow silk, approach the boulder, and Kyoko descends. The four Librarians stand in an awkward quadrangle until Unisa breaks the silence.

"Have you come to see us off?" She directs the question at Alba.

"Not exactly," Alba responds, lifting her bag and slinging it over her shoulder. "I volunteered to join you on your mission."

Unisa's lips curve into a smile. "What an honor to be under your guidance."

Alba's cheeks burn crimson and Kyoko stifles a chuckle.

"Are you well-packed?" Alba asks. Unisa nods. "And you've brought the book with you?"

Unisa taps her bag. "I have it."

Alba turns to Rafael. "Follow Kyoko's lead. You're going to pass through a number of villages that were heavily affected by the war. Your tunics afford you diplomatic immunity, but I would stay cautious regardless."

Rafael nods in acknowledgement, and she addresses Kyoko next. "That goes for you, too. Cautious and alert. Don't draw any unwanted attention, and stay hyper-vigilant of local laws. Committing a crime, even unintentionally, can be dangerous. Remember —"

"I get it, Alba," Kyoko laughs. "I promise, we'll be careful."

Alba smiles and wraps her arms around Kyoko, who takes in her mentor's warmth, along with her sea salt and citrus scent.

The angi swivels her head, searching. "Where is the chauffeur?"

Alba laughs. "Will this trip be financed from your own pocket, or the Prime's?"

"Uh, well, um," Unisa mumbles awkwardly.

"I'll be walking. You're welcome to fly."

Unisa shakes her head. "No, no. I'll walk." She turns and embraces Rafael. "Stay safe."

"I'll see you in a few days," he says before turning to Alba. "Take care of her."

Alba nods. "There is no one she'd be safer with."

Unisa and Alba step onto the dirt path, leaving Kyoko and Rafael standing together awkwardly.

"We should head out, as well," Kyoko suggests.

"That's a good idea."

The path heading south can easily fit two travelers walking side-by-side, yet Kyoko notices Rafael walking on the bare forest floor next to it.

Is he doing that deliberately? she wonders.

"You can walk next to me on the path, Rafael," she insists. "I won't bite."

"I'm comfortable here." His tone is so cold it nearly sends a shiver down Kyoko's spine.

I need you to laugh at my jokes, Rafael, or it'll be an unnecessarily long journey.

Kyoko's thoughts drift to the road ahead, and the places she might find familiar from her journeys with Alba. She reaches into her bag in search of a map, but comes up empty, so she stops walking to look more thoroughly.

"What's wrong?" Rafael asks, pausing to look back at her.

She closes her bag and hoists it back over her shoulder. "Did you bring a map, by any chance?"

Rafael nods. He produces the one he's brought and hands it to Kyoko. She examines it as they walk.

"It's outdated," she states with a frown. "We need a new one."

"How can you tell?"

"Some of these villages have different names now. Others have been conquered and merged, so these borders don't exist anymore."

"Is that relevant?" Rafael asks with a tinge of snark in his voice. "It's the same land we're walking through, regardless of what its name is or who owns it. The map is fine."

Kyoko's taken aback by his opposition. "No, it isn't. You should always be aware of whose land you're on, or whether a village is available for a stop."

Rafael holds his hand out and Kyoko gives the map back to him. "I think you're making a bigger deal of this than it needs to be."

Kyoko takes a deep breath, ignoring his tone. "I've been Alba's Vice for six years, Rafael. You've been within the city walls for the last eight. There's a reason Alba asked you to follow my lead."

She didn't intend for her statement to hurt, but injury and insult flashes in his eyes. He nods silently and continues walking.

What a wonderful start.

The silence grows painful by the second, until, an hour later, Kyoko loses her ability to maintain it. She gestures to the jewelry on Rafael's wrist and says, "That's a stunning bracelet."

There's a pause in which Kyoko thinks he might ignore her, but then he responds with a tone no warmer than earlier. "Thank you."

"Alba gave a similar one to Ana. It's a mari sibling tradition, right?"

He nods stiffly. "My sister gave it to me."

"How sweet. You must be very close."

Rafael takes a deep breath. "I don't want to talk about my sister."

Kyoko nods. She's unintentionally struck a nerve, so she attempts to change the subject. "How long have you and Unisa been together?"

He stops walking. "What?"

"Oh." Kyoko's cheeks glow red. "Are you not a couple?"

"No." He shakes his head and steps forward again.

She worries about being perceived as overly emotional or dramatic, but she does want to understand Rafael's coldness. "Have I done something to insult you?"

He looks genuinely confused. "No. Why?"

"You've just been very" — she pauses to find the right word — "closed off. Since we started walking."

"I'm sorry," he responds quickly, but it doesn't feel genuine. "I'm nervous about going to EverEmber."

Finally, more than two words.

"I understand. I have my own reservations about it."

"Didn't you grow up there?"

Kyoko nods. "I did, but there are people there I'd like to avoid."

"That's not the same thing," Rafael comments abruptly. "Your concern is an inconvenience. Mine is a matter of life and death."

"Life and death?" she says, her tone incredulous.

"Yes, life and death," Rafael snaps. "The igni and the mari just ended a war."

"Rafael, the war ended years ago. Everyone has moved on."

He pauses before he responds. "Not all of us can do that."

"What do you mean?"

"Nothing," he responds quickly. "I just don't feel safe around the igni."

Kyoko chuckles uncomfortably. "You're traveling with an igni, Rafael."

Rafael takes a deep breath and replies almost inaudibly, "I would never have willingly chosen that."

Realization strikes Kyoko with the force of a hailstone. What she had perceived as a standoffish demeanor was actually an intense prejudice. Rafael's reservations bleed into more personal sentiments toward her.

And now she's trapped, traveling for days with a man who's judged her before the journey's even truly begun.

CHAPTER 13

CereCenter Forty-Two

The Dissolved Nations Merchant
Date 19th Day of Month 6, Year 1628 DG

THE PROTECTIVE FOREST AROUND THE Library has been long left behind. Rolling meadows and vast fields of crops blanket the landscape as far as Unisa can see. Hand-drawn images in books do not measure up to the magnificence to which she now bears witness. The world beyond the walls is filled with such greenery and grandeur, her eyes water.

The journey thus far has certainly felt like a blessing in disguise. Unisa feels so starstruck around Alba, she's remained silent for the hours they've traveled.

A bead of sweat drips over her temple and she wipes it away.

"You don't have to walk," Alba says. "I have angi colleagues and friends. I don't think I've seen them walk ten minutes without stretching their wings, let alone hours."

Unisa breathes a sigh of relief. "Thank you!"

Alba continues walking as Unisa stretches her wings, flaps them twice, and launches into the air. She circles Alba overhead, taking in more of the sights around them. The treetops are inundated with rare, colorful birds. Golden light cloaks the terrain, and bracing breezes give life to layers upon layers of fields and farmland. In the distance, rivers intimately penetrate mountains and bring forth more glamor and elegance.

Had their schedule permitted, Unisa could've remained in the air for days, soaking in the grace of the world.

"How did it feel?" Alba asks her when she returns to the ground.

"Incredible."

"I'm glad," Alba says with a smile, before pulling out a flask and pouring water over her face and fins.

"You must be roasting." Unisa recalls Rafael's urgency to hydrate his drying, mari skin under intense sunlight.

Alba takes a long sip, then puts the flask away. "I'm alright. I've walked this journey enough times to know when to hydrate."

"You haven't checked the map once," Unisa notes. "I'm sure you know exactly where we are."

"I do. We're in the Dissolved Nations. These lands were once dominated by prosperous kings and queens, ministers, councilmen, and presidents."

Unisa adds, "Until that prosperity was driven up into the hands of a fraction of their populations. Poverty plagued the lower classes, while greed reigned amongst the wealthy, leading to collapse and ruin. And each nation in the region was named for the most common occupation of the residents there: Merchant, Bard, Cobbler, Courtesan, and Smith."

"You know your history well," Alba praises her.

Unisa's cheeks burn with humility. "I read. More than I'm required to."

"That's impressive. The heyday of the Dissolved Nations isn't among the more well-known eras. Just south of here is where Merchant once stood."

"And directly northeast was Courtesan," Unisa displays the depth of her studies.

"You study maps more than required to, as well? Are you a cartophile, like I am?"

Unisa's excitement grows. There's something fascinating about the personal details that humanize idols. "I'm not, but geography and history are..." She pauses to think of the right word.

"Sisters," Alba completes her sentence with a smile. "Have I ever told you about my sister?" Unisa shakes her head and Alba continues. "Ana. She's a Nysabaani translator and researcher."

"How old is she?"

"Twenty-nine. She was a year old when we arrived at the Library. I was ten. I carried her through the gates myself." She turns to Unisa. "You were four, right?"

Unisa nods.

"I remember Ora mentioning it. How did she feel when you told her about this journey?"

Unisa responds carefully, measuring her words. "She was surprised, and worried, as anyone would be for an assigned daughter."

"Hmm," Alba replies thoughtfully. "I've never heard someone emphasize that they were assigned to a Librarian when they were accepted for youth education. Do you always refer to her as your *assigned* mother or to yourself as her *assigned* daughter?"

"Shouldn't I?"

Alba laughs. "No, you shouldn't. Ora raised you. Fed you, clothed you. She put you to bed every night and let you sleep in her room when the thunder struck too close to your window. And she fostered that love of reading. By all accounts, Ora is your mother, and you don't have to qualify that."

Unisa had never before analyzed the way she talked about Ora, but everything Alba mentioned rings true. Ora is her mother, and she feels somewhat silly now, having felt the need to clarify how she came to be under the pixie's care.

"You're right," Unisa agrees. "Ora and Rafael are my family now. Do you have anyone you feel that way about? Someone who's *become* family?"

Alba pauses for a moment, then smiles. "Yes. It's actually funny you ask that question."

"Funny? Why?"

"Because you're going to meet him soon."

As the two Librarians cross the Dissolved Nations, the four suns race overhead, completing their arcs and diving below the horizon. When the last of them, Frona, descends in the distance, she leaves little light in the sky.

"Nightfall is near," Unisa mentions.

"We're almost there," Alba responds. She lifts a finger to a hill not far ahead. "Our rest for the night is just beyond the ridge."

Alba's geographic mastery holds true. From the apex of the mound, Unisa sees it: a maze of claystone buildings nestled into a valley. Surrounded by hills, the village is imperceptible to an unwitting passerby under the night's blanket of darkness.

The village is dim, but not quiet. Children of all species—human, Doruh, Mega—play together in the streets. Eateries come alive with villagers, friends, and neighbors laughing with one another. Workers close up their markets and make light conversation as they trek home.

As Unisa gazes upon the huddled homes and cordial crowds, she makes the connection and realizes what this place is.

"It's a CereCenter!" she exclaims.

Alba nods. "It is. CereCenter Forty-Two. One of four in the area."

"Where are the Educators?" Unisa asks, searching for red linen tunics amongst the masses.

"Likely home, by now." She looks up at the last rays of Frona's dwindling light. "Classes were dismissed over an hour ago."

"They just go directly home after?"

Alba laughs. "The Librarians aren't here to socialize, Unisa. Once the academic season ends, the Educators will return to the Library and likely won't be assigned to this Center again for years. Socializing will breed unwanted attachments."

"But what about management? Security?"

"That's their job." She gestures into the valley. Unisa squints and sees something she missed earlier.

Bravers. First, only a handful. Then, more appear. Some stand guard on the corners of the streets, while others play with the children. Unisa even spies one helping an elderly Doruh woman cross the road. The benevolence of the MegaFather's forces brings a smile to her lips.

Alba leads Unisa down into the valley through a path dug into the walls. As they make their way through the streets, the CereCenter reminds her more and more of the Library: a quieter, dimmer, less populated version. They walk for some time before they arrive at a small hut, and Alba knocks on the wooden door.

An angi man stands in the doorway when it opens, holding a lantern at eye level. A long, loose gown flows in the breeze, the greens and blues swaying playfully. He has a cloth turban wrapped around his head with a matching pattern, and thin, flat-sole sandals.

Unisa places him around Alba's age, close to forty. Light from the lantern glistens against the side of his bald head. His complexion is similar to Unisa's, or perhaps a little darker, and the sheen of his silvery feathers shimmers in the doorway.

"Alba?" he says. His eyebrows furrow in confusion, yet the corners of his lips rise into a smile.

"Good evening, Hassan," Alba responds cheerfully. "I'm sorry to disturb you so late. I see you've already changed out of your tunic."

"As soon as I get home," Hassan laughs. "What are you doing here?"

"We're traveling to SunSide." She tilts her head, gesturing to Unisa. Hassan moves the lantern to get a better look at the former Gatekeeper, who smiles and waves awkwardly, unsure of the stranger's preferred greeting.

"Again?" he asks, moving the lantern back toward Alba. "You and Kyoko just returned home."

Alba nods. "This mission was unplanned. Special business. I know we're imposing, but do you have room for us tonight?"

Hassan frowns. "Don't insult me. I have room for both of you, of course. Please come in, I was just about to perform my prayers and sit down for dinner."

He opens the door wide and moves aside, allowing the travelers to enter. As Alba does, they greet one another with a gentle kiss on each cheek.

Inside the modest dwelling, a cooking area sits to her left with a fire pit and some storage bins for rice, lentils, beans, grains, and flour. There's also a wooden table and a few chairs. To her right, a woven couch rests amongst straw boxes and a low table. A narrow hallway behind the couch leads to the back of the home.

Alba hands her bag to Unisa. "Would you mind putting our things away? I'll brief Hassan on our journey."

Unisa nods and takes the bag from her.

"Down this hallway, you'll find a bedroom to your left," Hassan explains. "That's where you both will be staying."

"Thank you," Unisa responds, trying to remain upright as she balances her own bag and now Alba's on each shoulder.

"You can take this with you, I have another." He shoves the lantern toward her and Unisa takes it. It's a relief when she gets to the end of the hallway and finds the room on the left. Smaller than expected, but there is a warm bed, which is enough.

She places the lantern down on a small wooden table in the corner of the room, and then drops the bags on opposite sides of the bed. There's a pause in which she thinks of Rafael. In the solitude of the room, amongst the soft bed and lantern light, she wonders how his journey with Kyoko is going, and how he must be feeling traveling with her. Their first day of travel is ending, as well.

Perhaps a day of forced proximity with an igni is all he needed to cleanse him of his visions, Unisa hopes, though she recognizes the naïveté of the thought.

She changes into a more comfortable outfit and then returns to the kitchen. The travelers volunteer to prepare dinner, allowing their host time to perform his prayers. He invites Unisa to join him, but she declines, concerned he'll judge her lack of connection to the angi faith. He simply smiles, nods, and continues to a corner of the room, where he lays out a soft mat and sits on it.

Unisa's eyes shift to him throughout the dinner preparation as she attempts to recall what little she knows about the religion. She's aware his mat is facing PeakHaven: more specifically, a temple called the Holy Summit. He folds his hands and speaks in Nysabaani, with his head tilted slightly forward in a reverent bow.

A sharp current of regret shocks Unisa as she witnesses the peace the prayer brings to the angi man. In her twenty-three years, she's never known what that feels like.

Hassan softly presses his folded hands against his face, and this appears to conclude the prayer. He returns the mat to its location in the corner of the room, upon a bookshelf holding holy texts and prayer beads, and joins his guests for dinner.

Unisa hadn't realized how hungry she had gotten during their travels. A mound of steaming rice and a deep bowl of rich lentils grace the table, near a glass container of mixed nuts.

They inhale the first round in silence, however, light conversation emerges during second helpings. Unisa talks about her life at the Library, and Hassan discusses his plan to return home once the season ends.

"I hope dinner was satisfactory," Alba comments when the rice and lentils have finished.

Unisa nods, pinned by the meal in her stomach. "It was delicious, thank you."

"Good," Alba responds, before turning to Hassan and holding eye contact.

Unisa notices the mari's hands, twinkling with sweat. She rubs them nervously and discomfort spreads across the room.

"What's wrong?" Unisa asks.

Hassan nods encouragingly to Alba, who turns and says, "There's something I wanted to talk to you about."

The growing cloud of discomfort accelerates Unisa's heartbeat. "Alright."

"Unisa," Alba begins, but doesn't continue.

The young Librarian forces a smile, hoping to disarm the Ambassador. "Why are you hesitating? Speak your mind. I'm listening."

Alba takes a deep breath. "This will be difficult for you to hear. But I need you to trust me."

Unisa's palms mirror Alba's. *Just say it.*

Finally, the Ambassador unburdens. "The letter you found, Hay-Ro's letter, is likely telling the truth."

Unisa's eyebrows scrunch together as she tries to make sense of the words. "Telling the truth?"

Alba nods. "Red-Lo likely fabricated much of the history in *The Everlasting Journey.*"

Unisa's heart slams harder against her chest. "How do you know this?"

"Because that is not all that's fabricated."

The young Librarian nearly laughs, but Alba and Hassan sit completely stone-faced. "You can't be serious."

"I am. The Library has powerful allies, and the history within its walls has been written and recorded in ways that protect those allies."

"You're talking about the MegaFather," Unisa guesses.

"Yes. Every MegaParent of this dynasty, and the Bravers they command, have been glorified through history, in ways that are inaccurate."

"Glorified? Alba, this dynasty is remembered exactly as it should be: in high honor. Benevolence and mercy personified."

"That isn't true, Unisa," Hassan joins the discussion. "This dynasty murdered the Doruh Alphocracy. They've committed innumerable war crimes throughout their reign. The least of which is the occupation in which the Bravers hold MoonSide."

Unisa stares, wide-eyed and astonished. The contradiction between what she knows and what these wise Librarians are expressing dizzies her.

She clutches the truth like a raft adrift at sea. "The Bravers are only in MoonSide to temper the battles with the radicals. They protect the Doruh civilians, maintain peace amongst the conflicts."

Alba sighs in exasperation. "I know what you've been taught, Unisa, but you have to believe me. The Prime's and the MegaFather's narrative has been used historically to vilify the Doruh. But it isn't a 'battle,' a 'struggle,' or a 'conflict.' One side has power, resources, and support, and they're slowly, but deliberately, trying to finish off the entire population."

"No," Unisa's voice barely escapes her throat. "Any violence committed by SunSide is in defense. You know this."

Alba shakes her head. "One who stands on the neck of another has no need for defense, Unisa. Their violence is fueled by greed and supremacy—the only forces that could influence warriors to attack civilians."

Unisa gasps at the accusation. "Civilians? Bravers wouldn't do that."

Alba closes her eyes and her expression morphs into one of agony. She takes a deep breath before opening them again. "I've seen Bravers bring their blades down first, and ask later if the deceased was their intended target. I've seen it in hospitals and temples." She pauses. "I've seen it in schools."

Unisa's stomach turns. She collects her words carefully. "Alba, you just walked through this CereCenter with me. We watched Bravers playing with children."

"What does that prove?" Alba questions. "The Bravers here exist in a place of peace. We'll be traveling through MoonSide tomorrow, and the Bravers there will be different. They'll be representing the true face of SunSide—a face the Library has helped mask for centuries."

Unisa lifts her hands to massage an ache growing in her temples. "Why are you telling me all of this now?"

"Because tomorrow you're going to witness the truth with your own eyes. And I want you to be prepared."

"This"—she pauses—"can't be true. The Library wouldn't allow fabrications at all, let alone to the degree you're implying."

Alba lowers her gaze to her hands and Hassan steps in to assist her. "It all starts at the beginning, Unisa. Hay-Ro is telling the truth: Drof-Fa didn't murder the MegaMother to usurp the throne for herself. It was all under Red-Lo's guidance. Then he wrote *The Everlasting Journey* to push the historical spotlight onto her, and away from himself."

Unisa's eyes narrow. "Your words attack the most honorable faerie SunSide has ever known."

"Where was that honor," Alba questions, "when the Doruh were in shackles?"

"What happened to the Doruh was horrific, but all blame can't be laid at Red-Lo's feet. Enslavement was the norm of his time."

"But it wasn't," Alba corrects her. "In Red-Lo's time, the Assembly was ready to liberate the Doruh. Years before the Uprisings. The day before it was set to happen, this *honorable* faerie commanded Drof-Fa to bring him the head of the MegaMother. Just as the shackles began to fall off, he put them back on."

Unisa's temples throb. "The Fully Bonded believe. The Fully Bonded believe. The history in the Catacombs is sacred and true. Where would you find these lies?"

"Some truths are given freely. Others must be sought out in books that have been banned."

Unisa laughs through her discomfort. "Banned? Who would ban books?"

Alba and Hassan exchange a glance before she continues. "Those for whom fear is a weapon and understanding a weakness. Who hold knowledge captive in the minds of the few, to inhibit it from spreading to the many. Like the Prime."

Heat rises to Unisa's cheeks. "The Prime encourages us to seek knowledge. It's part of being Fully Bonded."

Alba rises to her feet and walks around the table to sit next to Unisa. "The *knowledge* in his books and speeches feeds his ideology. The *knowledge* in the Catacombs glorifies his allies. He doesn't want you to have true knowledge, Uni. Knowledge empowers. As long as he knows more than you, he has power over you."

Unisa shakes her head. "I will not believe these lies. Look at all he's done." She turns to Hassan. "You're talking about the man responsible for crafting jobs, shelter, and resources for not only us, but for villages and nations drowning in poverty throughout the continent. What was this village like before it became a CereCenter?"

"I, too, often think of the good he's done," Hassan replies. "The CereCenters saved communities like these, but they've also become hubs for the Library's indoctrination. Intellectual enslavement. What's been branded as education is fiction."

Unisa pushes her seat back with her feet. "No. The Prime and the MegaFather are benevolent. Honorable. Merciful. This journey is proof of that; he could've punished me, but he didn't."

"Punish you for what?" Alba questions.

Unisa's speech slows in confusion. "For breaking the law, Alba. You know—"

"But what did you do *wrong*?"

She hesitates. "I removed the contents of *Witness* from the section."

"Why are those records not freely accessible to all? He wants to control the flow of knowledge, Unisa. History shouldn't be held captive behind Gatekeepers. You may have broken the law, but you haven't done anything morally *wrong*. Laws aren't inherently ethical. Sometimes they're the work of unethical authors."

"That may be the case in other nations and kingdoms, but not the Library. The Primes authored these laws ages ago. No one has a stronger moral code than they do."

Alba's soft eyes shift from tenderness to something that makes Unisa feel small.

Pity.

"Unisa…I understand your resistance. To accept the possibility of deceit festering in the Catacombs and CereCenters for centuries is to admit that we're all"—She pauses, struggling to complete her sentence.

Unisa obliges as her heart sinks. "Complicit. It would mean we're all complicit."

There's a deafening silence as Unisa's mind tries to reconcile the incoming information with the history to which she's devoted her life.

Alba breaks the silence. "The Prime is not who you think he is. I can prove that to you, and it'll help you understand what he's capable of."

Unisa's hands ache to cover her ears, but a small part of her wants to hear the slander she knows is coming, only so she can refute it. "Go on."

Alba turns to Hassan, who nods her forward. The mari resumes her eye contact with Unisa and says, "The Prime is my uncle."

Silence. Unisa can't speak.

"His moral fabric is shredded to scraps. You can ask Kyoko."

"Kyoko?"

Alba nods. "Yes. Kyoko came to the Library with her older sister, Kanako. They advanced through the academy quickly and caught the Prime's eye. Kyoko was only twelve, so I started protecting her the way I was protecting Ana, who was thirteen."

"Protect her?" Unisa interjects. "Why would you have to protect twelve- and thirteen-year-olds from the Prime?"

When Alba speaks, the pain in her voice is palpable. "Because there was no one to protect me from him when I was their age."

The air grows thick around Unisa as nausea squirms in her belly.

Alba continues. "I spent all my time mentoring Kyoko. For ten years, my missions were the only times we were separate."

"And, during those missions, I would look after Kyoko and Ana," Hassan adds.

"I wouldn't give the Prime access to Kyoko, so he dug his nails into Kanako. He said he was mentoring her, and I made the mistake of assuming that, being sixteen, she would vocalize any inappropriate experiences."

Alba looks down at her trembling fingers. Hassan gets up, walks over to her, and places a hand on her shoulder. She continues, her voice shivering. "As time went on, she became more and more withdrawn. Kyoko and I saw her less frequently. Anytime we would ask about her, the Prime would tell us she was busy studying or working. The days we saw her, it was difficult to communicate."

Her eyes grow moist. "It's my fault. He was isolating her. Inundating her with all kinds of lies and false promises."

"What happened to her?" the words race out of Unisa's mouth.

"Six years ago, my former Vice was promoted. Kyoko was the natural choice to replace him. Evidently, my uncle had promised Kanako the position without consulting me. He pleaded with me to agree, but I refused. Kyoko had worked hard for it, she deserved it."

"Kanako returned to EverEmber," Hassan continues. "She blamed Kyoko for 'stealing' what was promised to her. And the Prime blamed Kyoko for Kanako's departure. For leaving him."

"Leaving...him?" The words barely make it past Unisa's lips.

Alba nods. "It wasn't until after Kanako left that we found out the truth. He initially filled her ears with compliments, her heart with affection, and her mind with visions of a future together. But all of that changed after the isolation. She had no one to turn to. He turned himself into her only resource. He belittled her, devalued her, broke her. And then he took her to bed."

Alba holds eye contact with Unisa. "She was seventeen the first time. He was forty-three."

Unisa's breath catches and bile rises in her throat.

Alba continues, as if her tongue has finally come unchained. "It was years of manipulation. He made her promise she wouldn't acknowledge their relationship publicly."

Gently, she takes Unisa's hand in her own and leans forward. "He isn't honorable or merciful, Uni. Neither was any MegaParent in this dynasty. Those in power want you to choose them over everything. And when the time comes for *them* to choose, they will choose themselves, too."

There's a quiet beat as Unisa takes in what she's heard. "This is so inconsistent with his values, Alba. How do I accept that the man who helped so many could do something so horrific? This isn't who he is."

"It isn't?" There's a challenge in her voice. "Tell me something, Unisa. Are you *absolutely* certain your parents haven't contacted you in nineteen years by choice?"

Unisa's throat swells at the mention of her parents. She understands immediately what Alba is implying, yet she can't vocalize the response. *You're lying.*

"Your parents rescinded your assignment to the Library when they were told they wouldn't be able to come visit you. The Prime stepped in and convinced them he could give you a better life than they could. The words of this man you revere so much are the reason you were forsaken."

Unisa's voice comes out shriveled and feeble. "It's not true."

"It is. You refuse to believe he would isolate Kanako from her family to take advantage of her. And yet, he did it to you."

Alba's words strike Unisa's soul deep within. Tears erupt from the corners of her eyes. Alba wraps her arms around her as the former Gatekeeper buries her face in Alba's chest and releases the torment of her abandonment.

Her mind swirls as Alba's words thrum in her ears.

He doesn't want you to have knowledge, Uni. Knowledge empowers. As long as he knows more than you, he has power over you.

CHAPTER 14

THE MEGA OF NIVYAN HOLLOW

Theocratic-Monarchy *SunSide*
Date *19th Day of Month 6, Year 1628 DG*

THE CART BUCKS OVER BUMPS on a beaten path. Dust kicks up from the dirt below, and the branches of nearby trees reach into the cart and tickle the travelers like wooden fingers.

Salessa notices the light beyond the canopy growing dim. "Nightfall is near."

"We're almost home," Symin responds, pausing the nostalgic tales he and Ray-Mi have been sharing.

"We better be," Naina responds. "I've been inhaling dust for hours."

"Only been *one* hour, love," Ray-Mi counters.

If he calls me "love" again, Naina's voice appears in Salessa's consciousness, *I'm going to tear those piercings out one at a time.*

Salessa turns to her. *Have you been listening to their conversation? He's quite the storyteller.*

Don't do it, Lessi, she warns.

Salessa raises an eyebrow. *Don't do what?*

Let your guard down. When Lexona used to—
Stop. Don't say her name, I remember. I won't make the same mistakes again.

She turns away from Naina, but can't escape the lingering truth: the wolf is right. Salessa's trusting nature has led them to catastrophe in the past. Lexona is a name she never wants to hear again; a reminder of the suffering that follows emotional connection.

At the end of the dirt path, the Mega disembark. The density of the forest won't allow them to continue by cart. They travel now on narrow, leafy paths between thick trees that widen the further into the forest they go. The trees eventually become more spacious than the hut the twins called home.

The ground rattles, stopping Naina in her tracks. She places a hand on Salessa's wrist, stopping her as well. Thumping booms echo through the air, as if some behemoth stomps toward them. Symin and Ray-Mi continue walking, unaffected.

"What's that sound?" Naina questions them.

Symin stops and faces the twins. "It's a drum."

Salessa places her other hand on Naina's fingers. The wolf's rigid shoulders soften and Salessa leads her forward carefully.

"Let me show you," Ray-Mi, a few yards ahead, beckons them forth. He pulls the branches of two trees aside, through which they find a clearing. The drums grow louder. More instruments join, and an orange glow pours through the opening.

A fire rages at the center. Hollowed trees, turned into dwellings, trace the circumference of the clearing. Mega flood the area—on the ground by the fire, hovering in the air, and sitting in the trees.

They are laughing and smiling, singing and dancing, embracing and making love. Some are eating, others drinking. Some make music with instruments constructed from branches, pinecones, and animal horns, while others listen in.

They are old and they are young. They are shades of red and blue, green and yellow, purple and orange, teal and maroon, violet and crimson, and colors that the twins have never seen before. Some are clothed, some are not. They are male, they are female, and they are so much more.

Naina and Salessa have never seen such unbridled joy. The Mega are enraptured by their own ecstasy. None of them notices that the group of travelers has walked into their clearing.

"What are they celebrating?" Naina asks Symin.

"Celebrating?" Puzzled lines appear on his forehead. "They aren't celebrating. They're just living. Welcome to Nivyan Hollow."

The radiant joy before them exists in stark contrast with the bleak circumstances to which they've grown accustomed.

"Come with me." Symin breaks them from their trance. "I'd like to introduce you to my family." He strides toward the fire at the center of the clearing.

Naina hesitates, but, after a quick visual assessment of her surroundings, carefully steps forth, and Salessa follows.

"Where is Ray-Mi?" Salessa wonders as they walk.

Symin laughs. "Paradise." He points up and the twins look to one of the tree limbs above, where a group eats, drinks, and enjoys the music. At the far end of the limb, up against the trunk of the tree, Ray-Mi and a lime-green Mega kiss and frenetically remove one another's clothes.

Symin leads the twins to an occupied log by the fire. One of the Mega resting on it is elderly, with pumpkin-colored skin, while the other two appear younger than Symin, perhaps in their early forties. One of the younger Mega is clearly pregnant.

The elderly Mega rises when she sees Symin and opens her arms wide, embracing him. "I hope your journey was fruitful," she says.

"Indeed it was, Mother." He gestures toward the twins. "This is Naina, and this is Salessa. They've come to help us."

Symin's mother throws her hands up to her mouth. "Well, aren't you both so lovely."

Naina's forced smile betrays her discomfort with praise.

"Thank you," Salessa responds on their behalf.

"My name is Syma. Please come join us." The twins place their travel bags down and sit on the log next to the two younger Mega.

"This is my sister, Nypa," Symin introduces the pregnant Mega. "And her wife, Rona."

The twins nod, and Naina speaks first. "When are you due?"

"Any day now," Nypa responds with a smile. "Our third." She gestures to the other end of the clearing. Past the wide bonfire, two children fight over a doll made of twigs and twine. Nypa's smile drops. "Oh, no. Not again." She lifts a hand with her palm facing the children and then moves it quickly from side to side. An invisible wall separates the children, and the doll drops to the ground between them, out of reach.

"How long will you be staying this time, *mohuway*?" Syma asks her son.

"We're leaving in the morning," Symin replies. "We can't waste any time. The others are waiting."

Syma turns to the twins. "We'll make room in our tree for you."

"We don't want to impose," Salessa insists.

"We don't have a choice," Naina adds nonchalantly. "We don't know anyone else here."

Salessa glares at her, but Syma laughs. "Naina is correct. You are our invited guests; we'd be honored to have you stay with us."

The twins revel in the rhythm of the gathering. Salessa finds herself delighted by Nypa's tales of Symin's awkward childhood, and when she looks over to the other end of the log, she sees three unclothed Mega vying for Naina's attention. The wolf appears to enjoy the competition, a playful smile plastered across her lips.

"I can take your bags to Syma's tree, if you'd like," Ray-Mi offers, joining them from the base of the tree where they last saw him.

Salessa nods gratefully. She watches as Ray-Mi hoists the bags onto his shoulders, and confusion forces her eyebrows together. "Why don't you use the Radiance?"

"No Radiance for me, love. I'm a faerie."

Salessa's heart drops into her stomach.

There isn't enough time to stop Naina. As soon as the word "faerie" passes Ray-Mi's lips, the wolf leaps from the log, over her admirers. Her clothes tear under her thickening muscles, her teeth elongate and sharpen, and fur erupts around her body. Her eyes fixate on Ray-Mi as her enormous paws land on his chest and lay him flat.

She digs her claws into his skin. Her teeth are inches from his face as he pushes against her throat with his forearms.

"NAINA! STOP!" Salessa yells. The music ceases and all of the Mega look on in horror.

I told you! We can't trust them, Lessi, Naina conveys. It emerges from her throat as a bark.

Salessa attempts to reason with her. "If he wanted to harm us, he could've done it already. We didn't know what he was."

I don't feel safe.

"Let him go, Naina. I'm right here. I will keep you safe." She steps closer to the growling wolf and kneels next to her. "You don't have to trust him. Just trust me."

Naina backs up a few long, unpredictable seconds later. She stops growling and removes her claws from the faerie's chest. Blood spots cover it. She shifts back and reaches her hand down. He hesitates, but then grasps it, and Naina helps him stand.

"Nearly took my head off, beautiful," he says with a weak laugh.

"Sorry," Naina apologizes. "We've had bad experiences with faeries."

He wipes the smiles from his face, and for the first time since they met him, his tone sobers. "Don't apologize. Why do you think I'm here? I don't trust them either."

Symin turns back to the musicians and gestures for them to resume. There's a moment of hesitation, and some anxious glances, then the atmosphere comes back to life as if nothing ever happened.

Salessa gently puts her hand on her sister's cheek and runs her thumb softly along her skin to calm her. "Are you alright?" Naina nods. "I'll get you some new clothes."

"She doesn't need clothes here, if she doesn't want them," one of her suitors says with a laugh.

Naina smiles and holds eye contact with him. "I'm fine like this."

The atmosphere doesn't die down until late into the night, and all but Naina, Salessa, and Ray-Mi return to their tree shelters. They remain quietly by the fire and enjoy the soft starlight, the cool breezes, and the tranquility of the resting forest.

"So this is what it's like," Naina says. "Freedom."

She's smiling, but Salessa recognizes the sadness sitting on the edge of her lips.

Ray-Mi laughs. "A forced freedom, I suppose. A curse turned blessing."

"What curse?" Naina asks.

"Red-Lo's curse," Salessa answers her. "Right?"

Ray-Mi nods. "Red-Lo decimated nymph and pixie neighbor-hoods—and Doruh holy sites—to build the Temple Complex. It drove the Mega out here to the Hollow, where their connection to the Radiance was strengthened, but it came at a cost."

"Ancestral suffering," Salessa adds.

"Was that when the Revolution began?" Naina asks.

Ray-Mi's gaze shifts to the flames. "It was. And it's been eight hundred years of pendulum swings since then: faerie violence, Revolution retaliation, over and over, back and forth. The Uprisings freed the Doruh and set up the Alphocracy, but the faeries came back stronger with new technology, or weapons, or just sheer numbers."

Salessa lowers her gaze. She knows where this gut-wrenching tale leads. "Those numbers formed the Bravers. Twenty thousand warriors at the onset, more than double that now."

The faerie turns back to the wolf. "The Radiance was the only edge the Revolution had against numbers like that. Hope died the night their connection to it did."

"Symin told us about it," Naina responds. "The Siege of the Castrum."

Ray-Mi sighs, heavy with disappointment. "That night was like nothing I'd ever seen. The hope was"—he pauses—"indescribable. His surrender was in reach, until we lost contact with our collaborators within the Castrum."

"Who were the collaborators?" Salessa wonders. "What happened to them?"

"Two Members of the Assembly: a Doruh theocrat named Sonali, and Saila, the Facilitator's daughter. They saw the ore and accepted that our defeat that night was the will of the Four. We had no chance."

"We can still use their help," Naina says. "If we can get back in touch with them—"

"We can't." Ray-Mi lowers his gaze to his fidgeting fingers. "We all have bounties on us, and the Facilitator is actively hunting you two. Saila is out of reach and Sonali"—he pauses to take a deep breath—"was executed yesterday."

"I'm sorry," Salessa responds.

"Thank you. Symin vowed to keep the fight going, after the defeat during the Siege. I joined him to continue my atonement."

"Atonement for what?" Naina asks.

Ray-Mi hesitates. "I was a Braver, Naina."

Salessa hears the low growl bubbling in her sister's chest. Naina's fingers dig into the log beneath her and it cracks from her strength. She's doing everything she can to hold back another outburst. Salessa places her hand on Naina's shoulder.

"Breathe. It's alright."

Naina follows the command.

"I understand the anger toward me. I deserve it. For years, I had convinced myself, as they all do, that my clan was under attack—that the nymphs, pixies, and Doruh were trying to replace us in the social and political structure. I drew so much innocent blood over it, but I couldn't take it anymore. I defected and joined the Revolution."

"That was brave of you," Salessa points out.

Ray-Mi shakes his head. "It was just the right thing to do. Symin agreed to help me atone. He joined the Revolution after Saith abducted and murdered his daughter, and he's still fighting for her. You never really get over losing a child."

Salessa feels a stab of empathy.

"The Facilitator took our parents from us," the wolf responds.

"Is that why you joined the team?" Ray-Mi asks.

The twins exchange a puzzled glance, then Naina replies, "Symin showed up at our door in the middle of the night and asked us to help. We haven't committed to joining anything beyond that."

Ray-Mi laughs. "None of us did, at first, but now we're all invested."

"Who's on this team?" Salessa questions.

"Other than me and Symin? There's Kruga, who was engaged to Symin's daughter. Then two pixies, Gina and Zakia."

Something catches Ray-Mi's eye behind Salessa and Naina. The twins turn around and see Ray-Mi's lime green paramour standing in the doorway of a tree shelter.

"Do you have to go?" Salessa asks him with a wry smile.

"I do, indeed," Ray-Mi responds, rising to his feet and looking directly into Naina's eyes. "It's conversations like these that build trust."

Naina nods, slowly. "Good night, Ray-Mi."

The faerie scurries past them and quickly disappears into the darkness of the forest with the other Mega.

Naina stands as well. "We should sleep."

Much of what Ray-Mi told them continues to swim in Salessa's mind. "Is it alright if I sit alone by the fire for a while?"

Naina's discomfort around their new companions tenses her shoulders again, yet she agrees and heads into Syma's tree.

As Salessa watches the flames dance into the night air, she's reminded of the joyful energy she witnessed. Generational joy, born out of a need for survival.

What began with the faerie quest for supremacy and led through centuries of bloodshed and ages of violence, ended in the freedom of the Mega of Nivyan Hollow. The history that caused her parents' deaths is the same history that bonded these Mega to the Radiance in ways the faeries could never penetrate.

Like a single kernel harvested from a vast cornfield, the good that follows evil can never reconcile the grief born from that evil. Yet, Salessa thinks, it speaks to the resilience of survivors, the unbreakable spirits of those who resist. And it speaks to life's attempts to find balance amongst chaos.

As the flames frolic freely before her, Salessa is reminded of the duality of every moment. Moments that spill blood on a Braver's hands but also make him yearn for atonement.

CHAPTER 15

THE TANTO AND THE ARROW

Gerontocratic Village Adera
Date 19th Day of Month 6, Year 1628 DG

SILENT STILLNESS FILLS THE FOREST. Hours of tense travel have left Kyoko drained. She had thought this would be an—albeit somewhat awkward—overall pleasant journey. The igni reels from the realization of how inaccurate her expectations were.

Adding to her anxiety is apprehension over returning to EverEmber and potentially running into Kanako—something she's been actively avoiding for six years.

The suns' rays break through the edge of the forest and light the way to open, green fields descending from the apex of a small hill. Beyond the fields, at the base of the hill, is a village. Clusters of small homes huddle on the outskirts, while a marketplace and lush gardens fill the center. A river runs through the gardens and a grand, gated residence nestles in the southeast corner.

"That's our first stop," Kyoko says, pointing to the marketplace at the center of the village. "We can find a current map there."

Rafael looks up at the position of the suns. "It's still early. Perhaps we should advance to the next village before we stop."

"That wasn't a question, Rafael."

Kyoko steps forward down the hill toward the village. Rafael's behavior has destroyed any potential for partnership. He forfeited his right to be included in decisions when he allowed his disrespectful thoughts to roam freely from his tongue. Kyoko vows to remind him that he *will* respect her as an outranking Librarian.

The architecture within the village is an unpredictable mix of modern edifices, made of metal and glass, and ancient stone structures with wide columns and sculptures of prominent figures from Doruh mythology. One such sculpture, the largest and most intricate, sits high on a pedestal right at the entrance of the village. It depicts a mother cradling two newborn infants to her chest, each suckling one of her breasts.

The sculpture fascinates Kyoko, stopping her in her tracks when she notices something peculiar: the mother has pointed ears, while the infants do not. The mother has no pupils in her eyes, while the infants do.

"Is everything alright?" comes Rafael's voice next to her.

"Yes, sorry," she says, keeping her eyes on the sculpture. "I noticed something unusual."

"So did I," Rafael responds. "Is this a CereCenter?"

Kyoko breaks her focus on the sculpture to turn to Rafael. "I don't think so. Why?"

He gestures to the locals around them. At least a third of the population is wearing red linen tunics.

A Mega Educator walks by them and Kyoko taps his shoulder. The Librarian stops and turns to them, taking in their yellow silk tunics. He nods respectfully. "Welcome to Adera, Ambassadors."

"Is this a CereCenter?" Kyoko asks.

The red-clad Librarian shakes his head. "Adera is not a CereCenter, no. But there are three not far from here, so Adera's inns remain occupied throughout the academic season."

"That explains it," Rafael says.

"Can you tell me about this sculpture?" Kyoko questions quickly before the Educator can walk away. "Who is this?"

The Educator raises an eyebrow. "That's Adera, of course. The one for whom this village is named."

"But why is she feeding those Doruh infants?"

"You're not well-read on Doruh mythology, are you, Ambassador?" the Educator questions with a snarky chuckle. Kyoko's cheeks glow red. He continues, "The infants are the Twins. The Doruh deities. Adera was their pixie mother."

Kyoko shackles her next questions, in fear of sounding ignorant, allowing the Educator to continue on his way.

"I didn't know any of that either," Rafael remarks, his tone sympathetic. It's a jarring switch from the coldness he's presented thus far.

Kyoko stiffens, unsure how to react. She ignores the remark and suggests they continue to the marketplace. They deftly slip through the crowds and find the map merchant a few stalls in. The old Doruh man boasts about his inventory, claiming to have any and all maps.

From the corner of her eye, Kyoko notices additional wares in the merchant's stall, behind the counters.

"Can I look through some of those items?" she asks the merchant.

He shrugs. "If you'd like to. There's nothing of value. Just some artifacts from the human war, left behind by their soldiers."

Kyoko turns to Rafael. "Find the map we need."

He nods and quietly accepts the order. While the merchant lays out a number of maps before Rafael, Kyoko walks behind the counter and examines some of the items in the merchant's inventory.

This isn't an artifact, Kyoko thinks when she finds a tanto, a traditional igni dagger often carried by EverEmber's warriors. She turns it around in her hands and assesses the keen blade, the solid hilt.

Kyoko removes a handful of stones from her pouch and places them onto the counter. "For the map and the tanto."

The merchant collects the stones, packages the map Rafael selected, and hands it to her. With a patronizing sneer he asks, "Can you handle a blade like that, young lady? Don't lose a finger." He turns to Rafael, hoping for reinforcement, but the mari remains stone-faced.

Thank you, Rafael, she thinks, earnestly.

"I would demonstrate, but then *you'd* lose a finger," Kyoko rebukes. The merchant's smirk dissolves and he turns away to help other customers.

They continue through the marketplace until they reach a narrow street with far fewer patrons and a row of eateries. Rafael's eyes shift from one window to the next and Kyoko hears his stomach begin to roar.

"We should have something to eat before we continue our journey," she says.

"That's a good idea," Rafael replies, nodding sheepishly. "Where would you like to—"

Before the words fall from his lips, a thin, young Doruh man steps up behind him and slips his fingers into the Librarian's pocket.

Rafael's sharp reflexes turn him quickly around, reaching for the man's wrist, but the pickpocket slips from his grasp and weasels through the crowd. The Librarian drops his travel bag and runs off after the thief with nothing but his bow.

Kyoko tightens the strap of her own sack and launches into the crowd behind them.

The pickpocket and pursuing Librarians slip through residents like smooth pebbles through streamwater.

Stop running, Rafael. A few stones aren't worth this.

The mari remains a few feet ahead of her, occasionally closing the gap between him and the thief, then falling behind again. The pickpocket reaches a footbridge over the river that runs through the village. He places the top of the pouch between his teeth, pulls off his shirt, and shifts into a hawk. His clothes fall to the ground as he soars into the air, Rafael's pouch dangling from his beak.

Rafael comes to a halt when the hawk rises into the sky. He drops onto a knee, holding the bow in one hand and an arrow in the other. Kyoko blinks in disbelief; the arrow appears in his hand out of empty air.

"Rafael, stop!" she exclaims when she reaches her subordinate.

"I need that pouch," he responds, his eyeline sharp against the arrow, focused on the rising hawk.

"That's an order, Rafael! No amount of stones is worth potentially murdering a villager, even if he is a thief."

She watches his shoulders relax as he hesitates, but then he resumes his aim and repeats, "I need that pouch. I'm sorry, Kyoko."

The arrow cuts quickly through the air until it reaches the hawk, and the arrowhead slices through the pouch, just under the beak. Kyoko's heart sinks like stone when the hawk begins to spiral downward.

No, no, no. He killed someone.

Before it hits the ground, the hawk shakes its head and resumes its flight, up and away from the village. Kyoko breathes a sigh of relief before realizing the pouch is dropping toward the river.

"It'll be lost to the current," she says.

"No, it won't." Rafael pulls the bow back onto his shoulder and lunges onto the footbridge.

"Rafael, wait!" Kyoko calls to him, as she grabs at the neckline of his tunic. He slips through her fingers and continues forward, launching himself into the air, over the rail at the edge of the footbridge. He meets the pouch above the water, catches it, and cradles it to his chest as he plunges below the surface of the raging river.

A knot develops in the pit of Kyoko's gut as she reaches the railing and peers over it. Tense silence envelops the crowd forming around her, waiting for Rafael to appear. She sees a thin wisp of red where Rafael landed, and sweat breaks out on her forehead.

Come on, Rafael, you're mari. You live in water.

Finally, he pops up out of the river, holding the pouch in his hand above his head. He swims quickly and masterfully to the riverbank, where Kyoko meets him and helps him up. He's filthy, and his tunic is torn at the shoulder, revealing a bloody gash.

"Are you alright?" Kyoko asks him, gesturing to the wound.

He takes a deep breath and nods. "The river wasn't as deep as it looked. But I'm fine."

"It could've been worse. You could've hurt someone. All for a few stones. Not only was this unwise, you directly disobeyed my orders." She realizes that with every sentence, her tone grows less concerned and more admonishing.

Rafael opens his mouth to respond, but something over Kyoko's shoulder catches his eye. "Is that a bison?"

Kyoko turns around and sees the large ungulate bounding through the colorful lanes of the gardens, heading toward them. "It is."

The violent rattling of its hooves against the ground slows until it comes to a halt at the riverbank. It shifts and takes the form of a woman in her early forties.

"I almost didn't believe it," she says, "when they told me there were Ambassadors in my village running wildly through the streets."

"I was pickpocketed," Rafael responds. Kyoko narrows her eyes to encourage him to remain quiet as she speaks to the Doruh.

"We didn't intend to cause a spectacle," she says, apologetically.

"The spectacle is the least of my concerns, Ambassador." The woman's tone is stern. "It's highly irregular for new Librarians to arrive without notifying the Headwoman first. Had you followed your protocol, we could've prevented all of this."

Kyoko tries to hide her embarrassment. The woman is correct; Alba often visited political leaders before exploring any new territory. Kyoko should have remembered to do the same.

"I apologize, Headwoman, but we—"

The woman shakes her head. "Not me. My grandmother is the Headwoman. I have to insist that you come to meet with her and discuss"—she gestures to the dripping wound on Rafael's shoulder—"exigent matters."

Kyoko realizes what she means. The Librarians' safety and protection are the leadership's responsibility as soon as they step foot into the village. Any violation of that responsibility could be considered an intracontinental crime.

But Kyoko doesn't desire any political outcomes from this incident. Not only would it raise questions as to why the Headwoman wasn't contacted in the first place, it would blow a simple matter into something it doesn't have to be, and provide the Prime further reason to despise her.

"We aren't going to report this back to the Library," she says to the village leader. The woman waits, hesitantly, expecting Kyoko to offer some explanation as to why she's being so merciful. Kyoko pauses, struggling to find a reason without admitting to her culpability.

Rafael stands. "It was my fault. I shouldn't have jumped into the river. You aren't responsible for my injury; there's been no violation of my immunity."

The woman's body frees some of its tension. She continues, "Regardless, I must still insist you come meet with the Headwoman. And our salvers can heal you."

"I don't need salvers," Rafael says. "I just need water. If I jump back into the river for a while, my body will heal itself."

At "jump back into the river," Kyoko's heart thumps faster. "No. We'll come with you to see the Headwoman."

CHAPTER 16

THE LAST REMAINING ARTIFACT

Gerontocratic Village Adera
Date 19th Day of Month 6, Year 1628 DG

A DIRT PATH BEYOND THE commercial center leads to the Elder's Estate at the southeast corner of the village. The gate opens to a two-story claystone home with a flat roof. Carved into the walls of the home are designs that depict the ancestry of the Headwoman's family. Kyoko finds some bears, otters, wasps, squirrels, hares, and raccoons in the murals, but the overwhelming strength of bison genetics in the ancestral line is evident.

Shifa, the Headwoman's granddaughter, leads the way up the front stairs between ornate columns. The lineage continues on these stone pillars, Kyoko observes, as she and Rafael ascend to the foyer.

He holds a balled cloth to his shoulder, keeping pressure on his wound. The rag—pristine white when Kyoko pulled it out of her bag— is now crimson.

"The salvers are through this hallway," Shifa says, pointing to a corridor to her right.

Rafael shakes his head. "I told you, I need water. That's how we heal. Your salvers can't fix this wound by morning. Submersion will."

"Alright," Shifa responds. "There's a shower here on the main level, and another up on the roof."

"The roof is perfect."

Shifa gestures to a narrow staircase at the back corner of the foyer. Rafael nods gratefully and moves gingerly toward it, keeping the cloth pressed against his shoulder.

Shifa turns back to Kyoko. "I can show you to your room, Ambassador."

"My room? We won't be staying long, Shifa."

"My grandmother is sleeping and she won't wake until dinner. It'll be dark by then and it would be unwise to travel at night before Rafael has had time to heal."

Discomfort nourishes Kyoko's hesitation. Alba's presence when traveling commands respect. Kyoko's never seen her forcefully invited to stay anywhere.

But Alba would never have been in this situation in the first place. Trying to imagine what the mari Ambassador would do is futile. The only thought circling Kyoko's mind now is that Shifa, though excessively hospitable, makes valid points.

Kyoko sighs. "Alright. Show me to my room."

Cold water cures all ailments.

Rafael can only speak for the mari when he thinks this. There's no greater relief than that of chilled immersion under glowing, warm sunlight.

He sits on the roof, in a corner, with the outdoor shower running over him. The stream hits the clay and drains into a gutter along the side of the house. He wraps his arms around his knees, water falling from the showerhead and slamming against his spine fins and shoulders.

He slicks his drenched hair out of his eyes, then looks up to the suns. It's been two hours since he sat down. Although it continues to throb and ache, the healing has begun.

Just a few more hours.

Footsteps echo from the staircase leading up to the roof. Rafael considers darting to the cot where Shifa laid out some clothes for him earlier, but he has neither the energy nor the interest to cover himself.

The footsteps reach the roof and stop. There's a moment of uncomfortable silence as Kyoko stands there holding a clear vial of blue liquid. Rafael grits his teeth and takes a deep breath when he sees her.

His sister's blood paints the igni Librarian like a canvas. It's on her hands, dripping from her eyes and nose, and dampening her clothes. The yellow silk is entirely red.

Every drop on Kyoko's person mimics the blood that was on Joaquina's corpse when they brought her back home, before Rafael washed her clean with his own hands.

He reminds himself that Kyoko isn't *actually* covered in anything, but even after he closes his eyes and shakes his head, the blood remains stuck to the igni's clothing and exoskeleton. A haunting vision that hasn't let him sleep properly in eight years.

Kyoko holds the vial up for him to see. "The salver asked me to bring this to you."

Rafael gets to his feet, making no attempt to hide his anatomy. He turns the shower handle until the spray dies, then struts to the cot to pick up a towel. "I told Shifa before, I need water, not medicine. My wound is nearly healed."

He faces away from Kyoko, allowing her to view the slit running over his right shoulder and down his back.

"No, it isn't," Kyoko says. "It's recovered remarkably, I'll admit, but it needs more than just water. The salvers asked me to remind you that 'underwater' and 'under the shower' aren't interchangeable."

"Why didn't they come up?" Rafael wonders.

"They were going to, but I" —she pauses— "volunteered."

Rafael turns to face her, raising an eyebrow. *Does she expect gratitude?*

"Thank you," he musters.

"I had to. You're still my responsibility."

Her words sting. For a moment, he thought she'd come up out of genuine concern. However, she's more concerned about "injured subordinate" appearing on her professional record.

"I get it, *boss*." The title drips with snark. He holds his hand out for the vial.

"I can apply it to the wound site."

"No, thank you."

Kyoko rolls her eyes. "Let me help you, Rafael."

He looks down at her hands, still crimson with his sister's blood. The idea of her touching him is nauseating. "That's not necessary."

She pulls the vial to her chest, tightening her grip until her knuckles become pale. "You can't reach all of it, Rafael. Don't be difficult."

Her stoney expression silences him. It becomes plain she won't budge, so he wraps the towel around his waist and takes a seat at the edge of the cot. Kyoko settles behind him, removes the top of the vial, and applies the ointment.

Her fingers are...soft. The igni exoskeleton resembles shimmering stone, yet it feels like any other human's warm skin. Kyoko's fingers move gently up and down on the gash, caressing from the top of his shoulder, down his back, adjacent to his spine fins.

"Where have you been the last two hours?" Rafael asks, attempting to destroy the painfully awkward silence.

"In my room. Evidently the Headwoman won't be available to meet until dinner. Shifa suggested we stay the night and depart in the morning. It'll give you an opportunity to heal."

He's grateful for the additional time. "Thank you."

"You're welcome," she responds with a measure of sincerity. "But, please, be more careful. Follow my orders and don't make this more difficult than it has to be. A small pouch with a few stones is not worth the trouble."

Rafael's consciousness floods with memories of his ascension from disgraced exile to Prime's Gatekeeper. The mari Librarian devoted himself to his academics and his career, putting everything he had into his second chance.

As little as he'd like to unload the intimate details of his decisions to Kyoko, he wants even less for her to question his competence.

"Can I show you something?" he asks her.

She abruptly moves her finger away from his back. "Al-alright."

Rafael reaches underneath the cot, wincing from the wound. He brings the pouch up and opens it, allowing Kyoko to view what's inside.

"Your bracelet," she says when she sees it, her eyes widening with realization. "When did you take it off?"

"I slipped it into the pouch when we were by the sculptures, to keep it safe. I know what I did was reckless, but it wasn't without reason."

Twilight sprinkles the blue gemstones and silver links. Joaquina's olive-toned wrist appears in his mind—the way she would match all of her outfits with the bracelet. Moisture builds in his eyes as his throat tightens.

Kyoko reaches forward and wraps her soft fingers around his forearm. "Rafael, what's wrong?"

He runs his fingers affectionately over the bracelet, holding his injured voice together as best as he can. "My sister's dead, Kyoko." *And your people killed her on a battlefield.*

The igni's eyes widen.

"When I was exiled from SeaBed, I was only permitted to take the possessions I had on the day of my arrest. Luckily, I was wearing this bracelet. This is all I have left of her, Kyoko. It's all I'll ever have of her."

He clears his throat before he continues. "I know I did something stupid today. But, I think people are willing to do stupid things when it comes to those they'll never get to see again."

"Rafael" Kyoko's voice is nearly a whisper "I'm not sure what to say. I didn't—"

"Know," Rafael completes her sentence. "You didn't know what was in the pouch, or why this bracelet was so important to me."

Her fingers tighten on his wrist. When she speaks next, her tone is void of admonishment or judgment. She speaks softly and leans in close. "You should have told me. Rafael, this journey will only find success if we work together, and that includes communicating."

He looks down at the bracelet again. The last remaining artifact of a former life, involuntarily forfeited. As the mari heal when they submerge underwater, Rafael realizes his healing will only begin when he plunges into his new life.

This mission is the dive. Kyoko is right; they have to work together. If this mission fails, so does the submergence.

He gently clasps the bracelet back around his wrist, and looks up at Kyoko. "Then we work together."

She smiles, and as the horizon swallows the last of the suns, he notices a change to Kyoko's appearance. The blood drenches her still, but the crimson sheen has become dull and subtle.

It's faded.

CHAPTER 17

LOST

Gerontocratic Village Adera
Date 19th Day of Month 6, Year 1628 DG

THE ELEGANCE OF TRADITIONAL DORUH attire compels Rafael to flaunt the girth of his forearm fins. At lavish gatherings in SeaBed, eligible men and women seduce partners with this display. He won't have the pleasure of taking part in these rituals again, but old habits take longer to break than iron.

A servant presented Rafael with a hide travel bag and several kurtas. Shifa offered the worker a hefty sum in exchange for his generosity, as all that remains of Rafael's personal items are one yellow tunic, his bow, and the collapsible arrows.

And Joaquina's bracelet.

Moonlight plays on the bracelet's silver surface, hopping jovially between the twenty links. Mari siblings purchase one for each other, and a single blue gemstone is added to each link on every birthday until their twentieth, when they've come of age.

Three of the links sit empty; Joaquina hadn't reached her eighteenth birthday. Rafael had saved money to purchase the next stone, however, he'd had to spend the money before he could.

On her shroud.

He remembers the last words she ever spoke to him, as she clasped the silver around his wrist.

Keep it safe for me. I'll take it back when I return. Take care of Mother. She kissed his forehead and said, *I love you, Rafa.*

He catches a bit of his reflection in the polished bracelet and turns away, looking to the sky. A heavy pit develops in his gut, and his gaze lingers on the glorious starlight above.

I would offer you every gemstone buried under a thousand different oceans, he projects to the heavens, hoping she'll hear, *if it meant I got to see you again.*

He descends the staircase to the main foyer to find a large portrait of Shifa and an elderly woman with a cane situated over the fireplace mantel. Someone stands with their back to him, staring up at it. The individual is clad in a colorful, front-wrapped garment with square sleeves and a broad sash, her hair wound in a tight bun atop her head.

Rafael stands awkwardly unnoticed until he clears his throat and the person turns. His breath catches as Kyoko stares at him in a traditional igni outfit. The mari can't decide whether his shock is born from the unexpected admiration of her garment, or from finding Kyoko in anything that isn't a tunic.

Either way, his tongue refuses to obey his commands. Its rebellion leaves him standing with his mouth agape.

Kyoko smiles and approaches him, evidently ignorant of his speechlessness. "Finally. I've been waiting."

"Sorry," his tongue finally obliges. A compliment descends from his thoughts to his lips, but they shut tightly when his gaze falls on her bloody fingers. The vision remains, leaving his mouth void of praise.

Kyoko's smile dims when she notices his discomfort. "Is everything alright?"

"I've never seen you off duty," Rafael replies, shifting his eyes back to her face and away from her hands.

Her smile returns. "This is a yukata."

"It's stunning," the compliment finally bursts from him.

Kyoko's cheeks burn pink and she nods gratefully, then leans her face forward and tilts her head to the side. Rafael recognizes her initiation of the traditional mari greeting. He's tugged between the desire to distance himself from the bloody visions, and the concern that she'll feel insulted if he doesn't oblige.

The sound of footsteps draws Kyoko's attention from the greeting. Shifa appears in the foyer, wearing a pink shalwar-kameez with a white dupatta around her neck and shoulders.

"Dinner is ready," she announces. "We'll be dining at the fire pit tonight. Amma—" she pauses "—my grandmother is already out there, waiting. Please, follow me."

She leads them through the salver's corridor to a wide gate at the rear of the estate, beyond which spread lush, maintained gardens. They step onto a walkway to a cleared area with stone tiles and a wide flame centered between benches.

The Headwoman sits in the middle of a long bench at the far end, clutching the head of her cane, clad in a magenta sari. She stares into the fire, expressionless. The cool evening air kisses Rafael's shoulder and brings comfort to his aching wound.

"Please, have a seat," Shifa invites the Librarians, gesturing to the spaces on the bench on either side of the elderly woman. "The servants will be out with dinner shortly."

She marches back through the gardens toward the estate, leaving Rafael and Kyoko awkwardly before the fire pit.

She isn't going to introduce us? he wonders.

As if she's heard him, Kyoko steps around the pit and gestures for Rafael to follow. When they reach the Headwoman, Kyoko bows respectfully.

"You must be the Librarians causing such a ruckus in my village," she remarks with narrowing eyes.

Kyoko's own eyes widen, mirroring Rafael's surprise.

"I was pickpocketed and—"

"And you began firing arrows in the most crowded parts of the gardens?" The Headwoman raises an eyebrow. "Why didn't you follow your protocol and come visit me upon arrival?"

"We weren't expecting to be in the village for long, Amma," Kyoko explains.

"Hm!" Amma grumbles. "Not an excuse. You should have received better training, Ambassador."

Kyoko's cheeks burn red and Rafael watches a bead of sweat form at her hairline. Although the ordeal began with him chasing down the thief, her competence is now under scrutiny.

He steps forward. "It was my doing. Kyoko suggested we visit you, but I insisted we gather supplies and continue on. Kyoko is a skilled Librarian who's received training from the best."

Amma leans back and scratches her chin. "The best, huh? And whom would that be?"

"Ambassador Alba," Kyoko replies.

The Headwoman smiles. "Many, many years ago, there was a summit for all of the Gerontocrats. Alba was sent by the Prime to record and facilitate. If you are her protege, the transgression is forgiven."

She leans forward, dissolves her smile, and lifts her finger admonishingly. "This time. Don't ever walk around my village again without notifying me. Understood?"

Kyoko nods. "Of course, Amma."

Amma's smile returns. "Excellent. Now, please, join me."

Rafael and Kyoko take a seat on either side of the woman, and when Rafael catches Kyoko's gaze, he sees her lips form the words, "Thank you."

He nods and passes her a reassuring smile.

Servants appear around the pit shortly thereafter and place long wooden tables end-to-end in a gazebo adjacent to the fire pit. The tables are covered with a shimmering white cloth, embellished with golden embroidery, and the servants lay out a feast of rice, aromatic flavors of naan, and an extensive spread of curries and stews.

The feast begins when Shifa rejoins them. Amma is served first, followed by the Librarians and Shifa, and finally the servants, salvers, and groundskeepers. Throughout dinner, conversation is light and pleasant. Rafael finds himself lost in the fascinating details of village governance. Periodically, he catches the light of the flames bouncing off of Kyoko's exoskeleton and notices how it makes her cheeks shimmer. It's a delightful observation until his eyes wander to her hands, which remain crimson.

After dinner, a sea of servants clears the table and lays out desserts. Though he's quite full, Rafael finds it hard to resist the soft, fried balls of milk solids swimming in syrup.

"Gulab jamun," Shifa names them. "We also have rice pudding."

"I don't think I can take another bite," Rafael claims, patting his stomach. "You've filled me up right before bed." He stands.

Shifa frowns. "Bed? No, no. You haven't even heard Amma sing yet."

Kyoko's expression implies that she was also hoping to retire to the guest room soon, but when she nods, Rafael takes his seat again.

Shifa turns to Amma. "What will you sing for us?"

Amma raises her fingers to her chin again. "Perhaps...*Ayuma Liyuna*?"

Shifa's eyes glisten as she gasps with delight. "Yes! A celebratory folk song in honor of our guests."

Amma clears her throat loudly and releases the tune into the crisp night air. The Headwoman's expressive voice echoes over the crackling flames, melting into Rafael's ears and drenching his heart. He's mystified by the union of raw power and deliberate tenderness in her vocals.

The lyrics of the ballad, all in Nysabaani, add to the sensations. They strike an unpredictable balance between hope and disappointment, lamenting the songwriter's own worthlessness, while praising those that he loves most.

Amma's voice cradles Rafael's eardrums. Kyoko appears transfixed, as well, and Shifa is nearly in tears. After a few moments, Amma stops and Rafael's heart beats harder, yearning for more.

"Why don't you show them the dance?" the Headwoman asks Shifa.

Shifa claps her hands quickly, excitedly. "Wonderful idea!"

"There's a dance?" Kyoko asks.

Shifa nods. "Oh, yes! Let me show you." She takes to her feet and reaches her hand out to Kyoko. "Will you join me?"

The igni hesitates and turns to Rafael, who nods to encourage her. Slowly, she takes Shifa's hand and rises. The song resumes and Kyoko follows her host's lead. Their arms swing horizontally as their hips sway softly. They move to the tips of their toes as they twirl around and find one another's gaze again. They come close, hands together, and then move apart.

The dance matches the ballad in the balance of both hope and pessimism. At some movements, Shifa frowns, while at others, she beams brighter than the suns.

Rafael tries to follow the lyrics as Amma sings. Part of the Librarians' academic curriculum is devoted to Nysabaani, but Rafael has not heard all of these words before. He's able to translate a portion of it as he listens:

> A lifetime in a day
> In your arms, I stay
> But now, I say
> I am in the way
>
> New lovers abound
> Devotees surround
> Deservingly crowned
> A role newfound
>
> Adera, bonder of rifts
> Heart of gifts
> The Queen who uplifts
> The Mother of Shifts

Adera. He remembers the name from the conversation at the statues, when they first arrived. The Educator told them it was both the name of the village, and that of the mother of the Twins. The pixie mother.

Rafael's concentration on the lyrics breaks when Kyoko quickly approaches him, takes his hand, and leads him around the fire to where she and Shifa dance. They form a small circle and Rafael attempts to follow along. He's never considered himself a skilled dancer, yet the simplicity of the moves helps him keep up. Hips swaying and toes twirling, the Librarians and the bison spin entirely in sync.

He continues to translate in his head, hoping the lyrics will help him remember the sequence of movements. The verses describe the songwriter's offspring.

> I see you in our daughter
> In all that you've taught her
> I see you in our son
> In all that he's done

The lyrics have been dripping with emotion since the start of the song, but Rafael is unprepared for the impact of the incoming verses. They strike his core, and his smile fades. One line at a time, the world around him closes in.

The swaying continues, the twirling remains, but the ballad wraps its cold fingers around his throat and squeezes. Breathing becomes difficult as he translates:

When they speak to one another
When the sister fights for her brother
When he protects her from the other
I see, in them, their mother

Rafael hears these lyrics and drowns in memories of a sister who fought, and a brother who failed to protect. When he translates, *I see, in them, their mother*, he's flooded with all that the igni took from him, including the chance to see his mother ever again.

He sways, then moves up onto his toes, and when the twirl completes, Kyoko stands before him again. Blood drips from her eyes, nose, and ears. Her hair and her yukata are drenched in it. The faint red on her hands grows bright and apparent, screaming out to Rafael about his sister's innards being lost to the battle. Everywhere she steps, she leaves a trail of Joaquina's blood under her feet.

Rafael stops dancing, and Shifa bumps into him. The dancing stops, and the ballad follows immediately after. Rafael's heart pounds against his chest as he takes in the sight of the soaked igni before him. Angry, aching guilt forms like a blooming seed in his stomach. These are the monsters that tore Joaquina apart, and now he dances with them.

Kyoko steps forward, reaching for his hand, but he backs away before she can touch him. "What's wrong, Rafael?"

Rafael opens his mouth, but only silence exists.

"Why are you crying?" Shifa asks, her expression laden with concern.

"I-I," Rafael stammers, as he continues to back away. "I can't..."

"You can't what?" Kyoko approaches again.

"No!" It comes out louder than Rafael intended. Kyoko jumps back, wincing. She seems hurt, but he doesn't care. They're responsible. For his mother's tears, his nation's losses, and his own exile.

He lifts his arms and quickly wipes the tears from his cheeks. He turns to Amma, whose eyes have narrowed, and bows his head slightly. "Good night, Headwoman." His voice is feeble. "I have to go to bed."

He doesn't wait for a response. With quick steps, he stomps through the gardens and back into the estate, hoping to put as much distance between him and Kyoko as possible.

It is hours of restraining his sobs before Rafael feels calmer. Before he can lay on his cot staring up at the stars and breathe evenly again.

Millions of white eyes stare down from the heavens, beady, bright gems raining down their brilliance, providing the only slivers of illumination on the rooftop. Their starlight feels like a bridge that might carry his words to Joaquina.

"I'm sorry," he whispers, hoping the starlight doesn't delay in carrying them to her.

The words of the ballad, and all of the memories they brought with them, stung his mind and his heart repeatedly until their power withered and he was finally able to lie down on his back peacefully.

The quiet darkness of nightfall envelops him as he tries, and fails, to sleep. He considers how he might explain his behavior to Kyoko, Shifa, and the Headwoman in the morning. They'll be wondering, looking for an explanation of some kind. Some words to make his abrupt reaction seem reasonable.

But it wasn't reasonable. There's nothing reasonable about the traumas that shatter the world.

Light springs forth from over the side of the rooftop and catches the corner of Rafael's eye. He sits up and sees orange illumination painting the stone of the estate. Over the rooftop's edge, he finds the most peculiar sight.

The fire pit is alive again. Amma sits on the bench, dressed in a nightgown. She holds powerful eye contact with the mari, then raises her hand into the air and motions for him to join her. He rubs his eyes to confirm he isn't dreaming, then hesitantly nods and makes his way down to the foyer, out of the rear gate, and through the gardens to the fire pit.

The Librarian and the Headwoman sit quietly for a few minutes, staring into the flames, until Rafael finally speaks up. "I assume you want an explanation for my behavior."

"Actually," she says, "I don't think I need one."

Rafael turns to her, surprised, and she continues. "It was *Ayuma Liyuna*, wasn't it? You are a Librarian. I know you understand Nysabaani."

Rafael nods. "We're all fluent." He pauses, reconsidering the accuracy of his words. "Relatively."

"Why did the song affect you so deeply?" She leans in.

Discomfort flows through him. The intimate details of his past are buried, and he isn't likely to take to the shovel for a stranger. "It's personal."

She resumes her upright posture. "Hm. That's fair. But we can talk about the song, generally. Translate the title."

Rafael obeys. "*Ayuma* means 'mother.' And *Liyuna* comes from 'to change.' So, 'the Mother Who Changes'?"

Amma shakes her head. "The Mother of Shifts. It's a double meaning."

Rafael nods, recalling the subject of the song. "The song is about Adera. The village is named after her. She's the Mother of Shifts."

"Very good, yes. Adera is responsible for the most significant historical event this world has ever known. The title of the song alludes to the truth that this pixie created an entirely new species: the Doruh."

"Wait," Rafael responds, confused, "the Doruh were created during the War of New Clans. SunSide's warriors used the Radiance to attack the teri humans, intending to turn them into animals. The human and animal essences merged, and the shapeshifters were born."

Amma shakes her head. "Librarians truly believe they know everything, don't they? If their narcissism were trees in a forest, there'd be enough lumber for a thousand ships." She laughs. "Your records, your Catacombs, your history, it's all wrong. SunSide wants you to believe the birth of our people was an act of war, an act of chaos. But it wasn't. The Doruh were born from an act of pure, unbridled love."

"The records are wrong?" Rafael juggles the words on his tongue. His mind spins back to Unisa. *She was right.* His chest aches with guilt, recalling the manner in which he spoke to her when she came to him for help.

"Yes, they are wrong. The truth is that Adera was a pixie who loved a human of the teri clan, and had left SunSide to be with him in MoonSide. Her father, a close friend of the monarchy, told the MegaMother that the humans held his daughter captive, and the War of New Clans began. SunSide invaded MoonSide to bring Adera home and slaughter her human lover."

"The teri were able to connect to the Radiance," Rafael notes. "Did they fight back?"

Amma nods. "There was resistance, certainly, but SunSide's warriors decimated nearly half of the teri population in one night. Men, women, children. They razed entire villages, in a display of savagery no one had ever seen before, and then they reached Adera's doorway. She and her lover, Anhum, used the Radiance to hold the fighters back as long as they could, but SunSide's forces quickly began to overwhelm them. In the end, Adera had an idea that would change the world forever.

"She used every ounce of Radiant energy she could access to inject Anhum's body with the essence of a bird, so that he could take its physical form and fly away undetected. It was an act of desperation, and an act of love, but her connection to the Radiance was beyond even her own control. She successfully merged the essence of the bird with Anhum, but she also unleashed a wave of Radiant energy that expanded out, hitting every human of the teri clan and creating the Doruh."

"So they were able to escape," Rafael infers.

"Indeed. Anhum and Adera came here. They founded this village and lived out their lives in service of the new species. This village is where their children were born, the Twins, who are prophesied to one day be resurrected and return to the world to save it in its darkest hour. Not only are they our deities, but they were the first naturally-born Doruh."

Rafael understands. "The title of the song, the Mother of Shifts. It's a double meaning because it alludes to Adera being both the creator of the shapeshifters, and the architect of the new era: the shift in history."

Amma smiles. "Correct. The song is written from Anhum's perspective. It is both hopeful in the idea that Adera and the Twins have a new role in leading the Doruh, yet it laments the fact that Anhum now feels inadequate."

"Inadequate? But he had also become Doruh."

"He had, yes, but he'd lost the ability to access the Radiance, which was all he'd ever known. Shifting was difficult for him to master, and the Mega accessed the Radiance differently than the humans did. Anhum's feelings of inadequacy evolved from the realization that human Radiance would be lost to history."

"What was different about the way the Mega accessed the Radiance?" Rafael wonders.

"I'm sure you've seen them do it," Amma responds. "They search for energy in external sources. The leaves, the rivers, their four deities in the sky. The humans would access the Radiance in a manner more natural and organic than that."

She reaches forward and places her hand on Rafael's chest, over his heart. "Emotions. The energy within. Adera learned to access the Radiance from the humans. That's the only reason the Doruh were ever created. Tree energy would never have achieved such a feat. Adera used her desperation, fear, anger, and above all, her love."

"Accessing the Radiance through emotional energy." Rafael allows the abstract to seep into his mind. "A human ideal, that's now been lost for over a thousand years."

"Nothing is ever truly lost."

Rafael raises an eyebrow. "What do you mean?"

"The things we call 'lost' are just waiting to be found again. If human Radiance hasn't been accessed in a thousand years, perhaps it simply needs someone to try again." She leans in and smiles mysteriously. "Emotional energy. Someone to try again."

Rafael chuckles sarcastically. "If any human were to access a form of the Radiance that has been dormant for a thousand years, I can promise you, I'm not the one to do it."

"Well," Amma says, widening her eyes in mock surprise, "now it appears we're talking about *personal* things. Why do you say that?"

Rafael hesitates.

"Speak up!"

"I'm an exile. Banished from my home. Unable to keep my sister safe. Now I'm on a journey to prove that my second chance shouldn't be revoked. I'm completely lost." His eyes move to the floor and he sighs. "Does that sound like someone with the potential to resurrect a long-forgotten resource?"

"More than anyone."

Rafael looks up quickly, unsure if he heard her properly. The Headwoman continues. "After all you've been through, I can't imagine anyone with more emotional energy than you. Use your grief. When you feel the Radiance approaching, promise me, you'll allow it to carry you."

Rafael finds it hard not to dismiss the Headwoman's claims. The idea that humans might still be able to access the Radiance, using a method erased from the pages of history, seems bizarre alone. But the insinuation that Rafael, of all people, can be the one to achieve it is a concept he cannot reconcile.

Exiles aren't meant for greatness. He lost the right to dream so grand a long time ago.

Amma speaks again, bringing Rafael's focus back to the conversation. "Time is fleeting faster than it ever has before, and the knowledge of human Radiance needs to be passed on. At my age, we learn to impart what we can, to whomever will listen, so that it won't be"—she turns to Rafael and smiles—"lost."

"And you thought I would listen?"

Amma chuckles. "I did. But I also don't have emotional humans sitting in my fire pit every night." She gestures to the rooftop. "Return to your bed. You'll need rest to continue your journey in the morning."

Rafael stands, feeling a sense of warmth and sincerity with the Headwoman. "Thank you."

Amma nods and the Librarian begins his trek back to the rooftop, but when he reaches the other side of the fire pit, she calls out to him again. "Rafael, tell her the truth."

"Who?" Rafael asks.

"Your companion. She'll want an explanation for your outburst, and you'll be tempted to fabricate an excuse."

Rafael stands quietly for a moment, considering how best to respond. "I can't tell her the truth. The truth is that when I look at her, all I see is"—*careful, Rafael*—"pain and suffering."

"And then you turn away from it, which only prolongs it. Stop turning away. Face it, address it."

Rafael shakes his head. "I can't. The igni—"

"*She* is not *all* of the igni, and she is not responsible for her clan's collective actions. She is an individual with whom you'll be spending some time, and holding the stone of hatred over her head will only be a punishment to yourself. Apologize and bare your heart. She'll understand."

Rafael smiles, realizing that the Headwoman was correct in her judgment. He *will* listen.

CHAPTER 18

THE FINAL ACT

Theocratic-Monarchy SunSide
Date 19th Day of Month 6, Year 1628 DG

THERE'S AN EERIE AURA OF disappointment overflowing the Theater. Saith watches from the window wall as Frona's light falls behind the city structures.

"How long are you going to stand and stare?" Zar-Lo sighs, running his palms over his robes to smooth them out. Long black fabric mingles with golden armor, and a shimmering gold cape.

Saith turns to face the MegaFather, the weight of his failure palpable in his muted expression. "I should've reached them before they entered the forest."

The ground trembles from the weight of Zar-Lo's steps as he approaches the Facilitator. "You should have. But what's done is done. You'll have another opportu—"

Like a needle shot from a bow, agony abruptly pierces Zar-Lo's skull. He drops to his knees, clutching the sides of his head and hunching forward. Saith places his palm over the MegaFather and uses the Radiance to ease the pressure in his mind.

It doesn't help much.

Zar-Lo releases a growl as the piercing becomes sound, voices burrowing like a chisel in his mind, into the inner depths of his consciousness. He holds his breath to keep from becoming physically ill.

"They've returned," Saith observes.

Zar-Lo grunts and nods. The feeling passes after a few moments and he straightens his back, still on his knees, eyes closed. Saith places his hand on the MegaFather's forehead, emanating Radiant energy from his palm, soothing him in the aftermath.

"Their timing is impeccable," Saith remarks. "Twenty years since the last contact, nearly to the day."

"Yes. Their arrival is painful, but expected. And they won't leave until they get what they want."

He wraps his fingers around Saith's wrist gently and moves the pixie's hand away from his forehead. "Thank you."

Saith helps the MegaFather to his feet. "Their demands will be met soon. Once the twins are found, I'll extract what we need from them, and the ancients will be satiated."

Zar-Lo shakes his head. "Six years of abductions, fruitless. Another twelve hunting the twins, wasted."

Saith meets Zar-Lo's gaze again. "They are in Nivyan Hollow, I know it. I will find them."

Zar-Lo smiles. "I know. You've been closer to me than a brother for all these years." The smile drops. "But even family can fail, and no failure is above punishment."

Saith nods tensely as the gravity of the MegaFather's words land on him.

"Now," Zar-Lo continues, "let's get this reading over with."

The walk down the tower stairs is lengthy, from the Theater at the top to the Forum on the main level. The stones creak and rattle with every step, a chorus venerating the MegaFather's formidable girth.

The Forum's heavy wooden doors boast artistic depictions of the Four, a tribute to the theocracy that stands shoulder-to-shoulder with the throne.

"A reminder, Father," Saith states. "Try to show some enthusiasm when you greet them. They may be catching on to the fact that you are…"

"Godless?" Zar-Lo completes the sentence.

"Atypically spiritual."

Zar-Lo grunts. "I'll do my best."

Saith seizes the handle and swings the doors wide open. "Rise for the MegaFather, king of SunSide. Glory to the Quad Gods."

The faerie monarch steps into the wide chamber, his cape dragging along the floor behind him. Light from the panels around the room strikes the gems in the floors and gives life to his glimmering turquoise skin.

The nine theocrats of the Assembly rise to their feet. Two of them, elderly faeries, struggle to stand without assistance, yet do so regardless, out of respect for the throne.

"The Four have blessed us with your presence, Father," the Members chant in unison, bending their fingers into a circle and placing it over their foreheads.

Saith catches Zar-Lo's attention and silently pleads for the MegaFather to reciprocate enthusiastically.

The faerie reveals his teeth in a wide smile, and proclaims, "I am fortunate to be in your presence, blessed Members." He lifts his hands and places four fingers on his forehead to convey his respect, and finds Saith nodding with approval.

They all take seats around a wide table and the reading of the Final Act begins.

One of the elderly faeries clears her throat and addresses the monarch. "It is important that Member Sonali's Final Act be read. Before we begin, however, we would like to ask you some questions regarding the events of the past two days."

"I am happy to provide any clarification you require, Member Xo-Rah," Zar-Lo responds confidently.

Xo-Rah smiles. "Excellent. Firstly, how did you discover the note that outlined Member Sonali's alleged collaboration with the radicals during the Siege of the Castrum?"

"The Braver General discovered the note in his chambers three nights ago. The author remains a mystery."

The other elderly faerie speaks next. "What happened after the note was brought to your attention?"

Zar-Lo straightens in his seat, actively maintaining the confidence in his posture. "I approached Member Sonali to discuss the allegation, and she confessed."

"Why wasn't the note brought to the Assembly first?" This question comes from a young nymph.

Zar-Lo softens his expression, attempting to feign heartbreak. "Betrayal. The Member and I worked closely together for many years. With allegations of regicide and conspiracy, I wanted"—he pauses, dramatically—"no, I *needed* answers directly from her. I acted on impulse, I understand, but I wonder: how would any of you have reacted to finding out that someone you trusted had aided those plotting your demise?"

"We understand the emotional impact of your discovery, Father," another nymph states, "however, you've executed a Member of the Assembly, publicly, without trial. This is new ground for SunSide's politics."

Zar-Lo breathes deeply and recalls the rehearsal, spewing Saith's response verbatim. "Every aspect of the Member's execution—the timing, the location, the method, the exhibitionism—was by her own request. This can be verified by my Facilitator, Braver General, and a number of Braver officers that were in the room."

Xo-Rah smiles. "Well, then. I believe your response sufficiently clears the matter up. We can proceed with the reading of her Final Act." She turns her head to another Member, and everyone at the table follows her line of sight to the pixie at the end of the table.

Saila rises to her feet, holding a thin hardcover text in her hands. Her green fingers, wrapped tightly around the text, are steady. When Zar-Lo's gaze meets hers, she smiles, sparking uneasiness in his chest.

Why is she smiling during the reading of her friend's Final Act? Something is awry. Zar-Lo turns quickly to Saith, silently instructing him to intervene.

Saith clears his throat. "Beloved Members of the Assembly, I'd like to be clear: the reading of Member Sonali's Final Act is a formality meant to honor age-old tradition, correct? It has otherwise been both legally and practically nullified."

Saila's smile widens and Zar-Lo's heart sinks. "Oh, no, Facilitator Saith. You are quite mistaken." There's a hint of thrill in her tone. "The

Final Act is entirely in effect, and will be acted upon as decreed by theocratic law."

Saith pops up onto his feet. "That's not possible, Saila."

"You will refer to me by the title of my station," she sternly instructs her father.

"I apologize, Member," Saith murmurs. "Surely, there has been a mistake. Member Sonali was executed as a criminal. Her confession nullified her right to a Final Act. *This* is theocratic law."

"I suggest you review the laws of the Assembly more thoroughly," Saila taunts.

Heat rises to Zar-Lo's cheeks at her insolence.

She continues. "The law states that the Final Act will be nullified if the deceased Member is *convicted* of certain crimes. Member Sonali, however, was never convicted because she wasn't afforded a trial."

Saith narrows his eyes and slowly lowers back into his seat.

Zar-Lo's jaw clenches tight. "Perhaps I haven't been clear, Member. She confessed and then requested to forgo a trial."

"Irrelevant." Excitement beams from her face, and Zar-Lo's stomach ties into a knot. "The fact remains that, without a trial, Member Sonali could not have been convicted. The law doesn't nullify Final Acts over allegations."

Zar-Lo's gaze pleads with the faerie Members around the table, desperately searching for support.

"I'm sorry," Xo-Rah says. "We objected, but she's correct. Regardless of her confession, regardless of her request for execution, Sonali is innocent in the eyes of the law." Her eyes fall to her interlocked fingers. "The Final Act must be read and honored."

Saith opens his mouth to speak again, but Zar-Lo places his hand on the Facilitator's knee under the table.

"Fine," he breathes out. "Get it done with."

Still smiling, Saila opens the book and begins reading. "This Final Act is bestowed by the almighty Four, vessels of the Radiance, unto Sonali, Member of the Assembly of the Radiance, of the species Doruh, as decreed by the law of SunSide's theocracy. It is hereby noted, in the preamble to the Final Act, that Member Sonali holds the Red-Lo Royal Dynasty, and each of its generational representatives, responsible for the following crimes against SunSide, the Assembly, and the citizens of the kingdom."

Zar-Lo scoffs. "*She's* holding *me* and *my family* accountable for crimes against SunSide? This is madness already."

Saila continues, ignoring the outburst. "767 DG, regicide against MegaMother Picana by the usurper, Red-Lo. 784 DG, the slaughter of nymph and pixie citizens who fought alongside the Doruh in the Uprisings, Red-Lo, the usurper."

"The conqueror," Zar-Lo attempts to correct her.

Again, she continues as if he hasn't said anything. "1380 DG, the invasion and illegal occupation of MoonSide, and 1381 DG, the assassination of the Doruh Alphocracy, both by Tya-Lo the MegaMother."

A furious growl erupts from Zar-Lo's throat. "Get to the point, Member." He fails wildly to control the unraveling of his tone.

Saila's smile reaches both ears as she ignores him again. "1422 DG, the theft of land from native MoonSidians for faerie settlements by Hof-Lo the Unflinching. 1622 DG, the incorporation of ore into the kingdom's infrastructure, severing a portion of the population from the Radiance, a gift of the almighty Four. By Zar-Lo the MegaFather."

"Enough!" Saith raises his voice.

Saila pauses the reading to raise her eyes and meet her father's. There's a tense moment that feels like gloating to Zar-Lo, until Saila looks back down at the page.

"Finally, Member Sonali holds the Red-Lo Royal Dynasty responsible for the faerie clan's inability to access the Radiance, for the premature execution of a Member of the Assembly without trial, and for the overarching goal of establishing and maintaining faerie supremacy over the other clans and species that make up the kingdom's diverse citizenry."

Zar-Lo's fist comes down on the ore table so hard that the resulting *clonk* echoes around the Forum into the streets. When he lifts his fist again, there is a soft dent in the metal. The Members exchange anxious glances.

"We're almost done, Father," Saila says, keeping her eyes on the page. "Member Sonali acknowledges that she cannot hold the dynasty responsible in any official manner, however, she hopes that this preamble acts as sufficient evidence that her Final Act is indeed justified. By her Final Act, Member Sonali hereby removes Zar-Lo of the Red-Lo Royal

Dynasty from the position of MegaFather, and bans all progeny of the Red-Lo bloodline from holding political power in SunSide henceforth."

There's a stillness in the room as Zar-Lo's rage climaxes. It takes all of his strength not to toss the ore table to the side and tear Saila's throat out.

He releases a long, trembling breath and speaks the only words his tongue is able to conjure. "I don't believe it."

"Then look for yourself," Saila responds. She slams the thin hardcover text down on the table and gives it a hard shove. It slides quickly across the ore surface until Zar-Lo stops it. He lifts the book slowly and opens it.

The wind escapes his lungs, and the room spins around him as harsh realization sets in. His entire body goes numb. All sounds become muffled and distant. Time feels as though it has completely stopped. His heart pounds rapidly and loudly, like the rhythmic *clank* of a blacksmith forging a sword.

"She wrote it." Nothing more than a whisper.

"Of course, she did," Saila replies. "All Members write their Final Acts."

"No." Zar-Lo rises to his feet, still clutching the text. "The anonymous note. It's the same handwriting." The Members stare at Zar-Lo—some blankly, some perplexed, and others with concern.

Saila's smile continues to widen.

"Don't you see?" Zar-Lo continues. "She planned this. All of it. Her execution. The Final Act."

Saila ignores his frantic eruption and announces loudly, "The Final Act has been read and, by the will of the Four, it shall be done. We, the Members of the Assembly of the Radiance, mercifully grant you, Zar-Lo of the disgraced Red-Lo Royal Dynasty, the traditional four days to conclude all business. On the fifth day, SunSide will act as a sole theocracy until a new royal line is appointed. It will be announced before the kingdom on the Twenty-Fourth, just before sunsdown. And you"—she points a harsh finger at Zar-Lo—"*Father*, will be just another citizen."

Zar-Lo's hand clutches the edge of the ore table and he squeezes, crumpling it like paper. Two of the Members gasp at the display. Another whispers, "How did he...?"

Saila maintains strong eye contact, completely unfazed.

"You cannot allow this," Zar-Lo growls, turning to the two elderly faerie Members.

Tears form in the corners of Xo-Rah's gray eyes. "I'm sorry, my dear. We made objections to the Final Act, I promise you. However, it seems the execution has insulted the other Members. We were outvoted." Her voice breaks as she utters the next words. "Saila is right, I'm afraid. It is indeed the will of the Four."

"*The Four.*" His tone is both incredulous and condescending. "Absurdity! Utter drivel!"

Various Members around the table gasp.

Zar-Lo raises his arm to gesture widely at the kingdom beyond the windows. "Look! Look at what my dynasty has built. Cities, kingdoms, and nations all over Aerthomni flourish on the back of *our* technology. This dynasty has ushered SunSide into scientific revolutions time and time again. We've conquered MoonSide and brought every godforsaken animal to their fucking knees."

He lifts a threatening finger and points at the Members around the table, his hand shaking, his turquoise complexion turning lavender from the hot blood rising to his face. "This. Isn't. Over."

He straightens firmly, taking a moment to scan every face, committing them to memory. His eyes linger on Saila's as his skin boils with rage.

Saith stands and speaks directly to his daughter. "You are, indeed, a disappointment to the family."

Saila's unfazed smile and silent acceptance speak volumes as to how much stock she puts into her father's words.

Zar-Lo turns toward the Forum's heavy wooden doors and begins the long walk back to the Theater, Saith at his heels.

CHAPTER 19

TRUST

Theocratic-Monarchy *SunSide*
Date *19th Day of Month 6, Year 1628 DG*

ILLUMINATED SQUARES TWINKLE FROM THE windows around the city, mimicking the stars above. Zar-Lo, hands folded behind his back, stands at the window wall and commits every inch of his kingdom to memory; in case his time to watch over it is limited.

Exhaustion plagues the MegaFather. Not that of the body, but that of the heart. Where he once had a natural enthusiasm for life, the faerie now finds apathetic actions and perfunctory performances.

After all this time alone, little keeps him involved in fleeting moments beyond the ancient voices piercing his skull and the threat of shattering the legacy for which so much has been sacrificed. Thanks to the treacherous animal, that legacy is in greater jeopardy now than it ever has been.

Will this disgrace be the final, lasting legacy of the Red-Lo Royal Dynasty? Who can he trust to save it?

"No one," he growls.

Saith, standing on the platform in the center of the room, steps toward the king. "I'm sorry, Father?"

"I can trust no one," Zar-Lo elaborates and turns to face the Facilitator.

Saith frowns while descending the platform steps. "I remain devoted to you."

Zar-Lo sighs. "And what good was your devotion when my legacy was being torn out from under me?"

Saith reaches the MegaFather and stands before him. "I will fix this. By any means."

Zar-Lo looks down at the empty robe sleeve tied at Saith's shoulder, then back up to his eyes. "Devote yourself to me the way you once did. When you sacrificed your arm and so much more to protect me. I need *that* Saith."

"I'm here, Father. I swear it."

A knock echoes from the massive doors.

"Our guest is here," Zar-Lo says, keeping his gaze on Saith. "Make him comply."

Saith nods. "I can do that."

Zar-Lo turns back to the window wall as Saith holds out his arm and closes his fingers into a fist. The doors of the Theater swing open and Vy-Ro enters. Saith releases his fist and the doors swing shut again.

Vy-Ro forms a circle with his fingers and places it over his forehead. Zar-Lo nods and the Braver General lowers his hand.

"Thank you for the invitation, Father," he says. "I am intrigued to discover what important matter has forced you to summon me in the middle of the night."

"Please, have a seat," Saith says, forcing Vy-Ro's attention.

The Braver General turns from the MegaFather to the Facilitator, concern growing on his expression. He's never before been offered a seat at the desk. As he ascends the circular platform, his hesitation is palpable in his stalled steps. When he sits, the clang of his weapons rings out against the metal chair.

"Do you have any idea," Saith begins, "how valuable trust is for a king?"

Vy-Ro looks to Zar-Lo and back again. "I have some idea."

"Invaluable, Vy-Ro. Everything Father and this dynasty have built exists only because of trust. Take your ancestor, for example.

Few individuals in SunSide's history have been as trustworthy as Hay-Ro was."

Vy-Ro's eyes narrow. "Forgive me, Facilitator, but why are you telling me this?"

"Because your MegaFather needs you. And he needs to be able to trust your discretion."

"Of course. You, and the MegaFather, can trust me with anything."

Saith nods. "Two hours ago, Member Sonali's Final Act was read. It decreed the deposition of the MegaFather, and the barring of his lineage from the throne."

Vy-Ro's eyes widen and a whisper escapes him. "Impossible."

"Evidently not. The execution was premature, leading to the lack of a criminal conviction. The animal died a martyr. There was opposition to the Final Act, which led to a vote amongst the Members, but the majority agreed to keep it in effect. The execution of a theocrat without trial was apparently more of a personal affront to the remaining Members than we realized."

Vy-Ro's volume climbs. "This is outrageous."

"We must maintain the MegaFather's grasp on the throne, Vy-Ro. This dynasty has empowered the faeries, driven out radicals, and conquered MoonSide. The legacy is in jeopardy."

"I agree. Tell me what needs to be done. Anything."

Zar-Lo faces the platform and silently watches Saith, assessing his ability to extract compliance.

Saith delivers the assignment. "It's time for SunSide to enter into a new era of its history. As a sole monarchy."

Vy-Ro straightens in his seat. His jaw lowers slightly as the truth of the request dawns on him. "You want to assassinate the Members. All nine of them."

"All on the same night," Saith clarifies. "Is that a problem?"

Vy-Ro's eyes shift again between the two leaders, but Saith's hard gaze conveys the truth: there is only one acceptable response.

"Of course not, Facilitator. I only hesitate because I'm thinking of SunSide. What will become of our kingdom? The Members are beloved by their supporters. They uphold the standards of theocracy, and the connection we have with the Four. The citizens will not take this level of violence lightly. The unrest in the streets will return one-thousand fold."

"Let it," thunders Zar-Lo's voice from across the room. "Let there be rivers of blood flowing through the streets. Once we've cleaned them out, the suns will rise on a new SunSide, where I am a survivor of the brutal assassinations. I will be hailed as the MegaFather who brought this kingdom together after tragedy. *That* will be the legacy."

Vy-Ro speaks softly as he responds. "And what if fingers are pointed in your direction, Father?"

"No one knows about the Final Act but the Members and the three of us," Saith informs him. "The announcement will be on the Twenty-Fourth."

"That's four nights," Vy-Ro realizes. "To plan nine assassinations."

"Five nights," Saith corrects him. "Or were you planning on sleeping tonight?"

Zar-Lo's heavy footsteps rattle the room as he walks toward the platform. "The sooner this can be done, the better; four nights is going to push this plan to the edge, and I'd like some room to breathe."

Vy-Ro's voice trembles as he nods. "Understood."

"The morning after the assignment is complete, Saith will appear before the citizens and announce that I survived the attempt on my life. I will remain out of the public eye as I heal."

He reaches the base of the platform. "I only make this request because I trust you the way my forefather trusted Hay-Ro."

Vy-Ro stands slowly. "It will be done."

"Good. Do you have any questions before I dismiss you?"

"Actually, yes. Just one." He turns and meets Saith's gaze, holding it steadily. "Are you comfortable with this assignment?"

Zar-Lo turns to Saith as well, intrigued by the Braver General's inquiry.

Saith pauses before he responds. "Saila chose her own fate today. I didn't choose it for her."

"She's your daughter." A trace of disbelief rests in Vy-Ro's tone.

Saith shakes his head calmly. "She's my blood, but she's not my daughter. Not after today."

"I hope you understand," Zar-Lo says, reverting the focus to the task, "she will require extraordinary measures."

Vy-Ro nods. "Yes, I understand what she's capable of."

"Excellent. Begin the preparations. You're dismiss—"

Another loud knock at the door interrupts him. Saith raises his fist again, and the doors to the Theater swing open. A Braver with a pink mask that matches his skin stands in the doorway, frantic and sweating.

"Fleet Master," Vy-Ro addresses him. "What's wrong?"

The Braver quickly and weakly salutes the MegaFather before speaking. "An igni vessel has been identified approaching the docks."

Zar-Lo's irritation grows. "You're the Fleet Master. What would you like *us* to do about it?"

"We believe Courtman Tomohiro is aboard."

Zar-Lo's eyes widen and he turns around to face Saith. "What does he want?"

"I don't know." He stands. "Come, Vy-Ro. Let's find out."

Hidden amongst the wide trees of Nivyan Hollow, Saith and Vy-Ro watch as the igni vessel glides into one of the docks off of SunSide's coast. The two officials wait for the traveler to disembark, then they step forward beyond the edge of the forest and onto the shore.

A human ties the large wooden craft to the dock as he wipes tears from his eyes. The moonlight shimmers against his exoskeleton. When he sees Saith and the Braver General, he takes a deep breath and charges up the sandy shore to meet them.

"Welcome back to SunSide, Courtman Tomohiro," Saith says, coolly. "Unless I'm mistaken, you have no scheduled meeting with the MegaFather tonight."

Tomohiro's jaw tightens, and rage fills his eyes and his tone. "He *will* see me."

Saith ignores him. "Perhaps we can schedule a more formal conference at a later time."

"No! He will see me today! Right now!" More tears begin to form in the Courtman's eyes.

"Lower your voice, Courtman," Saith says, his icy tone persistent. "It is in your best interest to remain calm."

"*Fuck you!*" Tomohiro's voice wavers. "You're all heartless, soulless creatures. How could you do this?"

"I'm afraid I'm not entirely sure to what you're referring."

"STOP LYING!" Tomohiro yells. His voice bounces off the trees and out into the open ocean.

Vy-Ro unsheathes a blade so swiftly and stealthily, it seems to appear in his hand out of thin air. "Keep calm, Courtman."

Saith places his hand on Vy-Ro's shoulder, and after a pause, the Braver General resheathes the blade.

"I know the truth!" Tomohiro continues. "I know what's happening on Lily Beach. Why you *selflessly* offered it to EverEmber, and why you wanted anonymity in return."

He drops to his knees in sobs. "You lied to me. Used me. I ended the war because of your gift. I didn't know"—a pathetic whimper escapes his lips—"what your Bravers were going to do there. And now, igni blood is on my hands, too."

His tone hardens and his gaze travels on flames. "How do you sleep at night?"

"Peacefully," Saith responds, smiling. "Return to EverEmber. Quietly. Before anyone even realizes you're gone."

Tomohiro nods. "Oh, I'll go back. And I'll tell everyone the truth. The igni, the mari, the angi, the Doruh, the nymphs, your own citizens! The world will turn against you when they find out what you're doing on Lily Beach. Tell your master. Tell him I'm not afraid."

Saith's patience expires. He lifts an arm toward the kneeling human and clenches his fist, paralyzing the igni leader. Saith pulls his fist toward his body and Tomohiro rises from the ground and moves through the air, stopping inches from the Facilitator.

"Threaten the MegaFather again, Courtman, and I'll skin your entire family and make you watch. *They* are on Lily Beach, as well. Who do you think can get to them first? Your wooden paddle boat or my ore fleet?"

Tomohiro cannot respond but his eyes betray his fear. Saith continues, "Step foot on SunSide soil again and you'll be buried under it. Is that understood?" A tear loosens and flows down Tomohiro's cheek. "I'll take that as a yes."

Saith begins walking back toward the forest, Vy-Ro in tow. He unclenches his fist and Tomohiro drops to the ground and erupts into heavy sobs.

"You're going to let him go back?" Vy-Ro asks when they reach the edge of the forest.

"He won't say anything," Saith responds. "And even if he does, no one will believe him."

"Are you sure about that?"

Saith smiles. "Trust me."

CHAPTER 20

RACE TO MOONSIDE

The Dissolved Nations *CereCenter Forty-Two*
Date *20th Day of Month 6, Year 1628 DG*

ONA AND LONA PEEK OVER the horizon, and a waterfall of
brilliant golden light lands softly on Unisa's face, prying her eyes open.
She sits up and rubs balled fists against them.

Rest escaped her all night. Alba's and Hassan's words toyed with
her peace. She even forgot to oil and wrap her braids before bed.

Alba sits on the edge of her side, one of the low tables pulled toward
her, her back to Unisa as she peruses something laid out on the tabletop.

Unisa finds her bag on the floor next to the bed. She reaches in and
pulls out a vial of natural oils, along with a scarf. It takes her a few
minutes to oil her hair, tie it up in a bun, and wrap the scarf around it.

The Ambassador's eyes are locked on a map of MoonSide when
Unisa joins her. Alba's travel sack sits at her feet and Unisa sees, for the
first time, just how many maps Alba has packed. The sack is overflowing with rolled paper.

"That's a lot of maps," Unisa remarks.

Alba's attention moves to her bag and then to Unisa. "It is. I have a map of Aerthomni, a map of MoonSide, a map of SunSide, a map of the Castrum, a map of the Library, and a few other pertinent ones."

Unisa sits next to her. "You were serious when you mentioned you're a cartophile."

A soft smile plays on Alba's lips. "I was. I don't think I can go any-where without them."

Unisa wants to offer her a smile in return, but the dense tension from last night is suffocating.

"I know last night was difficult. We shouldn't have unloaded so much on you at once, but we didn't have a choice. The things you'll see today, as we travel through MoonSide, will shake the foundation of your beliefs and your philosophies, and everything you know to be true. I just want you to be prepared."

Unisa recalls specifics from the conversation. "'They're slowly, but deliberately, trying to finish off the entire population.' Is that what you want me to be prepared to see in MoonSide?"

Alba nods. "The Prime's deceit includes forging tales of peace-keepers—assigning the role of hero to aggressors. That's not what the Bravers are, Uni. You won't find white-hooded heroes in MoonSide."

Unisa remains silent. She doesn't have the heart to tell Alba that her intervention hasn't swayed Unisa's understanding of the truth. Lies as old and encompassing as the ones Alba describes simply don't seem possible, no matter how much power the liar wields.

"I know you still don't fully believe me," Alba says.

Unisa's eyes widen, and she wonders if Alba read her mind, or her body language.

"By the end of the day," Alba exhales deeply, sadly, "you will."

"Is that what you're hoping for?" Unisa asks.

Alba's expression holds weight and she slowly shakes her head. "No. It's what worries me the most."

They pack for the day's travel and keep breakfast light.

"Thank you for your hospitality, Hassan," Alba says, her arms wrapped tightly around the angi Librarian as they prepare to depart.

"Always a pleasure." He releases her and turns to Unisa. "It was an honor to host you at the CereCenter. The next time we meet, I'll keep our dinner conversations lighter."

The edges of Unisa's lips curve slightly. "I would appreciate that. Perhaps it'll be in the Library after the academic season ends."

Hassan places his hand over his heart and bows his head slightly. "That would be wonderful."

It isn't until she and Alba have started walking away from the Educator and the CereCenter, that Unisa realizes her plans to meet Hassan again can only come to fruition if she still has a place in the city after they return.

If she hasn't been exiled, or worse.

The farmlands are far behind them. On this side of the CereCenter, Unisa and Alba trek through rolling meadows and wild grasses that crawl up to their knees. Green hills scatter amongst rocky ridges as far as the angi Librarian can see.

Her mind drifts back to the previous night, stoking the flames of conflict in her heart.

Can a man who advocates so strongly for knowledge and truth, who's revered by an entire society, be a pillar for ages of historical inaccuracy? Can he who personifies benevolence in sunlight, be wicked in shadows?

Can someone who preaches freedom be so hungry for power that he coerces the vulnerable into positions of powerlessness?

"You're awfully quiet."

The words shake Unisa from her trance. She turns to see Alba smiling at her and holding the map of MoonSide open in her hands.

"Sorry."

Alba rolls the map and returns it to her bag. "Is there something on your mind?"

Of course.

"We can talk about it, if you'd like."

I would not like.

"Or, we can talk about anything else."

Unisa nods. "That sounds like a good idea."

Alba smiles. "Alright. How do you think Kyoko and Rafael's first day of travel went?"

She can only hope it went better than hers. "I hope they're safe and well."

Alba waves a hand flippantly. "I'm sure they're fine. From what I hear, Rafael is quite the archer."

"Oh, yes. He started learning from his sister as a small child."

"Then they must be safe and well. Kyoko can protect herself. With any weapon." She turns to Unisa, pensively. "What about you?"

Unisa raises an eyebrow. "What about me?"

"What weapons are you comfortable with? A blade?"

Unisa doesn't know how to respond without sounding underqualified. "I've had tactical combat and weapon skills training."

Alba rolls her eyes. "Of course you have. We all have. I'm not asking about training. I'm asking if you've ever picked up a sword and used it to protect yourself."

Unisa hesitates, then shakes her head.

"What about an axe? A bow? A mace? A scythe, staff, or spear?"

"Outside of training in the Academy," Unisa admits, "I have no experience in combat. And, frankly, I'd really like to keep it that way."

Alba seems a bit taken aback. "Unisa, you do need experience protecting yourself. These aren't elective skills you can choose whether or not to hone. In this world, they're survival skills. I personally taught Kyoko real-world combat and weapons training. Far beyond what the Library will teach you."

"I'd like to think I can solve problems without violence."

Alba chuckles. "We'd all *like* to solve problems that way. But when a team of assassins shows up at your doorstep, good luck solving the problem without violence."

Dread pulls in the depths of Unisa's stomach. She hopes to never find herself in a situation where such skills would be required.

There's stillness and spirituality in the rich verdure that surrounds them. All four suns race across the sky to their midday positions. It's distant at first, but as Alba and Unisa continue through the meadows, the sound of flowing water gets louder and clearer.

"Take a look from up there," Alba says to her, pointing to the top of a hill. With two hard flaps of her wings, Unisa is up on the crest, looking down at the river that lies beyond. It extends out so wide that she can barely see the stone walls of MoonSide on the opposite end. This is the most water Unisa has ever seen in one place, at one time.

"The Red-Lo," Alba remarks, gesturing to the running river water. "Longest and widest river on the continent. The first village of Moon-Side, Evic, is just beyond."

Alba places her travel sack onto the ground and begins to remove her clothing.

"Why are you getting undressed?" Unisa asks.

"How long can you fly without a break? Or will I need to find you a bridge?" She leans in and whispers playfully. "I'll give you a hint: there isn't one."

Unisa smiles. "I can fly over a river without a break."

Alba stuffs her clothes into her bag, careful not to damage any of her maps. She then shuts the bag securely, flips it around so that it is against the front of her abdomen, and tightens the strap as much as she can. The fins on her back, along her forearms, and down her calves are now all exposed.

"You sound confident," Alba notes. "Are you fast?"

Unisa nods. "Fast and"—she pauses, pretending to gauge Alba's age—"about fifteen years younger than you."

The smile on Alba's face evaporates. She leans in close to Unisa. "I'll give you a one-minute advantage."

"I really don't need that, Alba, I can beat you without it."

"Fly, Uni," Alba asserts. She points to the sky over the river. "Fly!"

Unisa takes six running strides toward the edge of the hill and then leaps. She pumps her wings quickly, beating them rhythmically every few seconds, accelerating her body.

She smiles wide. *Alba has no idea who she's racing.* The angi turns her body and glances quickly behind her while flying backward in the same direction. She sees Alba on the riverbank, hunched over and ready to dive into the water.

There's no way she can catch up now.

She turns back around to face forward. The feeling of the wind in her face, beneath her arms, and between her feathers is exhilarating. For the first time in what feels like days, or weeks, or months, or years, she feels free.

Like she's floating.

And then her peaceful flotation is disrupted. She hears a noise below her, in the water. There's something there, a trail of bubbles along the surface. She flaps her wings harder but the bubbles match her speed, and then...

A head pops out of the water. Alba swims backward, matching Unisa's speed at the river's surface, smiling at the angi.

Her body weaves rhythmically, coursing through the water, cutting it like a warm knife through butter. The mari winks, then dives back under the surface. The trail of bubbles moves farther and farther. Faster it goes, until Unisa loses track of it.

Alba is long gone.

Unisa flaps and pumps her wings harder and faster than she ever has before. She gains speed, but her efforts are futile. She never catches up to the Ambassador.

Her wings start to fatigue, so she stops flapping and conserves her energy to get to the end. Gliding mostly, the angi spies Alba waiting on the riverbank for her—wet, but fully clothed again.

Unisa slows herself down and shifts her body vertical. With two light pumps, she descends onto the riverbank, falling onto her hands and knees next to where Alba is standing, sweat dripping from her brow.

Alba helps Unisa stand. "Not bad for a flier."

Unisa laughs. She severely underestimated how fast Alba can swim. "Maybe I'll get another opportunity to race you somewhere along the journey."

Alba's smile fades. She turns to her right and Unisa sees the narrow stone gateway into the inaugural village of MoonSide only a few feet away. She hadn't realized how close the entrance to Evic was to the river.

Alba turns back to Unisa and the tone of the air around them shifts. The lines on her face deepen as the color shifts to a bleak monotone.

"No more racing," she says, her tone dripping with apprehension. "Welcome to MoonSide, Uni."

CHAPTER 21

WELCOME TO MOONSIDE

Occupied Territory *MoonSide*
Date *20th Day of Month 6, Year 1628 DG*

ALBA STEPS TOWARD THE STONE gateway, and Unisa follows hesitantly. Alarm bubbles in Unisa's chest from the Ambassador's shift in energy.

Beyond the gates, Unisa's eyes are drawn to massive walls on opposing sides, narrowing the village between them. The walls are rooted in stone but covered in dark, powerful metal.

Ore.

With every step further into the village, the uneasiness grows. A mix of tension, discomfort, and helplessness envelops Unisa, as if she knows someone near her is in danger but can't identify who it is, or how to help them.

The village contrasts heavily with what she's learned of MoonSide from the Prime and those who've ventured beyond the city. Their words depict a utopia, free of violence and hardship, under the diligent guardianship of SunSide's forces.

Illustrations coat every inch of the walls; the colors remind Unisa of artists she knows back home. For them, art is a medium of pleasure, creativity. The images here are certainly creative, but they're entirely void of pleasure.

Violence. Bloodshed. Bravers brandishing weapons. The MegaFather with blood pouring from his eyes. Slogans filled with desperation, yearning for hope and salvation. Unisa turns her head away, attempting to ignore it, but there is no ignoring it.

It's everywhere.

Her eyes fall on a pile of rubble only a few feet from her. A mass of broken stone and clay around frayed furniture and a shattered bathtub. This was once someone's home.

At the very top of the pile is a Doruh man holding a white sack with crimson blotches seeping through. He lifts a dusty object from beneath stone and places it into the sack. It takes a few seconds for Unisa's mind to register what the item is, but when it does, she begins to feel her stomach return whatever she's eaten.

An arm. No longer connected to a body. One end hosts bloody fingers, the other is only torn tissue and broken bone. The scent of fresh decay fills her nostrils, and her stomach churns harder. She drops to one knee as steaming acid works its way up her throat. She takes a deep breath to steady herself, but she fails, and the liquid projects out of her mouth and nose onto the dry ground.

Her eyes well up as a heavy arm wraps around her shoulders and helps her to her feet. She turns to see Alba leading her through a crowd of perplexed Doruh citizens.

"I don't understand," Unisa mumbles. "There's a limb. Someone is dead under that rock and the body parts are being collected in a plain sack?"

"Likely a family member, Uni," Alba responds, leading Unisa steadily to two wooden stools outside of a juicery. "Collecting the parts to give them a proper burial." She withdraws a flask of water from her bag and hands it to Unisa. "Drink."

Unisa takes a long sip and a deep breath before continuing. "He's gathering a family member's body parts?" Her eyes find the walls again. "Where is the safety and prosperity the Bravers brought with them from SunSide? Where is the haven won during the Uprisings?"

Alba shakes her head. She speaks slowly and repeats her words from the night before. "The Bravers here represent the true face of Sun-Side. A face the Library has helped mask for centuries."

Brutal reality drops onto Unisa's shoulders like an imploded building. Alba and Hassan were telling the truth.

She forces out the singular response her tongue can form. "Why?"

"Because the Primes have always protected their allies. The MegaParents."

Unisa's breath catches in her throat. "No, no, no, no…" She repeats it until her throat goes dry and her eyes grow wet. Alba stands and pulls Unisa's face into her chest, holding her the way one would hold a child who is suffering a bad dream.

The angi lifts her arms and wraps them around Alba. The last time she remembers being held like this was the day her parents left her at the Library. It hadn't been her mother who had held her until she had stopped crying, it had been Ora.

"I'm sorry, Uni," Alba says after a few moments. "I know this is a lot, but we have to keep moving. Our schedule doesn't account for rest here."

Unisa unwraps from the embrace. The image of the torn limb, and all that it represents in the fracture of her cognizance, still swirls in her mind. She takes another sip of water and looks out into the crowd of Doruh continuing their daily business.

Her attention is captured by a crowd of young boys and girls. The oldest is around ten. The youngest is around the same age Unisa was when she arrived in the Library. Some of them share a resemblance to one another.

Perhaps they're siblings.

They all display the same stunning smiles. Pure childhood joy, as they play with a red ball. They kick it around and chase it, laughing.

And then the scene changes. It erodes and perverts and degrades. Unisa has never experienced an escalation like it before.

The red ball is kicked, harder than intended. It soars through the air and one of the young boys runs after it. He still has his smile. Pure joy.

The ball lands on an unexpected target—the top of a Braver's head. It was a mistake. The child recognizes it, and his smile fades. Unisa's heart drops. Her eyes widen as she rises from her seat. Alba looks out through the crowd to find the scene on which Unisa's focus is transfixed.

The Braver looks down at the ball, then at the child, and then back at the ball. He's holding a spear made of ore. Solid metal. Hard, sharp, dangerous. He lifts it high, then brings it down quickly.

Pop. The ball is dead. Punctured, the air leaving its body.

Tears well up in the young boy's eyes. They're filled with hatred and anger. His friends, or siblings, call his name from behind him. He balls up his fists and charges.

Little punches hit the Braver. Another mistake of youth and inexperience. The Braver grabs the boy's shirt, lifts him off the ground, and tosses him aside. Like garbage. The boy rolls along the ground. Blood drips from his elbows, knees, and face.

Unisa cries out to the Braver, but Alba's hand wraps around her wrist, holding her back. The former Gatekeeper turns around to look at her, and Alba silently shakes her head.

The boy cries harder now. Anger, humiliation, anguish. There's only one thing a young Doruh boy can think of doing. He shifts. The boy becomes a lamb. His fleece is a pristine white.

He's a child. Not a sheep, but a lamb. He charges the Braver, butting his small head into the Braver's leg. He doesn't even reach the faerie's hip. The Braver stumbles for a moment from the impact, but then quickly regains his footing.

Anywhere else, the young boy would've been scolded for hitting the Braver. He would've been punished with a loss of free time. Or with prohibition from shifting for a month. Or even with a spanking from a parent.

But this is MoonSide.

The Braver doesn't waste any time. He's holding the spear made of ore. Solid metal. Hard, sharp. Dangerous. He lifts it high, then brings it quickly down. Unisa tries to take another step forward, to stop the Braver, but Alba's grip is unnaturally tight.

Unisa is frozen. Every muscle in her body cries out for her to run forth, but she can't move. Time stands still.

The ore spear pierces the lamb's side. The attack is precise. Calculated. Left side of his body, low and toward the front. It cuts through skin and punctures his heart.

His friends, his potential siblings, scream for him. The grief on their faces is gut-wrenching. Some of them drop to their knees and cry out to the Twins for mercy. For salvation.

The lamb becomes the boy again. Bleeding out on the ground. Horror and shock on his face. A wide wound over his heart. Unisa tries to take another step toward him. To hold him and love him.

Alba's grip tightens further. The boy lies on his stomach, back exposed, Braver standing over him holding a spear made of ore. Solid metal. Hard, sharp. Dangerous. He lifts it high, then brings it quickly down.

Pop. The boy is dead. Punctured, the air leaving his body.

Unisa drops to her knees. She can't breathe. Air has been sucked out of the atmosphere. She puts her hands on the ground in front of her and nearly doubles over. She vomits again. This time, Alba kneels beside her and rubs her back.

Unisa's world fractures around her. The solid turns liquid, as everything she believed, everything she was certain of, melts into a puddle of duplicity. She's been complicit in glorifying the villains of centuries-old falsehoods.

She's been on the wrong side of history.

The boy's friends are inconsolable. The Braver calls two of his cohorts over. They carry the boy's body away. Unisa hears them refer to the boy as "another one."

Just another casualty of the occupation. A casualty of a settler kingdom that doesn't value the land, or the people, on which they've encroached.

Unisa recounts history as it is etched into her mind. Her years upon years of devotion to names and dates and places all come barreling into her mind at once. It hits her harder now than ever; everything she's devoted herself to is a lie. This boy's blood is on the Library's hands, too. On Alba's hands. On the Prime's hands.

On Unisa's hands.

What started as innocent childhood folly turned violent and deadly in an instant. Doruh life is meaningless to the faeries. This isn't the story of triumph and liberation written in the history books. This isn't what the Alphocracy envisioned for its people.

Alba tries to hand Unisa the water again but the angi's limbs revolt as the boy's face makes rounds in her mind. A face covered in blood.

Alba places her hands on Unisa's cheeks and stares deeply into her eyes.

"Unisa," she says, but the angi cannot focus. "Uni. We have to go."

Time is a blur as Alba supports Unisa. She wraps her arms around Unisa to help her rise to her feet, and then they continue walking. When they're a safe distance from the scene of the murder, Alba helps Unisa sit on a stone bench outside of a tea house with a sign in the window that reads "Sultana's Chai Palace."

Unisa puts her head in her hands, trying to reconcile the discrepancy between everything she's been taught, and all she's seen. Everything she believed, and everything that exists.

Her voice trembles. "Why are the faeries doing this?"

Alba sighs. "The faeries believe MoonSide belongs to them."

"But, it doesn't. The teri lived here and they became the Doruh. It's always been their land."

"The faeries disagree with that sentiment. They believe the Four created SunSide and MoonSide together, as one kingdom encompassing the mountain range, and then bequeathed that kingdom to the faeries. Just as they claim SunSide's land, they claim MoonSide's with it, and have used this ideology to sustain support from the theocracy."

Unisa's tone changes from frantic to enraged. "Governments shouldn't be able to weaponize theology to tear civilians from their homes and cause all this devastation. Their beliefs are their own, and don't justify violence against those who already live here. Why is none of this recorded in the Library?"

"Because everything in the Library is written in pen and ink." Her tone hardens. "Real history is written with weapons and blood."

She lifts a finger to point toward the scene they just witnessed. "That is the truth. The truth of the Doruh, the nymphs, and the pixies. It's raw and honest, and hasn't yet been washed and cleaned to make villains look like heroes."

Unisa shakes her head. It still doesn't seem possible. "All of the Ambassadors, the Supremes, the Prime. They all know this is happening. How do the lies thrive?"

Alba pauses before she responds. "Narratives remain afloat on vessels of psychological coercion. You don't need a physical door to imprison thoughts and perspectives."

"What about the refugees and exiles we take into our city? They've seen this and their thoughts aren't imprisoned."

Alba casts her gaze to the ground. "Their voices are. Vows of silence and obedience in exchange for a chance at survival."

Her forehead creases, as if she's trying to recall a long-lost thought or memory. "Since the alliance of the Primes and the MegaParents began, they've been painting their ideologies on the inside of everyone's eyelids, Uni. They can open their eyes at any time, but why would they, when they believe they've already seen it all?"

Anger thrusts its way into Unisa's heart. "But *you've* opened your eyes. So has Hassan. And I'm sure more have seen this and realized the truth. Why has nothing been done? Why can't we help the Doruh and nymphs and pixies?"

Alba sighs. "Sometimes there is no helping. This has been going on so long. It isn't our fight to get involved in. That's not our duty."

Unisa's heart shatters. *Isn't it? Isn't everyone who bears witness responsible for helping?*

Bravers are openly violent. But she didn't understand true cruelty until she saw witnesses turning their backs on oppressed people. On violent situations.

On murdered children.

She didn't understand true cruelty until she saw bystanders choosing ignorance. Or worse, neutrality. When people, hungry for help, cry out, and those with aid let them starve; *that* is true cruelty.

Unisa and Alba sit quietly for what feels like an eternity. The Gatekeeper watches the Doruh citizens walk by on the road and in and out of the chai house. She observes the homeless huddled by fires, only feet away from walls behind which settler faeries enjoy wealth, food, and resources.

The child. The lamb. His cold eyes, his bloody face, reverberate in her thoughts. She can't close her eyes without seeing him. She tries to picture his smile. She tries to hear his laugh, but all she hears are the other children's screams and cries.

Alba stands abruptly. "We have to go. I'm sorry, but we're not going to make it to Arlun by nightfall if we sit here too long."

"No," Unisa responds harshly. "I'm not going anywhere until you tell me everything. The Library, the Prime, MoonSide, SunSide. I want to know everything you know."

Alba looks up at the positions of the suns. "Uni, it's barely midday. That conversation will take until nightfall."

"Then find us somewhere to stay tonight. Here. We can head out in the morning after we've talked." She speaks her next words with a certainty and a confidence she hasn't felt since she left the Library's gates. "No more lies, Alba. Please."

Alba hesitates but, seeing Unisa's resolve, she simply nods and walks away.

Unisa knows the journey is stalled because of her. But she doesn't care. She doesn't want to leave the boy. He's still here. Somewhere.

Where is he? They carried him away. Do his parents know what has happened to him? How will they find out? When will they find out? Will the Bravers come to their door and tell them? Or will they have to find out from the boy's friends? Will they be able to mourn him? Say goodbye? He isn't just a number. He isn't just another casualty to add to the list.

She sits and stares blankly, completely numb. An echo of Alba's words slams her eardrums.

"Welcome to MoonSide, Uni."

CHAPTER 22

THROUGH HIS WINDOWS

Theocratic-Monarchy *SunSide*
Date *20th Day of Month 6, Year 1628 DG*

IT'S THE MOST COMFORTABLE SLEEP Naina has had in some time. She wakes to find Salessa neatly folding the soft blankets Syma provided the night before, and placing them onto a wooden table nearby.

The light of the first two suns drips in through windows carved into the tree shelter's walls.

"Get dressed," Salessa instructs Naina gently. "We have a long journey ahead of us today."

Naina gets to her feet and registers an irregular flutter in her sister's mind. The wolf places a hand on Salessa's shoulder. "I'm nervous, too, Lessi."

Salessa smiles and covers Naina's hand with her own. "Everything will be alright. We have Symin and Ray-Mi."

Naina shakes her head disapprovingly. "We have each other."

The Mega of Nivyan Hollow fill the clearing around the fire. They eat, drink, and laugh while passing around fresh bread and vegetables roasted over the flames.

The twins find Symin with his family, who offer breakfast. Naina reaches for a hunk of warm bread before Salessa pulls her wrist back and asks where they can wash their hands and rinse their mouths first.

I'm hungry, not dirty. Naina forces her voice into Salessa's mind.

You have wolfmouth.

If you said that to any other wolf, they'd tear you apart, feather by feather.

Your breath is tearing me apart.

Symin leads them through a section of the clearing that opens to a hill. They descend slowly and arrive at a riverbed occupied by hundreds and hundreds of Mega—bathing, washing clothes, swimming, and spending time together. Naina's eyes widen as the magnitude of the communities that reside within the forest dawns upon her.

"All of these Mega live in Nivyan Hollow?"

Symin nods. "Oh, yes. Our cluster is just a small sample." He smiles and gestures widely at the population of bathers and swimmers. "This is our community. Our family. We all protect each other and care for one another as we're able to."

Naina's heart splinters in her chest as something triggers deep within her that she hasn't felt in a very long time. Other than Salessa, she's forgotten what it feels like to be cared for.

To be part of a family.

They return soon after to Syma's clearing and enjoy a warm meal with their Mega companions.

"Be safe. May the Four keep you in their light," Syma says to the twins after breakfast. She kisses their cheeks and sends them off through the forest with Symin and Ray-Mi.

When they emerge past the tree line, they face a row of wooden docks, tied to one of which is an old sailboat. The hull's shine has faded into a dismal dullness, the warped wood of the upper deck bends irregularly, the rickety masts tremble in the breeze, and the sails have been patched with incongruent fabrics.

"I was a Legion Director in the Braver fleet," Ray-Mi says, standing next to Naina and staring out at the sailboat with a smile. "I spent so much time at sea that my feet started to feel unsteady on dry land.

After I defected, I needed a way to get back out onto the water." He waves to the vessel as if he expects it to wave back. "She's as beautiful as she is functional."

Don't do it, Nai—

"If that's the case, we'll never make it past the docks, let alone to Panaerth."

Ray-Mi's smile drops. Naina feels Salessa's muscles tense up next to her. There's a long pause as Ray-Mi registers what Naina said, then explodes into laughter and pats Naina on the back.

"That was a great one, wolfie," he commends her, then turns and joins Symin in readying the ship.

Naina turns to Salessa with a smile. *You have to lighten up.*

You have to be more respectful. Her expression goes momentarily rigid, but her lips quickly slip into a smile. *But that was funny.*

They turn back to the ship, yet neither steps toward it. Despite the ages of hiding, the idea of crossing oceans carries more weight than any prior journey.

Naina feels her sister's fingers interlock with hers, and Salessa's voice softly reminds her, *Change champions, Naina. Right?*

Naina exhales and nods. *Change champions.*

An hour later, the journey affects Naina far more than she anticipated.

She leans over the wooden rails bordering the hull and tries to focus on the glittering sunlight on the ocean's surface. Ray-Mi keeps the vessel as steady as possible from the helm, but the occasional turns and sways stimulate a sickness that threatens to launch Naina's break-fast into the water below.

"How much"—she burps—"longer?"

Salessa, holding Naina's hair away from her face and rubbing her back, looks up at the sky. "We've been on the water for about an hour, so." She hesitates. "Maybe two more."

"Three," Symin corrects her, rising from the hold, grasping a flask. He offers it to Naina. "Close your nostrils and drink this as quickly as you can."

Naina shakes her head and turns away from the flask. *I don't accept flasks from anything with ears that pointy.*

Salessa takes the flask from Symin and offers him a grateful smile, then forces it into her sister's hands and whispers, "Please. Don't be stubborn."

Fine, Naina growls. "Thank you, Symin."

She opens the cap, covers her nose, and dumps the warm liquid into her throat. The unexpectedly warm temperature nearly makes her gag, but after the initial surprise, she continues to drink. Her nausea dissolves almost instantly.

Naina removes the flask from her lips and looks down at it, her eyes wide with disbelief. "What was that?"

Symin smiles and takes the flask back from her. "A family recipe. Made from a rare batch of flowers grown in Nivyan Hollow."

"How did you figure out they settle seasickness?" Salessa asks.

Symin runs his fingers fondly over the flask. He takes longer to respond than Naina expects. "My daughter, Zynima, spent some time out on the ocean for work. She discovered the flowers and this special use during one of her voyages."

Naina notices the lines on Symin's forehead, the wounded scrunch of his nose, and the struggling quiver in his tone, as Ray-Mi's words from the night before echo through her mind.

You never really get over losing a child.

With Naina's seasickness addressed, Salessa finds a cot, similar to the ones on which they slept back in Evic, to rest. Within another hour, saliva is leaking out of the corner of her mouth, her chest heaving with every grunty snore. Naina lies next to her, eyes closed, trying and failing to sleep under sweltering rays.

She can't see any vivid images, but their telepathy allows her brief glimpses into Salessa's nightmare: a deep shade of green, a broken hut, a river of blood.

Two young girls holding hands and running off into the woods.

"Naina!" comes Symin's voice from the railing toward the front of the ship. Her eyes pop open and she sits up. Symin gestures for her to join him. Ray-Mi stands at the helm still, staring out ahead and squinting, while Salessa remains lost in a deep sleep.

Excellent work having my back, Drooly. What if he throws me overboard while you're snoring?

As she stalks toward the bow of the vessel, Naina's hands become paws with claws behind her back.

"I want to show you something," Symin tells her, pointing over the ship's side.

Naina hesitates and takes a step back, out of his arm's reach, before she looks over the railing.

When she sees them, Naina's claws retract back into human hands. Her eyes widen and all of her focus invests in the stunning sight below. The rays of the late morning suns strike the deep, blue ocean water and scatter specks of light across the backs and fins of a dolphin pod.

"Wow," she says quietly, an almost juvenile excitement rising in her chest. She turns to Symin, who matches her excitement. Only four or five are visible, at first. Then a few calves show up alongside their mothers. Then some appear behind the boat and on the other side.

"Come with me," Symin offers, walking past her toward the captain's deck. Naina follows closely behind him, rising up the stairs to where Ray-Mi stands.

"If you've never seen a dolphin before, wolfie, you're gonna love this," the former Braver teases.

At the stern, elevated above the rest of the ship, Naina spins and takes in the vision around her. Hundreds of dolphins swarm around them, swirling in a maelstrom of excited clicks, joyous whistles, and powerful breach displays. She's never seen anything like it.

"Are they Doruh?" Symin asks her. She hadn't even considered whether they were true dolphins or not. She holds the railing tightly in her grip and waits for another breach. One launches its body into the air, high above the water, and Naina focuses, holding eye contact for as long as she can.

And then she sees it. The dolphin's essence. It's curious and intelligent. Natural and whole.

"They're true dolphins," she informs Symin. "They have one essence. Not two incomplete ones, like we do. A whole, pure essence, as nature intended."

"Nothing exists without nature's intention," Symin responds.

Naina turns to him, surprised.

The nymph continues. "They are whole, certainly. But their purity has no influence on that of the Doruh." He turns to her, and she finds a brightness in his expression. "Wouldn't you agree, Naina?"

Naina hadn't ever given it much thought. All Doruh live under the assumption that their half-human, half-animal essences deem them unnatural, an abomination. A thought that, surely, a Mega drove into the Doruh psyche long ago, only to be passed down through the generations.

Naina nods. "We are pure. And intelligent and loving, and"—her gaze drops down to her hands, and she balls them into fists—"we are strong."

Symin shakes his head. "Your fists are not what make you strong. They've helped you survive the Pit, but strength thrives in change, not in muscle."

Naina's ears stiffen as the words enter them. Her body tenses and her breath catches in her throat. He says it so fluidly, so effortlessly, so obviously. The way someone else said it long ago.

"*Change champions, when fists fail,*" Naina whispers, almost inaudibly. A decade of submerged emotions claw their way up her chest and into her throat. Her father's voice, speaking the words, is torn violently from her memories and slammed against her eardrums. Her cheeks burn red.

Symin's smile fades. "Are you alright?"

"Repeat that. What you said about change."

Symin's mouth hangs agape in confusion. "Strength thrives in change, not muscle."

"Where did you hear that?"

Symin seals his lips and turns to look out at the pod. Naina waits, her impatience demanding a response, but Symin seems focused on something below them. Naina almost repeats the question more forcefully, but something in his sudden silence begs her to investigate what's grasped his attention.

She turns and looks out at the water, at the still breaching dolphins. She follows Symin's gaze until she finds two dolphins in his line of sight, an adult...and a juvenile.

"My daughter," Symin finally responds. "It was something she said often, and lived by. The idea that physical strength is inferior to one's willingness to adapt and learn and grow."

He sighs and Naina watches the muscles in his throat tighten around his grieved voice. "She's returned to the Radiance, but her legacy lives on. In our memories, and our devotion to keeping her values alive. This is how I keep her close to me."

Naina and Symin turn to each other, and something powerful surges between them. It occurs to Naina that she's subconsciously been keeping her parents alive in the same way: by filling her every breath with their legacy. She hadn't realized it until a Mega, a broken nymph, reflected her ache and broke the Mega-Doruh barrier between them.

Naina looks deep into Symin's pupil-less eyes and sees through his windows.

CHAPTER 23

THE STORY

Continent of Panaerth
Date 20th Day of Month 6, Year 1628 DG

"LAND!" THUNDERS RAY-MI'S VOICE AROUND the vessel. "Ten minutes to shore."

Salessa stands from the cot and stretches her arms overhead with a yawn. The suns' positions inform her that over half the journey was spent in slumber. Naina lies on her back, staring up at the clouds.

"Did you sleep?" Salessa asks.

Naina shakes her head, a dazed gaze glossing her eyes.

"Is everything alright?"

The wolf nods, lips sealed.

Salessa slyly attempts to pry open Naina's thoughts.

"Do it and I'll kill you," Naina threatens.

Salessa removes her consciousness from Naina's mind. "You won't tell me what's bothering you."

"Can't some thoughts just be private?" Naina responds, sitting up.

"Not really, no. That's not how telepathy works."

Naina rolls her eyes. "That's not how *your* nosy telepathy works."

"I'm worried, not nosy."

"Don't be, I'm fine," the wolf reassures her, rising from the cot. "I'm just processing."

Salessa's heart sinks. "Processing what? Did something happen?"

"Let it go, Lessi!" Naina growls.

After a long moment of gauging Naina's agitation, Salessa nods. "Alright, I'm sorry."

"I see Kruga!" Symin yells from the front rail of the ship, pointing to the coastline ahead. A crimson-skinned Mega stands on a narrow wooden pier, toward which Ray-Mi navigates the vessel. Kruga waves his arms in a pulling motion and the Radiance draws the boat in and anchors it, allowing the travelers to disembark.

Kruga has as many scars on his face and arms as Symin, and he's clad in an identical hooded cloak. If it weren't for the difference in age and skin tone, they'd look more like twins than Salessa and Naina do.

Symin embraces the crimson nymph and asks, "How've things been here?"

"Quiet," Kruga responds in a gruff voice. His eyes trace the twins. "I see your journey was successful."

"Indeed." Symin introduces Kruga as "The son I wish had been born to me."

Kruga laughs. "That would've made Zynima's and my wedding night far more uncomfortable."

"One Mega's discomfort is another's kink," Ray-Mi adds from behind the twins. "Enough chatter, don't you have a schedule to keep?"

Kruga nods. "We should move. Gina will be waiting at the rendezvous in an hour."

"An hour is just enough time," Symin declares.

Naina raises an eyebrow. "Enough time for what?"

The pink nymph brandishes the forearm scar, about which Naina questioned him the previous morning at PeakHaven Pass. "You wanted to hear the story about this scar, didn't you?"

Naina nods excitedly.

"It's time we talked about infiltrating the Bravers."

A long and bumpy road, carved out of coarse sand and broken shards of stone, rocks the cart from side to side. It isn't dissimilar from the rickety cart in which Ray-Mi escorted them through Nivyan Hollow.

Salessa keeps her focus on the scenery to distract her from the jolting. To the left, she finds the edge of a green, lush forest, and to the right, the glittering, golden sand of the shoreline leading into the ocean.

The twins sit in the front row, with Symin and Kruga in the back. Ray-Mi had remained behind with the ship, hoping to protect it while the others continued on to the ore processing center.

A glowing blue circle surrounds the cart, placed masterfully by Kruga to cloak them from the outside world.

Not long into the journey, a gurgling erupts into the air, and the travelers look around for the culprit.

"That's me," Naina admits. "Vegetables and bread won't keep a wolf full for long."

"Remarkably," Symin notes, "Salessa doesn't seem hungry at all."

Salessa thinks of a response as quickly as she can. "We have wildly different activity levels, so Naina digests quicker."

I would rather you don't speak than lie so poorly, comes Naina's voice. *They're going to figure out you're not a wolf.*

Oh, now you're comfortable with invading my thoughts? To insult me?

Yes. For that, I am.

Kruga lifts a hide sack at his feet and hands it to Naina. She pulls apart the drawstring, and the stench of dead fish wafts through the air. Salessa turns her face away as Naina begins to salivate and withdraws a whole, raw branzino.

She wraps her teeth around the fish and shoves the bag into Salessa's disinterested hands. The chaitender examines it for a moment, until something catches her eye at the edge of the forest.

Two small hummingbirds flutter about the branches of a tree. She sighs as her usual meal casually hovers in the distance.

It'll have to do, she thinks, the raw aromas brutalizing her nostrils. She cautiously withdraws a smaller fish and takes a tiny bite. Somehow, her stomach accepts the offering without protest.

"Time for the story," Naina says to the Mega, masticated fish flesh visible as she speaks.

Symin nods. "Telling you this story will give you both a better understanding of this team and the individuals you're fighting alongside."

Salessa agrees with him. She's trusted them to bring the twins thus far, but knowing their history can, she hopes, alleviate some of the mistrust plaguing Naina.

"I can't tell you about the scar, or the infiltration that precipitated it, without background," Symin prefaces. "Sixteen years ago, my closest friend, Zabeza, went missing. His wife, Ovida, and I spent months searching before we found...his body."

He breathes deeply, steadying himself. "He was unrecognizable—skeletal, as if all life had been torn from him. Translucent flesh, withered eyes, hairless. I'll never forget it."

"The following year," Kruga takes over, "Zynima suffered the same fate. We were nineteen, young scientists working in the Castrum's research labs."

Naina inhales sharply. "You worked for the MegaFather?"
Naina!

Kruga nods. "We worked on special projects, testing the effects of Radiant energy on chemical structures. The Ore Monger wanted to make stronger and more versatile materials than anything in existence. Those efforts continued until he discovered ore, after which they were...pointless."

Kruga's head tilts up toward the sky, pensively. "We were in the labs when Zynima was summoned by superiors. She kissed me goodbye, told me she'd return soon, and left."

Symin clears his throat. "That was the last time she was seen alive. Weeks later, we found her in the same condition in which we found Zabeza. Skeletal and lifeless." His eyes swell with moisture, but he wipes it away.

Kruga places an affectionate hand on his shoulder.

Salessa delicately poses a question. "When you came to us, you said the Facilitator took your daughter from you. Is he responsible for these disappearances?"

Symin nods. "He abducted them and discarded their bodies at the edge of the forest, as if they were worthless."

"Not just them," Kruga adds. "Other Revolutionaries share tales of their own loved ones' disappearances. The bodies were always found in the same condition. The Facilitator, under the MegaFather's command, had been abducting citizens. All of these events took place in the same six-year span."

"Did you tell anyone?" Naina inquires.

Kruga shakes his head. "There was no one to tell, Naina. Most faeries don't care about nymph and pixie lives."

"Kruga, Ovida, and I joined the Revolution," Symin continues. "Our cries were neglected, so we became unignorable. We pledged ourselves to avenge those we lost, and three years after we joined, the abductions stopped."

"That was twelve years ago," Salessa notes.

1616, Naina transmits to her sister. *The same year.*

Do you think there's a connection?

"What is it?" Kruga asks them, observing their silent glances.

I have to tell him, Salessa insists.

To her surprise, Naina looks at Symin, then nods.

"1616 was the year he killed our parents."

Naina adds bitterly, "We were eight."

"Do you think the abductions were stopped when he started hunting you?" Kruga asks.

Salessa shrugs. "He certainly invested substantial resources into finding us. It's possible those resources were redirected from one goal to another."

"Yes, it's possible," Symin agrees, before continuing. "We worked with the Revolution long after the abductions ceased. There wasn't much else to live for. Ovida and Gina conquered the ranks and became our Generals. Under their leadership, we attacked Braver facilities and continued to recruit members to the cause."

"But success would escape us, so long as the Castrum stood," Kruga says. "We needed to get inside."

A soft smile plays on Symin's lips. "That's when Gina escorted a uniformed Braver into the Revolution's hidden chambers. The tension was so thick, I thought we'd all suffocate, until the Braver removed his uniform, prostrated before Ovida, and wept."

"Ray-Mi," Naina surmises.

Kruga nods. "His connections within the Castrum, particularly Member Sonali, changed everything. She and Ray-Mi provided us with Braver uniforms, schedules, hierarchies, passwords, locations, everything."

"A number of us infiltrated their ranks, quietly, drawing as little attention as possible," Symin explains. "All while compiling information on their vulnerabilities and passing it off to the Generals."

"Was that difficult?" Salessa asks. "To grow close to the Bravers knowing your mission was to betray them?"

Naina scoffs. "You think it would be difficult to betray monsters with bloodstained hands?"

Salessa frowns. "Ray-Mi was one of them. Faeries following orders against their own consciences, to provide for their families."

"Many Bravers are not malicious," Kruga explains. "And many are. That uniform empowers faerie supremacy. Their personal character matters little in comparison."

Salessa nods, acknowledging his perspective.

Symin's expression dims as he continues. "The infiltration culminated in the Siege of the Castrum. Seven years ago. It was planned as an invasion, but a band of Librarians arrived earlier than expected, so the plan had to change. We besieged the fortress instead, hoping it would force the Bravers into a confrontation in the streets, honoring the Librarians' immunity."

"But when the Bravers emerged, they had the ore," Salessa says.

Kruga nods. "The Castrum gates spread wide and birthed the Ore Monger. He knew this discovery would put an end to the Revolution, make him invincible."

"The Siege survived two days, until they opened the gates. We had heard about the ore during the mission, but hadn't realized it was functional, applied to armor and weapons. When they emerged, it was like…" He looks down at his hands.

"Like losing part of your body?" Naina asks.

Kruga shakes his head. "Like losing part of your soul. It was like the day I lost Zynima. The connection to the Radiance was severed so quickly and forcefully, many of the Revolution warriors lost consciousness."

Symin gently runs his fingers over his forearm scar. "That night, more than half our forces were slaughtered. The rest of us managed to escape, but we'd never experienced anything so physically, spiritually, and emotionally catastrophic before."

"After the Siege, the Revolution dissolved. Symin and I wanted to find a way to rid the MegaFather of the ore and restore the resistance.

Ray-Mi and Gina joined us, but Ovida stayed behind. She said she needed to rest. And we understood."

"Most of us understood," Symin corrects him. "Zabeza's sister, Zakia, was heartbroken by that decision. She asked to join our team in the General's stead, but she was only thirteen. I refused, until her mother intervened. She trusted us to look after her daughter."

Kruga laughs. "She trusted *Zakia* to look after *us*. Pixie's a damn prodigy. When she was ten, she used the Radiance to build a track-proof safe house called the Bunker."

The edge of Symin's lips curve into a half-smile. "Seven years later, we're all still looking after each other. We all bring something to the team that contributes to the overall welfare and safety of the group: Zakia's connection to the Radiance, Ray-Mi's experience with the Bravers, Kruga's scientific background, and above all, the dauntless leadership of…"

He falls silent as something ahead of the cart catches his eye. The twins turn to see what it is.

In the distance, a chartreuse-skinned Mega sits on a boulder at the edge of the forest, daggers strapped around her waist. She seems focused and alert, her robust musculature evident beneath tight, tattered rags.

Symin finishes his sentence: "…our General, Gina."

CHAPTER 24

THE SONGWRITER

Gerontocratic Village *Adera*
Date *20th Day of Month 6, Year 1628 DG*

THEY MUST BE CROSSING MOONSIDE by now, Kyoko thinks of her colleagues, as she sits on the windowsill in the guest bedroom. Ona and Lona have risen, while the other suns remain beneath the horizon. It's still morning, but Rafael and Kyoko should have been on their way already.

She turns to the door but doesn't make a move toward it. Growing apprehension quickens her heart as she recalls Rafael's outburst. The gradual warming of their interactions has stalled again, washed away when the mari stopped dancing and distanced himself from her.

Kyoko shakes her head lightly, pushing these concerns to the back of her mind. The journey, the mission, is all that matters, and they are far behind schedule.

She steadies her nerves, slings her travel bag over her shoulder, and heads down to the foyer.

"Good morning, Ambassador," a servant greets her at the bottom of the stairs. "Your companion waits with Shifa and the Headwoman." He leads her through the salver's corridor, and then through the gardens, to the fire pit. Shifa, Amma, and Rafael sit closely together, talking and laughing. He's wearing the same yellow silk tunic as the day before, the only one he has left.

When his gaze finds Kyoko, palpable tension staggers her breaths and withers Rafael's smile. Discomfort wraps her like a wet blanket in subzero temperatures.

"Good morning!" cuts Shifa's voice through the tense air. "Come join us, Ambassador. Breakfast should be out shortly."

Kyoko clears her throat. "I'm sorry, Shifa. But we're far behind schedule. We can't stay for breakfast."

Shifa frowns, then nods. "I'll see if they can pack something for the road." She steps around the fire pit and offers the Ambassador a soft smile as she exits the clearing and heads back to the estate.

"We hope to see you again soon," Amma says to Kyoko. "Perhaps on your way back to the Library."

Kyoko bows her head slightly. "I will be sure to inform you of our arrival next time."

"Good, good," the Headwoman responds.

Slowly, Rafael rises and steps toward the igni. The closer he gets, the slower time seems to move. After what feels like hours or days, he reaches her and abruptly blurts, "I'm sorry."

Kyoko tightens her jaw to prevent it from falling open. There were a lot of things Kyoko expected to spring from Rafael's tongue, but an apology wasn't one of them. It snuffs out a portion of the tension in the air between them.

Rafael turns around and makes eye contact with the Headwoman, who offers him a smile and a nod. Then he faces Kyoko again and continues, "When I can, I'll try to explain my behavior from last night."

As the words reach her, Kyoko realizes she has no desire for his explanations or excuses. What justification exists for the prejudice he's shown her?

Silence escorts the morning travelers out of Adera, toward the border of the Gerontocratic Villages and the neighboring region.

The quiet is preferable to tension and hostility. Kyoko ascribes the lack of conversation to the lost look of deep thought in Rafael's gaze. He continues to massage one shoulder, as a travel sack full of donated clothes and flasks of water hangs from the other.

His bow, strapped tightly to the sack, wobbles minimally as they travel on a dirt path between vast fields of crop.

"The Agrarian Townlets," Kyoko reads from the new map. "If we can cross the Townlets today, we'll have caught up to our schedule."

"Then we shouldn't stop unless we have to."

"Agreed." She notices him wince as he massages his shoulder. "How is your wound healing?"

"Still red and scarred, but otherwise healed." He pauses, as if juggling between whether or not to continue. "Thank you for bringing the balm to the rooftop yesterday."

Kyoko nods, accepting the gratitude. She remains confused by his emotional fluctuations, and recalls the looks Rafael and the Headwoman shared before their departure.

What have I missed?

As if her thought reached him, Rafael responds. "I spoke with Amma last night."

"When?" Kyoko blurts out. The last time she saw him, he was escaping to the rooftop, distraught.

"In the middle of the night. She invited me back to the fire pit."

"Oh." Her curiosity piques.

Rafael waits awkwardly for more of a response, but when Kyoko offers none, he continues. "I thought she might have wanted an explanation for my" — he pauses — "outburst. That was part of it, but she also talked to me about the Nyasbaani folk song she was singing. She asked if I was able to translate it."

"We all can," Kyoko responds, flippantly. "It was about someone titled 'the Mother of Shifts,' and it was from the perspective of her lover."

Rafael stops walking and his eyes widen.

Kyoko turns to him, an eyebrow raised.

"Your Nysabaani is far more fluent than mine. I translated it to 'the Mother Who Changes.'"

Kyoko holds back a smile. She continues walking and Rafael follows. "Why did she want you to translate the song?"

"Because the lyrics provoked my reaction. The portion that speaks of a sister and a brother, fighting to protect one another."

Kyoko's throat dries as the realization dawns on her. She admonishes herself for not having made the connection between the lyrics and Rafael's loss. Only hours before the incident, he had confided in her.

"The song surfaced some trauma I have about losing my sister— some difficult memories."

"What memories?" Kyoko yields to her curiosity, allowing her tongue to move before her mind can chain it.

Rafael tenses. "There are some personal things I can't talk about."

Kyoko nods and allows him to continue.

"Amma explained that the song is about Adera."

The name clicks in Kyoko's memory. "The founder of the village, and the mother of the Twins."

"Correct. Though Amma elaborated that her role in history is far more significant than just establishing the village."

Rafael fills Kyoko in on the remainder of his interaction with the Headwoman. Kyoko listens without interrupting, but finds it difficult as he reveals the old woman's claims: that the Library has recorded the birth of the Doruh species inaccurately, that human Radiance could potentially still exist, and that Rafael could access it using ancient methods.

"I know it's difficult to believe, Kyoko, but how much of what she says do you think is true?"

Kyoko ponders the validity of the claims. She's well aware of the Library's willingness to alter history to protect its allies, which lends credibility to the Headwoman's words. But dormant Radiant energy that has gone untapped for over a millennium? This one is far more challenging to accept.

The igni considers whether or not to enlighten Rafael, akin to Alba's plans with Unisa, on the Library's true intentions with the Catacombs. Librarians are involved in SeaBed's historical education, so all he knows is what Educators have taught him.

He's going to think I've lost my mind.

Kyoko clears her throat. "I don't think her claims can be immediately discredited."

Rafael turns to her, astonishment clear on his expression.

He thinks I'm mad.

"Rafael, the Library's records are, in fact, modified to reflect Sun-Side's version of events. What Unisa discovered in Hay-Ro's letter is likely true."

Rafael hesitates before he speaks. "You knew about this?"

"We all do, Rafael. When Librarians wander beyond the city gates, they bear witness to the true nature of SunSide's historical impact, and the ways in which that impact has been cleansed for the Catacombs. The agreement between SunSide and the Library has been mutually beneficial for centuries."

There's a long pause in which Rafael's expression remains static. When he speaks, his tone is gentle. "If the Headwoman knows about the modifications to the Library's records, perhaps she's right about that potential to access human Radiance."

Kyoko nods. "Perhaps. Which means she could be correct about you being the one to do it."

Rafael scoffs. "That part, I don't believe. I have no desire to drown in my grief long enough to unlock some long-forgotten spirituality."

His eyes peruse their surroundings, from the apple groves to the tall corn stalks to the vast fields of agricultural land. "When I was young, I had an interest in agriculture from working in our family's olive groves. Joaquina, my sister, would swim up to the surface once a week and find books on farming for me to read."

He turns to one of the trees nearby and reaches up to an apple on a high branch. The mari holds it upward with the bottom facing the suns, then rotates it until it smoothly pops off the tree. He hands the fresh fruit to Kyoko, though he seems careful not to let her fingers touch his.

"It wasn't an easy journey for her. Swimming to the surface from SeaBed. But she did it. For me." He reaches up and pops another apple off the branch. They munch on the ripe fruit as they continue walking.

"Selflessness declares our love for others," Kyoko remarks.

Rafael smiles and runs his thumb affectionately along the bracelet, before clearing his throat and continuing. "That's why I don't believe I'm the one to access human Radiance. I'm not what Joaquina was: self-less and destined for significance. I'm not Adera; I'm the songwriter who laments his inadequacy as those he loves move on to greatness."

"How do you know that?" Kyoko questions.

"Because I've already squandered the life I was given—the one in which I could've achieved something, been someone."

Kyoko's heart constricts for all Rafael has suffered. She leans closer to him. "You are still someone, Rafael."

Rafael responds, his volume low. "All I am now is the exile."

CHAPTER 25

A COOL SWIG

The Agrarian Townlets *Guardleaf Grove*
Date *20th Day of Month 6, Year 1628 DG*

THREE SPHERES PAST THE ZENITH, the afternoon heat blankets the Librarians, falling from the sky and bouncing off the dirt path beneath their feet.

Rafael looks down at his hands, which have lost their olive tone in favor of a pale, sickly one. His forearm fins flake and crack, and he assumes his spine fins do the same. A scratchy dryness claws at his throat, and thick beads of warm sweat crawl down his face.

He reaches into the travel sack, rustles through the borrowed clothes, and finds one of the two flasks of water Shifa packed. He pulls one out and takes a long, cool swig.

Kyoko walks next to him, eyes locked on the road ahead. The stone of her exoskeleton shimmers in the places not painted crimson. There isn't a drop of moisture on her body—not a single bead of sweat. In fact, the more the suns' rays beat down on them, the more the Ambassador smiles.

Rafael returns the flask to the bag, and his eye catches the other one. It was meant for Kyoko.

A beady, shrill voice erupts in the back of his mind. *Don't offer it to her. She's bathed in Joaquina's blood. The igni don't deserve relief and refreshment. They killed your sister. Let her burn in the heat. Let her—*

Another voice, the Headwoman's, interrupts the vicious ravings of his grief.

Stop turning away from your pain and suffering. Face it, address it. She is not all of the igni.

The igni have caused his suffering. His exile. Joaquina's death.

But Kyoko truly is not responsible for the sins of all the igni. Perhaps, the sooner he can come to accept this, the sooner the visions will release him.

He withdraws the second flask. "Kyoko. Have some water."

She turns to him and he holds the flask out to her. Her expression betrays her surprise at the offer.

You and I both.

"Thank you, Rafael."

She takes it from his hand and he pulls his fingers back quickly, ensuring he doesn't make contact with the bloody exoskeleton. She takes a short sip and hands it back to him, but he shakes his head and insists she hold onto it.

A low rumble echoes around them after they continue the journey. Hard as he looks, Rafael cannot identify the animal from which it came. It isn't until he hears Kyoko chuckle that he realizes the source.

"That was my stomach," she admits.

"Oh. Are you hungry?"

Kyoko nods. "Quite."

"You can eat what remains of the provisions Shifa packed."

"We finished that long ago." She reaches into her bag and finds the map. "The next village is a few hours away, at the other end of the Townlets. I suppose we'll have to eat then."

"No, we don't," Rafael responds, his eye catching a patch of dark brown dirt, forming a bed of serpentine vines and large fruit. "Watermelon."

They march to it and Rafael kneels to examine one. "Heavy for its size. High water content. The belly is the right color, and there aren't any bruises or dents. Perfectly ripe."

"There," Kyoko says, raising a finger to a small stone cottage a few fields away in the center of the farm. "We can purchase it directly from the farmer."

A deep powerlessness bubbles into Rafael's chest as he realizes the pickpocket in Adera has left him reliant on Kyoko for funds. The idea of being in the igni's debt doesn't sit well with him.

As they journey through field after field to the stone cottage, Rafael's keen agricultural eye recognizes that a number of them haven't been sown.

"It's late," he says.

Kyoko eyebrows scrunch. "Yes, we're behind schedule."

"I mean it's late in the season for these fields to not be sown. I can count at least four that could have produced a harvest by now."

Kyoko shrugs. "Perhaps the farmer didn't find use for them."

Rafael shakes his head and laughs. "No farmer would let fertility like this lie wastefully."

A wide sign outside the cottage reads "Welcome to Guardleaf Grove." The travelers rise up the rickety wooden steps to the front porch, and Kyoko knocks on the front door.

Rafael remains distracted by the fields that lie unworked. *What a waste.*

The front door opens and a young, slender Mega stands in the entryway. Gray, barricading eyes, mauve-toned skin. She wears a dirt-splotched, tattered white dress and a wide-brimmed hat that pushes her height to six feet.

Her expression declares that the Librarians have infringed on her rest.

"Yes?" Her tone is cold and crisp.

Kyoko clears her throat. "Good afternoon. I'm sorry for disturbing you. My colleague and I have been traveling all day and haven't had anything to eat—"

The farmer raises a hand and Kyoko's sentence abruptly ends. "This is a farm, not a charity. May the Four provide for you."

"We have money!" Kyoko blurts out before the farmer can close the door behind her. "We'd like to purchase two watermelons." She reaches into her pocket to withdraw her pouch of stones, but Rafael stops her.

"Actually, we don't," he says.

Kyoko turns to him and whispers. "What are you doing?"

"Saving your money," he whispers back. "Trust me."

"Are you going to purchase the watermelons or not?" the farmer demands impatiently.

"We're not," Rafael says, before gesturing to the unworked fields. "I can prepare one of your untouched fields in exchange for the two watermelons."

The farmer raises an eyebrow. "I'm not a fool. Who would seed an entire field for only two watermelons?"

"A hungry agriculturalist."

"Agriculturalist? You?"

Rafael points to the piscine nares on his face. "I'm mari. If you have olive oil in your home, it comes from SeaBed, and possibly my family's groves."

"Why are you doing this?" Kyoko whispers, her tone harsher. "I thought we said we wouldn't stop today unless we absolutely had to."

Rafael turns to her. "We don't have my stones anymore, so whatever's in your pouch is all we have left. I can hand seed a small field in a couple hours. Let me do this and we can save your stones for when they're needed most."

Kyoko pauses, then nods.

Rafael turns back to the farmer. "Do we have a deal?"

"No, we don't," the farmer responds. "I can see your fins cracking already. The last thing I need is a dehydrated Librarian dying on my land."

"I'll help him," Kyoko says. "He won't exert enough energy to dehydrate."

The farmer still seems hesitant, but after a moment of consideration, she nods. "Alright. Seeds are over there." She gestures to the far end of the porch, where Rafael finds a pile of packed, unopened sacks.

"That's quite an untouched supply," Rafael responds quickly. "Are you overstocked?"

"No, I'm understaffed. The laborers I hired promptly resigned in favor of moving to SunSide. Evidently, the MegaFather is providing incentives for anyone willing to join the Bravers."

"He's bolstering recruitment?" Kyoko asks. "Why?"

The farmer rolls her eyes. "I don't know. When you're done, take your watermelons, and leave." She retreats into the cottage and slams the door behind her.

Rafael and Kyoko manage to drag the sacks out to a small, unworked field nearby. The mari begins to hand seed, but Kyoko stops him and insists that he teach her, so she can help. He hesitates, but Kyoko is adamant that she'd rather he be delayed than dead.

While he turns his face to hide it, something about her sentiment forces a smile onto his lips.

It doesn't take long. Kyoko is a fast learner and a hard worker. She's patient and devoted, and she seems to relish in the new experience. Rafael can't help but recognize the qualities that launched Kyoko up the Librarian ranks to Vice Ambassador before the age of thirty.

As they tend the field together, the work quickly dissolves into play. Rafael isn't sure when or how it happens, but he finds himself laughing and smiling along with Kyoko as they talk about their work, their likes and dislikes, and other aspects of their lives they were previously reluctant to share.

Out in the open, with nothing but fields as far as they can see, it feels as if he and Kyoko are the only two people in their little world. It begs him to recognize that she is not a thorn in his palm, but a cool swig on a hot afternoon.

When he looks upon her again, it becomes apparent to him: the bloodstains are faint, and her exoskeleton shines through.

Kyoko wonders whether she should inform the farmer that they'll be taking their earnings now. She uses their prior interaction as a barometer and decides against it.

Her subordinate sits by the newly-sown field, his legs bent with his arms wrapped around his knees. He tosses the flask frustratedly back into his bag.

"All out?" Kyoko asks him.

He nods weakly.

She withdraws the other flask from her pocket and holds it out to him. "Here. You can drink this, too."

"That's yours," Rafael insists. "You may be igni, but you're still human."

Kyoko feels the suns' rays cradling her body and smiles from the refreshing heat on her exoskeleton. "I don't need water the way you do. Drink it."

Rafael returns her smile. "As you command, *boss*."

The title emerges from his lips far more playfully than before.

"It's time to eat," Kyoko reminds him. "You have to pick two watermelons."

"I can't stand. You pick."

Heat rises to Kyoko's cheeks. "I'm not sure I can tell which is right for picking."

The mari smiles. "I'll guide you."

From where he's seated, Rafael lists the characteristics she should look for when picking watermelon: heavy, uniform size, a yellow or orange field spot, shiny not dull. Kyoko gets lost for a moment in Rafael's passion. It's moments like these when the true, talkative Rafael comes alive, exposing a feverish love she didn't know was there.

And there's something inexplicably magical about watching people talk about the things that bring their resting souls back to life.

Kyoko selects two watermelons, and Rafael's smile indicates approval. She removes the tanto from its sheath and cuts into the fruit. Sitting on the ground facing one another, they take a bite together, eyes locked.

Bite after bite, their mouths fill with watermelon meat and juice, until the juices flow down their chins. It satiates her and quenches her, evoking her happiest childhood memories. She watches as the color begins to return to Rafael's cheeks and full lips.

They've nearly completed the first watermelon when an idea strikes her.

"Suikawari!" she says excitedly.

Rafael raises an eyebrow, staring in silent confusion.

"Suikawari. Here, let me show you."

Kyoko stands and holds her hand out to help him to his feet. He looks from her face to her fingers and she can see a clear hesitation, as if there's something in her hand that is distressing him. "Are you alright?"

Rafael nods. Slowly and gently, as if he might burn by touching her, he places his warm, soft hand in hers.

She leads him to an open area of the field, hauling the second watermelon and placing it two yards in front of him. Using the tanto, she removes a branch from a nearby tree, and a strip of fabric from her tunic.

"This is a traditional igni game." She hands Rafael the branch and then wraps the taut fabric around his eyes. With her hands on his shoulders, she spins him around three times.

"This is impossible," Rafael says, coming out of the third spin shakily.

"No, it's not," Kyoko responds, suppressing her laughter. "Children play this. Just try to crack the watermelon with the branch. If you can get it to break into two equal halves, I'll give you a perfect score."

Kyoko begins to count the seconds in her head as Rafael takes wild swings at the ground. She continues to encourage and guide him, while holding in her laughter.

"You can do this, Rafael." Swing. *Miss.*

"Listen to my voice. Swing in this direction." Swing. *Miss.*

"Thirty seconds left." Swing. *Miss.*

Kyoko takes a deep breath and speaks quickly, but calmly. "Ten seconds left. Listen to my voice. Hear me. It's right here at my feet. Five seconds. Now, Rafael! Swing!"

The branch comes down at Kyoko's feet and lands hard on the center of the watermelon. It cracks into two nearly equal halves.

Rafael pulls the blindfold off. "Did I get it?" He stares down at his shattered target, then throws his hands up in excitement. Kyoko's heart floods with childhood joy as she cheers loudly for him.

Rafael opens his arms out and, instinctively, Kyoko leaps into them. He wraps his arms tightly around her, and she does the same.

It seems to last for some time, until it abruptly comes to an end when Kyoko feels a long, sturdy mass that wasn't there moments earlier brush against her thigh. Rafael quickly releases the embrace and turns around. His face has taken on the hue of a tomato.

"I-I'm so-sorry," he stumbles through.

"Wow," Kyoko teases. "I thought *I* really enjoyed Suikawari."

"Please stop."

Soon after, the Librarians find themselves on the path through the Agrarian Townlets again; and they remain on it until Frona is nearly halfway beyond the horizon.

"I don't believe it," Kyoko says, her eyes darting from the map to the sky and back again, "but we could actually make it to the next village by nightfall."

"It's an hour to dark," Rafael adds. "We'll have to walk fast."

The dirt path between the farms winds left and bounds right, but the Librarians remain steady and focused on the path. With bellies full of watermelon and the evening air keeping them cool, they feel fulfilled and confident in their ability to reach the day's goal.

Kyoko's eyes slide down to the bottom of the map. She reads the wide, daunting *EverEmber* label, and a rhythmic thump begins in her chest. The words glow on the page and burn through her pupils. She doesn't blink as the ink melts and runs over her fingers, trapping her in position.

Rafael leans closer to the map and asks, "What's wrong?"

"Hm?" Kyoko responds, breaking from her trance. The ink returns to the page, as it always was. "Oh, nothing, sorry." She quickly rolls up the map and places it back into her bag.

The dread of returning to EverEmber and encountering Kanako takes hold of her, silencing her through the remainder of the walk.

"Do you want to talk?" Rafael asks, pulling Kyoko back to reality once again.

"There isn't much to talk about," Kyoko deflects.

"We're getting closer to EverEmber. Are you thinking about the people you want to avoid?"

Kyoko keeps her expression still, hoping to mask her surprise that Rafael is able to decipher her concerns.

She takes a deep breath, trying to steady the thumping before she speaks. "My sister, Kanako. I haven't seen her in six years, and we left off in a bad place. I'm concerned about how uncomfortable it might be to see each other again."

"I'm sorry to hear that," Rafael says. "Six years is a long time. A lot can change in that time. For the better."

"Or the worse," Kyoko replies. "She might hate me more now than she did then."

"I'm sure your sister doesn't *hate* you, Kyoko. What happened between you?"

Kyoko responds as delicately as she can, so her tone isn't perceived as abrasive. "I'm sorry, Rafael, but I don't think I want to talk about this right now."

He nods. "I understand. Let's talk about something else."

Kyoko reaches deep into her cognitive catalog to retrieve the conversation topics they shared in the morning, and selects one to quickly change the subject.

"This morning you said you have no desire to drown in your grief, to unlock this human Radiance."

"Correct," Rafael says tentatively.

"There are many emotions other than grief. Any of them can provide you with energy and spirituality, be it joy, anger, relief, excitement, love."

Rafael pauses. "I hadn't considered that." He turns to her and smiles. "But perhaps I could."

Kyoko cannot deny that Rafael continues to show new sides of himself. Sides that are as endearing as they are shrouded. After all they've been through, after all the tense and inconsistent interactions they've had, Rafael's thoughts and feelings toward her remain unclear.

She questions whether he is a stone in her boot, or a cool swim on a warm evening.

CHAPTER 26

KNOWLEDGE EMPOWERS

Occupied Territory MoonSide
Date 20th Day of Month 6, Year 1628 DG

THE OLDEST LIES ARE THE heaviest.

That's how it seems to Unisa as she cradles the weight of the *Everlasting Journey* in her hands. She once thought it was a work of paper and ink, but it must be constructed of something stronger, more dense. It's lasted so long, and has been used in the foundation of the world's most deceitful institutions. It must be made of stone, iron, or steel.

Or ore.

Unisa flips the text to the final pages. Hay-Ro's letter, the only honest words in the Catacombs, stare up at her. A long breath escapes her lungs and she declares, "I'm ready."

Fading light of the setting suns drips through the inn's windows. Alba leans on the sill, her hands folded in front of her, palpable irritation in her body language.

"I'm not entirely sure what more to say, Uni."

"The entire truth." Unisa is prepared to remain seated in place, on this bed in a MoonSidian inn, until she feels liberated from the darkness.

Alba scans the room. As if the walls are iron bars, her eyes display recognition that she isn't going anywhere.

"Unisa, you were correct last night, when you said no one had a stronger moral code than the original Primes did. Their intention in forging the Library was exactly the ideal the world still believes the city to be today. But that all changed when that text you're holding entered the Catacombs."

Unisa's fingertips begin to burn. The book of lies that eroded an entire city's moral foundation. She places it down on the bed, as far as her arm can reach.

Alba continues. "The ruling Prime made a decision that bartered integrity for innovation. That spoiled the spirit of the city. SunSide's alliance with the Library has always been public, but has never been transparent. Together, the MegaParents and the Primes have spent ages playing an artful game of manipulation."

Unisa rolls the word around on her tongue. "Manipulation."

Alba nods. "Red-Lo's rewritten history, sullying his wife's legacy, painting her with his own violence and irresponsibility, became the precursor to SunSide's long history of modifying and influencing the records within the Library. It proved that the Primes were willing to sacrifice their ideals for their own benefit."

Unisa's face drops into her hands. "How does deceit run so deep that generations of Librarians are unable to weed it out?"

"I'll say it again: manipulation. The Primes created the ideas of the Fully Bonded and the Fully Broken as a means of control. One person-ified loyalty, conditioning Librarians to surrender to every word that sprang from the Prime's tongue. The other was demonized, assigned to anyone who thought critically about what they'd witnessed beyond the walls."

"Then why rehabilitate the Broken?" Unisa lifts her head, but her voice emerges barely louder than a whisper. "I've seen, with my own eyes, Librarians escorting the Fully Broken to rehabilitation."

"Where does the rehabilitation take place?" Alba asks.

The question catches Unisa by surprise, leaving her speechless.

"History is not all that's buried under the city, Uni. You'll find equal parts books and bones."

Unisa's heart drops. Nausea rises from the deepest trench of her bowels. "No."

"Yes. The extermination of the Broken is a fail-safe, in the event that the indoctrination breaks. The Prime expects eyes to be deceived when hearts and minds are under control."

Unisa steps off the bed and rises to her feet. The image of the young boy's corpse flashes in her mind, and her throat tightens. "Even when those eyes witness unforgivable evil? It doesn't wake them up?"

"Unforgivable evil is always preceded by dehumanization and desensitization. It doesn't matter what Librarians or citizens witness if they believe in the ultimate goodness of SunSide and its warriors, and the inherent violence and savagery of the Doruh."

Unisa falls back onto the bed, sitting on the edge in disgust and disbelief. "What about those like us? Who do see the truth?"

Alba pauses, but maintains a strong line of eye contact. "They must face reality. The truth that they are culpable in every drop of blood spilt by SunSide's swords."

The nausea builds and Unisa wraps her arms around her stomach. "I feel sick."

Alba's tongue runs with the current of a river. "We are all responsible. Generations of Librarians have been ranked and trained to perpetuate the lies. If any do wake from the control, they've already invested years, sometimes decades, to a code of ethics they believed to be morally sound."

"We educate the continent for him. We authorize and edify him. We give him credibility." The words seep into Unisa's heart and tear her world apart. "We've been lied to, but we aren't victims, are we? We're perpetrators."

Alba slowly steps toward Unisa. "That line was blurred generations ago. Librarians have given all of themselves to a false narrative; we've lost the ability to consent to what knowledge we pass on."

She stops walking and her eyebrows scrunch together, as if a wayward memory has found its way into her mind. "Remember what I said last night? About knowledge?"

Unisa nods. "Knowledge empowers. As long as he knows more than us, he has power over us."

"Correct. The Prime knows that the Catacombs paint evil as good. He knows that Red-Lo etched his lies into history. And he knows that, as long as the Librarians are ignorant, or as long as they feel responsible for the havoc, he's in control."

Unisa turns, grabs the tattered text, and forcefully lifts it into the air so Alba can see it. "What's the point then? Why send me on this journey for the truth when he knows it's a lie?"

Alba sits on the bed next to her. She holds her palm open and Unisa hands the text to her.

"Two days ago, you walked into the Prime's office and created a situation that's never existed before. No one's ever challenged the integrity of the city directly to a Prime's face."

"I walked straight into the lion's den."

Alba shakes her head. "No. You walked into its mouth. You gave him the opportunity to test the limits of his control. To toy with you. And with me."

"*Toy* with us? What do you mean?"

Alba's eyes grow soft and apprehensive, and Unisa feels the Ambassador's body tense. She swallows hard and speaks in a low, strained voice.

"Ana and I planned to leave the Library, Unisa. This week. I can no longer live as an ideal he forces others to strive toward. My presence in the Library feeds his control. The only way I can take that power from him is to vanish into anonymity. I told him I wouldn't let him use me anymore.

"When you walked into his office, he saw an opportunity to keep me under his grasp. Forever. He sent you on this journey to prove that his grasp on you would hold, regardless of what you saw. That you'd choose of your own volition to be part of the Library's continuing legacy."

Unisa shakes her head. "Never."

"If you return to the Library Fully Bonded, he wins. He'll allow Ana to escape, but I'll be forced to take his tunic after him. However, if you are awakened, he says he'll let both Ana and I go freely from the Library. That's why I came. To protect you, and to ensure your awakening. My freedom is now in your hands."

Alba's final statement burrows into the forefront of Unisa's mind. *Alba's freedom. In my hands.*

Every word he's written and spoken, every ideal Unisa has digested for him, all dissolves before her eyes. Hours, days, weeks, years—all wasted to the devotion of a city of lies.

"You were right. We're all playthings for him. But now he's lost. I've awakened to the truth." She turns to the mari. "You're free, Alba."

There's a long pause in which Unisa expects joy, excitement, relief. At the very least, acknowledgement that they are successful.

But there is none. Alba continues to run her fingers along the beaten text in her hands. "No, I'm not."

Unisa raises an eyebrow. "What do you mean? Of course you are."

Alba raises her eyes to meet Unisa's. "I've been so foolish. I didn't realize until now, he can only win this game. If you return Bonded, he gets me. If you don't, you'll be deemed Broken and end up in a grave. He knows I won't let that happen."

There's a long pause in which Alba's eyes dart back-and-forth. She appears to piece more of the puzzle together before she speaks again. "And that's why he sent Rafael on this journey to question the TreeKeeper. He knows it doesn't exist, so Rafael's mission can only fail. Even if you return from the mission Broken, he still has Rafael to ensure he wins. Rafael's his foolproof backup plan. The Prime knows he's won. One way or another, I end up in the black tunic; either because I couldn't break your indoctrination, or because I sacrificed myself to save you or Rafael."

Defeat weighs Unisa down like stone, iron, or steel. "What are we going to do?"

Alba closes her eyes, as if the next words she speaks are covered in thorns. "We are going to complete the assignment. Then you're going to return to the Library Fully Bonded and let him think he's won."

"What about your freedom? You'll lose it."

Alba's voice is little more than a whimper. "I never had it. I will die under his thumb." Water wells in her eyes. "But Ana can still be free. We can still save her."

Unisa considers her words carefully. "I understand the sacrifice you want to make for her, but how can I pretend to support SunSide after what I've seen Bravers doing to the Doruh? I can't indefinitely devote myself to that."

"What if it isn't indefinite? Once he's freed Ana, a new game will begin. One that will burn the Library to the ground."

Unisa shifts uneasily. "Burn it to the ground? Alba, what are you saying? It's ages old. Let him install you as his heir. Once you're Prime, you can change things."

Alba shakes her head. "The Supreme Librarians would convince the entire city I had lost my mind and become Broken. There would be a parade following my public execution."

"So your solution is to *burn it to the ground*? What about the strong moral code of the original Primes? Is there no way the city can be salvaged to revert it back to the good intentions with which it was founded?"

A half smile appears on Alba's face. "Your idealism and your optimism are remarkable. I'm sorry, Uni, there are always good intentions behind the things evil people weaponize. But do you think anyone cares what the swordsmith's intentions were, when the blade is at their throat?"

Her words strike Unisa's heart.

"We've been sharpening that blade for him," Unisa admits. "How are we going to wipe our hands clean? How will we carry out justice?"

"Justice is strange," Alba replies. "There is relief in conquering evil, but so much pain for all those who were hurt along the way. But the longer we allow the current to accelerate, the harder the river will be to wade."

"So that's our plan? Complete the mission, free Ana, and begin plotting the Library's downfall?"

Alba nods. "Others will join us, eventually, for the battles to come."

The word alarms Unisa. "Battles?"

Alba sighs. "There will be conflicts, Uni. This isn't a path that will be free of violence."

"I told you how I felt about that," Unisa reminds her.

"And I told *you*, not all problems can be solved peacefully. Particularly not ones of this nature. You're a Librarian, Unisa. You have to accept that at some point in your career, you'll experience bloodshed."

"How do you know this plan will even find success?"

A half-smile appears on Alba's lips. "As I said before, as long as he knows more than us, he has power over us. But the Prime is ignorant of the plan."

Unisa understands. "Knowledge empowers."

CHAPTER 27

THE DAUGHTERS

Continent of Panaerth
Date 20th Day of Month 6, Year 1628 DG

ELABORATE STRUCTURES RISE FROM THE sand at General Gina's feet, forming an intricate sculpture of a city, matching the rhythm of her contorting chartreuse fingers. She's oblivious to the cloaked cart of travelers approaching on the path along the shoreline.

When the cart comes to a rest, Kruga leans forward and whispers to the twins, "Watch."

He bends his knees, then explodes skyward, leaping over the Doruh, and landing on one knee in front of the cart. The crimson Mega yells, "GINA!" while raising his forearm to his chest, from which a blue circle of light extends.

Gina pops onto her feet and swings her arms at her sides, using the Radiance to launch six daggers from her waist. It happens so fast, Salessa only catches the blur of the daggers swiftly moving through the air and colliding with Kruga's light shield.

Gina's expression melts into relief when she sees Kruga kneeling and smiling. She forms a fist and then lowers it quickly, shedding the cart's cloaking and revealing Symin and the twins.

"These games are going to get him killed one day," she angrily says, directly to Symin.

Kruga drops the shield and waves his hand toward Gina. The daggers float delicately through the air and return to the sheaths around the General's waist.

"With the lives we've led," Symin responds while dismounting from the cart, "I think a little fun may be the only thing keeping us civilized."

Gina scowls. "The battleground is no place for fun. Particularly not from a forty-year-old."

"I'm thirty-five," Kruga corrects her.

"You'll be dead if you don't stop acting like a child."

Symin steps between Kruga and Gina and issues a firm glare to Kruga. "That's enough." He turns to Gina. "Mission was a success, General."

She turns to the twins, who have also now dismounted from the cart. "I can see that. What are they?"

"Wolves," Symin replies.

Gina sighs. "Wolves? It won't work. They aren't small enough. Send them back."

Naina raises a hand into the air and snaps her fingers, getting Gina's attention. "We weren't purchased from a street merchant. You can't just send us back after your stewards dragged us here. Understood, Greenie?"

She's chartreuse, Salessa inserts into Naina's mind.

Shut up.

"Stewards?!" Kruga exclaims, his tone injured.

Gina quickly approaches Naina, towering a foot over the wolf. "What did you call me?"

An unwavering smirk settles on Naina's lips. "You heard me."

The tension drives Salessa's heart rate up. She grabs her sister's wrist, but the wolf tugs her arm away, eyes locked on Gina's.

"I can end you so quickly there wouldn't even be a puddle of blood left," Gina threatens.

"Bold of you to mention bodily fluids when you're the color of vomit."

Tense silence thickens the air as Kruga, Symin, and Salessa stand completely still, waiting for something horrific to begin. The tension dissipates when a tiny smile appears on the edge of Gina's lips.

"Alright," she says to Symin. "They can stay."

Long after the Four have dropped below the horizon, the travelers continue through the forest toward the General's camp. Symin and Gina walk ahead, streams of illumination issuing from their palms, while the twins follow closely behind.

Kruga had remained with the cart, as Ray-Mi had with the boat, to protect it while the others continued on.

Gina's stories enrapture Salessa, tales of equal parts heroism and hilarity. Her perspectives are a wide departure from Kruga's. Where he sees unmet goals, she finds lessons. Where he sees setbacks, she finds opportunities.

Salessa makes out thin shreds of moonlight and starlight through the treetops, guiding the way to a wide clearing littered with dry branches and dead, crinkling leaves.

"Home," Gina says, standing at the center of it.

She spins and waves her arms in a wide sweeping motion, gathering the leaves and branches in a pile at her feet. Then a flame erupts from her index finger and pummels the dry pile in a wave of wildfire. Naina and Salessa spring back as the towering bonfire rises over their heads. Symin, replicating Kruga's movements, cloaks the clearing with a circle of blue light.

Naina and the Mega discuss mission specifics, sitting on old logs as the fire licks the air. Salessa's thoughts, however, drift to the fresh, fertile forest surrounding them. Her mind juxtaposes the verdant flora with tall stone buildings and dark, disturbing walls.

Salessa recognizes a discernible composure in her stature, an ease in her breathing, that she lost a decade earlier. Only a day without Bravers, without the tip of a blade at her throat, has brought it back.

You should be paying attention, comes Naina's voice. The wolf projects the words while maintaining her eye contact with Gina.

Sorry, you're right. Salessa turns her ears to the discussion.

"Symin's cloaking emits a Radiant-magnetic energy that diverts passersby around us," Gina explains, "but once we leave this clearing, the connection to the Radiance dies. The processing center is a few miles east. Densest concentration of ore in one place we've ever seen."

"And the heaviest Braver patrol outside the Castrum."

The smooth, delicate voice that speaks these words comes from behind rustling trees, unexpectedly, but not alarmingly. They drip into Salessa's ears like water droplets from an oasis.

Salessa's gaze locks on the young Mega entering the clearing. Two thin strands of hair dance playfully against royal purple cheeks, leading up to a messy bun. The moonlight catches the gray of her eyes, causing them to glow. Salessa estimates she can't be more than an inch over five feet.

Zakia, the Doruh assumes, smiles and the world trembles beneath Salessa's feet. Her heart bashes through her chest and heat rises to her cheeks. A hard ball forms in the pit of her gut, and she nearly loses her feet from under her as she fails to recall having seen anyone so breathtaking in her entire life.

Lessi? A voice rings in her ears and she silently prays that it is Zakia trying to reach out to her. *Are you alright?*

The world tremors again, until Salessa realizes Naina has gripped her shoulder and is violently shaking her.

Salessa shakes her head and breaks from the trance. "I'm fine." She pulls the wolf's fingers off her shoulder. "I've never felt better."

Naina raises an eyebrow. "You're acting bizarre."

Salessa ignores her sister and watches Zakia make her way around the fire to first greet Symin and Gina, then introduce herself to the twins.

"Welcome to the team," her velvet voice wraps around Salessa.

Naina introduces herself and then turns for Salessa to do the same. There's a long pause as Salessa clears her throat and wipes the perspiration off her palms.

"Sa-Salessa," she introduces herself.

"What a lovely name," Zakia remarks.

"Are you not feeling well?" Naina asks her sister, abruptly. "Why is your face so red?"

Salessa's hands shoot up and she covers her cheeks. "I said I'm fine!"

Gina's foot taps nervously against the forest floor as she finishes her dinner and finds an excuse to pull Symin away from the clearing.

"Can you show the twins how to set up the sleeping areas?" she asks Zakia. "Symin and I will check the perimeter."

Zakia nods and escorts the newcomers to the other side of the clearing, while Gina leads Symin to a secluded ridge. Unsure how to broach the subject, the air remains thick with silence until Symin breaks it.

"What's wrong, Gina? Why did you bring me here?"

Gina collects her thoughts, hoping to articulate them softly, empathetically. These aren't traits she's particularly familiar with, but she attempts for Symin.

"I just want to make sure you're alright."

Symin's perplexity grows. "In what way?"

This will be harder than she thought. The last time she had this conversation with Symin, he didn't receive it well.

"I know why you brought these twins back with you, and it wasn't for the mission."

Symin's expression hardens, confirming Gina's suspicions. "Enlighten me."

"The resemblance is eerie, I understand. With pink skin, Salessa could be Zynima's twin. You look at her the same way you look at—"

"Not this again," Symin sighs. "Gina, we've talked about this. I didn't ask Zakia to join."

Gina shakes her head. "No, you didn't. But you also agreed to bring a thirteen-year-old when she asked." She places a hand on his shoulder affectionately. "No one blames you for still being so affected by her death. But..." She pauses.

"Go ahead," Symin challenges her. "Say it."

"You can't put lives at risk to fill the void Zynima left behind. The longer you collect these surrogate daughters, the harder it'll be for you to heal. This isn't helpful to your grieving."

"Do *not*," Symin says and stops. He lowers his volume, but increases the ferocity in his tone. "Do *not* pretend to know what it's like to lose a child." His voice quivers. "I am not collecting daughters. Every one of them is here on their own accord."

"I know they are, but you invited wolves on a stealth mission. Are they here to help, or are they here because they fill the Zynima-shaped hole in your heart? These are dangerous missions, Symin. Are you prepared to lose *another* daughter?"

Symin pauses and Gina sees the pain in the hard lines across his face. "I will die one thousand deaths before I let a hair on their heads fall out of place."

Gina nods. "I know you will. I just want you to be healthy. This doesn't feel healthy."

Symin forces a smile through his obvious suffering. "I'm fine. Please, let it go."

Gina nods hesitantly and embraces him. She hears every word he says, but she doesn't believe a single one.

The twins watch Zakia shut her eyes, tilt her head back, and raise her arms into the air, closing her fingers tightly as if taking hold of the gently falling starlight. There's no immediate change to their surroundings. Not a leaf, nor an insect, twitches.

Naina turns to Salessa and raises her arms up mockingly, earning a sharp elbow from her sister.

Salessa lifts her gaze to the forest's canopy and finds hundreds upon hundreds of leaves floating in a stunning, circular pattern. They flow like a river; they play and glide as the hundreds become thousands. Twigs and branches join the melee, illumination dripping off every plant in the sky.

Zakia opens her eyes and turns to the twins. The moonlight drifts down pristinely and bounces off of her deep purple skin, forming a glowing field around her. Salessa fights the urge to bathe in her ambiance and relish in the glow.

Zakia pulls her arms down to the ground and spreads them out. The thousands of leaves, twigs, and branches descend to the forest floor in an idyllic waterfall of natural life. Tree sap hovers from the corners of the forest and drips onto the leaves to secure them together. The twigs and branches wrap around one another to form bed legs, and the connected leaf platforms land on top.

Five sleeping cots made of leaves, held together by sap, and hoisted up by twigs and branches sit before them.

"That was impressive," Salessa says.

Zakia offers her a grateful smile.

Gina and Symin return to the clearing and begin final preparations for the night. Zakia joins them and invites the twins.

"We're quite tired, so we're going to lie down now," Naina tells the Mega, holding Salessa back by the wrist.

I'm not tired, Salessa projects to her sister.

Yes, you are.

Zakia joins the other Mega, and the twins each lie down on a cot and face one another.

Have you thought about what we have to do tomorrow? Naina asks.

Salessa raises an eyebrow. *What is there to think about?*

Naina rolls her eyes. *Who's going in, Lessi?*

Obviously me, Naina. You're a two-hundred-pound wolf, and this is a stealth mission.

You've already lied and told them you're a wolf. How exactly are you going to shift without them realizing we're two different animals?

That was a mistake, Salessa admits. *I'll tell them the truth tomorrow.*

No, you won't. Naina growls, even in her thoughts. *The lie protects us. It always has.*

Symin doesn't know who the Twins are and that's the most basic aspect of the religion. He won't know the significance of twins who shift into different animals.

What about Gina and Zakia? Naina challenges her. *What if they're aware of the prophecy? If they see you shift into anything other than a wolf, they'll know why we're being hunted. It has to be me going in tomorrow.*

Naina, you're not going to put yourself in danger because they might know the prophecy. It's safer for me, I'm smaller and faster.

DO. NOT. SHIFT. LESSI.

The conversation dies abruptly when the Mega join them and fall onto the cots. Naina lies on her back, staring up at the forest canopy, her expression wrought with frustration.

Salessa has always put Naina's safety first. That won't change, whether that protection manifests in keeping their true identities hidden, or keeping the wolf caged.

CHAPTER 28

THE PROPHECY

Continent of Panaerth
Date 20th Day of Month 6, Year 1628 DG

TERROR PLAGUES HER AGAIN. THE horrific visions bring discomfort, cold sweats, and tightness in the chest. Two small girls hiding, a green-skinned Mega with one arm, barking wolves, and burning flesh.

The cool, calculated voice of the Facilitator. "I need them alive."

Salessa shoots up from the cot, heart thrumming painfully, tears painting her cheeks. She takes a few deep breaths and wipes them quickly. Naina, Gina, and Symin remain undisturbed in their cots, but Zakia's is empty.

A flickering light illuminates the clearing. The bonfire lives, and just over the tops of the licking flames, Salessa makes out the pixie's face. The chaitender cannot blink; her eyes are afraid of losing even a momentary glance.

The embers of the bonfire flow up and down rhythmically from the logs and weeds on which they thrive. Zakia's royal purple skin gleams and coruscates, shining in the light, then deepening in the shadows, back and forth, on and off.

Salessa can either attempt to sleep again, potentially inviting another visit from the green pixie, or she can spend time with the purple one.

Green or purple? Nightmare or dream? Past or future?

She can still see Zakia's face shimmering over the tops of the flames when she walks around the raging fire, toward the log on which the pixie rests. It isn't until she's entirely around the flaming mound that the realization strikes: Zakia may be up in the middle of the night for solitude.

Salessa stands frozen, as if remaining stationary will make her invisible. Inevitably, the pixie notices her, spawning discomfort in Salessa's chest, until Zakia smiles. Not a soft, polite smile—a wholehearted, toothy smile. The kind of smile Salessa finds on her customers' faces when she brings their chai to their tables.

Zakia taps the spot beside her on the log. Without any words spoken at all, Salessa no longer feels unwelcome. Heat burns her cheeks as she walks, but she's unsure if it's coming from the bonfire or from within.

As they sit beside each other, eyes on the flames, Salessa tries to think of something to say. The longer she thinks, the more silence fills the air.

"Thank you," Zakia says, abruptly breaking the quiet.

Salessa's eyes widen. "For what?"

"For coming."

"Oh, you don't have to thank me. I saw you over the flames and—"

She's cut off by Zakia's laughter, and the true meaning of the pixie's words hits her like tumbling timber. Salessa turns to the bonfire and wonders if it would be more painful to die in the flames, or in embarrassment.

"I was thanking you for coming on this journey. For the mission."

"You don't have to thank me for that either. Naina and I were intending to leave MoonSide anyway, but we didn't have a plan until Symin knocked on our door. I suppose we should be thanking you for the direction."

"Well, I wish the direction we provided you wasn't so..." She pauses, searching for the right word.

Salessa comes to her aid. "Dangerous? Terrifying? Unpredictable?"

"All of those things," Zakia agrees. "But I know Symin chose you for a reason. It was his idea to return to Aerthomni for Doruh assistance. He wouldn't have brought you here if he didn't think you were the best option."

It occurs to Salessa in this moment that she's never questioned why Symin chose them. Was it because he genuinely believed they could help? Or was it because he was able to leverage the twins' history with the Facilitator to make them comply?

She shrugs. "Perhaps. We're certainly familiar with danger, living under the occupation. Skilled at lying low and keeping a distance. It's the only real way to survive. The only time I leave home is for work and, even then, it's difficult to feel safe."

"What do you do for work?" Zakia asks.

"I teach at the village schools and orphanages during the daytime. And then work the evening and night shifts at the local chai house."

Zakia's eyebrows soar up her forehead and her smile widens. "You're a chaitender?"

Salessa nods.

"I love chai!"

"You've had chai?"

"Of course! When I was a little girl, there were chai houses in the Doruh districts of Larso. I would go with my mother and"—her smile fades and her volume drops—"brother."

Salessa recalls what Symin told her about his friend, Zabeza. "I'm sorry. Symin told us about him, and everything following his abduction."

"I was four when it happened," Zakia responds, her tone subdued, "so I didn't have a lot of time with him. That's why I joined Symin's team. To honor him. Avenge him. Do anything I can to find some semblance of justice."

"That was a brave decision at thirteen years old."

The faintest hint of pink sparks on her purple cheeks. "Thank you, but I don't think everyone feels that way. At least, not at first. Gina was angry with Symin for allowing me to join."

"Well, Kruga speaks very highly of you. He called you a prodigy and told us about the safe house you built in Larso."

The faint pink glows brighter. "That's embarrassing."

"You don't have to be modest. It's evidence of how powerful your connection to the Radiance is. I've seen you use it with an intricate fluidity I haven't witnessed in any other Mega."

"We all contribute to the team in different ways," Zakia echoes Symin's words.

Salessa laughs. "Symin said the same thing earlier."

Zakia rolls her eyes. "And I'm sure the humble nymph never even mentioned what he contributes."

Salessa thinks back, but doesn't recall any mention of his own contributions. "I didn't realize it before, but you're right, he didn't."

"He doesn't admit it, but Symin is the soul of this team. When we start to lose a sense of who we are, and why we're here, he brings us back. When we need a break or a shoulder, he's always ready to hoist us up."

She turns to the fire. "Above all, he reminds us that this cause, this mission, is bigger than us and our lives. He prepares us, so if the day comes when any of us has to give our lives for a hundred or a thousand others, we're ready to do so."

Salessa is silent, taken by her resolve and devotion. She's in awe of the pixie who is willing to sacrifice anything for the good of others.

Zakia continues. "And his connection to the Radiance is quite strong, as well. It may not be as strong as mine, but he's a Siphon, and I'm not."

Salessa's forehead scrunches in confusion. "A Siphon?"

Zakia nods. "He can feed off the Radiant energy of others in close proximity. It's incredibly complicated, but after decades of practice, Symin's mastered the art. He can stand behind a Mega and feed, and they'd have no idea."

"I didn't know that was possible," Salessa admits.

Zakia leans in closer. "Enough about us, tell me more about you and Naina, and your life back in MoonSide."

Salessa's smile fades and she releases a deep sigh. "There isn't much beyond the walls, the checkpoints, the shortage of resources, the lack of safety." She raises her hands and gestures at the towering trees surrounding the clearing. "There isn't any natural beauty like this."

"Natural beauty?" Zakia responds with a quirked eyebrow. "These old, hollow trees and crispy, fallen leaves?" She smiles. "I can show you natural beauty."

Salessa hesitates a moment, but Zakia's smile puts her at ease. The pixie stands and holds her hand out, and Salessa places her fingers into the warm purple palm. A jolt of elation buzzes from where their hands touch, up Salessas's arm, and into her chest, as the pixie leads her out of the clearing.

Hands clenched, they travel through the forest with a cloaking circle around them. As they make their way through hordes of trees and over carpets of leaves, they talk more about their experiences and ideas for the future.

With minor differences, Salessa and Zakia hold parallel visions for what's to come: a world without walls, without violence, without too much distance between them. Salessa basks in the infectious light of the pixie's aura, feeling hopeful for the future she describes.

They arrive at a tall, thick tree and Zakia releases Salessa's hand before floating up to a sturdy branch. Salessa remains on the ground, staring up at her, wondering how she's going to scale the trunk.

I can't shift and fly up. Naina would kill me.

"What's wrong?" Zakia calls down from the branch. "Can't wolves climb trees?"

"I don't want to tear my clothes," Salessa responds, hoping the excuse passes.

Zakia holds her hand out toward Salessa and then slowly lifts it, until it is parallel to the ground. Salessa feels her feet leave the dirt, as if a giant hand has grabbed hold of her, and she floats up to the branch where Zakia sits.

"*This* is natural beauty," the purple pixie says, pointing out into the distance ahead of them. It takes a moment for Salessa's eyes to adjust.

The branch on which they sit is high enough to gaze over the tree-tops. Past the canopy of the forest, Salessa sees the shoreline end and the ocean begin. Moonlight falls onto the water's surface, creating a blanket of silvery streaks that sparkle and twinkle and bring the ocean to life.

Breaking waves form patterns in the light, passing from one crest onto the next until they reach the shore and dissipate into shimmering specks. A flowing mist covers the sand, enhancing the moon's glow. The ocean dances with the illumination.

Salessa sits speechless, absorbing an experience so breathtaking for her, and inconceivable for MoonSidians.

"I found this weeks ago," Zakia says. "I didn't have anyone to share it with. No one on the team would appreciate it, but something told me you would."

Salessa's gaze breaks away from the scene and finds Zakia's eyes. Her breath fails her, moved by Zakia's desire to share something so special with her. After everything they've told one another, after the ways in which they've bared themselves, Salessa feels an undeniable intimacy toward the pixie.

Her gaze travels down from Zakia's eyes to her soft lips. Staring at them sends a shiver of desire through Salessa's veins. She feels something tugging her closer, but a name abruptly enters her mind, spoken in Naina's voice.

Lexona.

The last person Salessa kissed was Lexona, two years prior, only an hour before the twins found her betraying their trust. The memory tears all desire for a physical connection away from Salessa.

But, then again, Zakia isn't Lexona. There is a warm understanding between them, and if there is anyone with whom she could share her truth, it would be someone with whom she has rapport—someone who has equally shared their truth. Something Lexona never did in the time they were together.

Naina is definitely going to kill me.

"Zakia, there's something I'd like to talk to you about."

The pixie raises a curious eyebrow. "Alright."

Salessa takes a deep breath to steady the growing uneasiness in her stomach. This could very well be the Lexona situation all over again. But as she takes in Zakia's empathetic eyes, Salessa's uneasiness dissipates and she knows, somehow, that this will be different.

"This isn't something Naina and I discuss openly, but I feel comfortable telling you."

Zakia nods. "I'm listening."

"It likely may not even mean anything to you. How much do you know about Doruh mythology?"

Zakia's brows furrow as she tries to make sense of the inquiry. "That's a broad question, but, as I said before, I've spent time in the Doruh districts of Larso. I know of the Twins and a little of their history."

"And the prophecy?"

"The resurrection prophecy?"

Salessa's heart races. Her fingers tremble and beads of sweat break onto her forehead. *She knows. Naina was right, this isn't a good idea.*

It's too late. Zakia's eyes widen as realization trickles into her mind. "Are you saying…"

Salessa swallows hard as the open truth lingers in the air. Slowly, she nods.

"The prophecy is true, Zakia. Two sets of Doruh twins will merge, physically and spiritually, to bring the divine Twins back to life and prevent catastrophe. And those four Doruh, the two set of twins, will be recognized when they shift into four different animals."

"Which is," Zakia adds, "otherwise genetically impossible for Doruh twins, correct?"

"Correct," Salessa confirms.

Zakia's eyes widen further and Salessa worries her grays might pop out. "You're not a wolf, are you?"

Slowly, Salessa shakes her head. "I'm a falcon."

Zakia pauses and looks away, processing and organizing a number of thoughts at once. Salessa waits anxiously until the pixie turns back and speaks one aloud. "And that's why the Facilitator is hunting you."

"We don't know for certain, but yes, we think he's hunting us because he wants to control whichever Twin we will resurrect. Either that, or he wants access to the abilities the Twins have granted us."

Zakia leans forward, intrigued. "What abilities?"

"Naina and I have a telepathic connection. We're also stronger and faster than other Doruh. And we heal far quicker."

Zakia's volume drops until it's barely above a whisper. "You're a goddess."

Salessa laughs. "Technically, I'm half of a goddess. Who won't be resurrected until Naina and I"—she pauses, feeling an unfamiliar discomfort with saying the word aloud—"merge."

"What does that entail?" Zakia asks with a frown. "Will you cease being Salessa?"

Salessa's heart flutters seeing the genuine concern painted on Zakia's expression. "I don't know anything. How or when it'll happen, who the other twins are, whether or not they've merged yet."

"Perhaps they're in hiding, as well," Zakia suggests.

Salessa shrugs. "It's possible. This isn't something Naina and I tell people freely, and I don't think they would either. And it's why I avoid shifting. Naina has to, for her employment, so I let people assume I'm a wolf, too."

"Because if any Doruh found out you shift into different animals, they would know you're one of the twin pairs who are named in the prophecy."

Salessa nods. "Exactly. They would know we're meant to resurrect one of the Twin deities and that likely means the other pair is out there somewhere as well."

They sit quietly together for a few moments. Zakia continues to stare out at the vast ocean, and Salessa wonders if the revelation will affect the way Zakia sees and treats her.

"I'm still just a chaitender from a small village in MoonSide," Salessa breaks the silence. "Nothing's changed."

"Some things have changed." Zakia locks her eyes with Salessa's. "When all of this is over, maybe I can come to your village and you can make a cup of chai for me."

A warmth ignites in Salessa's core. "I would love that."

They break eye contact and sit quietly again, on a branch beneath the forest's canopy, with the starlight evaporating around them. As they watch the suns rise on a new day.

CHAPTER 29

How She Lived

The Agrarian Townlets *Innkeeper's Ranch*
Date *20th Day of Month 6, Year 1628 DG*

"INNKEEPER'S RANCH," KYOKO SAYS, READING the
label on the map. "Creative."

Rafael looks to the horizon to find Frona's final rays depart-
ing for the night. "I'm glad we made it by nightfall. Crossing the
Townlets was...eventful."

Kyoko agrees. "It was, indeed."

Rafael scans her face and the exposed skin of her forearms, noting
the faint transparence of the blood stains.

Casual conversation and friendly banter continues all the way to
Innkeeper's Ranch. This is the most time he's spent with a member of
her clan, and with his most painful thoughts pushed to the back of his
mind, he's been mostly successful in seeing through the stains to the
human beneath.

Amma's guidance lives on in his thoughts. *Stop turning away from
your pain and suffering. Face it, address it...She is not all of the igni.*

The village is more crowded than Rafael expected. Villagers should be seated at the dinner table, enjoying their nightly meals together; instead, they stand in the front yards of their homes, parents and children alike, watching a caravan of ore carts roll through.

Legions of Bravers sit tightly packed into them.

A young Mega child holding a slip of paper passes by, and Rafael asks to see it. The child glances at Rafael's piscine nares and forearm fins, then hesitantly hands the paper over.

"Just as the farmer mentioned," Kyoko says, as Rafael holds it out so they can both read from it. "The MegaFather's recruiting."

"For what purpose?"

She shrugs. "We should report this back to Alba and the Library, if for no other reason than proper recording." She turns to the young child. "Is it alright if we keep this?"

The child nods and walks away. Kyoko places the paper into her bag and they continue on until they find the inn at the center of the town.

Before Rafael can reach for the door, Kyoko stops him. "You were right, when you said we should save our stones for the journey ahead. I have an idea."

"Alright," Rafael responds, intrigued. "What's the plan?"

"Give me your things, then put your arm around my shoulders and follow my lead. Drag your feet and look...sickly."

Rafael hesitates, but ultimately trusts Kyoko's guidance. He hands her his travel bag with his bow strapped to it, and places an arm around her shoulders. As they enter, he begins to drag his feet.

To his surprise, though she is shorter than him, Kyoko carries his weight and his items effortlessly.

"Somebody help!" she yells.

Rafael allows his eyes to droop, and his jaw to hang slack. *I could've been an actor.*

They reach the front counter by the entrance and Kyoko assists Rafael in leaning on it. He contorts his expression as if he's in magnificent pain.

The sound of hustling feet is followed by the arrival of the indigo-skinned innkeeper from a small room behind the counter.

"What's wrong?" he asks as he examines Rafael.

"We need water!" Kyoko exclaims. "Quickly!"

"What's happened to him?"

"The heat, obviously! He's mari! He needs water and a room to rest."

The innkeeper raises an eyebrow. "There's only one room available. Will you be paying? Or shall we send the bill to the Prime?"

"Would you rather the Prime come to collect a corpse?" Kyoko retorts.

The innkeeper's eyes widen. "Alright, alright." He shouts through the doorway of the small room behind him. "Bring water! Quickly! And the key to room 104."

He reaches into a desk drawer and withdraws a lined sheet of paper and a pencil. "Allow me to check you in until your water arrives."

He scribbles Kyoko's information onto the paper, and a young Mega appears carrying a jug of water and a glass. She pours it and hands the glass to Rafael, who gulps it down quickly.

"How long have the Bravers been here recruiting?" Kyoko asks the innkeeper as he finishes writing.

Really? Rafael thinks. *Now?*

"They arrived late in the morning," the innkeeper grumbles. "The Ore Monger thinks he can send his goons into town whenever he'd like. He's wasting his time. None of my villagers will go to SunSide and forfeit the Radiance."

"Your villagers?"

The innkeeper nods. "My family has run this inn for generations, and the village was founded around it."

"That explains the name," Kyoko remarks.

The innkeeper places the key to the room on the counter. "There's only one bed in the room. Are you alright with that, or shall I prepare the cot in the stables for one of you?"

The Librarians make eye contact and, for a moment, Rafael worries Kyoko might not be comfortable sharing a bed with him. He opens his mouth to offer to sleep in the stables, but Kyoko responds first.

"We're comfortable sharing the bed."

Despite the lone bed situation, the room is spacious, with a curtained-off section hosting the tub. Shortly after entering the room, Kyoko opens her bag, removes some items, and heads straight for it.

She emerges from beyond the curtain in a yukata, half an hour later. Different from the one she wore the night before, the colors are brighter and the length shorter. The material also appears lighter, more comfortable, as it hugs the igni's curvature.

But it isn't what she's wearing that catches Rafael's eye, it's her flawless face. Not a drop of blood appears on it. The faint crimson is localized now to her fingertips, as if her bath has washed away much of his haunting visions.

Or perhaps Rafael's efforts to separate Kyoko from the trauma her clan has wrought are successful. Their journey has only been smoother because of it. Amma was right.

"I'm done," she says, walking past him and running a towel over her wet hair.

Rafael pulls an outfit out of the travel bag and enters the sectioned bathing area, drawing the curtain behind him. A bucket sits under a long pipe and faucet protruding from the wall, which he uses to fill the tub in the center.

He dips his entire body into the cold water, immersing himself for fifteen minutes at a time, letting his body soak in as much hydration as it can without coming up to the surface. The scar is healing well—at least, the portion of it he can see.

Submerging does more for his emotional and mental health than the physical. It transports him back to a time when he would freely exit the domed cities and villages of SeaBed, into the ocean, swimming up to the land with Joaquina.

It allows him to go home for a short time.

After he dries himself, he hangs the towel loosely on the edge of the tub, then gets dressed and tenderly clasps his sister's bracelet back onto his wrist.

Kyoko lies on the bed with her hands folded over her stomach, her eyes closed. The fieldwork clearly exhausted her. Her enthusiasm for it, despite her inexperience, impressed Rafael.

He considers getting into the bed alongside her, but decides to place his bag on the floor at the foot of the bed and use it as a pillow. Sleep nearly takes him before Kyoko's voice brings him back.

"What are you doing?" she asks, peering off the edge of the bed.

"Trying to sleep," he replies.

Kyoko rolls her eyes. "On the floor?"

"I didn't know if you were comfortable—"

"Bed, now. That's an order."

Rafael nods. "As you wish, boss."

The mari settles into the empty side of the bed, sitting up with his back against the headboard. Kyoko sits the same way next to him, a few inches dividing them.

"You're a fast learner," he says to her.

"Ambassadors have to be," Kyoko responds, "or we'd never make it through the trials." She turns to the yellow silk tunic lying over the top of her bag on the floor. "I suppose I don't have to worry about the trials anymore. We have the yellow silk, we just have to earn it."

"I'm not sure how we'll do that." Rafael's tone betrays his despondence. "The TreeKeeper is a myth—a children's tale. The mission is a fool's errand."

Kyoko solemnly looks down at her hands. "We just have to finish. To Tusa and back. And in the meantime, we can make the most of the journey." She turns and smiles. "Like we did with suikawari."

Her eyes widen and she turns her entire body toward him. "I know another game we can play! Give me your hands."

Rafael silently appreciates Kyoko's youthful excitement and turns to face her. He places his hands in hers, palms up toward the ceiling, and she describes a hand game she often played with her sister when they were growing up.

He pays close attention to her instructions as they play.

"You're a fast learner, yourself," she remarks.

Interlocking fingers and meeting palms bring their hands warmly together. Rafael is still in awe of the softness of her stone exoskeleton. His eyes dart back and forth from her hands to her smile. There's beauty in her happiness. It's magic he can't explain, watching people do the things that breathe life into them.

The game continues, and recognition sets in. Rafael's hands trace memorized patterns and he loses focus entirely. Deep, buried memories take hold of his muscles and like a wave, it hits him.

He's played this game many times before.

A loud thump echoes throughout the room as his heart beats out of his chest. The mingling fingers hold his attention. The pattern, and the ease with which his muscles have remembered, slaps him so hard there's physical pain in every cell of his body. Caged memories release from the depths at which they were imprisoned, reminding him that this was Joaquina's favorite game.

And he's playing it with an igni.

Igni. The word reverberates around his mind. Shimmering exo-skeleton reflects light so harshly that it pierces his eyeballs. Joaquina's bracelet shines daggers into his pupils.

Tears begin to well. He blinks quickly, trying to void them, but they grow until they break free and trample down his cheek. One falls from his chin and lands on a blue gem.

"Rafael, what's wrong?" comes Kyoko's voice. Her hands stop the game and she grabs his fingers tightly. Slowly, he turns his moist eyes up to her face, and through the haze of anguish, he finds blood.

Not only does it drip out of her eyes and ears and nose, it fills the gaps between her teeth and travels like veins down her neck and chest. It oozes from festering wounds that have erupted along her exoskeleton. It travels from her fingers onto his, staining him with red fingerprints.

Rafael's body involuntarily reacts to the sudden vision. "Fuck!" He falls backward off the bed and onto the floor.

Kyoko peers over the side. Joaquina's blood drips off her face and nearly lands on Rafael. He quickly begins to crawl backward.

"Rafael?!" she exclaims, her voice growing deeper, demonic. "What's wrong?"

He continues until his back hits the wall below the windowsill. "Just stay away from me." He covers his ears.

She joins him on the ground. "Rafael, breathe. This is exactly what you did last night." Her tone hardens and her frustration is clear. "What's happening to you?"

Rafael balls his fists and violently rubs his eyes with them, hoping the vision will evaporate when he removes them. He pulls his fists away and...

It works. Kyoko sits before him, the purity of her skin bringing him momentary relief, until Blood Kyoko returns and his heart drops again.

"Talk to me, Rafael," the demon demands through red, rotting teeth.

Tears flow harder now, as Rafael's throat tightens and closes up. He tries to speak, but his voice is strained and hoarse. His words stumble between ragged gasps. "H-Her blood. I c-can see her blood."

Kyoko's brow furrows. "Whose blood?"

"M-my sister's. She was killed in battle, and then I saw her co-corpse when they brought her back." A sob erupts as pain stabs his stomach. "I can't get it out of my head. The igni did that to her."

The blood vanishes. He's sitting again with the Kyoko he's gotten to know over two days. This Kyoko is a balm between the suffering. Her eyebrows rise.

"I'm sorry, Rafael," she says, her tone harder than the words. "But it was war. You can't judge an entire nation on the actions of its soldiers or its government."

The blood drips again, and Balm Kyoko dissolves into crimson.

"It was an igni blade," he musters out through a tight throat.

"But I didn't swing it," Kyoko spits harshly. "Warmongers profited from it; politicians incited it. But citizens were dragged through the same mud your sister was."

Rafael shakes his head and caresses the blue gems on the bracelet. "Sh-she shouldn't have b-been out there."

Kyoko's tone finally softens. "Your sister made a choice. A brave choice, but one of her own volition."

"Y-you don't understand," Rafael snivels through a torrent of sobs. "She wasn't c-called. I was."

Kyoko's eyes widen and her jaw hangs slack.

Nausea grows in Rafael's bowels. Joaquina's bloody, torn corpse appears at his feet. His hands rise to his head and he tugs his hair out, follicle by follicle.

As he gazes upon the dead sibling at his feet, with her bracelet on his wrist, the truth emerges from the darkest depths of his heart for the first time in eight years. The undeniable fact that Kyoko is right; he is holding the wrong people responsible.

No one is to blame for Joaquina's death but himself.

The words that he's never before had the strength to utter appear on his tongue. He tries to fight them back, but they claw his lips open. His skin pales to the sickly color of death.

"It's my fault." Hot bile rises into his throat and he swallows it back down. He releases one more sob before whispering the truth again. "She's dead because of me, Kyoko. It's not the igni's fault. It's mine."

Clutching his agonized abdomen, he weeps and allows the imprisoned guilt to flow freely. Impossibly, he feels both lighter and heavier, simultaneously.

Blood Kyoko vanishes, and his companion returns. The Librarian and friend whose persistent challenging freed the truth.

But Joaquina's blood hasn't evaporated. His gaze travels to his hands and he realizes it has simply moved to where it belongs. The mari slowly rises onto his knees and turns around, taking a long look at his reflection in the window.

The demon stares back at him.

"What do you mean," Kyoko questions, "she's dead because of you?"

He drops back to the ground and wipes his cheeks. "She-she wasn't called to the war. She w-went..." His voice still trembles, as he defeatedly struggles to form an explanation. "I don't think I can talk about her death anymore."

Kyoko pauses. Her eyebrows furrow for a moment and then rise. "Her death is all you've talked about for eight years, isn't it?"

Realization registers.

She's right.

In eight years, all he's ever talked about was her death.

"Don't tell me how she died, Rafael. Tell me how she lived. Keep her legacy alive."

He feels a sense of ease he lost the day he was exiled, brought back by the idea that he can still keep her alive in some way.

When he looks down at the ground, the torn corpse is gone. Warm, affectionate fingers caress his cheek, and he finds his beautiful sister sitting by him. No blood, no pain, no suffering. She's smiling.

"What are you feeling?" Kyoko probes.

Rafael closes his eyes, holding the pristine image of Joaquina in his mind. "Love."

"Then use your love, Rafael."

The words of Adera's Headwoman surface in his ears. *When you feel the Radiance approaching, promise me, you'll allow it to carry you.*

The words flow from Rafael effortlessly.

"She was two years older than me. We didn't get along when we were young, but that changed when I was around ten. I was injured during an archery lesson and salvers said I'd never shoot an arrow again, but after I had recovered, she put a bow in my hand and proved them wrong."

The memories appear in his mind like lost images found again. Rafael holding a bow with a nocked arrow, Joaquina behind him, whispering instructions. She's taller than him, and lighter in the olive tone of her skin. Her eyes are a golden brown and her chestnut hair is cut just under her earlobes. The fins on her forearms are exactly as Rafael remembers them, sharper and longer than his.

"I used to call her 'blade-arms.' She hated it, because she was self-conscious about how sharp they were."

Heat rises to Rafael's face and burns his cheeks. His throat begins to tighten again, so he clears it and continues, keeping his eyes closed still.

"She taught me how to be good to others. Through her example, I learned the importance of service, something she lived by."

"From what you've told me, I can tell she was special."

He smiles. "'Special' doesn't even begin to describe her. She taught me empathy, respect, sacrifice. I've never been religious, never believed in a higher power. I'd never had a reason to, having already seen an entirely benevolent being with my own two eyes."

The heat begins to spread from his face to Rafael's entire body. His heart starts to race as if he's panicked, but he feels a strange tranquility he's never experienced before.

Eyes still closed, all sounds and feelings become faint, and he starts to float as if he's being transported on a cloud. Buzzing energy, like small sparks on his skin, covers and soothes him.

When you feel the Radiance approaching, promise me, you'll allow it to carry you.

He gives in to the floating, to the buzzing energy. A mighty gust of wind forces him upright and he shields his face with his arms. His eyes pop open and he sees he's not in the inn anymore.

The darkness of an abyss engulfs him, a black void. He tries to speak, but the words don't emerge from his throat, they project from his mind.

Where am I?

Rafael? A voice echoes throughout the abyss. He recognizes it immediately and the sparks on his skin ignite.

Joaquina?

It's me, Rafa, her voice responds.

You're alive?

I'm not.

His heart sinks. *Where are you?*

There isn't much time. The voice begins to fade, as if she is walking away from him. *The connection is weak. You must come find me.*

Find you? He twirls desperately, trying to get closer to the failing echo. *Where are you, Joaquina?*

I'll see you soon. I love you.

I don't know where you are. What is this place?

The voice whispers, *You are with the Radiance now,* and vanishes.

The wind gusts violently again and when it dies, Rafael sits up, in the inn again. Kyoko squeezes his hand.

"What happened?" she asks, concern in her voice and expression. "You stopped talking and slumped back against the wall for a few seconds."

Rafael sits up and tries to steady his racing heart. Nothing remains of the experience but the buzzing sparks on his skin.

"I let the Radiance carry me," he says.

Kyoko releases Rafael's hand and cocks her head. "Carry you where?"

Rafael looks at his pulsating palms. "I don't know how to explain it. I feel"—he holds his hands out, toward her—"something."

"What does it feel like?"

Rafael attempts to describe it. "Energy. Sparks."

"Is it Radiant energy?"

Rafael lifts his gaze and looks around the room. There isn't much nearby but the bed, their strewn belongings, and the bathing area sectioned off by the curtain.

The curtain. Rafael raises his hands, focusing on the buzzing and attempting to project it from his palm like an arrow. His hand balls into a fist and he pulls it toward his body, hoping to tear the curtain off its rings.

The energy visibly dissipates into the air as a cloud of green light. He feels the release from all over his body, like the ripples of a lake after a stone lands on the surface. He breathes deeply, fending off nausea.

The curtain remains untouched, unmoved, unchanged.

"Nothing happened," he says, the dejection clear in his tone.

"Are you sure it was the Radiance?" Kyoko asks him.

He isn't sure what he experienced, but he is sure that, after all he's said and done, Kyoko is still sitting by him.

"I'm sorry," he whispers. "For everything."

Kyoko hesitates to respond, a cold distance in her eyes.

He doesn't blame her.

"We should try to sleep," she suggests. "We reach EverEmber tomorrow."

Long after she's gone to sleep, Rafael is awake, staring at the curtain, wondering how an experience so profound could be so inconsequential. That thought lingers until his gaze moves past the curtain to the towel lying on the ground.

The one he had hung on the edge of the tub.

CHAPTER 30

PARASITES

Theocratic-Monarchy *SunSide*
Date *21st Day of Month 6, Year 1628 DG*

THROUGH THE TREATED GLASS OF the window wall, Ona and Lona surpass the horizon, bringing fresh morning light into the world.

Saith holds a small blue book in his hands and blinks rhythmically at the blank pages. With every blink, words travel from his thoughts and appear in ink, completing the MegaFather's schedule.

Zar-Lo slumps on the ore chair behind his desk, his thick hand covering his eyelids.

Saith closes the small book and slowly begins to walk toward him. "How frequent are they now?"

Zar-Lo moves his hands from his eyes and slowly straightens up in the chair. "Fairly constant."

"I'm sorry, Father."

"I'm not," Zar-Lo responds. "I'll endure the pain as long as the ancient ones maintain patience."

Saith reaches the platform and ascends the stairs. "What happens when they lose it?"

"The headaches subside. Their voices become clear. They demand the sacrificial offering in person."

"Has that happened before?"

Zar-Lo shakes his head. "I have never, and will never, let that happen. If they arrive at my doorstep, no one will survive. The only thing standing between this world and annihilation"—he turns to gaze at his kingdom through the window wall—"is me."

"They will have their sacrifice, Father. I'll begin production of the changeling at once."

Zar-Lo turns back to Saith. "How do you expect to do so without the girls?"

"We're close to finding them. Nivyan Hollow is not vast enough to provide refuge for longer than a few days. Bravers swarm new forest communities daily."

The doors of the Theater swing open forcefully and Vy-Ro, sweating profusely, rushes in. His weapons clang erratically against his ore armor. He quickly makes a circle with his fingers and throws it loosely up against his forehead.

"Quite the intrusion," Saith admonishes as they watch Vy-Ro approach. "Entering the Theater without a knock."

"I assure you," Vy-Ro gasps, trying to catch his breath, "this cannot wait for a knock. Alba and another Librarian were seen in a small village at the outskirts of MoonSide yesterday. They spent the night there and will be journeying to SunSide this morning."

Zar-Lo's spine stiffens. The Librarian's timing couldn't be worse. He turns to Saith, whose expression contorts with concern. "If Alba reaches SunSide, you know where she'll go first."

Saith nods. "Saila."

The MegaFather's heart drops into his stomach. "Are you confident your offspring will keep the contents of the Final Act to herself?"

"Saila was born unpredictable, rebellious. She'll honor her word and announce it to the general public after the interim, but to her closest friend?" He sighs. "Unlikely."

"Then Alba must be stopped. She cannot find out about the Assembly's plans."

Saith's brow furrows. "How can I stop her without violating the statutes that protect her from detention?"

Zar-Lo's gaze travels down to Saith's shoulder, and back to his eyes again. The implication of the gesture emerges on the Facilitator's expression. The pixie's words from the night of the reading hang in the space between them.

I will do anything you ask. I can prove myself.

"Do anything, Saith. You have to persuade her to turn back. She can't be detained, but she can be deterred."

"She's crossed the Red-Lo, Father; she's likely been traveling for two days. It won't be easy to persuade her to forfeit that journey."

Zar-Lo's tone hardens as his frustration builds. "Saith, you have to do this. Your daughter is about to implicate me in her assassination two nights before it happens."

"F-father," Vy-Ro stammers out.

Zar-Lo unsuccessfully attempts to temper his rage. "What?!" His voice booms around the room so powerfully, the heavy ore desk rattles before him.

Vy-Ro clears his throat. "Not two nights. Tonight. When you gave me this assignment, you told me 'the sooner, the better.' You wanted breathing room. Well, they're ready. Now."

Zar-Lo turns back to Saith. "Alba will be in SunSide during the assassinations."

"After meeting with Saila," Saith responds, "she'll retire to the diplomat's chambers in the Castrum. When the havoc breaks with the dawn, she'll be protected within our walls."

"But her finger will be raised in my direction."

"Perhaps we should delay the assassinations until she leaves."

Zar-Lo strokes his chin, considering the idea, but the harsh truth sets in. "Delaying is futile. In three days, the Assembly announces my deposition. The assassinations must be done before then, and no Librarian has ever stayed for shorter than three days."

Vy-Ro clears his throat. It takes everything in Zar-Lo's power not to launch the desk at him.

"Forgive my audacity," he begins cautiously, "but if the Facilitator is unsuccessful and Alba reaches SunSide, we could"—he pauses—"dispatch a team for her, as well."

There's a long, tense silence as Zar-Lo tries to process the obtuse suggestion.

"Vy-Ro, I don't have time to elucidate the stupidity of that proposal, but I will say this: we cannot have Librarian blood spilled on our soil. The Prime won't respond well when his most prized disciple doesn't return from my kingdom."

"Beyond that," Saith adds, "Alba is the most lethal Librarian to ever leave the city. And she isn't alone. Two nights ago, you were hesitant to prepare for nine assassinations. Suddenly you're prepared for eleven?" He scoffs. "Stupid doesn't even begin to describe it."

Vy-Ro closes his lips and hangs his head, while the MegaFather turns to the Facilitator again. "There's only one option, Saith. You have to persuade her to turn back."

Saith nods, hesitantly. "It will be done."

He steps around the desk and descends the platform to where Vy-Ro stands, placing the small blue book into the Braver General's hands.

"What is this?" Vy-Ro asks.

"The MegaFather's schedule. Congratulations, you're promoted to Facilitator until I return. Delegate your tasks to your Legion Directors."

Vy-Ro's eyebrows scrunch together. "I don't know how to do your job."

Saith growls with exasperation. He points to the MegaFather. "Anything he wants, he gets. That's my job." He taps the book in Vy-Ro's palm. "Make sure he attends all meetings and doesn't miss a meal."

Before Vy-Ro can respond further, Saith marches to the window wall, uses the Radiance to phase through it, and disappears off of the side of the tower, leaving Vy-Ro and the MegaFather in tense silence.

Vy-Ro begins to flip through the book, mumbling, "What's first on the MegaFather's schedule?"

"I can tell you that," Zar-Lo interrupts him with an eager smile. "Breakfast."

Vy-Ro nods and, almost eagerly, departs the room, returning an hour later with Castrum cooks. The chefs wheel in three long tables covered in trays of delicious items.

Zar-Lo waves his hand to dismiss the cooks once the final table has been wheeled into the Theater and set up. Before him sits roasted boar, frog legs, soups and stews made with chicken, larks and quail, four different types of bread, and two large hills of cheeses.

Vy-Ro sees the meal, prompting a violent roar in his gut. Zar-Lo ignores it and uses a long boning knife to carve the boar.

"Explain your plan for tonight," the MegaFather commands as he packs heavy meat and slices of bread into his mouth at once.

"We have one team of Bravers per Member," Vy-Ro responds obediently. "Each team is set to arrive at midnight, and the assignments should be complete shortly thereafter."

"How many Bravers on each team?" Zar-Lo dips a thick wedge of cheese into the stew and shoves it into his mouth.

"There are two elderly Members, who will only require two Bravers each. Then, there are four faeries Members, who each have limited combat training. There will be three Bravers on each of their teams."

"Alright. The two nymphs?"

"Each has combat experience. There will be five Bravers on their teams."

Zar-Lo eructates loudly and wipes his mouth clean. "That leaves Saila. The lone pixie. Surely you've prepared a team of more than five for her."

"Indeed, Father. Twelve."

"Thirteen," Zar-Lo corrects him.

Vy-Ro's eyebrows meet. "Thirteen?"

"Yes, Vy-Ro. Thirteen. You'll be there as well."

Vy-Ro hesitates, processing the instruction. "Please accept my apologies, Father, I don't mean to question you, but I'll be coordinating and supervising all nine assassinations."

"Eight will be executed flawlessly, I'm certain of that. None of us has observed Saila threatened. You *will* be there to personally see to our success."

Vy-Ro swallows hard. "As you command."

"Indeed. As I command." Zar-Lo stands and finishes cleaning his hands and face. "And the aftermath?"

"Recruitment pamphlets have been distributed throughout the continent. By afternoon tomorrow, new recruits will arrive to deal with any undesirable consequences."

Zar-Lo nods. "Very good. When is my next meeting?"

Vy-Ro finds the schedule, then peers out at the positions of the suns. "In an hour."

"Get the cooks to remove the tables," Zar-Lo responds. "Then send for Saimiza."

The Braver General hurriedly looks through the book again. "The Head Salver isn't on the schedule today, Father."

"What did Saith say before he left? Anything I want, I get." He lifts his fingers and massages his temples. "I want Saimiza."

The clack of Saimiza's cane echoes throughout the Castrum as she hobbles up onto the platform, after her arrival an hour later.

Standing across the ore desk, she looks around the room, curiously. "It's been many years since my nephew has not been at your side. Where has he gone?"

Zar-Lo sits in his seat and rests his elbows on the desk, his fingers still massaging his temples. "He's been sent away on urgent matters."

"Oh?" Saimiza responds. She looks suspiciously at Vy-Ro, hovering at the bottom of the platform, then back at the MegaFather. "Then to what do I owe the honor of your summons, Father, if my patient is not here?"

"I'm your patient today," Zar-Lo grumbles. "I'm having some latent energy ailment."

Saimiza narrows her eyebrows. "What energy issues can plague a faerie?"

Zar-Lo chooses his words carefully. "It's a foreign energy."

"Foreign?" The word drips out of Saimiza's mouth with incredulity.

"Yes. Foreign." Frustration mounts under throbbing temples.

"I'm afraid I don't know what you mean by 'foreign.' I can't treat you if I don't know what's ailing you."

Zar-Lo sighs, his irritation apparent. He lifts his head from his hands. "Treat it the way you would Negative Radiance Infection. I've been infected by a foreign energy that was dormant for many years and has suddenly emerged. It's a parasite. Try to get it out of me or force it back into dormancy. Is that enough information?"

Saimiza hesitates, but she nods nonetheless. "Yes, Father. I think I understand." She moves around the desk and stands behind him.

Zar-Lo leans his head back until it's resting over the back of the chair.

Saimiza places her fingertips on his temples. The hum of the Radiance pulses on his skin. "Relax, Father. Your tension is blocking my access."

"I'm trying," he mumbles, closing his eyes. After a few deep breaths, he relaxes.

Saimiza closes hers as well, applying more Radiant energy and linking herself directly to the Megafather's inner thoughts and emotions—his feelings, ideas, fears, regrets.

She finds no happiness or comfort in him. There's some distant anguish, some terrible loss. But mostly, she finds ages of fatigue. A despondent weariness of life and a bleak yearning for death.

A scream rings out in his memories—a voice begging for salvation.

"Who is screaming?" she asks.

"Ignore her," Zar-Lo responds. "Her suffering will fade with the parasites."

Images flash before Saimiza's eyes.

Dark images. Shadows. Flames. Blood. Water. Caverns.

She feels textures, smells nasty scents. Heat. Moisture. Sweat. Feces.

She hears sounds. More screams. Laughter. Retching. Explosions.

Two figures appear. Not Mega. Not Human. Not Doruh.

"There they are," Zar-Lo says. "The parasites."

"What are they?" Saimiza asks in horror.

Nausea grows. From the sounds to the scents to the textures, she wants to end it and tries to pull her fingertips off of Zar-Lo's head.

The MegaFather's hands shoot up and grab her wrists, pulling her fingers back to his temples.

"You will continue," he says forcefully.

"I-I can't," she stammers. Her throat becomes tight as she struggles to breathe.

"Fight them!"

"What are they?" Saimiza repeats. Two figures, cloaked in shadows. She can't see any defining features. Just silhouettes. Maybe wings.

"They're hiding," Zar-Lo says. "Seek them out and remove them, or force them back under."

"Zar-Lo, I can't k-keep it u-up."

She ages. Her wrinkles intensify, her fingers melt into nothing more than bone. She tries to pull back again, but Zar-Lo holds her wrists firmly.

"Please, Zar-Lo," she begs, "I'll d-die." Her eyeballs rot, and her scalp releases hair. Her teeth shrivel down to a quarter of their size.

"What is happening to her?" Vy-Ro yells.

"They're fighting back," Zar-Lo replies, "and they're winning."

"Who is fighting back?" Vy-Ro asks.

Zar-Lo holds Saimiza's skeletal hands to his head until suddenly the Radiant energy stops coming. The sounds and smells and textures fade away. His headache resumes.

She failed.

Zar-Lo releases her wrists and hears a thud behind him. He takes a few deep breaths to collect himself, then stands and turns.

Behind his chair, Saimiza's body has fallen off the platform and onto the Theater floor. She is smaller than when she came in, curled up into a fetal position. Her body is far more wrinkled, and most of her hair has fallen out. Her teeth are nearly gone and her expression is stuck permanently in a state of horror.

Zar-Lo steps off the platform and kneels next to her body. He places a hand on her weak shoulder.

"You did well," Zar-Lo says softly near her decrepit ear. "I had hoped your bond to the Radiance would be strong enough to withstand the might of the ancient ones, but"—he sighs—"it's time to rest now. Your service to this dynasty is complete."

He rises and looks at Vy-Ro. "Call the salvers. Have them clean this mess up and prepare her for Radiance-Return."

He turns back to the wasted corpse and shakes his head. "Saith will not be pleased."

Following the cleansing of the Theater and the removal of the Head Salver's corpse, the MegaFather welcomes an afternoon of arid meetings. The only item on his schedule of any interest is an appointment with the hover chariots' Chief Engineer, a peculiar but brilliant faerie.

The MegaFather and the Engineer review three potential new designs for the next model of the chariot, before Zar-Lo selects one and the Engineer sets out for the Panaerth ore processing center to deliver the new plans.

As the suns start to reach the horizon and night approaches, the MegaFather stares out at the mountains surrounding the Pass, wondering how his Facilitator must be faring in his mission.

The Theater doors fly open, abruptly interrupting his thoughts. Vy-Ro, standing at the foot of the platform, withdraws two swords from their sheaths.

One of the Castrum's caretakers stands at the door, frantically catching her breath.

"Father," she says, "I beg forgiveness for my uninvited presence."

"Forgiveness lies at the root of the offense," Zar-Lo responds, plainly. "What brings you into my Theater so impolitely?"

"There is a human downstairs in the atrium. The Courtman of EverEmber. He shouts vile slander against you and demands to meet with you."

"Tomohiro," Zar-Lo growls. He turns to Vy-Ro. "I thought he was warned not to step foot on SunSide's soil again."

"He was," Vy-Ro confirms.

"Then it appears he does not value his life." He turns back to the caretaker. "You're forgiven. Send him up."

The caretaker nods and exits.

"Do me a favor, Vy-Ro," the MegaFather says as they wait for the Courtman's arrival. "Keep the human's tongue wagging. Distracted."

Vy-Ro nods. "As you command."

The igni man bursts through the doors, red and swollen with rage. "You filth!" he screams as he charges into the room. "You absolute filth."

"Welcome, Courtman," Zar-Lo responds with a smile. "What seems to be the problem?"

"Where is my family? What have you done with them?" Venom drips from the accusations.

"Absolutely nothing." Zar-Lo feigns innocence, though Saith has briefed him on the fate of the Courtman's loved ones. "As far as I'm aware, they're still perfectly safe on Lily Beach."

"I went there!" Tomohiro screams. "Nobody has seen them."

"Courtman, I have to ask you to reduce your volume," Zar-Lo says, coolly.

"I don't care! Everyone will know what is truly going on at Lily Beach." Tomohiro edges closer to the platform, but stops when he sees Vy-Ro step forward, sword in hand.

He continues speaking with a strained voice. "I want the world to know it was *you*! You came to *me* and offered me Lily Beach. *You* wanted anonymity and a Braver presence there. And I gave it to you. I trusted you and ended the war with SeaBed. I gave up Bibi Sands for *you*, not knowing what you were planning for Lily Beach."

He releases a soft, broken whimper. "I didn't know you were going to use it as your own personal slaughterhouse."

Zar-Lo gets up from his seat and tilts his head to Vy-Ro, gesturing to the ore chair. Vy-Ro sits as the MegaFather drops off of the platform, without using the stairs.

"It would help if you relaxed, Courtman," Vy-Ro says. "Please, take a seat." He points to the seat across from Zar-Lo's on the other side of the desk.

"I don't want to sit. I want to know where my family is."

"I will be happy to explain," Vy-Ro responds. "But only when you're sitting calmly. The Bravers keep organized records of our activities on the island, and I can locate your family in a heartbeat. Please join me."

Tomohiro stares at Vy-Ro, hesitating. Cautiously, desperately, he steps forward and ascends the platform to the desk.

Once he is seated, the MegaFather quietly steps up onto the platform again behind him.

"Excellent," Vy-Ro says. "When was the last time you spoke to your family?"

Before Tomohiro can respond, Zar-Lo's massive hand lands on top of his head, pushing down. Startled and frightened, the Courtman screams and violently thrashes Zar-Lo's hand, to no avail.

"No, no, *noooo!*" Courtman Tomohiro screams. "LET ME GO!"

His demands become visceral, primal pleas for mercy, but the MegaFather has no intention of obliging. He swiftly jabs Tomohiro in the back of the neck with his free fist, directly on the spine. Dark, gooey blood spurts from the igni's mouth and his arms go limp.

The human sobs as Zar-Lo wraps his fingers around a portion of Tomohiro's spine that has come exposed through the igni exoskeleton. Tomohiro's cries dampen from the blood filling his throat. Zar-Lo feels him losing the ability to breathe and function, feels the life fading away.

One strong pull is all it takes for Zar-Lo to tug the human's spine out. Vertebra after vertebra pops out of the stone exoskeleton from within, all the way down his back. Tomohiro vomits blood and bile on himself, the desk, and the astonished Braver General.

Blood and gelatinous inner flesh spray out of his back with the spine. Zar-Lo holds his trophy delicately, admiring it. Courtman Tomohiro's limp body drops off the chair and onto the ground in a pool of his own fluid, innards, and shredded exoskeleton.

"What..." Vy-Ro can barely form the words. "What have you done?"

"I attempted to draw blood from stone." He holds up the spine. "And I was successful."

"How? How did you break through an igni exoskeleton with your bare hands? Faeries can't do that."

"This one can," Zar-Lo responds, placing the spine gingerly onto the desk. "Those parasites aren't the only ones who benefit from our relationship."

CHAPTER 31

ONWARD TO SUNSIDE

Occupied Territory *MoonSide*
Date *21st Day of Month 6, Year 1628 DG*

A NEW DREAM TAKES FORM — NOT one that remembers the past, one that examines the future.

Unisa stands at the gates of the Library, wearing the black tunic. She smiles widely at tight, ore cages filled with Doruh children, including the boy from yesterday.

Her lips part and Alba's voice erupts from her throat, stating, "Welcome to the Library."

She jolts awake. Sweat charges down her temple, her heart racing. Deep breaths settle her pulse as the boy's face evaporates. Alba's harsh words from the night before echo through her ears.

We are all responsible.

Unisa watched a Braver murder him. Alba watched. The world watched and did nothing because of the festering lies. Because everyone believed a dangerous radical was trimmed down before it bloomed, and a valiant warrior was simply doing his job.

Unisa runs her hands over her face and pushes the thoughts from her mind.

Alba's bed lies empty and neatly made. Her bags sit on it, packed and ready. Rolled paper peeks from one, reminding Unisa of Alba's cartophilia.

A short wooden table between the beds holds three plates of food, a note wedged between them: *I had to step out. I'll be back shortly. Have something to eat and be ready to leave by the time I get back. -Alba*

There's an uneasiness in Unisa's core when she reads Alba's name. A loss of respect, and a lack of trust, stemming from the realization that revered Librarians like Alba can look away as an entire species gets slowly strangled into extinction. That they can remain silent as the lower ranks continue to be unwittingly manipulated.

The wafting aromas from the plates of food command her attention, and her mouth begins to water. A sign reads "Alu Paratha" next to a stack of flavorful flatbreads with seasoned potatoes inside. Another plate carries three eggs prepared with runny yolks, and at the center of the table is a cup of masala chai.

Unisa attacks the breakfast. She's experienced traditional Doruh cuisine from the restaurants in the Library, but there's no comparison between roses in a vase and those in a garden.

Before packing up, Unisa oils her braids, letting them drape her shoulders like long black tendrils cascading down the side of a glorious oak. She then wraps them in a tight bun for the journey.

The door creaks open and Alba enters the room, igniting Unisa's uneasiness. The Ambassador's eyes dart down to the empty plates and then to Unisa's packed bags.

"I see you found my note," she says, plainly.

"Where were you?"

"Arranging transportation to PeakHaven Pass. The original schedule was to reach SunSide by nightfall today, and we still may be able to make it."

Taking up their bags, they exit the inn into a crowded MoonSidian marketplace. They pass Sultana's Chai Palace, the tea house outside of which Unisa sat the day before, and the angi notices a sign in the window reading "New Server Needed." It's a reminder that this village of broken homes, depleted resources, and suffering citizens is more than just idle, available land for an occupying force to consume.

It's a community.

Alba leads Unisa through an alley between two buildings and into an open field with a stout stone wall at the far end. Standing at one of the gates built into the wall is a tall wooden buggy.

The back of the buggy is a long cart with short benches along the inside, upon which Unisa counts seven travelers. Some wear shalwar kameez or saris, others are in casual kurtas and loose lounge pants. The travelers huddle together, staying close and quiet, bags at their feet and anxious glares in their eyes.

Unisa follows Alba to the front of the buggy, where three Doruh stand: a man, a woman, and a young boy, who is maybe twelve or thirteen years old. The boy is the only one clothed.

Alba drops a handful of colorful stones into the woman's palm. "Thank you for waiting for us, Diya."

Diya smiles and nods. "Of course, Ambassador. It is our family's honor to assist your journey. My son"—she gestures to the boy—"can help you to your seats."

"That won't be necessary. Do you remember our deal?"

Diya nods again. "You will be in SunSide by nightfall. I will increase our speed and surpass as many stops as needed. The other travelers have been notified."

Alba smiles. "Wonderful, thank you."

The Librarians hoist themselves onto the cart from the rear, and slowly wade through hunched, isolated travelers. They find two seats next to an older woman with her arms wrapped around a young girl. Unisa estimates she is younger than ten.

The angi leans back over the edge of the cart and peers to the front, where Diya and the nude man shift. Their deep golden skin turns into a lighter brown as their necks elongate and sprout manes of thin hairs. Their arms and legs stretch, and the nails on each hand and foot thicken and widen, wrapping around to become sturdy hooves.

Their transformations complete into two massive, majestic horses. Diya's son straps driving harnesses to them, then climbs onto the driver's bench and gently instructs them to move. With an unexpected jerk, the horses pull the buggy and the final leg to SunSide begins, leaving Evic behind.

Buggies aren't built for comfort, but Unisa feels safer as they get further from the Bravers and the occupation. She recognizes the ludicrousness of this feeling—a protected Librarian amongst huddled masses, yearning for freedom. How must they feel, leaving everything behind for an uncertain future?

The buggy winds through narrow paths between fields of farmland. The anxious postures and troubled expressions of the old woman and the young girl next to them remain intact throughout the journey. Despite the distance from Evic, none of the travelers appear to feel at ease.

Unisa continues to thrust her uneasiness with Alba to the back of her mind, but the reverent image she once held of the Ambassador, and all Librarians of her rank, has become stained. Alba periodically sparks conversation, and Unisa tries to maintain cordial banter to hide her feelings.

"Unisa," Alba says after long minutes of tense silence, "I'm sorry for the way in which you discovered the truth, and for the role I played in it."

Unisa's heart sinks. She hadn't realized her body language betrayed her concerns. "Last night was…difficult."

"I know," Alba acknowledges, "but we are still a long way from SunSide. I need to know that you can put what you're feeling aside, and we can address it later. It's the only way I can protect you."

Protect. The word carries Unisa to realization: Alba has *been* protecting her, since before the journey began, and she continues to do so.

Despite their silence, despite their blind eyes, revered Ambassadors were once Gatekeepers and Scribes and Recorders, manipulated all the same. Alba more so than anyone else, having lived a life under the Prime's nose.

And yet she stands against him, freedom in jeopardy, to protect Unisa. The realization banishes her uneasiness. She smiles and nods, allowing her body language to convey her trust.

The farmlands eventually give way to more stone buildings, and settlement walls grow from the landscape. Traveling high on hilltops, Unisa peers into the prosperous communities beyond the walls— endowed with plenty, never having to wait or want for anything.

A stark contrast to their Doruh neighbors.

The Bravers return with the walls, causing the huddled travelers to pray and release rigid breaths. Unisa's concern for their safety mounts.

The buggy comes to a sudden stop and Diya's son turns to address the travelers. "We've reached a checkpoint. Keep your heads down and speak only when spoken to. If you must, speak quickly. We'll be back on the road as soon as possible, with no trouble."

His mature presence of mind is sharply juxtaposed with his age. It's eerie and somewhat sad. *What does this boy know of childhood?*

The travelers follow the boy's instructions. Their heads are down again, their body language consumed by fear. Adults hold tight to their children. Bags are pushed into the center, hoping to be checked quickly and returned, without a word.

Bravers surround the vehicle, and one in a red mask, hood raised over his head, climbs up onto the back of the buggy and begins rummaging through bags violently, dumping out the contents and throwing the empty sacks back down onto the bed of the cart.

The travelers wait for the Braver to move on before they reach down for their unpacked items and gather them into the bags again.

Unisa's blood boils at the scene.

The Braver reaches Alba, Unisa, the old woman, and the young girl. He looks first at the Doruh, then turns to the Librarians and smiles.

"Ambassadors," he says with a serpentine tone. "What brings you to MoonSide in such"—he examines the cart and passengers—"dire transport?"

"Necessity," Alba responds, coolly. "Finish up your checks a little quicker. We're on a schedule."

The Braver's eyes narrow and he reaches down for the old woman's bag, pulling open the drawstring. He seems to be nearly finished when his hand finds something hard and wide at the bottom.

He withdraws a small black case and pops it open. Unisa sees a number of sharp objects inside: little knives, along with a small roll of bandages and some other tools that Unisa doesn't recognize.

"What is this?" the Braver asks angrily.

"My tools," the woman replies, wrapping her arms tighter around the young girl. "I'm a salver."

The Braver looks from the woman to the tools and back up again. He snaps the case shut, then turns and tosses it off the buggy to another Braver standing behind it. "Your tools are being seized."

"No," the woman whimpers. "I need those. I don't have money to buy more. I've spent everything I had to get us to SunSide."

"You're close to Arlun now, and you can't pass through the city with potential weapons."

The woman's tone hardens, but she keeps her volume in control. "I've saved lives with those."

The Braver's hand flies to the back of the woman's head and he grasps a thick handful of her hair, tugging at it. "Watch your tone, animal."

The slur hits every traveler there, and they shudder. The young girl screams and starts to cry. Unisa instinctually pulls the Braver's fingers off the woman's head and pushes him back a step.

"Let go of her!" The words shoot off Unisa's tongue before she can stop them. The involuntary action catches even her by surprise, as her eyes widen and she tightly purses her lips.

There's a long, tense pause as the Braver processes: a Librarian twisted his fingers and shoved him backward. The old woman's jaw hangs open.

The Braver's gaze locks with Unisa. "You just assaulted a Braver."

"I-I'm sorry," Unisa stammers, her voice catching in her throat.

Her heart slams against her chest as the Braver raises his hand again, aiming for Unisa. She's stuck on the bench with nowhere to go. The Braver gets closer until...

It's stopped. Mari fingers grab tightly onto the Braver's wrist and halt it.

"Have you lost your mind, or are you just stupid?" Alba asks the Braver, angrily. "She's a Librarian."

"I don't care," the Braver responds. "She assaulted me. That's a crime."

"Her *crime* was teaching you to use your words, not your hands. You're about to violate intracontinental statutes. Big difference."

The Braver growls. "Her immunity became void the moment she touched me."

Alba's tone is clear and calculated. "That's not how immunity works, you imbecile. Pull your hand back or you're going to lose it."

The Braver scoffs and, with Alba's fingers still tight on his wrist, continues to reach for Unisa. Alba bends the Braver's arm and then jerks it sideways. A loud *crack* resounds, and the Braver stumbles backward, screaming. Alba withdraws the sword from the sheath on the Braver's hip and in one fluid swing, severs his hand at the wrist.

The Braver falls backward off the rear of the carriage as blood sprays from his severed limb. Alba tosses the Braver's sword off the back of the cart and onto the ground.

Standing tall and calm, she turns to another Braver, this one in a blue mask. "Director, the next time an officer tries to touch myself or my colleague, I'll break them into so many pieces, you'll have no idea how to put them back together again. Our immunity *will* be respected, or there will be momentous consequences. We will be neither touched, nor addressed, in a manner that we perceive unfit. Do we have an understanding?"

The Braver in the blue mask stands quietly for a moment, her gaze sizzling, then nods. "We do, Ambassador."

"Good. Let every legion from here to SunSide know. This buggy will not be stopped again until it reaches the Pass. I don't have time to mutilate more of your officers."

She returns to her seat next to Unisa. The travelers hug their belongings and their loved ones tighter than they did before.

Unisa nearly jumps when a hand lands softly on her shoulder. She turns to see Alba, concerned, staring at her.

"Breathe, Unisa," she says. "The color is draining from your face."

The buggy moves, leaving the Bravers and the walls behind once again.

Arlun arrives after hours of watching verdant hills roll by.

"There are so few Bravers here," Unisa notices, as they pass by the Doruh citizens on the city streets.

"Beyond city limits is PeakHaven Pass," Alba explains. "Bravers assigned to Arlun are typically posted at the Pass to monitor the influx of travelers going into SunSide."

Unisa lowers her voice as she speaks, so only Alba can hear her. "Why don't more Doruh settle here? Instead of the occupied villages?"

"This is where the Alphocracy was massacred. Would you feel comfortable living in a place where even your warrior-leaders weren't safe?" She turns to the suns. "We have about an hour and a half until sunsdown. I can't believe it, but they actually got us here before nightfall."

They reach the city limits and traverse a rocky path leading to the Pass. Something catches Unisa's gaze that she hadn't expected to see for many more years.

The PeakHaven mountain range towers over the gates of the Pass. The city of PeakHaven rests atop one of the snow-covered peaks. The place where she was born, and the place where her family still lives.

The family she had always believed had abandoned her. Alba's words spring back up into her ears.

The words of this man you revere so much are the reason you were for-saken. You refuse to believe he would isolate Kanako from her family to take advantage of her. And yet, he did it to you.

Where once she held love for the Prime, she now finds hate. He has been toying with the lives of others since the beginning.

Where the field begins, Diya's son stops the buggy and unhooks the harnesses, allowing his parents to shift back into their human forms. After thanking them, the Librarians continue through the field to join one of the lines leading to the gates.

The field is crawling with Doruh, Mega, and humans. There are far fewer humans than the other two species—a set of wings here, an exoskeleton there, fins elsewhere. And, of course, there are Bravers.

Everywhere.

Stationed in tents or at gates. Waving faerie families through the Pass with a smile, while turning Doruh away in tears. The contrast between the two classes of Bravers is stark: the class of Braver at the CereCenter, playing with children, and the class in Evic, murdering them.

Or, perhaps, the Bravers are the same and it's the environment, the situation, that dictates their class.

As Unisa studies the field, she's alerted to two Bravers standing uncomfortably close to her and Alba. They approach with their hands firmly on the hilts of their weapons. Two more Bravers approach from the other side in the same fashion. It isn't until she makes a complete circle that a stark realization hits her.

They are surrounded.

Unisa taps Alba's shoulder to get her attention, but the Ambassador has already noticed the approaching Legion.

"Good evening, Ambassador," a Braver with a blue mask addresses Alba.

"How can I help you, Director?" Alba responds, the frustration evident in her tone. "We're on a tight schedule."

"Apologies, Ambassador, but before you make the trek into Sun-Side, you'll have to come with us."

Alba sighs. "The last Braver who attempted to detain us lost an appendage."

The Braver raises her hands defensively. "No one desires to detain you, Ambassador. We wouldn't make that mistake. This is a request."

"Request denied."

"Unfortunately, Ambassador, you'll have to deny the request to the one who made it."

Alba raises an eyebrow. "And who would that be?"

"The Facilitator."

Alba turns to Unisa and holds eye contact for a moment, as if trying to make an assessment. She then turns back to the Legion Director and nods.

"Stay close," she whispers to Unisa as they follow the Director back to one of the tents. The Bravers keep pace with the Librarians, and their perfect perimeter never wavers.

The Director enters the tent and gestures for the Librarians to follow, while the remaining Bravers stand guard at the front. The tent is nearly empty, save for a table holding a bottle of ale on the right, and a green-skinned, one-armed Mega in the center.

The MegaFather's Facilitator. She's heard of him, read of him—a shining example of loyalty to SunSide's throne, something Unisa once thought was a virtue.

Not anymore.

"Alba," he says in a silky voice, with a toothy grin. "How unusual of you to return to the kingdom so soon after you were just here."

"This unprofessional request is unusual," Alba counters.

"Unprofessional? How insulting."

Something moves in Unisa's peripheral vision. The bottle of ale and three empty glasses lift up off the table and hover toward them. The Facilitator is the only Mega in this tent, yet he isn't moving a muscle.

How is he doing that?

"Is it unprofessional for us to share a drink?" Saith asks as the bottle hovers between them and begins to pour.

"Entirely," Alba responds, flatly.

The bottle stops pouring, and Saith stops smiling. A gentle breeze blows and, as the moving air makes contact with the glasses and the bottle, they begin to disintegrate into tiny dust particles. The dust floats away with the breeze, as do golden streaks of evaporated ale.

"Get to the point, Saith," Alba says. "We don't have time for theatrics."

The Facilitator's tone hardens. "The MegaFather has been busy since you left, Ambassador. Whatever questions you have, I am here to answer them on his behalf."

"You cannot provide the answers we seek. Only the MegaFather and the Members of the Assembly can do that."

She turns quickly, taking Unisa's hand and leading her back toward the tent's exit. They stop when Saith speaks again.

"I urge you to reconsider, Ambassador," he says, his tone almost frantic now.

The hairs on Unisa's arms stand.

"My offer is beneficial for you, as well. Don't prolong this journey unnecessarily."

"Tell me something, Saith," Alba says, facing him again. "How did you know we were coming?"

Saith pauses before he responds. "The Bravers are not only our warriors, they are also our eyes and ears."

"Then I suggest you train them to stay far away from us. Or you'll end up both blind and deaf."

She turns quickly and leads Unisa out of the tent and through the field toward the gates. Unisa feels every Braver eye on them.

Alba leads her past the lines, directly to a gate.

"Wave us through," she says to the Braver there.

"There's a line," the Braver responds.

"And we were removed from it involuntarily. Wave us through."

The Braver looks past her, over her shoulder, back down the field. Unisa turns and sees that he is making eye contact with Saith, who is angrily standing at the entrance of the tent, staring at them.

Alba snaps her fingers in the Braver's face, an inch from his nose, until he turns his attention to her.

"Listen to me carefully," she says to him, "open the gate and wave us through. You don't need to look at him for confirmation. I don't take orders from him. Do you understand me?"

The tension mounts, as Unisa's knees tremble. The Braver stares angrily into Alba's eyes for some time before he nods and waves to the Bravers controlling the gate. It opens up.

Without another word, or a look back, Alba leads Unisa through the gates of PeakHaven Pass and in between the towering mountains.

Onward to SunSide.

CHAPTER 32

THE FALCON

Continent of Panaerth
Date *21st Day of Month 6, Year 1628 DG*

A NEW DAY DAWNS UPON Ona's light.

Zakia and Salessa enter the clearing again, and the pixie inactivates the cloaking circle. The pair find Gina and Naina strategizing the mission, while Symin extinguishes the morning bonfire.

Where were you? Naina asks Salessa.

Early morning perimeter check, Salessa responds, as Zakia instructed her to.

When Gina verbally asks Zakia the same question, she delivers an identical response, followed by a knowing glance to Salessa.

Salessa forces memories of the night out of her mind, in case Naina decides to telepathically probe her.

"We have to be at the processing center by afternoon," Gina commands. "Let's get moving."

One by one, the travelers cross the threshold, into the forest where the Radiance is void. They stay close together as they travel, eyes wide for Bravers. Gina safeguards the rear of the pack, with Zakia leading and Symin in the middle with the twins.

Without her access to the Radiance, Gina remains on edge, a dagger in each hand. Symin and Zakia, however, appear unfazed. They're alert and guarded, but exude a calming aura, focused on the path ahead.

When the Four reach their peak overhead, Salessa hopes the protests in her stomach aren't audible to the remainder of the group.

"It's midday," Gina announces. "We should stop to eat. The center isn't far now."

Maybe she heard.

Gina moves quickly around the surrounding trees and secures their perimeter, while Symin and Zakia take to the branches and gather fruit.

Salessa sits with her back against a tree, and Naina plops down next to her.

We have to finish our conversation from last night, the wolf demands.

Salessa juggles offering her the truth: Zakia knows who they are now, and the others are ignorant of the prophecy. They have no reason to hide the falcon.

But when she meets Naina's eyes, her nerves take over.

My feelings haven't changed, Naina. It has to be me. A wolf can't safely complete this mission, and I won't put you in danger.

We will be in danger if we reveal who we are. Did you forget, it's the reason we're on the run? We can't trust Mega, they'll want to use our abilities, or the Goddess herself.

Salessa breathes deeply to temper her anger. *You're lying to yourself. I'm in your head and I know your feelings have changed. I don't know how or when, but this untrusting, tough exterior act has started breaking down around Symin. I know you've seen through his windows.*

There's a long, silent pause as Naina tries to form a response, a denial.

Salessa continues. *Change champions, remember? What greater change is there than relieving ourselves of the things holding us back?*

Hiding the prophecy protects us, Lessi.

Hiding the prophecy HAS protected us. But not anymore. Now all it does is isolate us. We've been alone for twelve years.

She turns to the Mega around them and Naina follows her gaze.

I told you before, we need community. We don't need to protect ourselves alone anymore, when we have a community who will protect us.

Their eyes meet again.

It's time to change. It's time to stop hiding who we are.

Naina seems to take the words in. She stops transmitting thoughts to Salessa, but her gaze lingers on their companions as they continue the journey to the processing center.

The Braver presence grows heavier as the ore facility draws closer. The Mega instruct the twins to walk more carefully, avoiding sounds under their feet. They move away from beaten paths, walk slowly between trees.

They arrive at their destination on schedule, resting at a vantage point on a hill that overlooks the entire center. High up at the edge of the forest, the hill descends into a narrow, grassy valley, where the processing center sits. It's massive, with a gate on one end that opens to allow hover trucks, carrying raw ore, into the center.

Gina and Naina crouch behind a pile of stones, the others finding trees to hide behind.

"Where does he get it?" Gina wonders aloud. "If we knew the source of the ore..."

"We can follow the trucks," Naina suggests.

"We've tried," Symin responds. "They arrive on fleet vessels, coming in from all different directions. An intentional strategy to hide the originating location."

"I'll try to find a source while I'm inside," Naina says, sending Salessa reeling.

She had assumed their discussion had changed Naina's mind.

Gina shakes her head. "A wolf on a stealth mission is risky enough without poking around for information." She finds the suns. "Their guards are about to change shifts, we'll have a short window where you can slip in. Be ready."

There isn't much time. This is Salessa's final opportunity to change Naina's mind.

"Take a walk with me," she suggests to her sister. "I'll help you get centered."

"Don't go far," Gina commands them.

Naina follows Salessa until they are out of earshot of the rest of the group.

I thought we agreed, Salessa says.

You thought wrong. I have to protect us, and that includes keeping the prophecy from them.

As the seconds draw on, Salessa feels the pressure clenching her throat. Naina is moments from entering the processing center, and there's only one way to stop her.

Naina, we can tell them about the prophecy! Zakia assured me it was safe.

The words slip out before Salessa can cage them.

Naina is stunned into momentary silence, before a growl rumbles in her chest.

Don't freak out, Naina, please.

I'M GOING TO KILL YOU. Naina's fury burns into Salessa's mind.

Naina's muzzle erupts. Elongated canines and sharpened teeth show in her vicious snarl. Fur erupts all over her head.

Below the neck, she is still Naina, while above, she's a fierce canine. The growl simmers, low enough that the Mega are still oblivious.

HOW COULD YOU?

Salessa takes a step backward. *I'm sorry. You don't understand—*

How dare you lecture me about trust and community when you've been lying to me all day? I can't even trust my own sister.

Naina, please, that's not true.

Of course, it is! I saw the way you were looking at her. This is the Lexona situation all over again.

A sharp, pricking pain stabs Salessa in her heart.

I've apologized for that countless times, Naina. You can't hold it over my head forever. This is completely different.

Is it? Any time a pretty girl smiles at you, you completely lose all your senses. Are you going to give Zakia all of our money, too?

Her words become a long, thin dagger to the chest, as Naina invokes memories of the poor decisions she made years ago. Naina knows that Lexona betrayed Salessa's trust as much as she betrayed the wolf's. Salessa didn't *give* her anything.

She took it.

The pain translates quickly into anger. Salessa acts without thinking, turning to the Mega before Naina can stop her.

"I'm a falcon," she announces.

The Mega turn to her, raising an eyebrow at the abrupt declaration. She continues. "I lied to you earlier. I'm not a wolf."

Zakia opens her eyes far too wide and places her hands on her cheeks. "What a surprise!"

Gina and Symin exchange a look.

"You're a falcon?" Gina confirms.

Salessa nods.

"And you're clearly a wolf," she says to Naina, who is still canine above the neck.

"Aren't Doruh twins supposed to have the same animal forms?"

Salessa's heart drops. Gina knows Doruh genetics, but does she know their religion?

"We're a genetic anomaly," Salessa responds, her heart pounding, hoping Gina accepts the excuse.

Another look between Gina and Symin, and then a shrug.

"Falcon is better than wolf," Gina says. "You're going in."

Salessa nods and the Mega turn back to the processing center.

"I hope you're happy," Naina whispers to Salessa, fully human again. "You took a risk for both of us."

"I did it because I love you."

"Bullshit," Naina responds quickly. "You did it out of anger. There was no discussion or agreement. I don't know this lying, selfish Salessa."

Gina interrupts them. "It's time. Let's go."

Salessa turns back to Naina, hoping to explain that, regardless of how it appears, she only wants to protect her sister.

But Naina's words silence her. She's correct about Salessa's behavior. There's nothing more to say. Salessa got what she wanted, yet, she feels emptier now than she did before.

The twins join the group again, and the General hands Salessa a short cylinder that expands into a long wooden tube with a circular pane of glass on one end.

"What is this?" Salessa asks.

"Put it to your eye. It'll help you see small details about your route from here as I explain it."

Salessa hands the tube back to Gina. "I don't need this."

"Are you sure?" Gina raises an eyebrow.

Salessa points to her eyes. "Falcon."

Gina presses the tube to her eye. "See the back wall? There's a square hatch about a quarter of the way down from the top."

"I see it," Salessa confirms with a nod.

"It's a duct for the cooling systems. Naina was going to slip into the maintenance corridor, but if you think you can fit in the duct, it'll make this a lot quicker and easier."

"I'll fit."

"Good. Follow the ducts until you reach a small room with three compression tanks. They'll be connected by hoses. Wait for the room to clear, then disconnect each hose and reconnect it to a different machine. Once that's done, you'll only have about a minute, maybe two, to get back through the duct and into the sky, before the center joins you among the clouds."

Salessa nods. "Understood."

"Any questions?"

Salessa peers harder and notices the workers bustling about. "How will I alert the workers?"

Gina raises an eyebrow. "Alert the workers? It's a stealth mission, Salessa."

Salessa pauses, trying to understand the General's intention. "Gina, look at the Mega down there."

Gina puts the tube to her eye again. "The Bravers?"

"No. Everyone else. The engineers, scientists, laborers. Mega with families, friends, lovers."

All eyes lock on Salessa as she continues. "I have no issues completing this task with Bravers inside. But the rest of them came to work this morning to feed their families. They didn't come to die."

"This is war," Gina says. "It's ugly."

"Those aren't warriors," Salessa counters. "Is there another time we can do this? Tonight, after they go home?"

"Salessa," Symin says, his tone gentle. "They aren't here for the day, they're assigned for weeks and months at a time, and they sleep in the complex. Timing is irrelevant, everyone there is going to be caught in the blast."

Salessa hesitates. "It'll kill them"

"They're faeries, Lessi," Naina chimes in.

Salessa looks up at her. "That's not a crime."

"As far as I'm concerned, working for the Ore Monger is." She turns to Gina. "I can go in and do this. I have as little problem with faeries being caught in the blast as they do with cutting down Doruh in Evic."

"Wait," Symin's cool voice slips in. He turns to the falcon. "Salessa, I admire your empathy. But this is the only way."

Salessa's eyes dart from her sister to the Mega. Uneasiness grows in her stomach. Her expression morphs into one of reluctance.

"Maybe the wolf *should* go, after all," Gina taunts her.

"No," Salessa responds, putting an end to the conversation. "I'll do it."

Slowly, reluctantly, she backs away from them and removes her clothes.

"Good luck." Zakia offers her a smile.

Salessa turns to her sister and they hold eye contact. The betrayal hangs between them, as Naina remains cold and quietly says, "Good luck."

Salessa waits another moment for an embrace, or some form of affection from her sister before she embarks on a potentially fatal mission, but nothing comes.

"How far does your telepathy reach?" Symin asks.

Gina's eyes widen. "Telepathy?"

Symin nods. "Evidently, a twin thing."

"We've never tested distance," Salessa admits.

"You'll test it today," Gina commands. "I want updates."

Naina nods and coldly turns away from her sister.

Salessa closes her eyes, and her limbs shorten. Dark feathers pop from her arms, while lighter ones grow from the rest of her body. Her feet harden and turn yellow as long talons spring from them, and her mouth and nose elongate into a sharp, curved, black-and-yellow beak.

Naina can't remember the last time she's seen Salessa shift. A sense of pride fills her chest, knowing that her sister is traversing her comfort zone for the mission, but the betrayal overpowers it and she remains silent.

Guilt joins the pride and betrayal in her heart, for bringing up Lexona. Salessa has apologized countless times for her mistakes, and Naina had forgiven her.

Salessa shoots up into the air. Zakia, Gina and Symin stare in awe as the small bird takes flight.

Seconds later, Salessa is circling high above the wide building, a mere speck from the ground. And then she dives, and all three Mega's jaws drop to the forest floor.

"Is she teleporting?" Gina asks.

"No," Naina responds. "She's faster than you can follow."

The falcon perches on the edge of the roof, waiting for a group of Bravers to stroll around to the side of the building, from where she isn't visible. She lowers herself and uses her beak to open the duct's flap, before slowly floating in and folding her wings close.

"Tell her to keep in contact," Gina says once the hatch drops behind Salessa.

Naina nods. *Stay in touch.* She keeps her tone frozen.

It works, I can hear you.

"Has she found the room?" Gina asks impatiently.

"Not yet."

I'm above the first room. Large, full of machinery. Barrels of ore emptied into vats and melted. I'm going to keep moving.

I'll let Gina know.

"She's at the first room," Naina announces to the team. "The factory. She's going to keep moving."

Gina and Symin nod in acknowledgment.

After a few minutes of light descriptions, Salessa finally says, *I've found it.*

"She found it."

Gina smiles. "Excellent. Remind her to be quick on the way out."

Get out quick when it's done. Gina's instruction.

Salessa pauses before she responds. *Thanks, I will. There're workers in the room.*

We'll stand by.

What is that noise? Salessa's irritation comes through.

What noise? Naina asks.

Nothing, sorry.

Naina turns and relays the falcon's position to the group. Gina and Symin draw in a long breath, anticipating the moment they've been waiting for.

Salessa's voice rings again. *I have to go check.*

Check what?

The noise. Someone's yelling in the next room over.

Naina battles frustration to keep her tone steady. *Forget it. You're on a mission.*

No, wait. This might be important.

Lessi, stop.

Silence.

One. Two. Three. Four. Five.

Lessi?

Silence.

Naina's heart pounds through her chest. *Lessi?! Say something!*

"What's going on?" Gina asks, looking up at the wolf's scrunched eyebrows.

"Nothing," Naina responds quickly.

"Nothing? Naina, you're frowning and sweating."

"She's just waiting, alright? Relax."

Lessi, please, talk to me.

Silence inundates her mind, and Naina's heart shatters, realizing the last opportunity she had to embrace her sister was wasted. If something happens to Salessa, the last thing she heard was Naina's frozen tone. The wolf waits, and time slows as she begs the Twins to let her sister's voice come through again.

And they oblige.

It's a foreman, comes Salessa's voice. *He received a message from the Chief Engineer, who just left a meeting with the MegaFather.* Pause. *Something about a new chariot order.*

Naina releases a long-held breath. *Thank the fucking Twins. Lessi, you scared me.*

"Naina, what's wrong?" Symin's voice breaks Naina from the telepathy. "You're crying."

The wolf's hand shoots up to the corner of her eye and she wipes away the relieved tear. "Nothing—she's going into the room now."

Lessi, I'm lying for you here. Please go back to the room.

Lily Beach. Sacristone.
What?

The skies and the forest fill with the echo of a piercing alarm. Bravers around the center scramble to designated locations.

"What's happening?" Zakia asks. "Is she okay?"

"I-I don't know," Naina stammers out. "Let me ask."

Are you okay, Lessi?

Silence.

Her pulse quickens again. *Lessi?!*

"What's going on, Naina?" Symin asks urgently, his tone dripping with concern. "Is she safe?"

"I don't—" Naina doesn't know what to say. "I don't know."

"You don't know?" Gina's tone is incredulous.

"Look," Naina's voice breaks as her concern mounts, "I said I don't know, alright?"

"There she is," Zakia says, squinting and pointing toward the processing center.

Naina tears the magnifying tube from Gina's hands and places it to her eye. The black-and-yellow falcon beak pops the flap of the duct system back open and Salessa launches up and away from the building.

Seconds later, she dives through the treetops and lands gracefully on the forest floor in the exact place from which she departed earlier. A wave of utter relief washes over Naina, and before her human form has fully returned, the wolf's arms are wrapped tightly around her sister.

Water wells in her eyes, but she doesn't wipe it away, not wanting to let go of Salessa for even a moment.

"You're choking me, Naina."

"I'm sorry for bringing up Lexona," Naina whispers in her ear. "I know what she did wasn't your fault."

"I'm sorry, too," Salessa apologizes. "For everything."

There's a pause as Naina holds onto her sister and sniffs, and then Salessa pops into her head. *Wait, are you crying?*

No. Shut up.

The wolf finally presses the tears away with her palms before she releases the embrace.

"What was the alarm about?" Symin asks.

Salessa's cheeks burn red. "That was an accident. I tripped it on my way out."

"And the burners?" Gina asks.

"I didn't do it," Salessa admits.

"I hope you have a good reason," Gina taunts. "That was the entire purpose of dragging you here."

"Lily Beach," Salessa says.

Gina and Symin exchange perplexed glances.

Salessa continues. "The ships bringing the barrels of raw ore. You wanted to know where they're coming from. Lily Beach. They're mining something called sacristone there."

Gina's eyes widen with realization, but Symin's eyebrows remain furrowed.

"You have the wrong target," Salessa advises. "Destroying this processing center is a minor inconvenience. You want to cut the Ore Monger off? Go to Lily Beach and eliminate the sacristone."

Naina allows her pride to burst forth. "You did it, Lessi."

"And you did it without harming the Mega," Zakia adds, handing Salessa her clothes.

"Back to Nivyan Hollow to regroup and refresh," commands the General. An eager smile widens on her face. "Then…to Lily Beach."

CHAPTER 33

ENTER THE HEARTHBARK

The Agrarian Townlets *Innkeeper's Ranch*
Date *21st Day of Month 6, Year 1628 DG*

MORNING RAYS THRASH THE LIBRARIANS. Flasks filled, rations stocked, it hasn't been long since they left Innkeeper's Ranch behind.

Rafael avoids bringing his hands into view, as they're now covered in the crimson visions once painted on Kyoko. He keeps his eyes on the path ahead—the path to EverEmber and the TreeKeeper.

If such a creature even exists.

The warm rays on his back contrast against the cold wall between him and his igni companion. She's endured two days of erratic outbursts and prejudiced mistreatment. A cold wall is merciful.

She examines the map as they walk, providing Rafael an opportunity to break down the silence between them.

He leans over to gain a clear view of the map. "How far do you expect us to reach today?"

"If we keep to the schedule, we'll be sleeping on the Mother tonight."

"The Mother?" Rafael's forehead scrunches together.

Kyoko points to her native homeland. "EverEmber's largest island is called Roba; hub of commerce, recreation, government, and residences of the upper class. We call it 'the Mother' because of Mt. Mother, the volcano at the center."

Her finger descends south. "These two smaller islands are Sila and Tusa, referred to as 'the Sisters.' Sila houses the lower and middle classes, while Tusa, where the Prime is sending us, is nothing more than dense forest. An untouched look at EverEmber from before human exploration. Popular with explorers and archaeologists."

"Further confirmation of the pointlessness of this task," Rafael realizes, discouraged.

"Perhaps he means to humiliate us. It won't take long to search for the TreeKeeper, given Tusa's size. Had Courtman Tomohiro not discovered Lily Beach, we'd still be at war for Bibi Sands. They'll take any island that can be put to greater use than a small preservation."

At mention of the war, Rafael's gaze falls on his red fingers, and he shudders.

"I'm sorry," she apologizes.

"Don't be," he responds earnestly. "It isn't your fault."

It's mine.

Clay paths wind between towering hills on one side and thick trees on the other. As the suns arc overhead, warmth and humidity encapsulate the travelers.

"Let's take a break," Kyoko suggests when they pass two short, flat-top boulders. Rafael leans on one, trying to relax, until he hears footsteps approaching from the path ahead.

A caracal approaches, four feet long, maybe fifty pounds. The feline's strides are soft but confident, agile but aggressive. Hunched slightly, its mouth hangs open, baring sharp teeth in an angry hiss that stiffens its pointy black ears and tugs at its short snout.

It stops, blocking their path.

Rafael leans over and whispers to Kyoko. "True or Doruh?"

She examines it, assesses it. "Doruh."

The caracal's ears shrink to the sides of its head, and its fur turns to golden brown skin. Human facial features form from the snout and it lifts onto two legs as short gray hair with a matching mustache erupts onto his face.

The elderly man is taller than both Librarians, however, he seems to be struggling to straighten his back. The caracal was spry and light-footed, but his human form is quite frail.

"Correct," the old man says, a snarl on his face. "Doruh. Your journey on this path ends here."

"We're on a tight schedule, Caracal," Kyoko replies, calmly yet confidently. "There is no other path for us to take than this one."

"There is." The Caracal lifts his arm and gestures into the forest to their side. "The HearthBark has many paths to the south, if you are able to find them."

"We don't have time for riddles," Rafael insists.

The Caracal remains firm. "Your war used our village as a battleground. Our homes are in ruin, our children scarred. Your fins and exoskeletons will terrorize them again."

He gestures to the forest a second time and his tone softens. "Please."

Rafael finds deliberation in Kyoko's expression, while his own thoughts swirl around the far-reaching devastation of war—the unjust truth that even the uncommitted can be injured and exploited. Though his hand never touched a blade, the Caracal's truth racks him with guilt.

Kyoko nods. "We'll go through the HearthBark. Your people won't see us."

The Caracal bows gratefully.

Kyoko and Rafael hoist their bags once more. They find an opening into a pathway between two trees, and enter the HearthBark.

Just as they step into the forest, the Caracal's voice echoes behind them. "And beware *Reyu Paleyu.*"

Rafael turns to Kyoko. "Did he say *Reyu Paleyu?*"

Kyoko nods and translates the Nysabaani. "The Vine Demon."

Leaves and twigs crunch beneath Rafael's feet as he steps over colossal roots and chittering rodents. It feels like hours pass this way, stepping slowly and cautiously. His eyes dart up to Kyoko, a few feet ahead holding the map, and then back down again to secure his steps.

They reach a fork in the natural path, and then another, and then another. And then they find an intersection of many paths, until finally there are no paths at all.

The HearthBark quickly transforms from a forest, to a maze, to a prison.

Rafael steps quicker to close the gap between him and his companion, peering over her shoulder at the map. He wonders how Kyoko is able to navigate when no specified paths are outlined.

"Have you found the next path?" he asks, curious.

"Do you see any paths?" she responds sharply.

He shakes his head.

"Then how can I find the next path?"

Though he understands her distance from him, her contempt surprises him.

She rolls the map and exhales deeply. "I'm sorry, Rafael. Truthfully, I haven't even been looking for a path. We're getting closer to EverEmber, which means..."

"Closer to your sister," Rafael completes for her.

Kyoko takes a long pause. "Yes. Kanako lives on Sila, but works and spends all of her free time on the Mother."

"I know you think she hates you," Rafael recalls, "but I stand by what I said. Six years is a long time. People forgive. They move forward."

"Not after they claim you've ruined their life," Kyoko counters. "It's best we complete this journey without seeing her."

"I understand. But what will you do if you *do* see her?"

Kyoko pauses. "Let her be."

Joaquina's face flashes through Rafael's mind. If he were able to beg her forgiveness, he would. Without a moment's hesitation.

"Don't close your heart to the possibility of forgiveness. Where a tree was once cut down, a new seed can be planted. As long as your sister breathes, you have the opportunity to build something new."

He makes eye contact with her. "Some of us, who no longer have that opportunity, would give everything for it."

CHAPTER 34

THE VINE DEMON

Sub-Oceanic Stratocracy *SeaBed*
Date *43rd Day of Month 4, Year 1618 DG - 10 Years Earlier*

"LOOK AT ME, RAFA," JOAQUINA says, placing a hand on his chin and tilting his head up until his moist eyes meet hers. "Those who never fail cannot recognize success."

Rafael nods and wipes his tears away. "I'll try again."

Joaquina smiles, bends forward, and places a soft kiss on his forehead. "Forget the salvers. I know you can do this."

Rafael locks his sights on the bow at his feet, fingers trembling—a lack of steadiness in his hand that, salvers say, will halt his archery permanently.

But Joaquina bought him a new bow and quiver for his birthday. He can let neither her money, nor her faith in him, go to waste.

He grasps the bow firmly in his hand, hoping to steady his fingers. The siblings return to the olive tree they were using for target practice before Rafael angrily stormed off. Light falls from the panels at the top of the dome around the city and illuminates the entire grove.

"Nock an arrow," Joaquina instructs.

Rafael's hands remain still by his side.

"Nock an arrow, Rafa."

Again, Rafael doesn't respond.

Joaquina steps in front of him. "What's wrong?"

He speaks softly, eyes on the bow, releasing the question from its home in the back of his mind. "Do you think Dad's going to die?"

Joaquina's eyes widen and she stands in silence.

"Is that why you're pushing my archery lessons so hard? Because you think he named me his undersoldier and they're going to call me up when he gets killed?"

Joaquina's wide eyes relax only when she takes a deep breath and a long pause.

"Rafa, we don't know who Dad named as his undersoldier. It could be either of us."

Rafael scoffs. "The groves are the family legacy. They mean everything to him, and you've got his olive thumb. Dad's not going to risk the legacy by having you called up to fight in his place. Dad would have no problem sending me to war in his place when he dies on the battlefield."

Joaquina places both hands on Rafael's cheeks. "Dad is not going to get killed, and this war will end soon. No one else will have to fight, particularly not you. *If* Dad dies, I'll fight in your place.

"That's illegal," Rafael reminds her. "They'll exile both of us."

Joaquina's tone never wavers. "Illegal or not, it's my duty to protect you."

"I would never let you go for me."

Rafael pulls an arrow out of the quiver and nocks it to the bow, then gestures for Joaquina to move aside, which she does, revealing a clear path to the target hanging from the olive tree.

He draws the arrow, holds it as steadily as he can, and keeps his eyes locked on the small red circle in the center of the target. Dead center.

Joaquina steps close to him and whispers in his ear. "What are you shooting for?"

"Dead center," Rafael responds.

"I mean, why are you training?"

Rafael keeps the arrow drawn, and his line of sight focused on the target, as he speaks. "Battle."

"Why?"

Rafael pauses. "To defeat the igni."

"Wrong, try again."

He understands. "To protect the people I love." He feels her smile behind him.

"Imagine Dad. Imagine Mom. Imagine me. Remember why you're training. It's not about the warrior on the other side, who has left their family, too. It's about you protecting yours."

Rafael keeps the images of his loved ones in his mind as he takes a deep breath and releases the arrow. It cuts confidently through the air.

And it hits dead center.

Joaquina wraps her brother in her arms. "Always remember, Rafa, fear, hatred, and the desire to kill—these are the wrong reasons. Protecting the people you love is the right one. It will guide you."

The HearthBark
Date 21st Day of Month 6, Year 1628 DG

TIME STANDS STILL IN THE HearthBark as the canopy blocks the view of the suns.

Few words have been traded between the Librarians, as Kyoko leads him through the trees, but after some time, their surroundings look eerily familiar. Rafael wonders if they might be going in circles, but cages his tongue.

The scurry of wildlife around his feet is most irritating. He prefers the marine life that avoided him, or played enthusiastically, as he swam from the domed cities and villages of SeaBed to the surface. It was always one or the other, never a middle ground.

The scurrying and brushing against his ankles grows to be such an annoyance that he looks down to find the creatures and scold them, but all he sees are vines.

A bed of green, serpentine flora forms a network of veins across the forest floor. They cover the trees, slithering up branches and wrapping over roots. The few animals visible hurriedly try to escape from the expanding, breathing tentacles.

There are so many intertwined vines, Rafael would never be able to trace a source. The Caracal's warning comes to life.

Beware the Vine Demon.

Rafael quickly unstraps his bow from his bag. Ahead of him, Kyoko continues forward, unaware that a vine is slithering to her ankle from behind.

"Kyoko!" Rafael yells to get her attention, but he's too late. Before she can turn, the thick vine closes around her ankle, lifts her into the air, and then slams her back down onto the ground. An audible *crunch* rings out through the forest, and Rafael silently prays that her exoskeleton withstood the blow.

He drops the bag off his back and pulls a collapsible arrow from his waist. The vine lifts Kyoko again and Rafael takes aim. He lines the arrowhead with the vine around her ankle and fires. It cuts through the air quickly and makes contact, sending Kyoko tumbling toward the ground again.

But she doesn't land. A thicker vine catches her from the air and wraps tightly around her body, pinning her arms to her sides.

"No!" Rafael screams, pulling another arrow, but he quickly becomes the target of the demon's wrath.

Bow gripped tightly in one hand, arrow in the other, the vines drag him along the forest floor, on his front, toward Kyoko. Rafael musters strength to turn onto his back and stab the arrow through the vine around his leg.

It releases him, and a primal roar erupts throughout the canopies. The thousands of vines wrapping and penetrating the forest recede into one spot, beneath the limb holding Kyoko. Rafael feels momentary relief, until the ground trembles.

The vines conjoin cohesively until a head and face forms, followed by a body, legs, and claws. The vines wrap around one another until they give the beast, the monster, the demon a form.

The creature emerges from the vines as if the forest floor has birthed it. It doesn't reach the canopies, but it is certainly taller than any living being Rafael has ever seen. The Vine Demon boasts the dominating face and muscular body of a lion, with thick green vines forming a mane around its head. More vines extrude from its spine, flitting about like a hundred tails.

The rest cling to its body, forming patterns and designs along its sides and back. If it didn't pose such a threat, Rafael would've considered it a work of art. A miracle.

Its gaze challenges the mari to attack, before the beast opens its mouth wide to release a robust, violent roar that shakes the trees. The vine holding Kyoko releases her and she drops, landing hard on the ground a second time. She shakes herself off and crawls away from the creature. The tanto glints in her hand.

A hungry grimace crosses the demon's expression when it sees the Librarian escaping. A vine pounces forth, from the mane, to retrieve her. Rafael arms his bow and fires another arrow, severing the vine at the base, close to the beast's head.

Another roar bellows and it turns its sights on him. Rafael turns on his heels and quickly puts distance between him and the monster, hiding behind trees when possible.

The beast sends five vines, then ten, then twenty, until Rafael can no longer outrun or hide from them. The tendrils follow until they capture him, wrapping tight around his body and separating him from his bow.

They carry him into the air until he is inches from the Vine Demon's face. The raw stench of its breath bathes him as it growls deeply, reverberating through the vines and shaking him.

It pulls Rafael closer and opens its mouth.

His fingers fiddle with an arrow on his waist, trying to loosen one, but the effort is rendered pointless when the Demon releases him with an irate, guttural roar. Rafael lands on his side and pain shoots into his shoulder, arm, and hips.

Kyoko, armed with the tanto, stands on the Demon's neck, an open wound bleeding down the side of its face. Two vines rise up behind Kyoko—one knocks the tanto from her hand, the other wraps around her head, covering her nose and mouth. Her fingers latch onto the vine over her face, clawing at it violently as she struggles.

It's suffocating her.

Rafael wildly searches for his bow, finding it captive in a vine's grasp far above the monster's head. There's no way of reaching it before Kyoko asphyxiates.

Think, think, he demands, but no plan materializes. He watches, helplessly, painfully, his heart thrashing in his chest, his eyes burning. Rigid muscles, numbness around his body, the truth becomes clear.

He's losing her.

Rafael drops to his knees. The burning in his eyes spreads to his entire face, and throughout his skin. It's happening all over again; he feels fifteen years old, standing at Joaquina's funeral, feeling the weight of someone he cares about dying because he couldn't save them.

Seeing their red blood painted all over his hands.

The guilt clenches around his throat and strangles him. Nausea rises and his vision goes red with anguish. She will die, and he won't be able to save her.

And then, he's no longer on his knees; it feels like floating. Tranquility enters him. His eyes close and his fear of losing Kyoko, and his concern for her, manifest in an energetic charge buzzing around his body.

His eyes open again to an entirely red world, and he realizes the colored vision isn't part of his emotional state, but the physical one. The energy pulses up through his veins and into his eyeballs, searing the sockets. He screams from the burning nerves.

He simply *knows* what to do next, as he feels the connection to the Radiance guiding him. Kyoko's clawing fingers begin to go limp as her consciousness withers. The Radiance tells him to release the energy from his eyes and cut down the vines, but to take care not to hit Kyoko.

Joaquina's words from his childhood archery sessions echo through his ears. *Protecting the people you love is the right one. It will guide you.*

The burning in his sockets climaxes and he forces the energy out, releasing two thin beams of red light from his eyes. They travel faster than an arrow is shot, making contact with the vine around Kyoko centimeters from her ear.

A roar rattles the realm again, and the vines drop from Kyoko's face. She inhales sharply, then vomits and drops off the beast's back. Rafael bounds forward and catches her before she hits the ground, carrying her away from the injured Demon.

Rafael lays her down behind a tree, placing a hand on her face. "Kyoko?"

She struggles to conjure a voice, but nods and breathes deeply.

Rafael looks beyond the trees, and the Demon locks eyes with him. It creeps forward, but neither he nor the igni are in any shape to escape. He has nothing with which he can continue the battle. Only one option remains.

Pacify it.

He emerges from behind the tree and raises both hands in the air. "Stop! Please!"

Charging vines freeze. The Demon awaits his plea.

"We want to leave the HearthBark. We are not here to harm you or the forest."

The Demon growls and the vines advance once again. He closes his eyes, attempting to summon the Radiance, but fails. A single vine reaches Rafael, but doesn't attach to him; it slowly presses the tip against his chest, over his heart.

A familiar gust of wind rises and Rafael lifts his arm to shield his face from the violent blow. When the wind stops, Rafael finds himself in the void again. In the abyss of the Radiance. And the Vine Demon joins him.

Why have you brought me here? Rafael questions him.

To show you, growls a gruff voice in his mind. Images appear around the void. Rafael spins and takes them in. The first depicts a hooded figure in the HearthBark. A green-skinned Mega with only one arm.

SunSide's Facilitator, Rafael says.

Six years ago, the gruff growl continues. *Brought me here.*

The next image depicts the Facilitator with his hand raised, and a wide crack opening in the air.

Brought you here from where? Rafael questions.

The gruff growl becomes a pained, sorrowful moan. *Home.*

A third image. The Vine Demon on the ground, writhing in agony, as the Facilitator blasts him with two red beams from the eyes. *Evil creature. Made me kill.*

Kill who?

Witnesses.

Confusion racks Rafael. *Witnesses to what?*

I don't know.

The Radiance connects them. Rafael feels the anguish in the Demon's heart.

Do you know how to get us through the HearthBark?

The Demon pauses. *Yes. Then you send me home.*

Rafael hesitates. *I don't know how to do that.*

Then you stay lost.

Rafael sighs. *I can try. Take us through the forest and I'll try to send you home.*

The Demon nods, then the vines crawl toward Rafael and press against his chest. The wind gusts and returns Rafael to the forest.

The Vine Demon's wounds have healed.

"What happened?" comes Kyoko's voice.

Rafael finds her standing behind him, eyebrows scrunched, their bags and his bow at her feet.

The igni hands him the bow. "You've been standing here with a vine touching your chest and your eyes closed."

The Vine Demon turns to face south, then lowers onto its knees, its belly against the ground. Rafael understands.

He turns to Kyoko. "I found the path out."

CHAPTER 35

STEMS FROM LOVE

The HearthBark
Date *21st Day of Month 6, Year 1628 DG*

"WHAT WAS SAITH DOING IN the HearthBark?" Kyoko wonders aloud.

Seated on demonback, clutching vines for stability, Rafael relays his experience in the void. Their belongings sturdily rest on the creature's rear, strapped by green tendrils, as Rafael's hands wrap tightly around Kyoko's waist.

"He brought *Reyu Paleyu* here from" — Rafael pauses — "somewhere."

"I meant, where was he going?"

"Perhaps to EverEmber."

"In a hood? Any igni would recognize a green pixie with one arm." She shakes her head. "He was hiding from someone."

Rafael shrugs. "A mystery for the Prime to solve."

They sit quietly for some minutes before Kyoko's curiosity stimulates her tongue again. Encountering the Vine Demon was terrifying and dangerous, but, along with providing a way out of the HearthBark, it melted Kyoko's walls.

"What does the void look like?"

"Darkness," Rafael responds. "I can see my hands and my body, and evidently others within the void"—he gestures to the Vine Demon—"but nothing else."

"Sounds terrifying."

"It isn't. Tranquility accompanies the floating sensation. Once I've entered the void, I remain calm while I'm there."

Kyoko strokes her chin. "Where is 'there'? Physically, your body remains here. Perhaps it's a psychological or spiritual place?"

"Or an emotional one. I heard Joaquina's voice in the void last night."

"What did she say?"

Rafael closes his eyes and invokes Joaqina's comments. He repeats what he remembers. "She said my name. I asked if she was alive, and she confirmed she wasn't, but then she told me to come find her. She said our connection was weak."

"Come find her? How can you find her if she isn't alive? Did she say anything else?"

Rafael shakes his head. "Only that she loves me."

Kyoko pauses, then treads lightly in response. "I can imagine it must have been painful to hear her voice again."

Rafael nods. "There are now more questions than before."

"I know you aren't comfortable discussing your past," she speaks slower, treading even lighter, "the exile, your sister. But I believe in unburdening yourself from the mountains on your shoulders."

She's right. The blame he projected onto the igni has kept him from truly opening the gates of his grief. All he ever noticed was her exoskeleton, but with the visions gone, he can see Kyoko.

A friend, willing to shoulder some of his burden.

Rafael takes a deep breath, steeling himself for something he hasn't done since he told Unisa about his past, years prior.

"My father was killed in the War when I was fifteen and Joaquina was seventeen. He had named me his undersoldier."

He pauses to explain. "An undersoldier is a warrior who is called up for duty in the event of—"

"I'm aware," Kyoko stops him. "EverEmber is the only human city without a military-based government. I've spent time researching both PeakHaven's and SeaBed's political structures."

Rafael continues, impressed. "We received his helmet and uniform for memorial, along with another set in my size. I was terrified. Joaquina had sharpened my archery, but combat was never something with which I was comfortable. She and I were well aware this was a death sentence for me.

"Joaquina had so much more courage than I did. She was fearless. The night before my deployment, I cried myself to sleep in her arms. I woke in the night and she was wearing the uniform, heading out of our home. I tried to stop her, but—"

The scene plays out in his head, and his eyes begin to moisten. His throat clenches shut, so he swallows hard to release his voice, as he watches his sister leave again.

"She convinced me to let her go. She told me to take care of our mother, and that she loved me." A tear loosens and falls down his cheek. His voice wavers. "The next time I saw her was at her funeral."

The weight pressing down on his heart slowly rises. He runs his fingers over the gems of her bracelet.

"Had I performed my duty, she would still be alive." He looks down at the blood dripping from his fingers. Joaquina's blood. "Her death is on my hands."

There's a pause, until Kyoko offers her thoughts. "I never knew your sister, Rafael, but I know she made her choice to protect you. And I don't think that's something for which she would want you to feel responsible."

"It doesn't matter what she would want," Rafael responds. "She's dead, but it should've been me."

"Then it would've been her talking about losing her brother, eight years later. Except, she wouldn't have been exiled, and she would never have gone to the Library. Which means she would never have learned about human Radiance."

Rafael juggles the intention of Kyoko's thoughts. "Different life paths, with different outcomes."

Kyoko nods. "Loss is never easy, but perhaps it is purposeful. Perhaps the path you're on, to the Radiance, is exactly where you were meant to be. Maybe that's what 'Come find me' means. Look for her within the Radiance."

Comfort blooms in Rafael's heart at the thought of finding Joaquina's spiritual or emotional presence within the void.

Kyoko's words bury into his mind. *Loss is never easy, but perhaps it is purposeful.*

"Loss *is* purposeful, yes, but there are other emotions that can be purposeful, as well. My access to the Radiance today was paved by a sense of protection. For someone I care about."

Heat from her body burns against his chest. His eyes lock on a branch hovering above. Vibrant yellow bursts of petals eject from the branch upon thorny stems, like small collectives of sunrises.

He plucks a flower, stem and all, and hands it to Kyoko. "Grief. Love. Protectiveness. Loss. All parts of one flower." His fingers hover over the petals, then over the thorns. "Grief can be beautiful and life-changing, or it can be painful."

The thick, fibrous stem catches his gaze. "Either way, it grows and blooms from something benevolent."

He wraps his arm around her waist again. "It all stems from love."

Rafael can't see Kyoko's face, but, somehow, he can feel her smile.

The suns indicate midday when they breach the edge of the HearthBark. By some stroke of luck or divine favor, they're still on schedule.

The narrow beach ahead is a thin shore, where Aerthomni bleeds into the waters of the ocean. The waves dance with the rays of the suns, inciting splendid sparks to paint the surface gold.

Reyu Paleyu steps beyond the tree line and allows the travelers to dismount. It releases their belongings, placing them on the ground gently with its vines. The gargantuan creature rises to its feet and faces the Librarians.

"You promised to send it home," Kyoko whispers.

"I said I would try," Rafael responds, his volume low.

"Then try. I'm going for a walk."

She steps backward so swiftly, Rafael has no time to question her.

"I know I said I would try, but the Radiance is new to me."

A vine approaches from the top of the mane and rests gently over the mari's heart. Rafael closes his eyes, and the wind begins to gust.

This time, Rafael doesn't cover his face. He inhales deeply, allowing the air to envelop him. The floating sensation returns and Rafael is soaring amongst the clouds, not resting upon them.

Entering the void feels natural when he allows the Radiance to carry him.

The Vine Demon joins him. *Send home.*

Rafael looks down at his hands and tries to conjure some emotion. He thinks about Joaquina, about his mother, about his exile. He thinks about Unisa and the Prime and Kyoko. But he's unable to manufacture something that should be organic.

And then, as his thoughts linger on Kyoko, an idea strikes.

Loss is never easy, he says to the Vine Demon, *but perhaps it is purposeful. There was a reason you were torn from your home and brought here.*

For evil, the creature responds.

Rafael shakes his head. *Evil was only a vehicle. You helped us today, and perhaps that was the reason. Now, you can give your loss, your anguish, a purpose.*

There's a long pause where the stoic being remains still, and Rafael wonders if it understood. Then, the creature's eyes grow moist.

You've served your purpose here. Use that ache to take you home. Close your eyes and let the Radiance carry you.

The Demon's eyelids purse tightly, and a powerful gust forces Rafael's to follow. When it ceases, he opens them and finds himself standing on the beach again, at the southern tip of the continent.

Alone. The Demon has gone home.

Rafael turns to the HearthBark and smiles. *Thank you, Reyu Paleyu.*

"You sent him home?!" Kyoko exclaims, standing behind Rafael on the beach.

Rafael shakes his head. "No. The Radiance carried him back."

Kyoko raises an eyebrow. "I don't know what that means, but I'm glad."

"Where did you go?" Rafael asks her.

She turns and gestures to a small wooden rowboat docked by the shore. "There's a Doruh fisherman who will be walking home a little wealthier today."

Rafael frowns. "I hope you didn't have to spend too many stones on it."

Kyoko laughs and points to the vessel. "For that rickety, hollowed tree trunk? We saved money at the farm yesterday; this was a necessary expense."

Rafael agrees and with a plunge into the ocean, the journey to EverEmber's volcanic islands begins. Cold ocean water blankets and comforts the mari, who keeps pace with the speed of Kyoko's rowing above his head.

The water enters his nares and he can feel them strip the oxygen from it and deposit it into his lungs. Nictitating membranes cover his eyes, allowing him to witness the glory of the underwater world in which he once lived, loved, and thrived.

The journey to the Mother, Kyoko mentioned, is about an hour by boat, perhaps a little longer with the teetering little vessel Kyoko navigates. Rafael spends that time swimming around the boat, then leaping up onto it to speak with Kyoko. Much to her evident discomfort, it rocks unsteadily every time he emerges from the ocean and lands on it.

Their conversations are light, and they laugh often as the walls between them seem to grow thinner and thinner.

Until Kyoko's smile fades and a sickly paleness takes over her complexion.

"What's wrong?" Rafael asks.

She looks past him and points. "I can see the Mother from here."

Through the fog on the open water, he spies the outline of enormous walls and gates springing up from the ocean. Behind them, the monstrous silhouette of the volcano towers into the sky.

His heart pounds as he realizes his proximity to the nation with which his homeland was at war. He breathes deeply to temper the anxiety, and gets dressed.

As Kyoko continues to row them closer to the massive metallic walls, a warm tension overwhelms him, trembling his heart and sending adrenaline through his veins.

"If those walls were meant to be daunting, they're doing an excellent job."

"They weren't always," Kyoko explains. "They were carved out of volcanic rock, from Mount Mother, displaying cultural designs and patterns. Now, they're fortified with ore plates. A gift from SunSide that forged an alliance with EverEmber, but erased the culture etched within."

The gates become clear through the fog and enlighten Rafael as to why SeaBed's warriors were never able to breach the city. It truly is a fortress, protecting Mount Mother and the igni infrastructure around its base.

The closer they approach, the warmer the tension on Rafael's body gets. He sweats profusely as the air burns hotter and hotter and sets him alight. In a swift movement, he removes his clothes again and jumps back into the cool water.

"Are you alright?" Kyoko asks him.

His head pops out of the surface. "Why is it so hot?"

"Hot air rises from the volcano and settles out here, just beyond the gate. It's a natural defense for the island, and one of the evolutionary functions of the exoskeleton is to protect us from it. Stay in the water for now."

A wide door built into the towering gates swings open. An igni guard crew in a much larger ore-plated warship glides out of it. The Captain steps to the edge of the vessel and looks down at the travelers.

"Librarians? Courtman Tomohiro is away and hasn't informed us of when he'll return. We have no dispatch of your arrival."

"We're not here to see the Courtman," Kyoko clarifies. "We're here on Library business that requires us to visit Tusa."

The Captain turns to another guard with a raised eyebrow. The guard shrugs.

"Tusa? You're igni. You know there's nothing there."

"The Prime doesn't share that belief."

The Captain pauses and scratches his chin. "Well if you're here for business and not for pleasure, we can't allow you entry into the city without a Courtman or Courtwoman's sign-off."

"Then get it," Kyoko demands.

The Captain's expression hardens. "As I've said, we have no indication that any EverEmber official has business with you."

Kyoko points to Rafael, still disrobed and swimming by the boat. "Does *he* look like he's here for business? He's not wearing a tunic."

"You are," the Captain says.

Kyoko rises to her feet, lifts her tunic off, and shoves it into her bag forcefully. "Now we're here for pleasure."

CHAPTER 36

THE MOTHER

Court Democracy *EverEmber*
Date *21st Day of Month 6, Year 1628 DG*

THE GUARD SHIP ESCORTS THE Librarians to the shore of
EverEmber's largest and most populous island, leaving them to dress
again in their tunics after it's departed.

The burn of the descending heated air dissipates, granting Rafael
respite until Kyoko says, "Welcome to EverEmber, Rafael," heighten-
ing his discomfort.

The mari takes a deep breath and steps forth into the igni stronghold.

Busy adults and playing children fill an intricate network of streets
and roads and lanes. Sprawling black stone architecture weaves around
projections of volcanic rock erupting from the ground. Lanterns depicting popular igni figures, both historical and fictional, hang in doorways.

The infrastructure is a fascinating web of blacks and grays that
bring out the purity of the ethereal, white ceramics and porcelain of the
decorations on every doorstep and in every windowsill.

Rafael's palpable rigidity denies him a moment's repose to appreciate the rich culture. He feels the burn of a hundred thousand igni eyes on his fins, but cannot discern a single obvious source.

Kyoko's hand gently lands on his elbow, and the tension melts, momentarily. She directs his attention to a wide clearing, from which a colossal stone landform, Mount Mother, launches into the clouds.

"The city was built around her," she explains.

"By 'her,' you mean the volcano?" Rafael clarifies.

Kyoko nods.

"That's dangerous."

A smile widens on her face. "No. It's home."

Kyoko's expression reflects a sentimentality that mirrors the emotions Rafael felt as he leapt into the ocean.

"I'm proud of you," Rafael tells her, earnestly. "Despite your concerns, you're here, and you're happy."

Kyoko's gaze scans the crowd around them. "And I'll remain so, as long as I recognize the places, but not the faces." She points to a populated area beyond the clearing. "The marketplace. We should find supplies and a place to stay the night, so we can leave for Tusa first thing in the morning."

Rafael turns his fins inward as they needle through the packed market. They wouldn't puncture the igni exoskeleton anyway, but he takes great measures to avoid an altercation in what feels like an eruptive environment.

The marketplace hosts sturdy wooden stalls, and stone vehicles he's never seen before. A mother freely feeds her newborn. A teacher engages in a lesson with his students on the side of the path. Young lovers hold hands, kiss, and browse wares.

The experience engenders a widening disparity between the smiling citizens and the murderous exoskeletons upon which he pinned his sister's demise—the savages he's been taught to hate.

He hasn't seen a single one.

They see a group of children playing suikawari and Rafael's gaze meets Kyoko's, lighting flames on his cheeks. She smiles and winks at him, and he considers pushing an igni, hoping they will end his misery there.

Through one row of stalls, Rafael realizes the breadth of the marketplace. "We'll never visit each stall by sunsdown if we don't split up."

"Agreed," Kyoko says. "I'll come find you in half an hour?" She reaches into her pocket and pulls out a pouch of stones.

"You don't have to," Rafael hesitates.

Kyoko rolls her eyes. "Of course I do, you have no stones. Take half of mine and you can pay me back when we get home."

Rafael swallows his ego and nods, accepting the pouch. As he browses the stalls, he considers what supplies they'll need for the return journey, and his thoughts quickly drift to Unisa, hoping that her adventure has been uneventful and effortless.

He reaches a stall selling arrowheads—some new and functional, others ancient and decorative.

Do arrowheads qualify as supplies? he wonders, unable to resist the allure.

Holding a freshly-forged piece in his fingers, something wraps around his shin. It startles him, but he maintains composure and looks down to find a child, a young girl, embracing his leg. She's no more than two or three years old and gazes up at him, smiling. Her arms release him and she raises them, a nonverbal request to be held.

Rafael looks around, hoping to find the child's parents rushing toward them, but no one comes. He turns to the merchant, who shrugs and helps other customers.

Thanks.

The child's expression slowly deteriorates as her insistence grows frantic. He's held few children in his life, but is well aware of where a refusal to oblige will lead.

He sighs and lifts the child up into his arms. She's lighter than he expected, and her exoskeleton hasn't fully developed yet. Some of her gelatinous inner skin is still visible on her hands.

The child tugs the arrowhead from Rafael's fingers and laughs as it shines. He cannot hold back his smile as a joyful warmth spreads inside his chest. Her sprightly giggles evaporate the stillness between them, and the Librarian finally releases a breath he had subconsciously drawn.

This small child has done more to ease him than any experience he's had around igni in eight years.

"Natsumi!" echoes a silvery voice through the crowd. Rafael turns to find a woman with long, dark tresses in a vibrant yukata walking toward him. Though worry paints her face, he silently recognizes how beautiful her shimmering eyes are. He feels drawn to their familiarity.

The igni woman reaches him and holds her arms out to the child, who laughs and leaps into them, still holding the arrowhead. The woman takes it from the child and hands it back to Rafael.

"Sorry," she says. "Natsumi is very friendly."

Rafael smiles. "I have young cousins who've done the same. Don't apologize."

The woman returns his smile, then scans Rafael from head to toe. He addresses the obvious in an effort to shatter her discomfort.

"Not many mari here, are there?" he says.

She shakes her head. "It was your tunic that captured my attention, not your fins."

Rafael raises an eyebrow. "Ambassadors can't be that uncommon."

"They aren't, but I actively avoid them."

Inexplicably, her words sting harder than he expected. Avoiding mari is expected, but Librarians?

"Then I'll let you continue to avoid them," he says sharply, turning back to the arrowheads.

She clears her throat and then her silvery voice emerges into the air again. "I didn't mean to offend you. I hold no malice toward Librarians, I just"—she purses her lips tightly and pauses before continuing—"never mind. Thank you for keeping my daughter from wandering. Enjoy your arrowheads."

"Wait!" It slips from Rafael's tongue, louder than intended, before he can stop it. Something in her hesitation, in her discomfort around the tunic, and in the familiarity of her eyes, draws him curiously toward her.

"Have you been to the Library? Do I know you?"

She speaks slowly, pronouncing each word carefully, as the color drains from her lips. "I have, but no, we've never met."

"I see. Well I do hope that, perhaps one day, a lasting, positive experience with a Librarian can eradicate the echoes of past hardships."

He offers her a smile, and to his surprise, after a moment's hesitation, she returns it.

"Natsumi is a good judge of character. Perhaps you are right."

She turns and disappears into the crowd with Natsumi looking over her shoulder. Rafael resumes his browsing, though his focus on the inventory wavers. The woman's eyes simmer in his mind, robbing his attention from the arrowheads, the merchant, and the marketplace.

"Arrowheads?" says a silvery voice behind him. It has the same tone and texture as that of Natsumi's mother. "That's not supplies."

Rafael laughs as Kyoko approaches the stall. "I got distracted."

Kyoko shakes her head in reproach. "Well, finish up quickly. We have to check into the inn and then I'd like to show you more of the Mother this evening."

A smile widens across her lips. "As I remember it."

CHAPTER 37

THE MEGA AND THE MARI

Theocratic-Monarchy SunSide
Date *21st Day of Month 6, Year 1628 DG*

THE UNEXPECTED MEETING WITH THE Facilitator, and the violent interaction that preceded it, arouses a rigidity in Alba's body language that leaves the air fraught between her and Unisa.

The angi keeps her gaze lowered as Alba steps quickly and fluidly over the stone path of the Pass. About halfway through, the road forks. The path on the right continues on to SunSide, while the left leads to a trail venturing up the side of the mountain, at the top of which sits PeakHaven, a city where the altitude allows only angi to breathe easily.

The sign at the entrance of the trail reads "PeakHaven: *Alasa Belita, Alasa Nekita.*"

"Unlimited Skies. Unlimited Love." Unisa translates the Nysabaani in a whisper. Her heart aches knowing that she would have received a modicum of that unlimited love, had the Prime not manipulated her parents into abandoning her.

And then she devoted her life to him, his teachings, and his malevolence.

"That's not your home," Alba says, bluntly shaking her from her thoughts.

"What home do I have?" Unisa gestures to the sign. "The city that left me, or the city that lied to me?"

Without hesitation, Alba responds, "Home is where your mother is. Always."

Memories of Ora, the pixie who defines "unlimited love," flood Unisa's thoughts.

"I've never been away from her for this long."

Alba gently places her hand on Unisa's shoulder. "This assignment has tested you in every way, and you've conquered it, proving your resilience." She smiles. "Nothing reminds me more of Ora than that. She may not be with you physically, but everywhere you go, you bring her with you."

Unisa returns her smile. Everything she's accomplished has been on the shoulders of the greatest pixie she's ever known. She turns away from the sign, finally leaving PeakHaven behind her.

SunSide welcomes them with an image of the MegaFather, smiling, holding a chunk of ore. Written under it is "The Future is Forever."

The image is so unnerving, Unisa turns away with a shiver.

The Pass opens to a wide, grassy field, with a predictably daunting presence of officers. The north side of the field is sectioned off by waist-high ore barricades and a fence of Braver shields. On the opposite side are Doruh families, anxiously anticipating the arrival of their loved ones from MoonSide.

Unisa finds a mix of joyous, grateful reunions, and despondent agony. While some wrap their arms around the loved ones who made it through the Pass, others drop to their knees and release cries that shatter Unisa's heart.

The mountainous, metallic gates in the distance hide Larso and the monarch. Hover chariots litter the field, accepting customers who haven't previously made travel arrangements. Unisa's read about the vehicles, and the ore roads built to give them life. She admits, they're quite impressive.

"Alba!" a voice excitedly rings out as the Librarians move toward the chariots. A young, jade-skinned Mega approaches them. She's dressed casually in soft fabric pants that cling to the legs, and a loose top with long, flowing sleeves and a drawstring near the low-cut neckline.

Unisa has only seen her in pictures: Member Saila of the Assembly. Despite her appearance, every Braver she passes stops to face her and place four fingers over their foreheads to salute her. After she acknowledges them, they resume their work.

The confidence she exudes can be felt yards away.

She wraps Alba in a tight embrace, which the Ambassador happily reciprocates. Unisa was entirely unaware that the Mega and the mari shared such a warm bond.

"Your letter completely shocked me," Saila says to Alba. "You're back so soon."

"You know my uncle," Alba responds, "he keeps me busy. I'm just here to facilitate Unisa's first assignment."

She gestures to the angi, whose awe has silenced Unisa.

"Marvelous," Saila responds. "Welcome to SunSide, Unisa."

Saila's hover chariot flows smoothly along ore plates as the theocrat and the two Librarians enter the city. Unisa rests in the back row; though she would've been far more comfortable in the sky, she didn't want to refuse a theocrat's generosity.

Intricate designs telling magnificent tales have been etched into the city gates. The artwork here is in stark contrast to that on the settlement walls of MoonSide. Where one depicts the MegaFather and the Bravers as violent monsters and tyrannical beasts, the other hails them as benevolent heroes and empowerers of the faerie clan.

"The Assembly and the Four are absent," Unisa notes aloud. "The gates show the monarchy and the military as champions, but don't represent the theocracy or the Four at all."

Saila sighs. "Those gates are made of ore, and they memorialize only those whom the forgers worship. Metalwork is just another industry in which the Ore Mong...sorry, the MegaFather has replaced nymphs and pixies with his clanmates."

Unisa's jaw nearly drops, hearing a Member of the theocracy referring to her colleague, and the reigning monarch, by a pejorative, regardless of recent revelations.

Saila continues. "Alba can tell you more about the MegaFather's industrial influence tonight after you all have rested."

"You know more than I do, Sai, you can give her a detailed account." Alba turns to address Unisa. "We'll be staying in Saila's home tonight."

"Oh." Unisa's forehead scrunches in confusion. "Isn't it protocol to stay in the diplomatic chambers in the Castrum?"

Alba nods. "It is, but we'd be far more comfortable staying with Saila during such an" — she pauses — "atypical assignment."

Unisa can hear a voice in her head, admonishing her for disobeying protocol, but she can't tell if it's her own, or the Prime's.

"Unfortunately, I won't be able to tell Unisa much tonight," Saila admits. "I'll be leaving the city as soon as I drop you both home."

Alba frowns. "I'm sorry. Had I known you were busy, I wouldn't have imposed."

"Oh, please." Saila rolls her eyes. "You know you're always welcome. My mother isn't well. I have to return to the village to care for her. I'm meeting with the village salver tomorrow morning."

Alba's eyes widen. "You have a meeting in Eloa *tomorrow*? Sai, it's at the other end of SunSide — even you can't fly that fast."

Saila's jaw drops in mock insult. "I most certainly can."

Alba smiles. "How long will you be gone?"

"Not long. I'll be back on the Twenty-Fourth around sunsdown. The Assembly has a massive announcement planned."

"How massive?"

Saila pauses before she responds. "Historic. It's actually rather serendipitous that you've come here. This announcement will change SunSide forever, so it'll need to be recorded for the Library."

"Sounds significant," Alba comments. "We'll record the announcement before we return to the Library."

The mari turns to Unisa again, though no words are exchanged; Alba's expression relays the thought, *Sorry*.

Unisa forces a smile, communicating, *I understand*, while her heart sinks anxiously. She'd never willingly prolong this torture.

"Will your father be part of this announcement?" Alba asks the pixie.

"Hmm"—she places a finger on her chin—"indirectly."

"I see. And will he be joining you to visit your mother?"

Saila scoffs. "You know he wouldn't do that. He's too busy fulfilling his duties as Zar-Lo's pet. Why would he suddenly care about anyone but himself? He doesn't even know I've been called to her bedside."

"We saw him in Arlun. He tried to stop us from coming to SunSide."

"What?!" Saila's volume rises. "Did he detain you? I can inform the Assembly. There can be consequences."

"Wait," Unisa jumps in, as a spark goes off in her mind, "the Facilitator is your father?"

"Unfortunately."

"I'm surprised someone had a child with him," Unisa blurts out loudly before she can stop herself. "Apologies. I simply meant he doesn't seem very...fatherly."

Saila laughs. "Spot-on instincts. He isn't much of a father. Never was. Always chose his duty over family. Even over his own arm."

Unisa is hesitant to pry, though the pixie's last comment invites her. "What do you mean?"

"During the nymph and pixie rebellions here in Larso, twenty years ago. I was fifteen and had spent the majority of my life in Eloa, my mother's village. But when she started to fall ill, I was sent here to live with my dear daddy."

"Your father brought a teenager to Larso in the middle of a rebellion?"

"He did. His paternal instincts have always been wrapped in a bit of"—she pauses—"carelessness. While the rebellion fought for land rights, my father was a Braver."

"A pixie Braver," Alba specifies, shaking her head. "Defending a monarch who was stripping his own clan of their rights."

"A rare breed of traitor," Saila continues. "He was convinced that they could keep the *radical scum* at bay, but the Bravers lost control of the skirmishes rather quickly. My connection to the Radiance was in its infancy; I barely survived when the battle came through our neighborhood and decimated our home."

"Where was your father?" Unisa asks. "He didn't protect you?"

"He was in the Castrum, losing his arm for the only one who's ever mattered to him."

"Father of the Century," Alba scoffs.

Saila nods. "He was named Facilitator that day. Sacrificed his arm and his daughter for a promotion. I lost all respect and what little love I had left for him. I vowed never to share a roof with him again."

"Did you go back to the village?" Unisa asks.

Saila shakes her head and smiles. "Oh, no. I stayed in Larso after a Doruh family took me in. They had a daughter around my age, Sonali. We pursued our education together and even started the same political apprenticeship."

There's a long pause in which her expression dims, but she quickly shakes her head and continues. "I worked myself ragged until I joined the Assembly. He opposed, of course, but my resolve never wavered. In fact, I think the more he opposed, the stronger my will became."

"Sai's sharp wit and unwavering ambition terrifies him," Alba says, shooting a look of admiration at the pixie.

"I stayed focused on my goals regardless of his offers, wanting him to see me around the Castrum as a reminder of what he'd lost— what he'd willingly forsaken for an individual he barely knew at the time."

She exhales deeply. "Above all, I wanted him to know I didn't need him. That I was better off without him and that I could make real change in SunSide."

"An ambitious goal," Alba comments. "One that often feels impossible since the monarchy feigns devotion to the Four to fool the theocracy into support."

A soft smile presses onto Saila's lips. "We might die in the pursuit of the impossible, but hope never does. Perhaps it's closer than we think."

High population density with limited space plagues the outskirt districts of Larso. Towering stone buildings stack residents on residents. A maze of streets overflow with the homeless. Outside of the ore infrastructure and the lack of faeries, there isn't much that differentiates these communities from those in MoonSide.

"The Doruh who migrate here, and the nymphs and pixies who chose to stay after the displacement, settle in these communities," Saila explains. "They travel into the main districts for work, but can't afford to live there since the faeries, dragging generations of wealth behind them, thrust property values into the sky."

"The land around the Castrum was once evenly distributed amongst the three Mega clans, back before this dynasty," Alba adds. "As were basic social and economic resources. None of those resources followed the lower classes out to these neighborhoods."

Unisa sighs. "This is all history. I'm a Librarian. I should know this."

"Your tunic is the very reason you *don't* know any of this," Alba reminds her.

"How do the faeries justify treating the Doruh and the other Mega clans this way?"

"Fearmongering," Saila responds. "These neighborhoods in the outskirts have slightly higher rates of crime, so the faeries use those statistics to label others as violent."

Having studied the rise and fall of kingdoms and nations throughout history, the truth seems glaring to her.

"Of course crime rates are higher in these neighborhoods," Unisa says. "Crime follows poverty and desperation. The faeries don't keep crime low because they're faeries; they keep crime low because they've surrounded themselves with plenty. With abundance. With luxury."

Saila nods. "While all of that is true, there's also the fact that crime statistics come from faerie researchers. It's hard to gauge how much of those findings actually exist, and how much is manufactured."

As they leave the outskirt districts behind, residences become mixed with commerce. Mega marketplaces, Doruh bazaars, small teashops and merchants; the non-faerie residents of the outer districts slowly become scarce. Faeries are found in their chariots, or on Doruh chauffeurs, dressed in clean, pressed clothing, laughing and enjoying a life where all basic needs, and more, are provided for them.

"Larso University is in this area," Saila dictates. "Classrooms are packed with faeries whose parents have either paid handsomely to educate them or have leveraged friendships and status to enroll their children."

"Meanwhile," Alba continues, "the non-faeries are offered *generous* sums of money to attend classes by wealthy faeries to whom they'll be indebted for the remainder of their lives."

Saila sighs. "And possibly their children's lives."

Unisa's brow wrinkles as she tries to pull weeds of fallacy from the gardens of SunSide's society. "I don't understand. Educating the populace benefits the kingdom."

She holds her gaze to Alba's. "Knowledge empowers, right? Why would a society obstruct empowerment with financial burdens that bar citizens from education?

Alba and Saila exchange a long look and allow Unisa's question to linger as she arrives at the conclusions on her own.

Because pouches of colorful stones can be weighed, and societal success cannot.

They finally arrive at the center of the city. Similar to the middle districts, there is a mix of commerce and residences, but none that seem overly crowded. The ore streets weave like thick vines around buildings, and more chariots appear on the roads, including longer ones carrying thirty or forty passengers at a time.

"The Castrum complex is not far from here," Saila explains. "All government operations are run from there."

"That much, I'm aware of," Unisa responds.

Saila stops the chariot outside of a stout, two-story home. She and the Librarians disembark with their belongings and walk up the stone steps.

Unisa finds herself facing a number of wide, open rooms on the first floor, with a staircase in the center of the home leading up to the bedrooms on the second. To the right of the staircase is the kitchen, and to the left seems to be a study with enormous, full bookshelves lining the walls.

Starlight drips into the home from a transparent glass pane on the ceiling.

"The skylight window is my favorite feature," Saila remarks before she points to the staircase. "Bedrooms are upstairs. Choose any. I wish I could stay, but I really have to leave."

"You've done so much for us," Unisa responds gratefully. "Thank you."

Saila smiles. "It's my pleasure. I'll see you on the Twenty-Fourth. The announcement will take place at sunsdown. I'll be back then."

Alba embraces her. "Fly safe. Take care."

With a final wave and smile, Saila takes to the skies, fully expecting to return to the same SunSide from which she now departs.

CHAPTER 38

THE FALCON AND THE WOLF

Theocratic-Monarchy SunSide
Date 21st Day of Month 6, Year 1628 DG

CALM OCEAN WAVES CARRY SEVEN companions back to
their home continent. Soft breezes tickle Salessa's cheek as she sits with
Zakia, listening to Gina and Kruga plan the infiltration of Lily Beach.
Naina stands on the upper deck with Symin and Ray-Mi, discussing
the navigation back to SunSide.

There's an indescribable tranquility engulfing the vessel. Serenity,
comfort—a far departure from life in MoonSide. Salessa wonders if
they deserve it, as if they're living a moment that belongs to someone
else. The twins belong in MoonSide, surely, alongside their people.
Living the life fate has ascribed to them.

But they were plucked from that life five days ago, and thrust into a
community that gave them some semblance of family for the first time
in over a decade. A family that never questioned their contributions,
that invited them to belong.

Family. It's not lost on Salessa that this word holds too much weight for five days. It's an extreme response to twelve years of deprivation — twelve years without trust, when trust was all Salessa craved. She'd made the mistake of trusting too quickly before, and had promised Naina she wouldn't repeat what had happened with Lexona.

Somehow, though, this feels different. The vulnerability isn't one-sided. Symin's grief is worn on his sleeve. Ray-Mi's history is etched into his atonement. Gina's, Kruga's, and Zakia's suffering is palpable in their steadfastness.

Ten gray eyes, ten windows, and Salessa feels as though she's seen through them all.

Five days is extreme for family. But extreme moments require extreme decisions. And Salessa has made an extreme decision.

She turns toward her sister standing between Symin and Ray-Mi, and sends a thought into Naina's mind.

Naina, it's time. Everyone on this vessel has opened up to us. They don't deserve to be lied to anymore.

Not again, Lessi, comes Naina's exasperated voice. *How can we trust —*

We're on a ship with them, in the middle of the ocean. We've just completed a mission for their cause. We know who they are and how they came to be here.

Naina pauses, considering. *And if telling them our truth reels them into our danger?*

Look around, Naina. They're already in danger. Vulnerability and honesty forge bonds that can't be broken. Secrets keep us isolated. We need allies and a community.

There's a long pause, during which Salessa anticipates an explosion of rage and aggression. But there is none. Naina takes a moment to look around at their traveling companions.

Do it. Whatever comes after, I'm with you.

Always?

Yes, Lessi. Always.

Naina leads Symin and Ray-Mi down to the lower deck. The two trailing suns near the horizon; nightfall is less than an hour away. Salessa takes a deep breath, clears her throat, and addresses the travelers.

"There's something Naina and I would like to share," she says. "The truth. About why the Facilitator is hunting us."

"Well, why we suspect he is," Naina clarifies.

The group exchanges looks of interest, but remains silent, allowing the twins to continue.

"It's important for us to tell you, first, about the Twin deities of the Doruh religion. Naina told Symin a little about them already, and Zakia is aware of the mythology, but, for the rest of you, the Twins are a pair of siblings, a brother and a sister, who are prophesied to be resurrected one day to prevent catastrophe."

"I do enjoy a good myth," Ray-Mi says, rubbing his palms together eagerly. "Story time."

Salessa continues. "Shortly after the creation of the Doruh, a set of twins were born to a pixie named Adera and a former teri human named Anhum. The twins were the first naturally-conceived Doruh and—"

"Lessi, quicker," Naina admonishes her. "They're not your students, they don't need a history lesson. Just the basics."

Salessa nods. "Sorry. One night as the twins slept, they had a vision. The same vision, on the same night. They witnessed their rebirth as deities: glowing skin, wings, engaged in a catastrophic battle against an indiscernible evil force."

The Mega lean in, intrigued.

"When they awoke the next morning," Naina continues, "they told all of their followers about the vision."

"Did anyone believe them?" Symin asks.

"Oh, yes," Salessa responds. "Most of the Doruh did. They formed a group of devotees to the resurrection of the Twins, calling themselves the *O'raha*."

"Group of devotees," Naina scoffs. "Call them what they were, Lessi. A cult."

Salessa sighs. "The *O'raha* eventually grew to become dangerous extremists, but that was long after the death of the Twins. They kept oral records of subsequent visions the Twins had. Visions that foretold details of their rebirth."

Salessa clears her throat to recite the declaration verbatim:

"One from the land, one from the seas
One from the skies, one from the trees
Two sets of twins will be conceived
Their souls and bodies will be weaved

The God and the Goddess will be retrieved
And peace on the All-Sphere will be achieved."

She continues, elaborating, "Two sets of Doruh twins will be born, and each set will merge, physically and spiritually, to resurrect one of the Twin Deities. Genetically, Doruh twins must shift into the same animal. If one is a tiger, the other will be a tiger."

Naina continues. "But the four Doruh who will resurrect the Twins will all shift into different animal forms: one from the land, one from the skies, one from the trees, and one from seas. That's how the Doruh will recognize that the time for resurrection has come."

Symin's eyes widen with realization. "The falcon and the wolf. The skies and the land."

Salessa's breath catches in her throat as her heart's pace quickens. She feels uncomfortably bare as their secret is thrust into the open.

"Yes," Naina confirms. "According to the myth, we are one set of twins who will resurrect the God or the Goddess in the world's darkest hour."

"Do you know who the other twins are?" Kruga asks.

Naina shakes her head. "We don't even know if any of this is real. We told you earlier that our differing animal forms are a result of a genetic anomaly. That could very well be the case, and all of this could be mythology — folklore."

Salessa warns the group further. "But we think that the Facilitator and the MegaFather believe the myth to be true, which is why we told you the truth. You deserve to know who's at your side, and what risk is posed traveling with us."

"We appreciate the transparency," Gina finally speaks, "but it doesn't change anything. Risk is inevitable in this life. How did you expect us to react to your little children's story?"

"Gina!" Zakia exclaims. "Naina and Salessa just opened up to us about something—"

"Something they admitted could be a waste of breath." She turns to the twins. "Do you have any evidence that this myth could be true?"

Naina and Salessa exchange cautionary looks before Salessa responds. "There are a few things, the biggest one being telepathy."

Symin chuckles. "So it isn't just a twin thing."

Naina adds, "We're also impressively difficult to kill."

"What do you mean?" Zakia asks, wide-eyed.

"I've had bones torn from my body and lost limbs. My head's been turned around entirely. I've found myself on death's doorstep at least once a month for the past few years. As you can see"—she gestures to her body—"I healed."

"There's also…" Salessa continues, "the feeling. It's hard to explain, but Naina feels like an extension of myself. It's more than love. It feels like we're—"

"Two halves of the same being," Naina completes.

Zakia turns to Gina with a smug grin, though Gina seems unfazed. "Do you have any evidence that what you described is unequivocally *not* the result of a genetic anomaly?"

The twins remain quiet. There isn't any evidence of that.

Gina turns to Kruga. "You're a scientist. Tell them."

Kruga raises a finger and strokes his chin. "From a scientific perspective, any of that could be the result of genetic mutations."

A smile widens on Gina's face, only to fade when Kruga continues.

"However, that doesn't invalidate the idea that mystical factors are influencing your lives in some way. Science and mythology aren't necessarily exclusive of one another."

Gina scoffs and opens her hands to gesture to the twins. "Come on, Kruga. These two? An ancient, powerful Goddess incarnate?"

A low growl develops in Naina's throat.

Ignore her, Salessa says.

"Myth or science, it doesn't matter," Symin addresses the group. "Salessa and Naina are in danger because of it. Now, more than ever, they need our support, our protection, and"—he locks eyes with the twins—"our community."

Salessa nods gratefully and turns to Naina, who, for the first time in a long time, wears the hint of a sincere smile on her face.

A blanket of darkness unfolds over the sky as they approach Aerthomni. Moonlight guides the vessel to SunSide's docks. Gina steps off first and onto the pier. She stretches out her arms and legs, then takes a deep breath and turns toward the visible edge of Nivyan Hollow.

"I can feel it," she says. "The Radiance. I never want to be near another crumb of ore again."

"We're heading to Lily Beach in the morning," Kruga reminds her, stepping onto the dock. "We'll likely find more ore there than anywhere else."

The travelers make their way through the wide trees until they reach Syma's clearing. They find themselves among the familiar tree shelters, but something has radically changed since the last time they were here.

It's quiet. No music, no singing. No food, no drink. No celebration. The clearing and the treetops are filled with nothing but silence.

"Mother," Symin whispers, staring at Syma's tree with horror.

He steps quickly forward, lifting his hands, and then pulls them apart forcefully, as if tearing a hole into the air in front of him. When his hands separate, he disappears and then immediately reappears in front of the dwelling. He places his fingertips on the wood of the door and then phases through it, entering smoothly as if it weren't even there.

The twins and remaining Mega wait with bated breath, in stunned silence, until Symin and his mother emerge from the darkness of the tree hut. He leads her out slowly, and Salessa holds back a gasp.

Her eyes are sunken and her skin is withered. She's distraught.

She steps past all Mega, directly up to the twins. "You are in grave danger, my darlings." She moves her hands about rhythmically until a piece of paper materializes between her fingers. Salessa slowly takes it from her and Naina leans in to read it.

At the top of the sheet is a drawn image of two young women, resembling the twins. The words underneath state: *Doruh Twins. 19-21 years old. If found, inform your local Braver authority. Any false reports or harboring of fugitives will be tried as treason. Do not approach. Do not engage.*

Salessa's heart drops into her stomach and she makes eye contact with Naina.

He knows we're here, Naina's voice pierces into her mind.

"What is it?" Gina asks. Salessa hands her the paper. She reads it and passes it along to the others.

"They're making rounds through the forest," Syma says. "The Bravers are holding entire communities hostage until they get information."

A look of panic crosses Naina's face and the elder nymph continues. "We haven't told them anything. Everyone has gone into hiding."

"This is our fault," Salessa says, guilt sitting like a stone in her gut.

"What do we do?" Naina asks Symin.

He now holds the paper and stares down at it intently, focused but not alarmed. His gaze rises to Gina and they hold eye contact, as if they, too, are telepathic, and Gina's stern stare forces a nod from the nymph.

He turns to Salessa, a sad half-smile emerging on his face. "You're shorter than her, and your skin isn't pink. But the day I walked into the teahouse, I thought I had seen my Zynima."

He turns to Naina. "There's no pain in this world like losing a child. And no one can take that child's place. But for a short time, I think part of me wanted to feel whole again. And that's why I invited you to join me on this journey."

Gina offers him a reassuring nod and he holds up the "Wanted" flyer.

"I can no longer put your lives at risk to fill the void Zynima left behind." A tear loosens down his cheek. "You have to go."

"Go?!" Naina's volume rises and her tone stiffens. "Where, exactly? You pulled us out of MoonSide, we can't go back now. Not with—" She gestures to the flyer.

"Panaerth," Gina suggests. "You can take our old vessel and hide there."

"We're coming with you to Lily Beach," Naina insists forcefully. "That's the plan. One you wouldn't even have had if it weren't for Lessi."

"Lily Beach is swarming with Bravers," Symin counters. "It's not safe for you to come with us anymore. You can't stay here, and you can't go back to MoonSide. Panaerth is the safest option."

There's a long pause in which Salessa tries to generate some kind of response to dissuade Symin from his decision. But by the end of it, she accepts that they won't be able to change his mind.

"After all of this," Naina growls, "you're just going to abandon us?" Her voice shakes, but not with anger.

Naina's hurt.

Symin takes Naina's hand in his own. "I'm not abandoning you. I'll come find you after this is over."

Naina pulls her hand back fiercely. "I knew you couldn't be trusted."

Symin's jaw falls agape. He clears his throat and turns to Zakia. "Escort them to the old ship. Then meet us back here."

Zakia nods and, reluctantly, the twins say their goodbyes to each of their former companions. Salessa's throat tightens as she embraces

Symin and thanks him for facilitating their escape from MoonSide. Naina presents him with a brusque nod, and the twins follow Zakia through Nivyan Hollow again, back to the docks.

What's the plan? echoes Naina's voice as they wade through the trees.

Salessa remains stone-faced, hoping to hide her confusion from Zakia. *We're going back to Panaerth.*

I'm not complying with their horseshit idea, Lessi.

I don't have a different plan, Naina.

I do. Follow my lead.

Naina, wait—

"Hold on," Naina says to Zakia, who abruptly stops walking. "Change of plans. We need your help."

Zakia turns to Salessa, who shrugs apologetically.

"With what?" the pixie says.

"Take us to Larso."

Again, Zakia turns to Salessa, who is glaring at her sister, bewildered by the wolf's penchant for dangerous situations.

"I'm definitely not going to do that," Zakia replies. "The Facilitator can track you, remember?"

"Not in the Bunker, he can't," Naina replies. "Your safe house. Kruga told us about it."

The pixie turns to Salessa. "Are you sure about this?"

Salessa looks to Naina. *Are YOU sure about this?*

Yes, Lessi. Please.

Salessa sighs. "We're sure. The Facilitator will not stop looking for us, even on Panaerth. The only place he won't expect us to be, is right under his nose."

Zakia's hesitation is apparent. "But he'll be able to feel you in the city from the time you enter the gate, until you get into the Bunker. It's risky."

Salessa recalls Gina's sentiment. "Risk is inevitable in this life. We're tired of being hunted. It's time we do the hunting."

Zakia turns to Naina. "Symin is not going to be happy about this when he finds out."

"Does it look like I care what Symin thinks?" Naina responds, turning and walking in the direction of the city. "He'll live."

CHAPTER 39

FATE

Court Democracy *EverEmber*
Date *21st Day of Month 6, Year 1628 DG*

THE YUKATA OFFERS FAR MORE comfort than a tunic. After two days of hard travel, Rafael finds peace in the tightly wrapped garment covering the crimson blemishes creeping up his chest.

The visions survived eight years on exoskeletons, whenever Rafael saw them, and they'll likely last longer on him. But it's a fate he's accepted.

The preserved inn is a two-story wooden structure with a thatched roof, a flavor of older igni architecture that has since been largely replaced by volcanic stone.

Rafael steps down from the front entrance to find Kyoko waiting for him on the stone path. Behind her is a railing, protecting passersby from the waters of the canal below.

"I should be upset with you for making me wait this long," Kyoko teases with a devious smile.

Rafael's cheeks burn red. "Sorry, I closed my eyes for a minute and woke up…later."

Kyoko looks up at the falling suns. "Well, it's almost dark now. The ryokan gave us a pass to a local onsen, but we'll enjoy it more in the daytime."

"Um," Rafael clears his throat sheepishly, "Ryokan? Onsen?"

Kyoko's smile widens and she gestures to the inn. "Ryokan." She then turns to the water beyond the railing. "This is a hot spring village and the springs are onsen."

Rafael's eyebrows scale his forehead. "That sounds fun! Perhaps we can use the pass on the return trip."

Kyoko nods. "There is something else I can show you before dinner."

She leads him through softly lit streets lined with willow trees, where he takes in the calm ambience of the hot spring village. Families, friends, and couples travel leisurely through the alleyways and over small bridges above the canal. There's a peace penetrating the place like faint droplets of mist.

But this peace is interspersed with moments of quiet hostility. Periodic backroads feature revolted igni glances and low mumbles, and individuals who march in opposing directions when they see the man with piscine nares walking toward them.

Rafael initially believes his paranoia toys with him, but when Kyoko holds a prolonged moment of disappointed eye contact with him, he realizes she's noticed it as well. A part of him is relieved to see a predictable response. In many ways, the feeling is mutual.

"Ashiyu," Kyoko says, identifying their destination upon arrival at the other end of the village.

A foot bath, set up outside a local merchant's shop on the side of the road, sits before Rafael. Stone pillars hold a sturdy roof over the warm spring water and wooden benches where people relax while their feet soak.

Relief shoots through Rafael when his feet hit the warm water. His eyes close instinctively and he releases an unintentional moan.

Kyoko laughs. "I can't articulate the joy of watching you experience this for the first time."

Rafael surrenders to a relaxing reverie, oblivious when Kyoko mentions she's going to enter the merchant's shop and will return in a few minutes. Rafael nods absentmindedly, allowing the warmth on his feet to crawl up his legs. He much prefers the cold of the ocean, but he cannot deny the curious allure of new experiences.

Footsteps soon approach the bench next to him. Someone takes a seat and he assumes Kyoko's returned. "Find what you were looking for?"

"Evidently," chimes a familiar, silvery voice.

Rafael's eyes pop open and he finds the woman from the marketplace smiling at him. "Natsumi's mother."

Her eyes widen and Rafael feels drawn to their familiar shimmer again. "You recognized me."

"You recognized me, too."

The woman laughs softly. "There aren't many fins here."

"You can't even see my fins under the yukata, unless you've been inspecting me," Rafael states confidently.

A mild pink glow burns on the woman's cheeks. "You stick out more than you realize."

"Trust me. I realize." He looks over his shoulder and can still see sparse passersby giving lingering looks of disgust.

He turns back to the woman. "Are you going to tell me your name, Natsumi's mother?"

"Yala," the woman responds.

Rafael pauses, mentally tracing the origin of the name. "That's Nysabaani, not igni. Are you trying to hide your real name from me?"

Yala shakes her head. "It's a nickname. I don't really use my igni name anymore."

"Why is that?"

Yala's smile starts to fade and the mari realizes he's invaded her privacy. Quickly, he moves the subject. "Why don't you put your feet into the ashiyu?"

She sits reversed on the wooden bench, with her sandals on the stone path, her back to the water.

Her smile recovers. "I should probably be returning to the store across the street. Natsumi is there with some of my friends and she's going to get impatient if I'm gone for too long."

"I appreciate that you came to see me," Rafael says with a polite smile.

"You haven't told me your name, Ambassador."

"Rafael."

"It's good to meet you, Rafael. Perhaps I'll see you around more while you're here."

"I won't be here long. My"—he pauses, realizing "coworker" doesn't feel entirely accurate anymore—"friend is here with me and I think we'll be leaving in the next couple of days."

Yala stands. "It appears fate brought us together twice in one day, on EverEmber's most populous island. Either it has some grand intention of bringing us together, or some other force is drawing us to one another. Something tells me I'll see you again."

Rafael nods. "Then I'll see you soon."

Yala's eyes scan Rafael from head to toe. "You look better in the yukata than in the tunic."

"Are you saying I look handsome?" he teases.

Yala laughs. "I'm saying you look better in the yukata than in the tunic. Take from that what you will." She steps forward and returns over the bridge to the merchants across the canal.

Something she said continues to ring in his ears long after she's gone and Kyoko's returned.

Either it has some grand intention of bringing us together, or some other force is drawing us to one another.

Kyoko sips gently as warm soup flushes her insides with cozy satisfaction.

The restaurant was a short walk from the ashiyu, but it helped her work up a rather aggressive appetite. Her jaw tightens around salivary glands when her gaze finds a bowl of rice and stir-fried lotus root.

Rafael's appetite rivals hers, but less for food and more for water. The two goblets resting about her meal are no match for the eight around his. It leaves little room on the table for his dinner, yet he somehow manages.

They solidified their morning plans before the food arrived: a short trip to Tusa, confirmation of the TreeKeeper's absence, and then return to the Mother, where they've decided to stay an additional night before journeying home.

Their mouths have now become too full for talking, though Rafael will occasionally pass a comment to Kyoko, which she will minimally register. It isn't until Rafael says something truly peculiar that she pulls her mouth from her bamboo chopsticks and raises an eyebrow.

"I'm sorry, what did you say?" she asks.

"I said I recognize someone at another table." He peers excitedly over her shoulder.

Confusion washes over Kyoko. "You've never been to EverEmber, how can you recognize someone?"

"I actually just met her today," Rafael clarifies. "Twice actually."

"Oh," Kyoko spits out, still confused. "Where?"

"First in the marketplace, and then at the ashiyu while you were in the store. Her daughter wandered up to me in the market and we ended up talking."

Kyoko turns around to look across the restaurant, but the dining crowds make it hard to discern who he's talking about.

She turns back to Rafael. "You're welcome to invite her to join us if you'd like."

Rafael raises a finger to scratch his chin. "I don't want to disturb her dinner, but perhaps I'll just walk over to be polite."

Kyoko offers him a reassuring smile. "That's a good idea."

Rafael stands and crosses the restaurant. Kyoko turns quickly back to her food, enjoying every bite of the delicious meal. A nostalgia grows in her stomach as she tastes flavors she hasn't experienced since she left sixteen years prior.

Rafael returns quickly and places a hand on Kyoko's shoulder to get her attention. She looks up from her plate.

"My friend wanted to meet you," he says, a wide smile on his face.

Kyoko smiles politely and stands as Rafael introduces his friend. "Kyoko, this is Yala."

The name strikes forcefully, like an arrow shot from Rafael's tongue. Every muscle in her body tenses and her breathing stops entirely. A hundred thousand thoughts and emotions flood her mind.

By some violent stroke of misfortune, her sister stands inches from her. The one person on this planet she was actively avoiding now stands so close, they breathe the same air.

Kyoko's throat closes and she tries to hide her physical reaction but fails miserably. Heat rises to her cheeks and her eyes start to burn.

Kanako's jaw has lowered and her eyebrows have come together in an obvious display of regret. A moist coating slowly begins to develop over her eyes.

Kyoko's heart pounds furiously, as the last words Kanako spoke to her creep back up into her ears. Words she'd long buried in the grave-yard of her mind.

I never want to see you again. You have no idea what I've been through, all for a prize that you stole from me. I hate you. Don't ever come back to EverEmber. If I see you again, I'll tell everyone what you did.

And now, she stands in front of Kyoko. Here in EverEmber. The cruelty of fate knows no bounds.

Rafael looks between the two women and the truth seems to dawn on him. The brightness of his expression fades quickly as his eyes widen so far, Kyoko thinks they might fall from the sockets.

He turns to his new acquaintance. "Your igni name is Kanako, isn't it?"

There's a hesitant pause, and then Kanako nods, slowly. She turns quickly on her heels and, somehow, it feels like fresh rejection—anoth-er stabbing pain in Kyoko's gut.

"Wait!" Rafael says, and Kanako stops. "Please, don't go."

"I have to," Kanako's voice emerges, little more than a pained whisper.

"Please," Rafael begs and then turns quickly to Kyoko. "Do you remember what I said?"

Kyoko shakes her head. She can't hear anything but Kanako's voice saying, *I hate you.* Her breathing hastens as the room grows cloudy and she takes in as much oxygen as she can. "Rafael, I can't do this."

He steps closer to her and takes her hand in his. "Kyoko, do you remember what I said in the HearthBark?"

Kyoko finally focuses on something other than her sister's long-uttered words. She takes a deep, rattled breath and shudders as she thinks back to what Rafael said to her earlier this morning.

Don't close your heart to the possibility of forgiveness. Where a tree was once cut down, a new seed can be planted. As long as your sister breathes, you have the opportunity to build something new. Some of us, who no longer have that opportunity, would give everything for it.

She places his words into perspective. Her sister is alive, standing in front of her. Kyoko can still be forgiven.

"This is your chance," Rafael whispers to her. "Build something new."

Kanako speaks again, her voice more strained this time. "I'm leaving."

Rafael hurriedly calls out to her. "You said it yourself, not three hours ago. Fate brought us together for some grand intention." He gestures to Kyoko. "What intention could be greater than this? I refuse to believe you don't see that."

There's a long pause in which Kyoko is certain Kanako will simply walk away. But all sense is lost when her sister turns back around to face her, her eyes lowered to the ground.

Rafael turns back to Kyoko. "I'm going back to the ryokan. Join me after."

Kyoko is at a loss for words, reeling from the ghosts of her past, but she allows Rafael's words to reverberate through her mind again.

Some of us, who no longer have that opportunity, would give everything for it.

"Please," she says to Kanako, her voice quivering through a clenched throat, "join me." She gestures to the place where Rafael sat.

After six years of silence and one last, hesitant pause, Kanako takes five tentative steps forward and sits at the table.

CHAPTER 40

KANAKO

Sovereign City-State *The Library*
Date *39th Day of Month 8, Year 1622 DG - 6 Years Earlier*

"YOU CAN DO THIS," ALBA encourages her Vice Ambassador.
"Don't let her leave without an explanation."

Kyoko's eyes remain locked on the igni woman loading bags onto
a camel chauffeur. "If Ana were in my position, and you were in Yala's,
would a sense of sisterhood even matter to you anymore?"

A gentle smile plays on Alba's lips. "It is the only thing that
would matter."

Alba's words seep in and Kyoko nods. Family is all that matters.

She steps forward from the Library's gates and breathes deeply as
she approaches the edge of the forest where the path south begins.

Yala turns to her and, when their eyes meet, a pang of guilt tears
through Kyoko's chest. Her throat tightens as she witnesses the lines of
stress across her sister's face, and the sunken, sleepless eyes.

"Please, don't leave me," Kyoko's voice creaks out. "Let me
explain, Yala."

Yala's finger rises to within an inch of Kyoko's face, and her cheeks flare crimson. "Don't you *ever* fucking call me that again. Mama told you to call me Yala because it means 'Protector.' But I will not protect anyone who" —she pauses and moisture gathers in her eyes—"betrays me."

Kyoko pushes the words out as best as she can. "I'm sorry. I didn't know he had promised it to you. I'll find a different Ambassador to work with. You can have Alba. Just, please, don't leave me."

Yala continues to load her baggage to the camel's back. "He isolated me from you. From everyone. I have no one here." She turns again and holds stern eye contact. "How many times have you seen me in the last ten years, Kyoko? How many times did you come looking for me?"

Nausea rises from the depths of Kyoko's shame. Her words emerge broken and scattered as she tries to find a response. "I d-didn't know, Yala. W-what he was doing to you…"

A tear breaks free and journey's down Yala's face. "You didn't know? Or you didn't want to know, as long as it didn't interfere with your ambition?"

Kyoko shakes her head. She's unable to find the words to express how wrong the accusation is.

"He stole everything from me, Kyoko. Years of my life. My self-worth. My ability to know whether I would have made it here without him. And you watched it happen while climbing the ranks and taking the one thing that was promised to me. The one thing for which I actually agreed to isolation."

She displays an accusatory finger to her younger sister. "I never want to see you again. You have no idea what I've been through, all for a prize that you stole from me. I hate you."

She turns quickly and mounts the camel, speaking her final words over her shoulder as it steps forward. "Don't ever come back to Ever-Ember. If I see you again, I'll tell everyone what you did."

Court Democracy EverEmber
Date 21st Day of Month 6, Year 1628 DG

PARALYSIS ACCOMPANIES DISTRESS. NOT A physical paralysis, though that follows closely behind, but the paralysis of time.

As Kyoko sits across the table from her sister after six years, time has stopped. The music has silenced, the patrons and staff are frozen in place, and even the wings of the flies remain stagnant.

Nothing lives, nothing breathes, but Kyoko and Yala.

Yala's lips purse tightly, though her expression isn't void of emotion. Her cheeks flare red, the way they had at the edge of the forest. Kyoko isn't sure how a conversation of such weight should begin, so she utters the only words that spring from her thoughts and into her mouth.

"You have a daughter," she says. It isn't a question, it's a reaction to Rafael's description of how he and Yala met. A reminder of how distant Kyoko and her sister have become.

Yala nods and a soft smile springs onto half her face. "I do. Natsumi. She's two."

Kyoko forces an equally half-hearted smile. "You have a life now. A *real* life. I'm happy for you."

Yala swallows hard and the smile fades. "It feels like my third life. There was one before the Library, one while I was there, and now, the one after."

Kyoko doesn't recognize the woman in front of her. Memories flash before her eyes of a bright, exuberant teenager, whose hopes and dreams carried them across the continent for a chance at a better life.

But the woman before her has a dimmer shine, the dregs of suffering scarring her expression like a brand on the flesh.

"You built this new life," Kyoko responds. "You deserve all the joy it brings you. I mean that."

Yala nods. "Building this life wasn't easy. When I walked away, I had the body of a twenty-six-year old, but the mind of a sixteen-year old. I lost all of that time and had to start over again."

The world grows blurry as the guilt in Kyoko's chest tightens her throat and fills her eyes with water. "I know I failed you."

There's a long pause as Yala inhales deeply and releases. Her next words fall on Kyoko like a lightning bolt. "It's not your fault."

Kyoko is in disbelief. She dreaded facing Yala after all these years because she knew the opposite to be true. Her eyebrows scrunch. "What?"

"It's *his* fault, not yours. He used my innocence against me, forced me to believe there was no room in my life for anyone but him. At first, he lovingly urged me to confide in him, and then used my insecurities against me."

She shudders as her voice strains. "And then, he kissed me for the first time."

A single word breaks free from Kyoko's rigid vocal chords. "When?"

"When I was sixteen. And he was forty-three."

The tears release down Kyoko's cheeks and the realization haunts her. "It started right away."

Yala nods. "When I tried to reject him, he threatened to resign as the Prime. He said the city would blame me, so I continued. I was dealing with a demon who had promised me that the Vice Ambassadorship with Alba would make me more powerful and successful than I could ever hope to be. I waited for that day—for Alba, and for you to come save me."

Kyoko's eyes fall as tears drip from her chin onto her lap.

"He victimized us all, and then he put us in roles to victimize others. That's always been his plan: to keep it going as long as he can. He refers to it as the Inner Catacomb. It wasn't just me. There were other young women and girls there, who he'd use to find and recruit more."

Kyoko breathes deeply to quell the nausea rising in her chest and throat. "How was I ignorant to this?"

A sad half-smile plays at Yala's lips. "You had Alba to protect you."

Kyoko loses command of her emotions as a soft sob rips from her throat. None of it is fair. Her bright, beautiful, intelligent, ambitious sister didn't deserve to have her light dimmed at the hands of a monster.

"I-I'm sorry," she sobs.

Yala softly shakes her head. "It's not your fault. I'm sorry for blaming you the day I left, but six years of reflection and treatment helped me remember that."

Kyoko has borne witness to gruesome situations and heartbreaking testimonies throughout her life and career. But nothing has remained with her the way her sister's words from six years ago have. While Yala appears to be absolving her of her wretched guilt, her mind refuses to accept it.

"You were right. I should've protected you. I should've known what was happening."

"How could you? The Prime was in control. He would tell me I was Fully Broken if I resisted. He made me feel tremendous shame for wanting the love of someone my own age. I still felt that shame even when I met Natsumi's father."

Kyoko's eyes wander to Yala's fingers, but she sees no rings.

Yala shakes her head and continues. "Our relationship didn't last. I was so accustomed to his control that this gaping abyss grew into my life when I returned to EverEmber alone. I sought out a relationship, not for love or affection, but for a remedy to the void. It wasn't healthy or sustainable. It'll take years before I'm fully ready to allow someone to love me."

Kyoko wipes the moisture from her eyes. "You don't deserve this. I'm sorry."

"Forgive yourself, Kyoko. Fight the shame. That's his product inside of you. We buy it every time he sells it. The whole city does. It kept me away from you."

Kyoko raises her gaze again. "Is that why you never wrote to me?"

"What makes you think I never wrote to you?" The question lingers between them and amplifies the silence of Kyoko's confusion. "I wrote to you, Kyoko. Hundreds of letters over six years. Apologizing for what I said. I just never sent them. Shame kept me from doing that."

Another sob escapes as Kyoko's heavy heart registers the truth. "You don't hate me?"

Yala smiles and places her hand tenderly on Kyoko's. "How could you ever think I meant that? You are my family. I would restart my life a thousand times to protect you."

Kyoko shuts her eyes tight and drives her face into her hands. She's overcome with the simultaneous sadness and relief of Yala's admissions. She feels lighter as the mountains of burden slowly begin to drift away.

They sit quietly for a few minutes until Kyoko's breathing conquers her sobs.

"I want to show you something," Yala says. She reaches into her pocket to withdraw a small picture and hands it to Kyoko. There's a little girl in the image, all dressed up with a bright, colorful flower in her hair.

"Natsumi," Yala says. "She resembles her Aunty Kyoko."

Another tear loosens from Kyoko's sore eyes as a smile widens on her lips. Natsumi shares the shimmering eyes of their family, and her picture is nearly identical to some of Kyoko's childhood images.

"Is she here?" Kyoko asks.

Yala's smile fades, and she responds hesitantly. "She is, but I've never mentioned you to her."

Kyoko's heart sinks. *Of course she hasn't.*

Yala continues. "But I can. After I've had some more time to talk to her and to…" She seems to search for the right word.

"Heal," Kyoko finishes her sentence. "I understand. I just want you to know: as long as I'm alive, there's always an opportunity to build something new."

Yala's genuine smile returns and she rises to her feet. "I look forward to that."

The paralysis of time ends. The music plays again, the staff and the patrons resume their activity, and the wings of the flies flap once more.

Everything around them comes back to life as Kyoko utters the most difficult words she's spoken in six years. "Goodbye, Kanako."

Her sister shakes her head and says, "Please, Kyoko. Call me 'Yala' again."

Kyoko nods and begins the journey back to the Ryokan. It somehow seems longer than when she and Rafael walked there. When she arrives, her feet carry her almost instinctively to his room.

She sits on the edge of Rafael's bed and he plops down gently beside her. Silence lingers in the air. She assumes he is waiting, listening, for her to speak first, and she appreciates his patience.

"Thank you," she says, expressing the thought most present in her mind.

Rafael's eyebrows scrunch together. "For what?"

"Allowing us the space we needed to heal old wounds. Things aren't perfect, and they likely won't be for a long time, but we've taken steps toward one another."

Rafael smiles. "I'm happy to hear that."

"Shame, on both sides, was keeping us apart, and we've started the process of stripping that away. You were right. While Yala and I are still able to, we should find a way to forgive. After all she's been through alone, it's time for me to be there for her."

Words release from her tongue like river water through a broken dam. She reveals the truth of what her sister has been through, the role that she and Alba played, and the true monster of the heinous crimes perpetrated against her.

By the end of it, Rafael has buried his hands in his hair, resting his elbows on top of his thighs. "I idolized him."

"Everyone idolizes him. Because of him, I failed my sister."

Rafael turns to her and takes her hand affectionately. "It's not your fault. He failed us all."

Kyoko looks down, almost in disbelief, at the mari fingers wrapped warmly around hers. Not three days prior, he'd kept a yard's distance between them at all times.

And now, as she turns up to his eyes, she sees a kindness in them that he's never directed at her before.

He looks down at their interlocked fingers as well. "I'm sorry, Kyoko. Truly. For how I've acted toward you." His eyes linger, but he doesn't seem to be looking at their clenched hands anymore; his gaze drifts to his own forearms.

He continues. "It was easier to place my guilt on the igni than to shamefully admit where it truly belonged. I may have been misplacing my guilt on others, but you have been misplacing it on yourself. You were led astray by someone you thought—we all thought—was the ultimate good. Place the guilt where it belongs."

Kyoko isn't sure how to respond. She tries to digest what he's saying, but for the remainder of the night, her heart and her mind require rest. She tips her head onto his shoulder. "Thank you."

The Librarians sit this way, hands clenched tightly and tenderly, her head resting on his shoulder, until Kyoko's eyes fall shut and she drifts into exhausted slumber.

CHAPTER 41

A Night of Death and Rebirth

Theocratic-Monarchy SunSide
Date 21st Day of Month 6, Year 1628 DG

THE THRUMMING OF RAINWATER RAPPING against the window wall spreads across the Theater. Zar-Lo breathes deeply as Frona completes her descent, leaving the stars and moons to illuminate the sky with their solemn sparkles.

The storm rages as the heavens weep over the kingdom, and the king stands alone, soaking in his domain as it unwittingly sleeps on the edge of a new era.

"Tonight," he whispers, as if the nine Members of the Assembly stand within earshot, "I enshrine the legacy of what she and I built. Tonight, I end ages of exhausting sycophancy—eons of endowment—in exchange for paltry shreds of respect."

As droplets slam the glass, he ignores the voices that have all but replaced the headaches.

Bring us what is owed to us, Faerie. We have an agreement. Bring us the sacrifice. We are starving.

He ignores them and continues. "Tonight, I step into the era of my sole guardianship over this world, as it always should have been. And I do it all for her, whose memories sustain my essence, despite its enervation."

The doors creak open and the Facilitator enters. Zar-Lo's eyes remain on the city below as he listens to Saith's footsteps approach.

"Is it done?" he asks.

After a moment of hesitation, and perhaps defeat, Saith replies, "No, Father. Alba and her colleague have crossed into SunSide. They've likely reached the diplomatic chambers by now."

To Zar-Lo's surprise, he feels nothing but the constant exhilaration of his plan's inevitable success. "So be it."

"And what of her potential enlightenment to the Final Act's contents? If my daughter has revealed the truth, Alba will ensure your name has 'Murderer' etched alongside it."

"Do you remember what I told you the day of the execution? Kings are illusionists. And history is our greatest illusion. Nothing that is written cannot be rewritten." He turns to face Saith. "Bid farewell to your daughter. It is her final night."

Saith's gaze moves to where his arm once was, and back to the MegaFather. "I remain committed to you, and to this dynasty, as I always have."

"I know. Once we've managed the chaos and the streets are cleansed of dissent, we can turn our attention to finding the girls and forging the changeling. It has to be perfect, Saith. Authentically organic, from skin to bone to blood. The ancient ones cannot know that it wasn't made from my loins."

"It will be. They'll believe it to be your offspring. With Vy-Ro and the Bravers searching the forest, we cannot be far from the twins."

A soft snicker escapes the MegaFather's lips. "The twins. They think they've outsmarted us, but it isn't the sharpest in the room who survives." His eyes narrow on the forest. "It's the most desperate."

Saith's eyes shift to the ore desk and his eyebrows rise as if a thought has occurred to him. "Speaking of desperation, how was your day with Vy-Ro? What have I missed?"

Zar-Lo hesitates, knowing that the answer to his subordinate's question will distress the Facilitator. He spits the information out as quickly as he can.

"That *spineless* igni Courtman returned, shouting accusations in the Castrum."

Saith shakes his head. "I'm surprised. I told him to stay away for his own safety."

"Well, now he's dead."

There's a long pause, in which Zar-Lo is painfully aware of Saith's staring. "Please, Father, tell me you didn't—"

"I did," Zar-Lo admits. "You threatened to do the same."

Another long pause. Saith must be biting his tongue. "Not in broad daylight. Were there witnesses?"

Zar-Lo shakes his head. "Only Vy-Ro. The body was taken offshore on the igni vessel, which now rests on the ocean floor."

Saith exhales deeply. "Anything else happen while I was gone that I should know about?"

Zar-Lo weighs his next words carefully. "This won't be easy to hear, Saith."

"What is it?" There's genuine panic in his tone.

"Believe me, it was never my intention for anything to happen to her."

"To whom?"

Zar-Lo turns to lock Saith's gaze. "Saimiza has made her radiance-return."

The color slowly begins to drain from Saith's face. His jaw falls slack and his nostrils flare. "What happened to her?"

"I was hoping she'd be able to subdue the presence of the ancient ones in my consciousness. Evidently, I was wrong."

Saith steps backwards, as if Zar-Lo has physically pushed him. A layer of moisture spreads across his eyeballs and he attempts to blink it away, but tears begin to form. "Father, I'd like to be dismissed for the night. I can resume my duties in the morning."

Zar-Lo hesitates to allow Saith a reprieve on such an auspicious night, but he sees the Facilitator wiping tears from the corners of his eyes. "Alright, Saith. Rest tonight and return before the suns rise."

"Thank you, Father," he says with a quiver. The pixie turns and begins to exit the room, but Zar-Lo's voice stops him.

"I understand you're about to lose your daughter and your aunt on the same day. You're welcome to mourn tonight, but when your eyes open in the morning, they should be dry."

Without another word, Saith nods and leaves Zar-Lo alone in the Theater. The MegaFather turns back to the window wall and watches the raindrops hammer the streets, envisioning rivers of red blood flowing into the gutters.

The king stands, ready to celebrate a night of death and rebirth.

CHAPTER 42

A BEAUTIFUL PLACE

Theocratic-Monarchy *SunSide*
Date *21st Day of Month 6, Year 1628 DG*

ALBA SLIPS OUT OF BED, her throat clenched shut with a desperate plea for moisture. The skin on her forearm fins cracks from aridity.

Rainwater raps against the window, a light thrumming filling the air. She peers out, hoping to find the positions of the moons through the clouds. The sparkling illumination is faint, but she manages to reconcile that it is close to midnight.

She's trained to travel without water on long journeys, but training can only outsmart biology for so long. Hoping to alleviate some of the heat in the room, while preventing too much water from slipping in, she cracks the window open slightly, then heads to the kitchen to bathe her throat as the raging storm does the kingdom.

The guest room in which she sleeps is at the end of a long, tiled hallway on the second floor of Saila's home. Across the hallway is the other guest bedroom, where Unisa stays. Alba walks softly on bare feet until she reaches the angi's door, then slowly opens it and pokes her head inside.

Unisa is sound asleep, snoring lightly. Alba stifles a laugh, realizing she's checking on Unisa the way she checks on Kyoko—the way she's been checking on Ana since she was a little girl.

Old habits, she thinks.

She's impressed by the silence of the staircase, which she expected to creak and moan as she descends. She finds the cooling box in the kitchen. The light inside springs out into the darkness of the kitchen, providing enough illumination that Alba doesn't need to activate the lighting panels.

She reaches into the box, removes one of the small jars of water, and ravenously pours it down her throat. As she drinks, enjoying the cool sustenance, a sixth sense kicks in—one she's developed and honed throughout her career.

A sense that has saved her life on many occasions.

Her heart rate bounces up, and sweat breaks out on her temple. Her skin comes to life with chills and small bumps, alerting her to some impending danger. Something is wrong. Something is happening.

Instinctually, her fingers release the glass jar from her lips, and before it even reaches the floor, Alba turns completely around and snatches something small and sharp out of the air.

A throwing dagger, hurled at the back of her head, now rests innocuously on her palm.

Slowly, she lifts her head as the sound of the glass jar hitting the ground and shattering rings out around the kitchen. She meets eyes with the individual who threw the dagger.

A faerie in an atypical Braver uniform. The usual white hood and colorful face mask are replaced by stone gray and black, as if the Braver is attempting to blend into the ore of the city, and the darkness of night.

The two stand silently for a moment as Alba processes. The Braver's eyes are wide. He speaks, but his voice emerges barely louder than a whisper. "You're not Saila."

"How observant," Alba responds coolly.

The sixth sense bursts to life again as a minuscule twitch in the faerie's fingers alerts Alba to his intentions. Before he can reach for another dagger, Alba has launched the one in her hand. The Braver's body hits the ground with a loud *thud* as the small knife digs through his eyeball and into his brain matter.

Alba looks down at the shattered glass around her feet, reeling. *Bravers. Camouflage. Thought I was Saila.* The truth drops on her like mighty bolts of lightning.

It's an assassination.

She moves as quickly and intentionally as she can through the kitchen. Using the light escaping the cooling box to guide her, she finds four thick cooking knives held in place on a long wooden block secured to the wall. She picks the two longest of these knives and tucks them into her waistband, then heads back to the staircase.

She steps over the body of the dead Braver. Only one thought exists in her mind. *Get Unisa out.*

As she rounds the corner out of the kitchen and reaches the base of the stairs, her sixth sense comes to life again. A dagger narrowly misses her face as she twists her body back around to the kitchen.

She stands with her back against the wall, listening to the Bravers on the other side beyond the staircase.

"Tell Vy-Ro we have a problem," one Braver says to another. "Alba's here." She hears the other Braver exit to retrieve Vy-Ro, and the dagger-launcher speaks to her.

"This isn't personal, Alba."

Alba breathes deeply to swallow her rage. "If you've come for Saila, it's personal."

She looks to her left and finds a wooden cutting board sitting on the counter. An idea forms. She grabs the board and holds it in front of her as she swings around the corner and out of the kitchen again.

She hears the familiar *whoosh* of knives cutting through air as she swings the cutting board around, catching one knife after another. Alba advances on the Braver, and by the time six knives have lodged themselves deeply into the wooden board, she's within striking distance.

She tosses it toward the Braver, who swipes it away with an open hand, and before she can reach for another dagger, Alba has slashed her forearm fins across the Braver's throat. The Braver falls backward, clutching to control the crimson spray, until Alba pulls a dagger off of her person and stabs it into the side of her head. The Braver's hands fall limp as her blood begins to pool around her.

Alba turns quickly back toward the stairs and launches up two steps at a time until she reaches Unisa's door. She enters the room and, in a moment of quick resourcefulness, blocks it with a stout armoire.

"Alba?" Unisa asks, sitting up in bed. She rubs her eyes and takes a long look at the mari. "You're covered in blood!"

Alba approaches her quickly and takes her hand to lead her out of bed, to the window. "You have to go, Uni. Now. They don't know you're here."

"They? They who?" Unisa says, jumping up out of bed as Alba tugs on her arm.

Alba takes a deep breath and locks eyes with Unisa. "There's no time to explain. Everything's going to be alright, but you have to leave. Now."

"Leave and go where?" Unisa questions frantically.

"Back to the Library. My bedroom window is open. Fly to my room and get the bag with the maps. You can follow the map of Aerthomni back home."

While Unisa begs for answers, Alba tugs her to the bedroom window and opens it as wide as it will go.

"Why are we going back to—?"

"Not we. Just you. If I go with you, they're going to hunt us both down. But they've only seen me for now, so they don't know you're here."

Unisa takes a step back from the window, her eyes wide with panic. "Alba, you're scaring me. Please, tell me what's happening."

Alba's bloodied hands shoot up to the sides of Unisa's face. "Please, Uni. Listen to me. This is important and I have very little time."

Slowly and reluctantly, Unisa nods, and Alba lowers her hands. "Get the maps and go home, immediately. Do *not* come back into this house, no matter what. As soon as you're out of SunSide, send a letter to Saila. She's with her mother in Eloa, remember? Tell her there was an assassination attempt on her home, and Alba didn't make it."

Tears brim in Unisa's eyes. "Alba, what are you saying?"

Alba shakes her head and places a finger over her lips, then continues. "Promise me that you'll make sure Ana gets out of the Library."

Unisa hesitates, then, with a trembling voice, she utters, "I promise."

"Tell Ana, Kyoko, and Hassan how much I loved them." She bends forward and affectionately kisses Unisa's forehead. "Always remember how proud I am of you."

Unisa whimpers as a tear rolls down her cheek, the lines on her forehead contorting with confusion. The sound of a fist loudly banging against the bedroom door echoes violently around the room.

"Alba!" comes Vy-Ro's voice.

Unisa's expression descends into horror. "Who is that?"

Alba brings the angi's attention back to the instructions. Through her apprehension, she smiles and imparts her final thoughts to the angi.

"Remember what we talked about last night? As long as the Prime is in the dark, you can still change things. You don't need me. Take his power out from under him."

Unisa releases a soft sob. "Alba, I can't do this without you."

Another series of knocks threatens to annihilate the door.

"Promise me, Uni. Promise me you'll end him." She speaks her final words slowly and deliberately. "Do whatever is necessary."

Unisa nods and lowers her gaze as more tears roll down her face. Alba guides her to the window, and before the angi can protest further, the Ambassador shoves her into the storm. Unissa topples from the second story, hurtling toward the ground until her instincts kick in and she takes control of her descent, flying back up to the window.

Alba closes the window and pulls the curtain, standing alone, hoping Unisa will retrieve the maps from her room and head back to the Library.

And that she'll keep her promises.

Vy-Ro's voice and violent knocking continue. Alba smiles, knowing Unisa's escaped while the Braver General is ignorant. Vy-Ro won't let Alba leave alive, but she can at least give Unisa a head start. If Unisa follows through on their plan, Alba will have saved Ana, and contributed to the fall of the Prime.

These truths alone give her the peace she needs to accept her fate. She can die now.

She pushes the armoire away from the door, then steps back to address the Braver General. "What have you done, Vy-Ro?"

The knocking stops. There is a chill in the air as silence settles in, before Vy-Ro speaks again, far more softly. "This wasn't the plan, Alba. Why aren't you in the Castrum? Where is Saila?"

"Does Saith know you've come here to assassinate his daughter?" The silence resumes and, from it, Alba extracts the answer to her question. "He gave the order, didn't he?"

Silence again. "Speak, Vy-Ro!"

"The Assembly has voted to remove the MegaFather from the throne." It's nearly a whisper when it comes out, but it hits Alba's ears and she understands.

"The announcement."

"You know?"

"Only that something historic is on the horizon."

"It isn't anymore. Saila is the only Member left. Tell me where she is."

Alba scoffs. "We've known each other for years, Vy-Ro. We're both *well* aware of how this will end. I'll refuse to tell you where Saila is, and then your Bravers will try to kill me. Perhaps we should skip the interrogation and proceed to the fun."

Vy-Ro takes a long pause, but when he speaks, his tone is pregnant with genuine regret. "They forced me to do this, Alba."

Alba's blood boils. "Apologies, I seem to have left my sympathy back at the Library. Where is your honor?"

Vy-Ro's tone hardens. "My honor is in my duty."

"Correct. And your duties are those of the Braver General. Not those of a subservient lapdog, ready to commit crimes against the theocracy for a pat on the head."

There's another long pause before Vy-Ro speaks again. "Any final words, Alba?"

"How many Bravers are out there?"

"Ten."

"Including you?"

Vy-Ro sighs. "Eleven."

"Can they hear me?"

"They can."

"Good. I'd like you all to know: you're entirely fucked. None of you will make it out of here alive."

There's no response. Vy-Ro's footsteps return along the tiled hallway until he reaches the top of the staircase, or somewhere near it. All ten Bravers must be strategically placed between the bedroom door and the middle of the hallway, where Vy-Ro waits.

It's not an incredibly long distance; they'll likely attack her all at once.

Her mind races to establish a strategy. *Don't let them see your back. Number them to keep track.*

She takes a deep breath, approaches the bedroom door, and places an ear on it. She can hear and feel them on the other side, ready to attack her as soon as the door opens. Her heart feels ready to burst from her chest.

Excitement, not fear.

Both cooking knives are still in her waistband. She withdraws one and, with her free hand, turns the doorknob and quickly pulls it open. As soon as she does, a Braver with a wide sword, whom she dubs One, charges into the doorway and brings his blade down quickly.

Without hesitation, Alba swings around from behind the door and jams the knife upward through the soft tissue behind his chin. She keeps his body in front of her as she pushes out of the door and into the hallway.

The Braver's body rattles as throwing daggers are launched in her direction and hit her faerie shield. She takes the sword from One's hand as Two and Three approach her from her sides. Two wields a sword as well, while Three has ore knuckles loaded on her fists.

Alba throws One's body down and avoids Two's slashes, dodging until there's an opening to swipe her own sword upward between Two's legs. It makes contact, spraying blood from his groin onto the ground as he screams and covers the wound.

Three's hand falls on Alba's shoulder and violently pulls her toward a swift jab with the ore knuckles, to Alba's jaw. The mari falls onto her back as blood fills her mouth and the room starts to spin.

DON'T LET THEM SEE YOUR BACK, she reminds herself angrily.

Three kneels over her quickly, unleashing a flood of fists. Alba raises her forearms and blocks them, so the faerie moves to her abdomen, where Alba hears and feels the blows crushing her ribs.

Alba jams her forearm fins into Three's eye and, with the faerie off-balance, pushes her in the way of Four's oncoming daggers.

Five approaches with a long spear, bringing it down on Alba, who reaches up with both hands and grasps the wood, pushing against the Braver's downward thrust. The spear hovers in the air just over Alba's chest, both the Librarian and the Braver pushing it with opposite but equal force.

Alba shifts the point from her chest to her shoulder and allows it to drop. She clenches her teeth from the pain but uses her now-free hands to pull daggers from Three's corpse and launch them at both Four and Five. The daggers both strike between the eyes and the Braver bodies fall.

Alba rises to her knees and pulls the spear from her shoulder, recognizing the choice is likely unwise.

Five down, five to go.

Six, Seven, and Eight approach together and attempt to encircle her. Alba picks up the fallen sword at her feet in one hand, while tugging another throwing dagger out of Three's back and holding it tightly in the other. Wet blood drips from her shoulder and travels down her arm. Her ribs throb as all three Bravers advance on her at once, imploding their circle.

Eight brings a long-pole scythe down on Alba and she raises her sword to block him, aiming and tossing the throwing dagger at Six. It hits his throat and he drops to the ground with his axe.

Alba kicks Eight to push him back as Seven swings her mace at the Librarian's head. Alba grabs the handle of the weapon and swipes her sword at the Braver's wrists, severing her hands. Seven drops to her knees, crying out, as Eight swings the Scythe horizontally at Alba's abdomen.

Reacting solely on instinct, Alba twists her body in a fluid motion that allows her spine fins to divert the blade of the scythe away from her, leaving Eight off-balance long enough for Alba's blade to find his neck. His body falls as his head hangs on to his shoulder by a thin shred of flesh.

She hears Nine's and Ten's footsteps on the tile. As cleanly as she can, the sword departs from her hand and finds Nine's chest, tearing it open and knocking her backward.

Ten is all that remains, his knuckles augmented with short ore spikes. The battle has come down to a blow-by-blow flurry of fists between the Braver and the Librarian.

His flying fists are stronger, but she is quicker. With lightning precision, she evades his jabs and lands every one of hers on his side, chest, and throat. He slows down further, losing steam.

He finally lands a blow to Alba's side, and then to her stomach, each fist digging sharp points into her skin. She stumbles backward, blood pooling at her feet. He charges at her and she continues to block and evade, but he's gotten a second wind and lands another blow, this one to her face.

She falls backward, blinded in one eye, red vision in the other. The Braver comes down on her and Alba does her best to block through spinning surroundings and half her vision.

As her body presses against the ground, she realizes she still has one cooking knife in her waistband. Without hesitation, she reaches back for it and jams it as hard as she can through the Braver's eye, then tears it up and out through the top of his head, showering her with brain matter.

Ten's body drops onto Alba and she uses what little remaining strength she has to roll it off of her. As she lies on her back, bleeding from the face, shoulder, and side, her ribs destroyed and her eye socket demolished, she smiles knowing they're all as dead as she is.

All except Vy-Ro.

She hears him approach and kneel down beside her.

"Let me bring you to the Salvers, Alba. They can heal you." His tone feels oddly remorseful. "Tell me where Saila is, and I promise I'll save you."

Alba uses all the strength left in her body to sit up on her elbow, then gathers all of the bloody saliva in her mouth and launches it at Vy-Ro's face. It covers him, and he jerks his head back in disgust.

"Fuck you, Vy-Ro. And good luck."

"I don't need luck. I'll find her."

Alba drops onto her back again and smiles. "I know. I meant good luck surviving her when you do."

Those are the last words that Alba speaks before her eyelids close. She can neither hear, nor respond. Her throat has collapsed, and the pain of her wounds evaporates. Warmth and coolness wash over her body simultaneously. Comfort, in its purest form, as if she is falling asleep in the arms of a loved one.

No pain, discomfort, or worry. No hesitation, grief, or sorrow. She simply goes, slowly, to a place of love. Her senses fail, her mind stops, and her heart pumps a final beat. Her last thought lingers in the emptiness of her dwindling consciousness.

I am in Saila's home. What a beautiful place to die.

Endless bliss cradles her essence as a loving parent cradles a newborn. It lasts only for a moment, until her eyes pop open again.

She sits up quickly as her senses return. She is conscious, but she feels no emotion—no fear, no confusion. She simply is.

She raises her hands and looks at them. Her body is whole and there are no wounds on her. There is no blood, no injury, no ache. In fact, her skin glows like an ember in a dark room.

She's clothed in a white outfit; light, airy material covers her from the shoulders down, wrapped around her body. She gets to her feet to observe her surroundings. A verdant forest, more stunning than she's ever seen before. It feels alive, breathing around her.

What a beautiful place to be reborn.

An entity appears. A grotesque, deformed figure, yet there is still no fear. Somehow, Alba recognizes the entity.

"I know you," she says to the being, "yet we've never met before."

The entity nods. "All who pass from the world of life come to this place. It is a bridge to the world beyond, and I am its keeper. I am familiar because you are void of emotion, so I cannot feel unfamiliar, frightening, or perplexing to you."

"Why do I feel no emotion?"

"Because you have no heart. You are simply an essence. And your time has come to move on."

The essence stands. "I am ready."

"I must ask you first: are you satisfied with what became of Alba's life?"

The essence pauses, and in the span of a blink, Alba's memories flood her vision. "I never got the chance to save my sister from the Library."

"Did you do your best with what you were given?"

Alba pauses again to consider. "I tried."

"That is all that matters."

The entity gestures to an opening in the clearing between two wide trees. The space begins to glow with the brightness of the suns. "Come, essence. Reap what you've earned. Live in love—now and for all time."

The entity begins to move toward the door, but the essence stops her. Something Alba knew—something in Alba's memories—is important for the entity to know.

"Wait. Before I go, there's something I have to tell you."

CHAPTER 43

AN ACT OF WAR

Theocratic-Monarchy *SunSide*
Date *22nd Day of Month 6, Year 1628 DG*

DEATH CAME FOR BOTH THE Ambassador and the storm. Unisa sits on the flat roof of Saila's home, arms around her knees, braids wrapped. She should be shivering, but the numbness keeps her still.

Ona's light falls from clear blue skies. It's as if the storm never happened, as if the world has been reborn and Death has erased all traces of what once was.

The sun's natural light descends into the skylight window, a square pane of glass next to Unisa. It lands in the second-floor hallway where the angi watched Alba fight for her life.

The hallway where Death took Alba, bloodied and broken.

Alba's maps sit next to her, as well. Other than the clothes on her back, it's all that Unisa has left. All of her belongings, everything that was important to her, had to be left behind.

As did Alba.

Bravers killed her. Unisa's eyebrows cling to each other as she tries to draw a reason as to why SunSide's military would assassinate a peaceful diplomat. This was an act of war. Of evil and barbarism.

If it weren't for Alba, the Gatekeeper would've been bloodied and broken in the same hallway. Small polyps of anger spring into her chest. At the Bravers, at Alba, and at whatever force governs the wanton movements of fate—be it the Mega's Four, the Doruh's Twins, or any other almighty being.

Unisa's gaze rises to the inching Ona and she realizes she's been sitting in this one position for hours. Yells capture her attention. Angry, distressed voices that she attempts to ignore until they build into the riotous roar of a crowd screaming obscenities.

She rises to her feet and stretches her wings, then steps forth, crouched and concealed, to the ledge that envelops the perimeter of the roof and peers over. Braver's stand guard behind an ore-chain fence barricading the front yard of Saila's home. Searing bile rises into Unisa's throat at the sight of them.

The crowd beyond the fence grows angrier and more violent as the moments pass.

"Is Member Saila safe? Why haven't you given us any information?"

"Who did this? We demand justice! This is treason!"

A Doruh man speaks up next, standing in front of an amber-skinned faerie with narrowing eyes.

"Don't believe the Bravers! They know who did this and are hiding the truth!"

"Be quiet! The Bravers put their lives on the line every day to protect you scum!"

"Watch it, faerie! The Bravers come into our neighborhoods and antagonize us. This has their fingerprints all over it."

"Perhaps if you all didn't resist—"

"What did you say?!"

Insults and taunts continue until the crowd dissolves into fisticuffs and chaos. The Bravers discharge weapons into the crowd in an attempt to contain the melee as they usher the faerie away and brutally arrest the Doruh.

With the Bravers distracted, Unisa turns on her heels, seizes the maps, and launches herself into the rear yard of the home with a few cursory flaps.

She's lost almost immediately, wandering from one alleyway to the next. The crowded streets of Larso, and the unpredictability of the riots breaking out around her, drive panic through her bones.

She's pushed and shoved and knocked to the ground, but she gets back up every time and keeps moving. There's no clear destination. Alba instructed her to return to the Library, but paranoia keeps her wings strapped to her back. The less attention she attracts, the better.

It's too late. From the corner of her eye, she spots two Bravers whispering and pointing in her direction. She hops laterally into an alleyway between two tall buildings and continues her escape, until she finds another Braver watching her and is forced to change direction yet again.

She reaches a street with a Braver on each end and only one alley-way—the one through which she came. The warriors begin to move in on her. Unisa looks up at the sky and realizes her only escape would be upward, whether she likes it or not. Her wings slowly begin to extend until a gentle hand lands on her shoulder.

"You don't want to do that," says a young Doruh woman Unisa hadn't noticed standing next to her.

"I don't have a choice," Unisa responds. This is the first time she's spoken since the night before. Her throat is dry and her voice is hoarse.

"You do," the Doruh assures her, gesturing to the alleyway behind them.

"I just came through there, it leads to another street with more Bravers."

The Doruh shakes her head. "Not the alley."

She gestures again and Unisa realizes she's talking about a small wooden panel at the foot of a wide, ore building. "Tunnels under the city that the Bravers don't know about."

She takes Unisa's hand and, reluctantly, the angi follows. The Doruh removes the wooden panel, revealing a staircase leading underground.

"Enter, quickly," the Doruh urges.

Unisa hesitates. "I don't know you."

The Doruh glances over her shoulder with urgency in her eyes. "The Bravers are looking for a young female angi Librarian. You may not have a tunic, but you check most of those boxes. I promise you, you're safer with me than on the streets."

Unisa's heart drums against her chest as she tries to reconcile following a stranger into a dark underground staircase with the danger on the streets.

The Doruh sighs and continues. "You cannot fight or fly your way out of this situation. You have to change—adapt. When fists fail you, change will be your champion."

Her words remind Unisa of Alba's final statement.

Do whatever is necessary.

Unisa's been playing by the rules and following a script her entire life. Her survival hinges on her ability to change—to do anything necessary.

She nods and steps down the cold, dark staircase into a tunnel lit by torchlight, and the Doruh joins her after closing the wooden panel.

"Why are you helping me?" Unisa asks, before they continue.

"Because you're not the only one the Bravers are looking for. They're after my sister and me, as well. We have to stay together."

"What's your name?" Unisa wonders.

The Doruh smiles. "Salessa."

CHAPTER 44

THE APPLE AND THE FLIES

Theocratic-Monarchy SunSide
Date 22nd Day of Month 6, Year 1628 DG

"I DON'T UNDERSTAND, LESSI," NAINA barks. "You're the smartest person I know, but you're also the dumbest."

Salessa keeps her eyes lowered and her hands folded calmly on the wooden table. She accepts Naina's scolding patiently.

The wolf isn't wrong; venturing through the tunnels that branch out of the Bunker might be safe, thanks to Zakia's track-proofing, but emerging into the streets of the city wasn't. She accepts the admonishment.

"Don't be so hard on her," responds the older pixie at the table. She places her royal purple hand over Salessa's affectionately. "She was only out for a few minutes, and she saved so many from the riots."

"Please, Zalona, don't make excuses for her," Naina pleads. "Her decisions could have put us into a lot of danger. What if the Facilitator tracked her while she was streetside?"

Zalona nods. "I understand. I don't disagree that it was risky. But had she not gone out, she never would have saved the Librarian."

Naina turns back to her sister. "This Bunker is a safe house. Not a shelter for stray humans."

"I'm sorry for the risk I took, Naina," Salessa finally speaks, lifting her gaze. "But I'm not apologetic about saving Unisa. Obviously, there was a reason I felt compelled to go topside and help."

Naina scoffs. "Let me guess. Fate?"

Salessa nods. "As of last night, she has the same target on her back that is on ours."

"Then she better be able to fight alongside us when the rest of the team returns from Lily Beach. If she's useless, I want her out of here."

Salessa sighs and shakes her head. "We're not going to force her to fight."

"Then why is she here, Lessi?"

"The same reason we're all here." She pauses. "To survive. You and I may be here for justice, but in the short conversation I had with her, Unisa told me she needs to get back home. That's why she's here. So we can help her."

"She's right," Zalona agrees. "The entire kingdom has been thrust into chaos overnight. Rivers of blood flow through the streets. Theologians cry out for retribution. Braver supporters are inciting riots at even the slightest accusation that the monarchy or military might be involved. Unisa is safest here and if she just needs a path home, that is the goal."

"She won't survive without us, Naina," Salessa continues. "With the Bravers' recruitment efforts, and the recall of officers from around the continent, the city is a fortress."

Naina sighs dejectedly. "These assassinations couldn't have happened at a worse time. We don't need more Bravers crawling around."

Disappointment rises in Salessa's chest. Her tone hardens. "I'm sorry the assassinations of innocent Mega weren't convenient for you, Naina."

"They were SunSidian politicians," Naina growls. "There wasn't an innocent among them. You won't find me shedding a single tear."

The bedroom door abruptly creaks open. Unisa enters the main room of the Bunker wearing a shalwar kameez suit that Salessa gave her.

She takes a seat across the table from Zalona, her eyeballs inflamed with red, finger-like streaks. Salessa thought the Librarian would have slept for longer than an hour.

"How did you sleep?" Zalona asks.

"Not well," Unisa responds, her voice feeble. "I've never been to SunSide before, and the person I was with..." She falls silent and looks down at her folded hands on the table.

"We understand," Salessa says, passing her a smile.

"Can I get you something to eat?" Zalona offers.

Unisa shakes her head. "I'm not very hungry."

Zalona gestures to a bowl of apples, pears, and other fruit at the center of the table. "If you do start to feel hungry, eat something. I can bring you a more filling meal later."

She rises to her feet. "The staff upstairs is a bit overworked current-ly, with the influx of survivors we've taken in. But if I can find a third cot available, I'll bring it down."

"Thank you," Unisa responds softly, before Zalona ascends the steps to her inn.

Unisa turns to Salessa. "And thank you for the clothes. I'll find a way to return them to you once I'm home. They'll help me blend in as I pass through MoonSide this evening."

Salessa's smile drops and she turns to Naina. *Does she know what's happening outside?*

Great, she's useless and oblivious.

I'm serious, Naina.

She obviously doesn't know.

Naina turns to Unisa abruptly and spits out, "You're not leaving any time soon, Feathers."

Unisa's brow furrows. "Excuse me?"

Tactful, Naina.

Sorry.

Show her the flyer, Salessa instructs.

Naina opens a sliding drawer on her side of the table and riffles through sheets of paper until she finds the two she's looking for. She hands them to Salessa, who places them in front of Unisa, one face up, the other face down.

"This is our 'Wanted' flyer," Salessa says, pointing to the sheet fac-ing up. "The Facilitator has been hunting us since we were children. As of this morning, he's hunting you, too."

She flips the other paper and Unisa's eyes expand quickly. At the top is a drawn image of an angi in a yellow tunic. The words underneath state: *Angi human. Age unknown. Key suspect in the assassinations of the Members of the Assembly. Entered Larso wearing the uniform of a Librarian. If found, inform your local Braver authority. Do not approach. Do not engage.*

Unisa looks up from the paper, her jaw hanging open and panic in her eyes.

"So did you do it, Feathers?" Naina blurts out.

Salessa reaches forward quickly and slaps her sister on the shoulder. "Naina!"

"We need to know who we've dragged into our safe house, Lessi," Naina defends herself. "If she's an assassin, we have a right to know."

"I didn't kill anyone," Unisa clarifies. "This is a lie."

Naina scoffs. "Disappointing. We could've used someone experienced."

"Can you tell us what happened to you last night?" Salessa asks.

Unisa nods and clears her name to her two new companions. She talks about her mission to correct records from the Library, her journey through MoonSide, and her arrival at Member Saila's home.

"She and my colleague are" — she pauses and winces — "were good friends. Member Saila wasn't there during the assassination. Alba woke me up, gave me some instructions, and then told me to leave. I watched from the skylight as they…"

Tears begin to well up in her eyes, and Salessa feels the urge to place a comforting hand on her shoulder, but she resists.

Naina turns to Salessa. "Why would Bravers want to assassinate the Members?"

"Remember what Ray-Mi told us? Maybe they found out that Saila was working with Sonali and the Revolution."

"Why assassinate the entire Assembly then?"

Salessa raises a finger to stroke her chin. "Perhaps the Ore Monger is staging a coup."

"Unlikely," Unisa says, and the twins lean in. "The monarchy was sanctioned nearly two thousand years ago by the Assembly itself, toward the tail end of the Teri Age. They're two sides of the same coin, meant to keep balance in the government; one side represents the liaisons to the Four, the other the liaison to the citizens."

"You seem to know a lot about faerie politics," Naina remarks.

Unisa shakes her head. "History, not politics. I'm a historian."

Naina points upward to the city streets. "Well, Feathers, the history happening out there is the reason you can't go anywhere. As soon as you flap your pretty wings, they'll put ten arrows through each of them."

"I can't stay here," Unisa responds calmly. "The Prime has to know what happened to Alba. A Librarian was murdered. Do you have any idea what the political consequences of that are?"

Naina turns to Salessa and rhetorically asks, "Is Feathers ignoring me?" She turns back to Unisa and speaks slowly and loudly. "You. Can't. Leave."

Unisa's expression hardens as she responds. "My name is Unisa, not Feathers. And I heard you the first time. I recognize it won't be possible until my name is cleared."

"Good. Now that you're here, you can help us."

Unisa raises an eyebrow. "With what?"

"Procuring justice. The Facilitator killed our parents and has been hunting us, but things changed recently and we're doing the hunting now. You can either help, or see how you fare out there on your own."

Unisa's wide-eyed expression grows alert. "Why did he kill your parents? Why is he hunting you?"

Should I tell her about the proph—

Don't even think about it, growls Naina's voice in her head.

"We're valuable to him," Salessa responds vaguely.

Unisa's anxiety is palpable. "This is a suicide mission. The Castrum is, quite literally, a fortress."

"We have allies in a team of former Revolution fighters. They're on a mission at the moment, but they'll be back soon."

"Then you don't need my help," Unisa concludes.

"We have a common enemy," Naina points out. "Are you naive enough to believe that the Ore Monger will simply allow you to walk out of Larso and go home? There's only one path to freedom for you, and it's the same as ours: take them out. For good."

"I won't fight," Unisa admits. "I've had basic combat training, as all Librarians have, but I've never actually used that training. Nor do I intend to."

"What about justice for your friend? Alba?"

Naina's words initially strike a nerve, as Unisa's lips straighten into a hard line, but then her expression melts.

"Alba believed that violence is inevitable in the path to justice."

Naina smiles. "Smart woman."

"I didn't agree. And I still don't. Violence is not the only path to justice."

"Welcome to SunSide," Naina responds. "Violence is the only language faeries understand."

Unisa sits silently for a moment, then reaches for an apple from the basket of fruit and places it between her and Naina.

"If I leave this apple here, untouched, it'll begin to rot and invite flies. You can swat as many flies away as you want, but you won't find a solution until you identify the problem: the rot."

She picks the apple up and returns it to the bowl, then turns back to Naina. "Violence will only beget more violence until the problem is rooted out."

Naina scoffs. "You're a historian, right? So tell me: what is the solution to a problem that the Revolution has had for eight centuries? They've been fighting back, but clearly haven't found a way out of this battle. What are they doing wrong?"

"I'm no one to question the tactics of an oppressed clan. But I think it's important to realize that the problem is deeper than physical oppression; that's the flies, not the apple. The problem is that, like the Prime, the MegaFather has grown too powerful. Support from other sovereignties, idolization from followers, the physical might of a warrior organization. Their power is the apple."

"What's the solution?" Naina repeats her question.

"Education. Experience. The citizens of both SunSide *and* the Library have been fed a healthy diet of lies for centuries. They don't know what truth tastes like. They don't know what it's like to experience friendship with *others*. Hatred is taught, and it's all they know."

Naina scoffs again. "Easy words for someone who's lived behind golden gates, and not between ore walls. Education isn't saving anyone in a war zone. You know what will? The Ore Monger's head on a platter, and the Facilitator's in a trash bin. We need solutions *now*, not this long-term bullshit."

There are a few moments of tense silence until Unisa's eyes widen with a sudden realization. "I may not be willing to fight with you, but I can still help."

She runs back into the bedroom. Naina and Salessa exchange a glance and Salessa shrugs. Unisa returns holding the bag with which she arrived and withdraws a long sheet of paper, rolled tight.

"A Librarian's map of the Castrum," Unisa says excitedly, rolling the paper out onto the table and stepping aside for the twins to examine. "Passageways and tunnels, hidden chambers, all superficial buildings and towers, everything is here. By international law, foreign governments are required to be transparent to Librarians about the physical makeup of their facilities."

Naina's demeanor transforms. Her tense shoulders fall slack, her eyes widen with excitement, and the hard lines on her face disappear.

She turns to Unisa and, sincerely, says, "Thank you."

Salessa reaches out and places a hand tenderly on Unisa's shoulder. "This is a significant gesture."

Unisa nods and places her hand over Salessa's. "I'm glad. After you helped me this morning, I owe you my life."

"I know it's not easy to be here, but this is the safest place for you right now. I'll help you find a way home as soon as it's feasible."

"I understand. And other than engaging in battle, I'm here to help you in any way I can."

"Consider us even," Naina says, still smiling as she salivates over the map. "Let the hunt begin."

CHAPTER 45

To Lily Beach

Territory of EverEmber *Lily Beach*
Date *22nd Day of Month 6, Year 1628 DG*

RARELY DO STORMS UPSET THE calm of Ardev Ocean.

The dull heave of the ship is as good as a lullaby. Four cots rest in a line, each with a Mega on them: Zakia, Gina, Ray-Mi, and Kruga. The scientist is the only one awake. Zakia and Ray-Mi snore lightly with carefree smiles stretched across their lips, while Gina sleeps on her back, a dagger clutched to her chest.

Kruga looks out and sees only one sun over the horizon. It's still quite early in the morning, too early even for breakfast. He hears footsteps as Symin descends from the upper deck holding a map. The clomp of his boots on wood wakes the rest of the team, who sit up sleepily.

"We're here," Symin says matter-of-factly, raising a finger ahead of the ship.

Kruga looks out at the open water and, just on the horizon, finds a vast landmass growing clearer through the mist. A line of widely-spaced ore ships sits between them and Lily Beach, each brimming with a crew of Bravers.

"A barricade," Ray-Mi recognizes. "Standard protocol. Forming a perimeter around the island."

"Can you get us to Lily Beach?" Kruga inquires.

"*To* Lily Beach isn't an issue. *Through* Lily Beach is."

"What do you mean?" Zakia asks.

"A map can get us there, but what we need are blueprints. How do we navigate and dismantle a facility we've never seen before?"

"By using what we know," Gina says, sheathing her dagger and rising to her feet. "Braver schedules, ranks, duties, how they run their processing centers, how they think. We use it all to our advantage."

She paces toward the front of the ship, her eyes locked on the island ahead. "Everything we've done and learned, from the Revolution to this very moment, has prepared us for today. This is the mission that will define them all moving forward."

Ray-Mi leans over to Kruga and whispers, "I get such a chill when she talks like that."

Kruga suppresses a laugh and raises a finger to his lips.

"Here's the plan," Symin says, rolling the map back up. "The island holds Braver facilities *and* igni settlements. The goal is to neutralize as much infrastructure and machinery as we can, denying access to the sacristone and stopping production, without alerting or harming any humans."

"What if the facilities are mixed into the human communities?" Kruga asks.

"They won't be," Ray-Mi replies confidently. "Bravers thrive on secrecy. Humans are naturally curious. The Braver complex will likely be on an isolated portion of the island, away from the settlements."

"Then we have to find the isolated complex first," Zakia notes.

"Not if Ray can get the Bravers at the barricade to lead us to it," Gina remarks, turning around to face the team. She holds her hands out to her sides, and then brings them quickly together in a loud clap. As the sound waves propel outward and hit the members of the team, their hooded rags transform into pristine Braver uniforms.

Symin, Zakia, and Gina wear face masks indicating they are offi-cers of low rank, while Ray-Mi has the blue mask of a Legion Director.

Kruga's mask informs that he is noncombat, typical for those in the scientific divisions.

"Once we get to the complex," Gina continues her instructions, "Kruga, Zakia, and I will recon. When we've devised a plan of attack, we'll come back for Ray and Symin. Any questions?"

The four Mega shake their heads.

Kruga looks out over the bow and realizes how close they are to the barricade. "You're up, Ray."

Symin rises to the upper deck to navigate, while Zakia and Gina busy themselves with various tasks around the ship, as a Braver crew would. Kruga and Ray-Mi stand together just behind the front railing.

The former Braver has his hands folded tightly behind his back, his eyes focused and unflinching, all indications of his true personality wiped clean. Years of training and Braver etiquette kick in, as he stands ready to communicate with the Fleet.

The Director of the nearest vessel hails the ship over and Symin follows direction. When the two boats are sitting side-by-side, Ray-Mi and Kruga approach the starboard railing and the Director speaks first.

"Legion code?" he asks in a gruff tone.

"854," Ray-Mi issues confidently and quickly.

The numbers summon a distant memory in Kruga's mind, of a Legion they incapacitated on Panaerth weeks prior.

"854?" The Director raises an eyebrow. "800-Code Legions are assigned to Panaerth. You're a long way from your assigned location."

Ray-Mi gestures to Kruga. "My crew is escorting this scientist to the Biochemical Engineering Division. Please direct us to the labs."

There's a long pause in which the Director eyes Kruga suspiciously. A mild sweat breaks on the scientist's temple, until the Director slowly nods.

"Follow the shore southeast until you reach the complex. If you pass the sea stacks beyond the headland, you've gone too far."

Kruga watches a sly smile twist onto Ray-Mi's lips under the mask, before the former Braver turns to Symin and whistles. The ship moves past the barricade and heads southeast.

To Lily Beach.

CHAPTER 46

THROUGH LILY BEACH

Territory of EverEmber *Lily Beach*
Date *22nd Day of Month 6, Year 1628 DG*

AN EMPTY STRETCH OF LAND divides the bustling human settlements and the gargantuan ore infrastructure of the Braver complex.
The faerie facilities tower over human homes and markets, causing the
early morning suns to cast a dark shadow over the igni.

Zakia recognizes a clear division between the human city and
the faerie sector from the vessel, as it circles to the southeast corner
of the island. As they approach the complex, the comforting buzz of
the Radiance along her skin begins to die. She feels suddenly bare
and unprotected.

"If all goes according to plan," Symin says, "they'll have no idea it
was us."

"If all goes according to plan," Gina corrects him, "they'll all
be dead."

Gina's words arouse memories of Salessa's hesitation.

The engineers, scientists, laborers. Mega with families, friends, lovers. They didn't come to die.

Zakia shakes her head to push the words away. The mission comes first, the team comes first. Innocent bloodshed is an unfortunate reality of war. Empathy has no place in battle.

Or does it?

The ship reaches the intended ports. Wooden docks lead directly onto the sandy shore, which rises into a rocky climb up to the Braver complex on a stone plateau. The reconnaissance begins when Gina, Kruga, and Zakia step off the vessel and journey up the rocky island, a short but tedious journey.

The complex is predictable—a mirror image of the processing center on Panaerth. Tall buildings crowded together, the smells of oils and gasses permeating the air, and the controlled clangs of metalwork echoing around.

Bravers stand firm, guarding restricted areas, while scientists and engineers hurry about from location to location. Workers and foremen, dressed in thick black fabric suits, hustle like bees, running in and out of buildings as directed.

The odors pollute Zakia's senses. "How do they work like this?"

Kruga inhales deeply through the Braver face mask, then moans as he exhales. "Brings back so many memories. We must be close to the labs. Should we start there?"

Gina shakes her head and whispers as she instructs, "If the goal is to cut off production, we need to identify the source of the sacristone and destroy it."

"Won't it be alarming to see three uniformed officers wandering around the factories?" Zakia suggests.

"Three, yes. Two, no," Gina responds. "Patrols make rounds in pairs. You two head to the factories. I'll try to gain access to the restricted areas."

Zakia hesitates to split up, but when Kruga nods confidently, she follows. Light perspiration coats her palms when they stroll into one of the towering factories. She pays close attention to how Kruga behaves while undercover, capitalizing on the experience of her first infiltration.

In the center of the tall, wide building is an array of machinery and long metal tables with workers and scientists all around them. Large chunks of dark, raw stones rest on the tables until workers chisel them into smaller pieces.

"We're in the wrong building," Kruga whispers.

"How do you know?"

"They're working on raw ore, the sacristone." He pauses as his eyes linger on the scientists' activities. "As fascinating as this is, we need to find the source. There must be a mine or something."

"How would we find that?"

Kruga's eyes move to the Bravers lining the walls and entrances. "We need an escort from another Braver—one familiar with the whole complex."

Zakia rolls her eyes. "No Braver will break rank to give us a tour. Why don't we just search each of the buildings on our own?"

"The longer we wander, the more unwanted attention we'll attract. Speed, accuracy, and stealth are the foundations of reconnaissance."

Zakia's gaze travels the walls and floors and machinery, searching for a plan, until her eyes fall on a ceiling panel with a flashing red light.

"An emergency," she whispers to Kruga, pointing to the panel. "If there's an emergency in the mine, they'll call Bravers, who will lead us right to it."

Kruga's brow furrows. "How do we manufacture an emergency?"

"We don't. They just have to *think* there's an emergency."

Kruga's eyes brighten and Zakia feels his smile through his mask. "Follow me."

He leads her to a Legion Director standing toward the building's rear exit. When they approach, he speaks to her quietly, but frantically. "Director, we need reinforcements to contain a contamination breach of the raw sacristone."

"I can't leave this assignment," the Legion Director responds. She turns to a subordinate. "You! Go with them to Intake. Use the shortcut."

"Yes, Director," the Braver acknowledges, gesturing for Kruga and Zakia to follow. She leads them to a narrow doorway on the far right wall of the factory and down to a damp, semi-lit underground hallway.

"Where's the contamination?" the Braver asks as they tread through the sticky tunnel.

Kruga clears his throat. "Intake."

The Braver's tone grows irritated. "I understand, but in which section of Intake? The hospital, the tunnels, the husking sections?"

Zakia's heart starts to race, knowing neither of them have an answer. Her thoughts circle around the Braver's question. *A hospital? I thought she was taking us to a mine.*

Kruga answers. "The orders weren't specific. Take us to where Intake begins and we'll secure each level."

Their conversation continues, but the voices drown when a painful odor strikes the inside of Zakia's nostrils. The smell of rot grows thicker and thicker until it becomes a sickening paste dripping down her throat.

And then she finds the source.

Cots, pushed up against the walls of the tunnel, piled high with igni corpses. Men. Women. Children. Stripped bare and dropped onto one another like logs in a forest.

Zakia's feet freeze. The hairs on her arms and neck rise to attention. Liquid comes up into her mouth, and she purses her lips to contain it. She falls backward against something.

Another stack of rotting human corpses. She pulls her mask down and vomits onto the ground as the half-skeletal face of an igni appears in her mind and won't go away.

Strong fingers wrap like tendrils around her arm and lift her. Kruga's voice enters her ears but she can't make sense of the noise.

"Are you alright?" his voice finally comes through, muffled. He gives her a light shake and repeats the question.

Her eyes move to the unconscious Braver on the ground by her pool of vomit.

"What happened?" she asks Kruga.

"You vomited and she grew suspicious. I had to knock her out."

"What is this?"

The crimson pixie sighs. "We found the mine. The sacristone is exoskeleton, torn from igni corpses. The tunnels connect to the hospitals in the settlements. Unwell and elderly settlers are dispatched, then funneled here before being taken into the factories to make the sacristone."

"Dispatched?" Zakia's eyes grow wide as she realizes what he means.

"They're killing igni, Zakia," Kruga confirms. "And tearing the corpses apart."

Zakia attempts to control her visceral reaction with deep breaths. "What about their families?"

Kruga pauses. "I didn't ask, but I'd assume they're told their loved ones didn't survive their illness or old age, and were taken to be buried."

Zakia shakes her head. "The igni don't bury their dead. They're thrown into a volcano on EverEmber. The families must think that's where the bodies have been sent."

"Instead, they're here. Rotting in tunnels."

"This is genocide." The smell creeps back up into her nostrils and her stomach threatens to spill its contents again. "Is this the recon we needed?"

"Not entirely. I need to know how they turn the exoskeleton into ore. Somewhere in this process is the answer to why the ore cuts off our access to the Radiance."

The infiltrating Mega ascend from the tunnels into another factory. The layout is identical to that of the first: workers and machinery in the center, Bravers patrolling the perimeter.

Kruga walks quickly with calculated attention, taking note of the various work stations, reading the signs to Zakia.

"Section One: Husking." Cots are carried from the tunnels to a long metal table where the igni body is dropped. Here, faerie workers use an ore hammer and chisel to pry the exoskeleton open and loosen it from the igni body.

Once removed, they break it down further into smaller shards and gently compile it into a cart to be hauled away to the second section, while the gelatinous flesh and organs are dumped carelessly onto a platform labeled "Discard."

"Section Two: Malleableizing." The exoskeleton shards are further beaten down until they can be more easily shaped and molded.

The third and final section is populated, not by laborers, but by scientists. They place the fragments of exoskeleton into a machine that resembles an oven. The device melts the shards into a fiery liquid. By the time the exoskeleton leaves this section, it no longer bears any resemblance to its original state.

"Section Three," Kruga reads the final sign, "Molten Ore Preparation."

Zakia's focus falls on the legion of scientists and the absence of Bravers. "Why are we the only Bravers here?"

"This section is a laboratory. It's just for testing."

He gestures to a smaller version of the superheating device sitting on the table next to them, shining fragments of raw exoskeleton littered around it.

"How angry do you think Gina would be if I changed the plan?" he asks, eyeing the fragments.

"Gina has one level of anger: extremely." Her brows furrow. "Why?"

He pauses, gaze locked on the exoskeleton. "I have an idea that could change everything." He waves a hand to attract a nearby scientist's attention.

Zakia swallows hard. *This is not a good idea.*

"Is everything alright, officer?" the scientist asks when she arrives.

"I apologize for taking time away from your research," Kruga begins politely, "but my colleague and I are enrolled in biochemistry courses in Larso University during the academic season. We're working on a project that deals with ore and we were hoping to ask you some questions."

The scientist's face lights up. "Stuck on this island, we don't often get the opportunity to impart knowledge on budding scientists such as yourselves. Please, ask away."

Kruga places his hand on the small machine. "What does this do?"

"It superheats the exoskeleton."

Zakia sees Kruga physically resisting the urge to roll his eyes. "Sorry, I wasn't clear. I meant molecularly."

"Ah, yes. When heat is applied to the exoskeleton, the Radiant energy in the molecules polarizes and projects outward. It's an exoRadiant chemical reaction."

Kruga's eyebrows scrunch together in confusion. "Radiant energy? Where do human molecules get radiant energy when humans cannot access the Radiance?"

"Well," the scientist begins, pausing to gather her explanation, "modern humans do not connect to the Radiance, that's true. But biochemically, there's really nothing standing in their way. They still have the molecular structure to absorb, maintain, and project Radiant energy, the way their ancestors did."

"I see," Kruga responds. "So the superheating causes the molecules to completely change polarity and act as a negative Radiant energy, which blocks our Radiance."

"Precisely," the scientist confirms with a smile.

"What would happen if the exoskeletons underwent the opposite chemical treatment? If they were supercooled instead?"

The scientist strokes her chin. "Theoretically, the opposite polar effect." She throws her head back and releases a hearty laugh. "Catastrophe! Imagine if the other clans discovered the truth and cooled the ore. We'd find superpowered nymphs and pixies ruling Larso in a matter of hours."

The scientist asks if they have any more questions, but Kruga, lost in thought, doesn't respond.

"That's it for now, thank you," Zakia interjects, before the scientist returns to her station.

Kruga's gaze snaps to the rounded exoskeleton fragments on the table, and the superheating device. He whispers to Zakia, "Stand behind me. Don't let them see."

Zakia obliges, awkwardly attempting not to draw any attention in their direction, but it doesn't work for long. Scientist eyes curiously peek up from their work at the two Bravers towering over laboratory machinery.

"Quickly, Kruga, they're starting to notice."

"One more minute."

He continues working as the scientist they were speaking with, and a few others, get up from their stations and begin to move slowly toward them.

"What's he doing?" come their voices.

"Are those Bravers touching equipment?"

"They told me they're students."

"Someone get a Legion Director."

While the others continue to approach, one of the scientists runs to a nearby lighting panel and pushes it. It depresses under his hand and, when it pops back up, flashes red.

Zakia's heart pounds in her chest. "Kruga, faster."

"Almost done."

Twenty Bravers appear, weapons drawn.

Zakia peers over Kruga's shoulder. He has removed the back panel of the machine and rewired the connections within. He throws a pebble of exoskeleton into the machine and turns the dial to its maximum. Through the glass door, Zakia watches frost develop on the exoskeleton pebble.

Braver footsteps grow louder.

"Did it work?" Zakia urges him.

"You tell me," Kruga says. He tears the supercooled fragment from the machine and places it into Zakia's palm.

There's an initial sting from the frozen fragment on her skin. Then, a familiar buzz erupts throughout her body; she feels it in every vein, every pore, every cell. Kruga's theory holds true. The Radiance is born within her and the feeling of powerlessness melts away.

She's whole again.

A Braver's blade comes down toward her face. The pixie squeezes the fragment, drawing more energy from it, and the Braver holding the sword freezes.

She lifts her other hand and places her palm slowly and gently against the Braver's chest. As soon as her flesh presses against him, the Braver's body explodes, launching organs, flesh, blood, and other organic matter all over Kruga, Zakia, and the onlooking faeries.

But the pixie, miraculously, isn't disgusted. She's smiling.

CHAPTER 47

ESCAPE FROM LILY BEACH

Territory of EverEmber Lily Beach
Date 22nd Day of Month 6, Year 1628 DG

STILLNESS. SILENCE. CONFUSION.

The scene is incomprehensible to the wide-eyed faeries who watched a colleague explode at the touch of a Braver.

"Nymphs?" comes one whisper.

"Pixies?" comes another.

And then a third. "Get them."

Twenty Bravers charge forth, weapons drawn. Zakia's forearm rises to her chest and an invisible defensive shield forms around her and Kruga.

"Can you teleport us out?" Kruga asks as the Braver weapons bash the shield.

Zakia tightens her fist around the fragment to gauge its strength. "I don't think so. It's given me *some* connection to the Radiance, but it's too small to counteract the amount of ore on the island."

She searches frantically until her gaze finds a window in the rear wall. "Stay close to me!"

The dome remains intact, Bravers pounding it uselessly as she keeps her forearm tight to her chest. More join as they approach the window; the twenty grows to a hundred or more. In the complex below, dozens more continue their patrol.

Zakia clenches her fist, drawing Radiant energy, and launches herself and Kruga out the window. They land on their feet in the center of the complex. Palpable confusion permeates again as the faerie forces around them take notice, freeze, and blink wildly.

The warriors withdraw weapons and rush the forcefield like a flood. They attack hard, forcing Zakia to exert more pressure on the fragment. Every fiber of muscle in her body tenses, and her knees tremble from weakness. There's too much ore counteracting the light connection.

"I don't know how much longer I can hold this."

A warm stream flows down the side of her lips and she realizes her nose is bleeding. Lightheadedness takes control of her body and she drops to her knees.

"Gina!" Kruga yells, pointing. Zakia follows his finger and sees their General limply kicking the forcefield, pretending to contribute to the assault. She reaches her free hand out toward Gina, and an opening forms in the forcefield. Gina quickly shuffles in before Zakia drops her free hand and the opening vanishes.

The world grows blurry as blood drips from her face onto the ground. She turns to Gina. "Take this from my hand and keep the dome up."

Zakia slams the ground with her fist, and a shockwave of blue Radiant energy spreads out and knocks the Bravers closest to them backward. It gives them just enough time for her to pass the fragment to Gina, who closes her fist around it and smiles. The invisible shield springs to life again.

"We have to get back to the ship," Gina says.

Kruga gestures to the path leading down the rocky hillside to the docks. A horde of Bravers stands between them and their escape. "How are we going to do that?"

Gina falls silent for a few long moments, eyeing the exit route, then turns to Kruga and Zakia with soft eyes, peace washing over her expression.

"Bravers will follow us down the hill. We don't need a dome, we need a wall."

"Will you be able to hold a wall up from the ship?" Kruga asks her.

A smile widens on her lips and she slowly shakes her head. "Symin's turn to lead."

She flicks her wrist at them and, like insects flung from a table, hurls Kruga and Zakia over the stony path, causing them to land harshly on the sandy shore by the docks.

Zakia coughs as the air slowly returns to her lungs.

Ray-Mi's cornflower-blue fingers grasp her arm and help her to her feet. "What happened?"

"She...she," Zakia struggles to explain through gasps.

"She made the sacrifice," Kruga blurts out.

They turn to the stone path leading up to the complex, where Bravers appear stuck behind an invisible wall blocking their descent.

"She won't be able to hold it for long," Ray-Mi comments as they reach Symin and the vessel.

"What do we do?" Zakia asks.

Pain in his eyes, Symin exhales deeply. "We accept her sacrifice. It's time to go."

"Go where?" Ray-Mi questions. "There's a fucking barricade out there, Sy."

"We can't stay here," Kruga points out. "We'll have to maneuver through it."

"Through the ore Fleet?" Ray-Mi scoffs. He turns quickly to a Fleet ship docked on the adjacent pier, then back to Symin. "Don't wait for me, just go."

"Ray, stop!" Symin shouts, but Ray-Mi is already bolting down the dock to the Fleet vessel, which he boards, and sets off toward the barricade.

Symin bounds to the upper deck and prepares to sail. Zakia watches Gina's wall fail and Bravers descend like an avalanche down the stony path toward the shore.

Arrows shoot from the top of the hill, landing on the ship and the sand nearby. As the ship departs, three Bravers reach it and hop aboard, each armed with a sword.

One lunges furiously at Kruga, who evades the blade and counters with a fist to the stomach, and another to the jaw. He knocks the sword from the Braver's hand, but before he can reach for it, another swordsman jabs a blade toward him. The Braver narrowly misses, then follows with a series of punches, bloodying Kruga's face and knocking him onto his back.

Zakia faces off against the third Braver. Without the Radiance, she has little combat experience to call upon. She avoids the swordsman's advances as long as she can, but his skill outweighs her dexterity, and the blade finds her face, slicing her cheek wide open. She drops to her knees as blood pours onto the ship's deck.

The swordsman approaches her quickly and raises the blade over her. Instinctually, Zakia puts her forearm under the descending blade and closes her eyes.

The sword doesn't sever her.

Her eyes pop open to find the swordsman frozen with the blade inches from her face. She spies Symin on the upper deck, his hand outstretched toward her attacker.

"Can you feel it?" he shouts at her. "It's back."

Zakia takes a deep breath. The buzzing around her skin returns and the lightheaded weakness evaporates. The energy fills her veins, her muscles, her cells.

She flicks her wrist and the blade flies out of the swordsman's hand. Symin releases him and he charges at the pixie, fists raised, but she chops her hand horizontally and severs his head cleanly from his neck.

Kruga, exhausted and bleeding, battles two Bravers at once. Zakia inhales, and her connection to the Radiance grows. She feels as though she can bend steel.

The pixie raises a fist and paralyzes both Bravers, then tugs her fist to her chest and tears the paralyzed Bravers' hearts from their bodies. With another loose flick, all bodies and organs plummet into the ocean's depths.

Zakia helps Kruga to the upper deck, where they join Symin.

"Now the barricade," Kruga says to Symin, still leaning on Zakia for support.

Symin, with a trembling tone, replies, "It's taken care of."

Ahead of them, the line of Fleet ships forming the barricade is open where Ray-Mi steered his hijacked vessel into it. A fire rages on the ocean surface as debris from the wreckage floats about. Metal, wood, and bodies litter the calm waters.

Amongst those bodies, Zakia assumes, is Ray-Mi's.

"We have a problem!" Kruga exclaims, panicked. Behind them, another Fleet advances.

"What are we going to do?" Zakia asks Symin, her heart thrumming wildly, her mind battling hopelessness. "They're going to catch up to us."

An unfamiliar despondency crosses Symin's face. For the first time in all the years she's known him, Symin truly has no idea what to do.

But she does.

The Radiance pulses through her cells with the force of a thousand blazing stars, and an idea takes shape.

She turns to Symin and confesses the burden caging her heart; she likely won't have another opportunity. "I lied to you."

"About what?" Symin responds, confused.

"Naina and Salessa are in Larso with my mother. At the Bunker."

His eyes widen. "Zakia…no."

"Yes. Please, Symin, don't rob them of their only chance at justice."

"It's not that sim—"

"It doesn't matter. They are destined for far greater things than all of us. It's their fight as much as ours."

"Why are you saying this now?"

Zakia takes a deep breath to strengthen her nerves. "You and Kruga have to make it back to Larso, or everything that happened here today was for nothing. I have to destroy the complex before they send word to the Ore Monger about what's happened."

Symin shakes his head and grabs her wrist. "The amount of power that would take…I won't let you."

"Promise me something," Zakia continues, ignoring him. "Tell Salessa that I'm sorry, I'm not going to make it back for that cup of chai, after all."

Her throat tightens as the truth of all she's losing washes over her. All of the experiences she'll never get to have.

Symin's eyes grow moist as he squeezes her wrist tighter. "I will *not* lose another daughter."

"Strength thrives in change."

His fingers release her wrist and he steps back, jaw falling slack.

Zakia smiles and places a warm, affectionate hand on his cheek. "Thank you for protecting me all of these years. It's time for a change. I have to protect you now." She tenderly kisses his forehead.

A tear breaks from his eye and words fail him.

Zakia snaps her fingers and the world dissolves around her. When it forms again, she is hovering in the air above the ship, which continues on toward the barricade as Zakia turns to face the island and the oncoming Fleet.

They launch flaming projectiles at her. Effortlessly, she waves her arms about in a silky, fluid dance that sends the fireballs back from where they came. They strike the ships that released them, causing massive damage. Some take on water, while others continue.

The pixie sweeps her hand horizontally in front of her body and then chops the air forcefully in a vertical movement. The ocean grows angry; waves begin to appear, moving the ships back and forth and sideways. She flips her hand over and the ocean swallows every elite vessel whole, crew and all, into the dark depths of the Ardev Ocean.

Zakia locks her sights on Lily Beach, taking in the entire island at once from her soaring vantage point. Again, she sees the clear division between the human settlements and the faerie complex.

She repeats the vertical chop movement, then lifts her hands to her shoulders as if some invisible, mountainous force is pushing down on her. The pressure is immense, her hands shaking from the sheer weight.

Slowly, she pushes against it, moving her hands upward, lifting the gargantuan mass. Every millimeter her hands rise, a crack forms in the island's crust. Stone crumbles under the Braver complex. The entire island stretches and rattles as the waves around Lily Beach grow furious.

The faeries scurry frantically like insects under a boot.

Zakia's arms extend fully overhead. Blood spouts from her ears and nostrils, and her eyes roll back. Her throat tightens and she can no longer breathe.

The island's cracked crust shatters, deeper and deeper, until the faerie complex is severed from the human settlements and rises into the air. Ocean water drips from the bottom of the island chunk. Faerie insects leap off the enormous floating mass of dirt and stone, into the water below.

The water is death, the island is death.

Zakia throws the giant, invisible weight away from her, and stone by stone, sand grain by sand grain, leaf by leaf, the island chunk is dismantled. The mighty ocean waves envelop and conquer the tiny particles of island, ore, and faerie bodies.

The water around the island turns red as Zakia's body drops. She cannot breathe, yet there is no fear, as if the Radiance cradles and comforts her.

As she falls through the air, warmth and coolness wash over her body simultaneously. Comfort, in its purest form, as if she is falling asleep in the arms of a loved one.

No pain, discomfort, or worry. No hesitation, grief, or sorrow. She simply goes, slowly, to a place of love. Her senses fail, her mind stops, and her heart pumps a final beat. Her last thought lingers in the emptiness of her dwindling consciousness.

How lucky I was, to be so loved, by so many.

CHAPTER 48

THE BRIDGE TREE

Court Democracy EverEmber
Date 22nd Day of Month 6, Year 1628 DG

THE FIRST RAYS OF MORNING light drip through the window. It's earlier than Rafael typically wakes, yet he's already dressed, his waist armed with collapsible arrows and his bag packed.

Half a day in EverEmber has swirled by in a blur. He hasn't properly had time to process the bizarre twists of fate that delivered Kyoko to her sister and somehow sanctioned Rafael as the courier.

EverEmber has not been as violent and terrifying as he's imagined, though a significant factor of that experience lies in his realization of misplaced blame. Joaquina might have found her end under an igni blade, but it was her brother who placed her in its path.

As he'd bathed earlier, he'd scrubbed his skin feverishly, hoping to rid himself of the bloody visions across his body. But it will take more than soaps and lotions to cleanse his mind and heart of what he can't escape.

Joaquina would have been living a peaceful life today had it not been for her cowardly brother who couldn't answer the call to war.

The bedsheets stir as Kyoko rises, yawns, and rubs her eyes. "What time is it?"

She's dressed in the same clothes from the night before, having fallen asleep on his shoulder, exhausted from the emotional toll. He'd lifted her into his arms and laid her onto one side of the bed, then changed into a more comfortable outfit and slept next to her. He hadn't wanted to disturb her sleep in attempting to carry her back to her room.

"Too early," Rafael responds with a smirk. "We should head out for Tusa soon."

Kyoko nods sleepily. "I see you're already dressed and packed. I didn't even realize I fell asleep here last night." She rises to her feet and walks over to the foot of the bed, where Rafael is seated.

"I hope you don't mind that I let you sleep here."

There's a pause in which Rafael cannot fathom what Kyoko may be thinking. He worries until her lips curl into a pleasant smile and she says, "I don't mind. I'll go get ready and we can head out to Tusa shortly."

She leans forward and tilts her head to the side, beckoning him to perform the mari greeting with a kiss on each cheek. At Shifa's estate, he hesitated, but he doesn't anymore. He places a kiss on each of her cheeks, and takes in a quiet moment of gentle affection.

When they pull apart, Rafael's gaze locks on the igni Librarian's. A realization falls upon him like the plunging weight of an avalanche. Yala's shimmering eyes and silvery voice, the attributes that amplified the comfort he felt when interacting with her, are Kyoko's.

It was never about Yala. It was always Kyoko.

The clearing from which Mount Mother rises is on the way back to their vessel from the ryokan. A significant crowd gathers at the base of the volcano, many of whom wear the same necklace, with three dark, volcanic pearls hanging from them. A small child approaches the Librarians and hands a pearl necklace to each.

"What is this?" Rafael asks Kyoko.

"Mourning Pearls," she answers. "It appears there's a funeral happening at the base of Mount Mother."

"Who's passed?" Rafael wonders aloud.

Kyoko shrugs. "Must be someone influential. There are hundreds, or thousands, of mourners."

"Should we go around?"

Kyoko shakes her head. "It'll waste time. The quickest way past is straight ahead."

She guides him into the thick collection of igni citizens, taking his hand and squeezing through as many people as they can. He clutches Joaquina's bracelet to his chest.

About halfway across the clearing, Rafael's eye catches a fascinating scene at the base of the volcano: a coffin on a stage and six individuals in formal igni attire saluting.

He tugs gently on Kyoko's hand and she stops walking.

"I've never seen an igni funeral before. I'd like to watch."

Kyoko nods and they stand side by side, observing as she explains. "This isn't a typical funeral. The deceased is someone in the government."

"How do you know?"

"That's the Court up there. All seven..." She squints and counts again. "No, only six of the members of the Court are present. It looks like Courtman Tomohiro isn't—"

Her eyes widen and her mouth falls open. She turns to an elderly woman next to her, whose cheeks are painted with streaks of tears. "Whose funeral is this?"

The woman raises an eyebrow. "Have you not heard? Somewhere off of SunSide's coast, Courtman Tomohiro's ship has sunk. He was aboard."

"That's terrible," Kyoko responds after a pause. She gestures to the coffin on stage. "They were able to find the remains?"

The woman shakes her head. "Found the ship, but no body. The coffin is empty."

Kyoko's expression remains solemn as she continues to watch the funeral with Rafael.

"I'm sorry," Rafael says, leaning toward her.

Kyoko looks up at him and smiles, but he can tell it's forced. "He was a rare breed of politician—one who actually seemed to care for the citizens. The discovery of Lily Beach influenced his decision to relinquish Bibi Sands and end the war. He always seemed to want the best for us, which is more than I can say about anyone else on that stage."

"It's unfortunate they couldn't find his remains to bury."

"Bury?" Kyoko asks, visibly confused. "We don't bury our dead." She points to the volcano. "The dead are fed to Mount Mother, coffin and all. An igni exoskeleton won't decompose in the ground. It has to be melted down by the volcano's heat. The liquified stone then flows through natural underground tunnels, depositing and solidifying around the island."

A loving smile spreads across her lips. "Eventually, we all become part of her."

Rafael realizes the beauty in the cultures he'd condemned; he laments how much he would have learned long ago, had his mind and heart not been imprisoned.

"I'm sorry, Rafael," Kyoko interrupts his thoughts. "Igni funerals go on for some time. We have to keep moving."

They do so, finding their boat from the previous day and trekking the same way they arrived: Rafael swimming in the water, while Kyoko rows above.

Tusa is exactly as she described — tiny and covered in dense forest. Rafael can see why the EverEmber government can't find practical use for it, and why it's preserved by archaeologists and explorers.

The search for the TreeKeeper doesn't last long. They enter the forest on the northwestern edge, walk east and then south, and begin to head back to where the ship is tied.

Kyoko masterfully guides them in patterns that reveal every tree, bush, and small cavern on the island. She knows it well. The search ends in a desolate clearing, covered with rotting logs, dead leaves, and colorless trees. It oozes eerie grimness, save for the northern boundary, beyond which is the shore and the ocean.

"Mission over," Kyoko says. "We've explored Tusa, as the Prime instructed, and the TreeKeeper doesn't exist. Alba and Unisa's journey is the only means of verification left for Hay-Ro's letter."

Rafael takes a seat on a large boulder and sighs, demoralized. Through the trees, the suns' rays play off the ocean's surface. The longer he watches it, the more he realizes there's a familiar buzz of natural energy on his skin. He feels it throughout his body.

Radiant energy.

"Kyoko," he says with a shaky voice, getting her attention. His heart pounds as the buzzing of the energy amplifies. "Something is happening."

And then the gust comes, the wind that twice before carried him into the void of the Radiance. He accepts it, allows the floating feeling to take him, and his eyes close. When they open again, he's still in the clearing.

He never entered the void.

Kyoko's eyes widen. "Is that...more forest?"

Where there was once an ocean and a shore, there are now thick branches and tall trunks, as if the island has grown. "Wasn't this clearing at the very northern boundary of the island?"

"The Radiance," Rafael says. "I felt it. It's leading us somewhere."

To me, echoes a familiar voice in Rafael's mind.

"Joaquina?" he says. "I can hear you."

You've found me, Rafa.

"Rafael?" Kyoko places a hand on his shoulder. "Who are you talking to?"

"I can hear Joaquina. She's calling me to her." He listens again.

Follow the forest and come find me, Rafa.

Heat rises into his cheeks and his feet move, beyond his control. "I have to go to her."

"Rafael, wait," Kyoko hesitates.

Any logic or reasoning is wiped clean the moment Joaquina's voice reaches his mind. He doesn't question what is happening or why, but a miraculous tug demands he enters the forest. And he cannot refuse its call, as hard as he tries.

He turns to Kyoko and holds out his hand. "I have to find her, Kyoko."

Hesitating still, Kyoko slowly places her fingers in his palm and he leads her out of the clearing and into the forest.

There is a vibrancy in the trees and bushes and leaves around them. Glorious greens and a bright, rich aura surround them. They smell fresh mud and morning dew on the playful leaves by their feet.

They arrive in another clearing, far larger than the one they left behind. It's filled with spirit and brilliant life. At the very center is a girthy tree with so many branches and leaves, it would take a millennium to count. It features colors Rafael has never seen before, and the interconnected roots expand out to every tree in this section of forest.

"Where are we?" Kyoko wonders.

An unfamiliar voice echoes from the canopy above. "You are at the Bridge Tree, where this world connects to the world beyond. And I am its keeper."

An entity appears. A grotesque, deformed figure with thin, raven hair that appears unattached to her scalp. Crimson eyes sunken in, sharp teeth, and a serpentine tongue. Her magenta skin is wrinkled, flaking off and blistery.

She is covered in a black garment that flows around her, like a dark cloud trying desperately to cling to her. Under the cloudy cloak, she appears muscular—the body of a warrior.

"The TreeKeeper," Rafael identifies her.

"Welcome," croaks her grimy voice, "I was forewarned of your arrival."

"By whom?" Kyoko asks.

"I cannot say. It is not yet time."

She turns to Rafael and points a diseased finger at him. "You. You have been holding her here."

"Holding who here?" he responds.

"She has wanted to go home. To the world beyond. And you have kept her here at the Bridge Tree."

Rafael's brows furrow as he tries to make sense of what the Tree-Keeper is saying. "Who are you talking about?"

The TreeKeeper moves aside, revealing a doorway in the Bridge Tree's trunk. Through it, a human steps into the clearing.

A young woman, with beautifully flowing hair. She has piscine nares and fins along her arms. Light, airy material covers her from the shoulders down, wrapped around her body. An enchanting calm emanates from her. She is ethereal and sublime.

The woman turns to Rafael and smiles. "Rafa. You've found me."

Rafael's mouth locks and his throat dries entirely. His heart rate quickens and sweat breaks out along every inch of his body. Emotions find their way up to his eyes, burning his tears out.

The memories of this young woman flood into his mind. Moments she cared for him, moments she taught him life lessons, moments of the love they shared. The energy pulses wildly and powerfully around his body, yet he's stuck, still.

All he can do is hope the apparition is real.

"Joaquina," he whispers. No other words come to him.

She approaches him and wraps her arms around him, and he melts into her embrace.

Warmth rises from her body, and he takes in her scent, exactly as he remembers it. She holds him like no time has elapsed since he lost her.

Like he's fifteen again.

Rafael leans back, separating himself from her a bit so he can look into her eyes. Slowly, he reaches a hand up and touches her hair, then her cheeks and her shoulders, and finally holds her hands.

Every blink unleashes new tears. His lip quivers and his hands shake. He tries to swallow but his throat won't allow it.

"It's really you," he squeezes out. He throws his arms around her and embraces her again, this time with all of the strength he has, as if he's compensating for eight years of lost embraces. He buries his face in her neck and her hand rises to caress the back of his head.

It isn't long before his grief enters the clearing through wailing sobs. He feels empty and full, light and heavy, mournful and elated. Words evade him as he soaks in the miracle standing before him.

Through his tears and sobs, only two words escape his lips.

"I'm sorry." What the utterance lacks in volume, it counterbalances with the colossal weight of his self-loathing. "It's my fault."

She releases him from the embrace and looks on him with confusion, reaching up to wipe the tears off his cheeks. "What's your fault?"

"I was Dad's undersoldier. If I had gone"—he takes a deep breath to compose the rest of his sentence—"you would still be alive."

Joaquina shakes her head and smiles. "Rafa, have you been living with this all these years? Why are you holding this burden in your heart?"

She pulls his forehead down to her lips, then runs her thumb lovingly along his cheek. "I chose to fight. To protect you. I'm your sister, that's my duty. And I would do it again. Over and over. I would die a thousand deaths to keep you safe."

At a loss for words again, he melts into a loud howl.

"Death was painless, like falling asleep. But now I realize I've missed years of your life. *That* is painful."

Her voice gets softer as she struggles to speak, tears twinkling from the edges of her eyes. "And I know I'm going to miss more. I won't get to see you grow old. I won't get to see you become the man I always knew you would be one day. I don't regret dying, Rafa. I just regret not being able to love you for longer than the time I was given."

"You can't go," Rafael says. He grips her shoulders tightly. "I won't let you go again."

Joaquina takes Rafael's hands. "That's the problem. You never let me go in the first place. Look over there."

She gestures to an opening in the clearing between two wide trees. The space begins to glow with the brightness of the suns.

"That is the world beyond. For eight years, I've felt it tugging at me. I yearn for the eternal peace that awaits me." She looks back up at Rafael. "But I've been stuck here."

She places her forehead against his and they close their eyes as she whispers to him. "You have to let me go. I miss you, too, but this isn't natural for me. I need to move on."

She caresses the bracelet on his wrist. "Keep this with you always. It is a small part of me that will remind you of the big sister you had. The sister who loved you more than her own life."

Rafael's heart shatters at her words. It feels as though he's losing her all over again.

"I haven't been the same since I lost you, Joaquina. I'm empty."

Joaquina places her hand over his heart. "I'm right here. I'm always right here. But you have to promise me something."

Rafael nods.

"Forgive yourself."

Her fingers trace his hands and forearms gently, and as they pass over the bloody visions anchoring Rafael's guilt to his heart, the red vanishes. His skin is clean again—unblemished as the days when Joaquina was alive.

She continues. "It feels like you've been waiting for me to forgive you. But *you* have to forgive, Rafa. What happened to me was *not* your fault. Promise me that you will forgive yourself."

Hesitantly and reluctantly, he nods again.

"I live in your heart now, Rafa. Don't make it a dark and sad place. Fill it up with light and love. Give me a nice home."

Joaquina's smile fades and the bright opening in the clearing begins to pulse. The TreeKeeper appears next to her and water builds in Joaquina's eyes.

"I have to go now."

Rafael shakes his head, the feeling of a thousand arrows burrowing through his chest. "I need more time."

She places her hand over his heart again and repeats, "I'm always right here."

He nods and releases her shoulders.

For the first time in eight years, he lets her go.

"I feel so lucky that, even if it was only for a short while, I was your sister."

"I was the lucky one," Rafael replies. "I never deserved a sister like you."

"It's time to say goodbye. Let's do it properly this time."

They embrace again and Rafael holds onto her as tightly as he can, as if it will, in some way, keep her there with him.

But he knows it won't. He knows that the universe, or perhaps the Radiance, has given him the opportunity to say goodbye one final time—to get the closure he needs to move forward.

"I love you so much," he whispers into her ear.

She squeezes him tighter as she says, "I love you, too. Live your life and let me rest."

Rafael releases her, stepping back. She is smiling and beautiful, just as he remembered her. As he'll always remember her.

Joaquina strides to the light between the trees. It reaches out and, finally, accepts her. Rafael's heart melts and he can feel it instantly: Joaquina's final peace. She's exactly where she belongs.

She's gone home.

Rafael drops to his knees and Kyoko wraps her arms around him. He allows his body to fall limply into her, sobbing quietly.

The TreeKeeper approaches them. "I am ready to answer the questions you've come to ask regarding Drof-Fa, the MegaMother."

Kyoko's forehead scrunches as she addresses the entity. "How do you know we have questions?"

"I was forewarned of your arrival," she repeats.

"What can you tell us about how the MegaMother perished?"

The TreeKeeper's hateful, crimson eyes soften, relaying pain and suffering. Her indifferent stance dissolves into one of shyness. She looks down at the ground by her feet.

"The MegaMother never perished." Her sad, lonely eyes meet Kyoko's. "I was Drof-Fa, the MegaMother."

CHAPTER 49

THE EVERLASTING JOURNEY

Theocratic-Monarchy *SunSide*
Date *8th Day of Month 2, Year 783 DG - 845 Years Earlier*

FRONA, THE FOURTH SUN AND the youngest of the gods, makes her way over the horizon and appears in the mid-morning sky, joining the others.

Drof-Fa stands at the wide windows of the royal bedchambers. She's watched Ona, Lona, and Throna, waiting for the Four to be together before she addresses them.

"Glory to the Four," she whispers.

She's alone in the room, yet she maintains a low volume to shield her words from the ears of those passing by the door.

"Are you truly glorious? As much as they praise you, you'd think they've all witnessed your glory. Yet, I haven't experienced a shred of it."

She releases a heavy sigh. "I've praised you myself, day in and day out for over a decade now. They are all convinced—the Assembly, the citizens—that my devotion is true."

She turns from the window and paces, her steps remaining in the light of the Four. "The Assembly waits on my every word, granting me all desires. Any legislation I want to pass, they jump to sign off on. They never did that for Red-Lo; they despised him. I've achieved more in three years than he has in the decade prior."

She stops pacing and faces the Four again. "And it's all because they believe I worship you. That makes you my tool, certainly, but it doesn't prove your divinity."

The MegaMother runs her hands down the front of her long, intricately-embroidered gown to smooth it out, a nervous habit. "I *want* to believe in you, but I need proof. I need to know you have a plan. Show me your plan."

Drof-Fa looks straight at the suns and ignores the burn in her eyes. "Show me that it's possible to bring my husband back to my side. That I haven't lost him entirely." A deep inhale, as she rubs her hands together anxiously. "If you do, I will raise my voice and, for the first time in my life, I will sincerely say, 'Glory to the F—'"

A knock at the door.

"Enter," she commands.

Hay-Ro steps into the room and closes the door behind him. As he approaches the MegaMother, he forms his fingers into a circle and places it on his forehead.

Drof-Fa rolls her eyes. "Please, stop."

"Apologies, Mother," he responds, causing the MegaMother to wince. "I've come bearing your assessment results."

A smile widens on his face. "You're healed. All of the damage from the infection has been repaired."

Her subconsciously bated breath releases. She has questions, but takes a moment to drink in her small victory first. After three years of treatments, assessments, and patience, she's finally well again.

"Will I—?" The question lingers; she's unsure of whether or not she wants to know the answer.

Hay-Ro senses her hesitation. "Yes, you'll be able to bear children again. Though, we would have to keep you under strict observation. That was my mistake last time."

Drof-Fa leans forward and places a reassuring hand on Hay-Ro's knee. "You have no blame in what happened. No one does. Not you, not me, and not Red-Lo. It was simply the will of the Four."

Switching the performance back on has become a habit; she doesn't even know what she's said until after she's said it. Her smile fades as she realizes how little she truly believes that the Four were involved in what happened to her three years ago.

"I don't believe your husband agrees," Hay-Ro mentions.

"My husband is not in any state, currently, to hold judgment on others."

Hay-Ro nods. "I can understand your resentment, after you've had to assume leadership of his kingdom."

Flames nearly project out of her eyes. "It is not *his* kingdom anymore. The citizens have barely seen him in three years. The weight of the entire *queendom* rests on my shoulders."

Hay-Ro's eyes widen. "Apologies, Mother. It wasn't my intention to offend you. I simply meant that, regardless of his involvement, he is still the MegaFather by title."

Drof-Fa releases a heavy sigh. "I don't need him to be MegaFather. The queendom is well cared for. But I am not. I need my husband back. My companion."

Hay-Ro offers her a gentle smile. "And you'll have him, Drof-Fa. He loves you more than he loves anyone or anything else. As do" — he pauses, as if he's reconsidering how to finish the thought — "the citizens."

Drof-Fa smiles. "You called me by my name."

Hay-Ro laughs and winks. "Apologies, won't happen again."

As he turns to exit the room, Drof-Fa says, "There should be a servant outside. Will you please ask her to retrieve Red-Lo from the study?"

Hay-Ro nods and leaves Drof-Fa in silence.

I need my husband back. The sentiment races through her mind, resentment raging in her heart. *I will demand my husband back.*

Red-Lo enters the bedchambers carrying a dusty book. The MegaMother hides the disgust she feels as she takes in the sight of what he's become.

His once bright face is now adorned with sleepless, sunken eyes and a long beard matted with grime. What was once a powerful body that held up the hopes of the faerie resistance is now a slight, stringy frame that hasn't been properly nourished since he abandoned the throne. Glowing, turquoise skin has now turned watery and translucent, and his royal attire has been replaced by old, torn rags.

"My love," he addresses her.

She fends off her discomfort quickly. "I'm sorry to disturb your research, Red, but I needed to speak with you about something quite important."

"Then it is truly serendipitous of you to send a servant to retrieve me; I was just about to come to see you with something important myself."

Drof-Fa takes his words as an opportunity to stave off the conversation a little longer. "Oh? What is it?"

Red-Lo moves quickly to a desk on the far side of the room and gestures for Drof-Fa to follow him. He flips vigorously through the tattered tome.

"Where did you get this text?"

"It was brought to me this morning by the Prime Librarian."

Drof-Fa takes a step back. "The Prime Librarian? He came all the way from the Library to personally deliver a book to you?"

"Of course he did. After all we've done for the Library, he'd deliver me a cow and slaughter it, if I asked for a steak." He gestures to the text. "This book belonged to the Sprites."

"It must be ancient, then, if it was written prior to their extinction."

Red-Lo's finger slams down on the page. "Here it is! Look at this."

A poem sits innocuously on the page:

Search no more amongst these pages
We bring word from the mages
A continent away, lies your claim
Find the water within the flames
Caged in the cavern below the knife
Free us; the prize is everlasting life

Drof-Fa attempts to hide her confusion. "What does this mean, Red?"

Red-Lo's smile fades. "It's directions, obviously. *A continent away. Find the water. Cavern below the knife.* Don't you see, it's…"

His voice trails off when Drof-Fa shakes her head and backs away from him. The MegaMother's internal struggle fails and her emotional turmoil, three years of accrued abandonment, roars out of her like an anguished tsunami.

"How. Much. Longer?"

Each word inhabits its own space in the thick air between them.

Red-Lo's mouth hangs open. If her love for him hadn't started fading, she might have felt sympathy for his obvious obliviousness. But all she feels now is contempt for his inability to understand how much pain he's caused her.

"How much longer will this go on? SunSide has lost a MegaFather, and I've"—she pauses, but can't chain her tongue quickly enough—"I've lost my husband. I have humored this search for immortality long enough. It is time for you to come back, Red." She sighs, holding the moisture developing in her eyes at bay. "I need my husband."

"Humored?" When he speaks, his voice quivers as if she has pierced him with an arrow. "I've been doing this for us, you know that. SunSide will be there for us to rule when we return."

"Return from what?" She fails miserably at keeping her volume low.

"From our journey. When we are immortal, we will come back and rule SunSide. Together, forever. That's the plan. It's been the plan, since…"

He stops.

"Say it," Drof-Fa challenges him. "Since we lost the baby?"

Red-Lo nods slowly, pain creasing his expression.

Drof-Fa is finally able to sympathize with Red-Lo. For the pain he's feeling. She feels it, too. "Hay-Ro was just here, Red. I'm well again. We can continue our legacy."

"No." His tone is solid. "I won't try that again. Do you have any idea what I had to do, Drof-Fa? Do you have any idea what it's like when Hay-Ro says that death is at your doorstep ready to claim your wife or your child, and you have to choose who it gets?"

His voice wavers. "Have you ever thought for a second, in the past three years, of the kind of agony I go through every time I close my eyes and hear Hay-Ro's voice asking me to choose who lives and who dies? I stopped believing that Hay-Ro had the answers a long time ago."

"Hay-Ro is—"

"I mean this with every strand of my being, Drof-Fa: *fuck* Hay-Ro. I will never put myself in the position to have to make that choice again." He points down at the poem. "This is the path. This is the journey to our immortality. That is how we continue our legacy. Not with an heir. But by sitting on the throne eternally."

Drof-Fa is lost. She's always believed that once she was well enough to carry a child again, he would snap out of this delusion. But she realizes, now, how limitlessly devoted to this cause he is. How her husband has lost the ability to discern reality from fantasy.

"Red, you are not alone in your agony. I've lost my child, as well. A child I carried inside me for months."

He steadily moves toward her and takes her hands in his. "And that is why we must go on this journey together. Let us make it so that, if death comes back to our doorstep, we reject it. We send it back to the darkness from which it came. Immortality, Drof-Fa."

She searches in his eyes for the faerie she once fell in love with, but comes up empty. "If we don't find anything, will you abandon this search and join me on the throne again?"

Red-Lo nods. "Absolutely. But we must complete this journey first." He lovingly places his hands on either side of her head. "Please, my love. I need you. Your husband needs you. What do you say?"

She catches the rays of the Four in the corner of her eye. Perhaps they have a plan after all. "Glory to the Four."

Continent of Panaerth
Date *48th Day of Month 2, Year 783 DG*

STRINGS OF STARLIGHT FLOAT DOWN around Drof-Fa and Red-Lo, who huddle together under a thick shawl, by warming flames, surrounded by the walls of a canyon. Days of travel have yielded minimal opportunities for rest or hygiene.

She remains committed, knowing the tortuous journey nears its conclusion. Their efforts to find the source of immortality have been fruitless. By the following night, if their goal is not achieved, they will finally return to SunSide.

We bring word from the mages. Find the water in the flames. Caged in the cavern below the knife.

Above all, she is delighted she'll never have to hear this meaningless riddle again. Immortality does not exist.

Death comes for all.

Red-Lo holds a fist toward the fire. The flames roar powerfully as they expand outward. They generate enough light to illuminate a wide margin of the canyon. Small animals and insects appear, hovering and crawling near their campsite.

The illumination reveals more than just the native fauna. Past the licking flames, carved into a wall of the canyon and hidden behind a bed of boulders, is the mouth of a cave with a symbol carved above it.

"Is that a sword?" Drof-Fa asks.

Red-Lo's eyes widen when he realizes what it is. "No. It's a knife."

Drof-Fa recognizes the thoughts running through his mind. "Red, it's not—"

"Caged in the cavern below the knife," he says. "We've found it."

She uses the Radiance to light a glowing ember over her palm and leads Red-Lo into the cavern. They trudge forth cautiously, and she keeps her free hand tight on the hilt of her sword, ready to draw it if needed.

The cave opens steadily the deeper they go, and the wet walls give way to a wide, egg-shaped space with torches along the walls.

Lit torches. As if someone has been here recently.

"It's warm here," she whispers.

"Not warm," he replies. "Hot. Too hot." He ventures further into the egg-shaped room, eyes wide.

"What are you implying, Red?"

His gaze is glued to the far end of the room. In the shadows between the torches, a column of rock stands four feet tall, unnaturally carved and placed with purpose. On top of the stone pedestal is a small clay pot with a lid.

"It's a shrine, I believe," Red-Lo remarks.

Drof-Fa flanks him and shuts her fist, extinguishing the flame. She bends forward to get a better look at the container. There is a design etched into the outer rim.

"Flames," she says.

"Find the water in the flames," Red-Lo repeats a verse of the riddle.

Drof-Fa's mind births a wild thought. *Perhaps Red-Lo is right.*

The MegaFather continues. "A continent away, in the cavern below the knife. If this pot has water in it, we'll have found the water in the flames."

His eyes are locked, as if he is alone with it. Gently, he reaches forth and pulls off the lid, uncovering the shimmering contents inside.

He leans forward to peer into it, then looks up at Drof-Fa and smiles. "It's wat—"

A vibrating beam of light erupts from the pot and blasts Drof-Fa off her feet. Red-Lo shrieks, covers his eyes, and stumbles backward. The cavern spins around Drof-Fa, and her temples pound, but she manages to gain her footing and help Red-Lo stand. She unsheathes her sword, and Red-Lo steps behind her.

Then, the light disappears back into the pot.

"What was that?" Red-Lo questions.

Drof-Fa scans their surroundings and finds that they are no longer alone.

Two figures, one male and one female, stand in the hot room with them. When she sees them, Drof-Fa employs every ounce of her strength to stop herself from retching. The only word that comes to her mind to describe the two beings is *grotesque*.

The two creatures are wet and naked. Water drips off their bodies, but they are also drenched in a number of other fluids, including blood, mucus, pus, and feces. Their faces, torsos, genitals, arms, and legs are covered in blisters, burns, and scarring, as if they've been through an intense battle.

Entirely hairless, they each have two pairs of arms: one pair at the shoulders, the other extruding from their ribs. Their eyes are small and crimson, their skin too decrepit to ascertain a color. There is an odor coming off of them that is so horrific, it changes the entire texture of the air, a mixture of years of decomposition and warm excrement.

They're so thin and skeletal that their arms, legs, and hips look as angular and raw as avian talons.

Their most unusual features, Drof-Fa notes, are what seem to be remnants of wings. Not light, feathery wings like those of the angi, rather, they seem to have once had scales or some surface covering what is now just interconnected loops of bone.

The two creatures are hunched over at first, grasping the top of the stone pedestal and breathing laboriously. Then, they turn to look at one another and when their eyes meet, they smile. Inside their mouths, Drof-Fa sees brown, degraded teeth and a long serpentine tongue.

The creatures embrace until their breathing normalizes.

"Brother," says the female, "we've been freed." Her voice is grimy.

"We have indeed, Sister," the Brother responds with a voice of similar quality. "Our imprisonment has ended."

The Brother and the Sister move their faces closer until their mangled mouths are mashed together. They slither their serpentine tongues into each other and moan loudly. The Brother is visibly aroused, and when the Sister sees this, her smile widens.

Before the depravity continues any further, Drof-Fa sheathes her sword and holds her hands out in front of her in a defensive stance, ready to use the Radiance.

"Who are you?" she calls out loudly.

The siblings turn in Drof-Fa's direction.

"Look, Sister. The ones who freed us from our bondage." The two creatures walk around the stone pedestal and stand in front of it.

"They are Mega," the Sister observes. "Our genetic cousins."

"Who are you?" Drof-Fa repeats herself, more forcefully this time.

"We go by many names, Mega," the Brother responds. "The Drowned Sprites. The Burning Succubi. The Ancient Ones."

"Sprites?" Red-Lo raises an eyebrow. "It's been over three thousand years since the Sprites' extinction."

"Three thousand years," the Sister sighs. "We've been confined for millenia, Brother."

"I cannot believe it, Sister. We are finally free again. We will find Vala's progeny and they will pay."

"How? I feel weak. It will take time for our strength, and our abilities, to return."

The Brother turns to the Mega. "Our new friends will help us grow our power. And in exchange, we will grant their desires."

"No," Drof-Fa growls. "You can waste away here in this cave. But we have a kingdom to return to." She grabs Red-Lo by the elbow. "We're leaving."

"You can grant our desires?" Red-Lo blurts out.

The Sprites smile.

"Yes," the Sister replies. "But we need strength. We need essences."

"Red, we have to leave." Drof-Fa tugs his arm, but he's stuck in place.

"Show me what it is you want," the Sister says. She holds her hand out toward Red-Lo and says, *"Lari Tinari."*

The Mega drop to their knees. All of their memories, from the day they were born to this very moment, come flooding into the forefront of their minds at once. They watch the entirety of their lives flash through their consciousnesses.

The sting of some foreign force, some unidentified presence, needles its way into their minds. It feels as though a long, thick nail is being driven into their temples. The Sprite siblings' voices come alive inside their heads.

They've entered the Mega's minds.

The Sprites' presence remains even after the pain has subsided. They are now joined, the Sprites feeding on their thoughts and memories and ideas like parasites.

Red-Lo helps Drof-Fa to her feet, and she turns angrily toward the Sprites. "That was a mistake."

She pushes her hands out in front of her and flames come roaring from her palms and toward the Sprites. Just as they are about to reach the two creatures, the Brother says, "*Xorol Norol*" and lifts his hand. His palm absorbs every flame, rendering Drof-Fa's attack futile.

"And that was your mistake," the Sister says, and then points to Drof-Fa and chants, "*Beesa Fureesa.*"

Drof-Fa feels every muscle in her body clench and tighten. She is frozen—paralyzed. The Sprite curls her finger and Drof-Fa lowers, involuntarily kneeling at the Sister's feet.

The Sprite leans forward and puts her lips on Drof-Fa's, allowing her revolting, serpentine tongue to slither into the MegaMother's mouth and down her throat. Bile rises up from her stomach at the nauseating taste and stench of the Sister's tongue in her mouth.

"Let her go!" Red-Lo lifts his hands, ready to use the Radiance.

The Sister pulls her tongue and lips away from Drof-Fa, who vomits all over herself.

"Relax, Mega," the Brother says. "There is no need for violence. We can come to an agreement."

"What kind of agreement?"

"We know what you want now."

"Immortality," the Sister says. "You've lost a child. The fragility of life is a torture for you. Let us end the torture and grant you immortality."

Red-Lo hesitates, then asks, "You can do that?"

"For a price," the Brother responds. "We need our strength. For that, we need essence. Life force."

Red-Lo pauses, considering.

"Offspring," the Sister elaborates. "Go back to your kingdom and find a new bride. Lie with her and raise offspring. When we call for you, bring us the child. We will feast on its essence, and then we will place your essence into its body. Your essence will continue on, strong and young, for another generation."

The Brother continues. "Generation after generation, you will spring forth new children, and we will feast on their essences, and you will live on in their bodies. Forever."

Red-Lo finds his voice. "That is horrific. I will never lie with anyone but Drof-Fa, let alone allow you to feed on the essences of my children for generations. Now let her go."

"Don't forget, Mega," the Sister reminds, "we are in your head now. We know what you truly think, even when you try to convince yourself otherwise. And right now, you are lying. You want this. You want your immortality more than anything. Maybe even more than"—she gestures to Drof-Fa—"her."

"Never," Red-Lo responds. "I've had to make an impossible choice before. And I chose Drof-Fa. I will always choose Drof-Fa."

The Brother smiles. "And that is exactly why she must die." He faces all four of his palms toward her.

"Wait!" Red-Lo yells. "I'll do it. If you spare her life, I'll agree to your plan."

"She is a liability. She is your weakness."

"Hide her from me. I won't search for her. Let her live, and I will bring you my offspring every generation. You can feed on the essences, and I'll claim their bodies."

"There will be consequences if the agreement is unfulfilled," the Sister advises.

"What consequences?"

"We will unleash the Three Deaths upon this world. A beast of the sky, a beast of the sea, and a beast of the soil. They will raze this world to the ground, and we will rise up to create our kingdom upon the ashes."

"That won't be necessary. I will provide an essence in every generation. I will serve you in my immortality. Just, please, let her go."

The Brother faces all four palms at Drof-Fa again and says, "*Amana Karana.*" She screams in agony as her flesh burns, blisters, and melts to the bone. Her consciousness fades until all sounds and sensations die with her.

And then her eyes open again, in an ethereal, verdant forest, next to a girthy tree with so many branches and leaves, it would take a millennium to count.

CHAPTER 50

THE TREEKEEPER

Court Democracy *EverEmber*
Date *22nd Day of Month 6, Year 1628 DG*

KYOKO AND RAFAEL SILENTLY DIGEST the tale. The mari's cheeks still shine with the sticky gloss of his sorrow.

Drof-Fa, the TreeKeeper, laments her age-old misfortune. Through the disfigurement, the once-glorious MegaMother shines through.

"There is no Zar-Lo," Kyoko speaks first. "It's Red-Lo."

Drof-Fa nods. "Zar-Lo did exist once. Red-Lo raised him to have a strong body and sharp mind. When the time came, he brought his son to the Sprites, who ate the boy's essence and gave Red-Lo his body. As they've done for over eight hundred years."

"The Sprites granted him immortality," Rafael states.

"Far more than that," Drof-Fa clarifies. "During each transfer of Red-Lo's essence to a new body, the Sprites instill their own energy into him. He doesn't have their magic, but he has their strength, their rage, and their resolve."

"Are you not bound to them?" Kyoko asks.

Drof-Fa shakes her head. "Not anymore. When they placed me here, I obeyed, ushering essences to the Sprites for consumption, instead of to the world beyond. I'd forgotten who I was, but I slowly began to remember again. I was racked with guilt, so I broke free from them, and from my servitude."

Rafael leans in. "How?"

"The Bridge Tree has kept my connection to the Radiance alive. Once I had resolved to sever myself from them, I imbued an essence with a Radiant infection that disconnected me. But there were unintended effects. My connection to the Sprites was successfully broken, but their magic is" — she pauses — "unpredictable. Once our connection was severed, it latched onto a new mind to form a new connection."

Kyoko's eyes widen as realization dawns on her. "Red-Lo's mind. You're connected to Red-Lo."

"I am, but only from me to him. I can hear what he thinks, and I can see what he sees, but he's unaware I'm there. That I have been for centuries."

"You never wanted this," Rafael empathizes. "The Everlasting Journey was Red-Lo's idea. Hay-Ro's letter revealed the truth."

Drof-Fa nods and a soft smile curves her lips. "Hay-Ro. Even in death, he still cares for me the way my husband never did."

"Your husband tarnished your legacy," Kyoko tells her.

She shakes her head and the smile fades. "The greatest irony is that I now have the immortality that Red-Lo desired, yet his agreement is close to collapse. His final days may be upon him."

"What do you mean?" Kyoko asks.

"Zar-Lo's body is unable to reproduce." Sadness fills her eyes. "I've watched as he has tried with so many Mega, over and over again, unable to impregnate a single one. The Sprites still require an essence from him. If it is not delivered…"

"The Three Deaths," Rafael completes.

"Yes. Red-Lo's plan is to forge a changeling in place of offspring — an organic copy of Mega genetics, grown to create flesh, blood, bone, and an essence. If he succeeds, the Sprites can feed on the essence, and he can have the changeling's body. But a predicament challenges his scheme."

Kyoko's brows scrunch together. "What kind of predicament?"

"Forging a changeling requires an amount of Radiant energy that Red-Lo cannot find. He and his Facilitator spent six years abducting Mega citizens, searching for a power source, until they accidentally came upon what they needed in two Doruh children. Those two young twins, the falcon and the wolf, have the immeasurable power of a deity."

"Where are these two Doruh now?" Rafael asks. "Does Red-Lo have them?"

Drof-Fa shakes her head. "They are hidden under his nose. For now. If they are found, he will use their power to forge the changeling, and deliver the essence to the Sprites, continuing his immortal reign."

"If they aren't found," Kyoko adds, "the Sprites will release the Three Deaths."

"Precisely. Red-Lo and I weren't aware, but the Sprites were too weak to carry out that threat in the cave. I have no doubt that, after eight centuries of feeding, they now have the ability to call the Deaths forth and raze this world."

There's a heavy tension in the air as Kyoko weighs the impossible choices: sacrifice two young Doruh to save the world, or sacrifice the world to save the twins.

She turns to Rafael. "What do we do?"

"What *can* we do?" Rafael counters.

There's only one person she knows who would be able to answer that question.

"Alba will know. We have to go to SunSide. She and Unisa are in danger if they're about to question Red-Lo about the death of MegaMother."

At the mention of Alba's name, the TreeKeeper rises into the air. "My duty to answer your questions has been satisfied. I have kept my promise."

Kyoko rises to her feet. "Your promise to whom? You haven't told us."

"Again, I will not. You are no longer welcome in my dominion, until your essence is ready to pass through."

She opens her arms wide and whips her dark shroud over them. It expands out and covers their surroundings entirely.

Kyoko instinctively closes her eyes and covers her face to protect herself. When she opens them again, she and Rafael are standing on the shore, by the boat.

"We're back," he says.

Kyoko turns up to the sky. "It felt like we were there for a few hours, but the suns haven't moved. It's still early morning, the same time as when we arrived on Tusa."

"She gave us time," Rafael concludes. "Our day has been reset to get to SunSide."

Kyoko nods. "Then we have to go, now."

"How fast can you row?" Rafael asks.

"Faster than you can swim."

Rafael begins to undress. "We'll see about that."

CHAPTER 51

THE SLAUGHTERHOUSE

Theocratic-Monarchy *SunSide*
Date *22nd Day of Month 6, Year 1628 DG*

THE MEGAFATHER AND THE FACILITATOR stand shoulder to shoulder, patrolling the kingdom from the window wall. The suns strike midday and illuminate the city below, aiding the Mega's surveillance.

"In the lodging district?" Zar-Lo asks to confirm.

Saith nods. "Yes, Father. The sensation disappeared before I could get there, but it was strong. They are at one of the inns."

Zar-Lo strokes his chin. "How are they cloaking?"

"I'm not sure, Father. I just need one more mistake. The next time I feel them, even for a moment, we'll have them."

Zar-Lo locks eyes with the pixie. "We'd better. This world doesn't stand a chance against the Sprites and their beasts."

He turns back to the city with narrow eyes, as if peering through every window of every inn. "I don't know why, but the lambs have entered the slaughterhouse."

"Perhaps they've awakened the Goddess."

"Unlikely," Zar-Lo replies. "If the Goddess were awake, we'd have met her by now."

A knock echoes from the door.

Zar-Lo sighs. "Is it him?"

Saith closes his eyes, focusing on the entity beyond the door. "It is."

"Let him in."

Saith raises his hand and waves it toward the door. It cracks open slightly, just wide enough for one individual to slip through.

As soon as Vy-Ro enters, the door closes behind him.

He forms the circular salute with his fingers and places it over his forehead as he approaches the window wall.

"Stop there," Zar-Lo bellows.

Vy-Ro's feet obey quickly.

"You've lost the privilege of walking freely through this room. Speak quickly, then get the fuck out."

Vy-Ro nods, holding in a tense breath. "I've come to keep you abreast of all situations. The search for both Saila and the Librarian are ongoing. I've spread flyers for the angi around the city, as well as proclamations detailing your survival from the attacks, and the length of your recovery period."

"In other words," Saith interjects, "you are doing the bare minimum to clean up your mess. Let alone employed, you're lucky to still be breathing. Particularly considering I had to remind you that another Librarian accompanied Alba into SunSide."

Vy-Ro swallows hard. "There is one new situation I must regretfully inform you of."

Zar-Lo launches swiftly forward in wide strides until his fingers reach Vy-Ro's throat. The faerie hoists him into the air with one hand. The Braver General sweats and gasps, his feet dangling two feet off the ground.

"What more could possibly go wrong? Saila lives. A Librarian is dead and another is a fugitive."

"Not just any Librarian," Saith adds. "Alba. The Prime will not hesitate to march onto our soil with the only military in the world that matches the Bravers' might."

Vy-Ro's puce cheeks start growing frantically purple as he sucks in jagged air.

Zar-Lo continues. "Saith, I command you. Tear this *new situation* out of Vy-Ro's skull. And please, don't be gentle."

Saith steps forward as Zar-Lo lowers the Braver General to the ground with the MegaFather's hand still tight around his throat.

Saith peers into Vy-Ro's eyes and the Braver General's face and head begin to tremble. His eyes roll toward the back of his head, and blood flows from his nose as Saith gleans the information from his mind.

"Oh, dear," Saith says. "What terrible news."

Zar-Lo raises him until he dangles at eye level again.

"I don't want to see your face until there is good news. The next time I see you, I'll strip you of your weapons and your armor and send you out into the streets where the sharks can feast on your pathetic meat. Do we have an understanding?"

Struggling to breathe, Vy-Ro nods desperately.

Zar-Lo launches him to the door, and the Braver General lands on his back, then turns quickly and crawls out of the Theater on all fours.

The MegaFather turns to Saith. "What is it?"

"Lily Beach has gone silent. Neither the Fleet ships nor their command posts return any correspondence."

"Send warships. We must be prepared for anything."

He turns, and with every step, he names another dilemma. "Ancient beings ready to decimate the planet. A kingdom on the verge of civil war. A general who's misplaced our most powerful enemy. A dead Librarian, and another on the run. Twins still hiding."

He reaches the window wall. "Eternity is exhausting when you're alone."

"If I may ask, why burden yourself with the Sprites' demands, Father? What's the point of sustaining your legacy and protecting the world when you've grown so weary of it all? Let the Sprites build their kingdom atop ash and ruin."

There's a long pause in which ancient memories of Red-Lo's life flood Zar-Lo's young mind. "For her. I loved ruling, but I was never a conqueror. She was. Eight hundred years later, I cling to this throne and this life because..." Magenta lips part in his mind, revealing a smile for which he'd set the world aflame.

"Because it's the last bit of her I can't seem to let go."

CHAPTER 52

THE GENERALS

Theocratic-Monarchy SunSide
Date 22nd Day of Month 6, Year 1628 DG

WHEN KYOKO TIRES, SHE CALLS out to Rafael, who leaps forth from the ocean to relieve her. Once she's rested, they trade places again, and the journey to SunSide continues.

They dock shortly after midday and she guides Rafael through Nivyan Hollow, on a path leading directly to Larso's southern gate. Kyoko's legs carry her briskly, her heart pumping with the rattle of an engine, her thoughts on Alba's safety.

They reach the edge of the forest and Rafael steps forward beyond the tree line, until Kyoko notices something peculiar and pulls him back to hide amongst the shadows of the branches.

"Why are there so many?" she wonders aloud. "I've been to this gate before, and there's never more than a single Legion here."

"There are four now," Rafael says counting the officers inspecting arriving travelers.

Kyoko shakes her head. "I count six Directors. Something has happened." Her apprehension mounts, fingers trembling anxiously.

"Do you think..." Rafael begins.

Kyoko brushes his thought away, as she did when she had the same one. "No, they're fine. Once we're in, we'll confirm and head home together."

She steps forward and gestures for Rafael to follow. "For now, there's nothing we can do besides wait in the queue."

Shortly after they take their places amongst the hopefuls entering the city, Kyoko finds all six Legion Directors approaching the Librarians at once, their fingers firm around the hilts on their hips.

"Follow my lead and listen closely for my orders," she instructs Rafael, who nods.

"Good afternoon, Ambassadors," one of the Directors slithers forth, reeking of forced diplomacy. "What brings you to SunSide?"

"Business," Kyoko responds vaguely.

"We would be delighted to escort you into the city ourselves." She gestures to a wide hover carriage nearby, floating in an ore-plated lot that connects to roads leading into the city.

Beads of sweat roll along Kyoko's palm. "We can manage on our own, thank you. I've been to the diplomatic chambers within the Castrum before; I know how to get there."

The Director tightens her grip on her sword. "Unfortunately, our escort is the only option today."

Kyoko, taken aback, freezes her expression to hide her emotion. "I'd be cautious with how you word your statements, Director. A single option implies detention, which you and I both know violates—"

"Laws that are suspended in an active war zone," the Director steps in.

Kyoko pauses, speechless. "Active war zone?"

"Your escort will explain on your way into the city."

Rafael awaits her command. She takes in the six eager Legion Directors, as well as the other travelers, who've now started to glance in their direction. A confrontation is unwise, and an explanation, needed.

She nods to the Director and they're led to the carriage.

Rafael leans down and whispers as they walk, "This is tense for a diplomatic escort."

"We're typically received by the Castrum as honored guests. Something is very wrong."

The Director opens the back of the hover carriage to reveal Vy-Ro sitting and waiting inside. The Braver General stands and approaches the rear of the carriage.

"Welcome back, Kyoko. I see you've acquired the yellow silk. Congratulations."

Kyoko's irritation bleeds into her tone. "What is all of this, Vy-Ro?" She gestures to the Directors. "Why are they telling me Larso is an active war zone?"

"For your own safety and protection, I can't allow you to wander the city streets. Please, allow me to explain as we escort you directly into the Castrum."

He holds out a hand to help Kyoko into the carriage. The hairs all around her body stand alert. Until she has some answers, she has no choice but to cooperate.

She ignores the Braver General's hand and steps up into the carriage on her own. Vy-Ro turns and follows her.

She hears Rafael moan behind her, "He didn't offer *me* his hand."

Vy-Ro appears purple in the carriage's dim light. The outline of wide, strong fingers glows around the Braver General's throat, and a small bubble of empathy ripples into Kyoko's heart, until she remembers to whom the throat belongs, and pops it.

From the transit time, Kyoko estimates they must be well into the city, yet no explanations have been offered.

"You promised me answers, Vy-Ro," she demands.

"There is active warfare in the city." He reaches into his pocket and withdraws a folded sheet of paper. He hands it to the Librarians and says, "This is the reason why."

Kyoko nearly falls off the bench when she unravels a *Wanted* flyer with an image of an angi Librarian drawn at the top, and a description that identifies the human as a key suspect in the assassination of the Members of the Assembly.

The igni's mind jumbles at the attempt to process so much new information at once.

Saila is dead? Unisa is a suspect? Where is Alba?

"What is this bullshit?" Rafael spits, in the least professional tone Kyoko's ever heard from a Librarian on duty.

She slowly moves her hand to his knee and redirects the conversation as professionally as possible.

"Nine Members were assassinated in one night?" she questions with a raised eyebrow. "Even Saila?"

Vy-Ro sighs sorrowfully. "Indeed. Last night, our peaceful kingdom was rattled by a despicable plot to assassinate all of our leadership at once. None of the Members survived, but, by the mercy of the Four, the MegaFather did."

A hard knot pulses in Kyoko's stomach. *Alba must be devastated.*

"I'm sorry," Vy-Ro continues. "I know you and Alba were both close to Saila."

Kyoko ignores his condolences. "You think *Unisa* crept through Larso in the night and assassinated nine Mega, and wounded a tenth?"

"So you know her," Vy-Ro says, leaning in.

Rafael growls, "Of course we know her."

Vy-Ro's eyes narrow at Rafael's tone. "I didn't want to assume all Librarians knew each other. It's a big city."

"This is clearly a mistake, Vy-Ro," Kyoko attempts to diffuse the tension. "This Librarian is—"

"At large," Vy-Ro informs them. "Tell me, Ambassador, why would a human be on the run if they are innocent?"

"Because she's terrified. You're wasting your time looking for her when you have an assassin on the loose. Where is Alba? She can very quickly clear Unisa's name."

Vy-Ro's gaze falls to his feet and he inhales deeply. "Unfortunately, Alba has disappea—"

White and orange light burn through the carriage as shards of metal and wood soar around them. Kyoko's eyes shut tight instinctually as searing heat ignites the air. It singes her hair, roasting the passageways in her nostrils. The smells and sensations of smoke inhalation char her insides as she coughs and vomits violently.

The torturous stings and flaming pricks of debris and disaster envelop her. She hears screaming and crying as she tries to orient herself, but the sudden confusion leaves her vulnerable to more damage inside and out.

Light pierces through the haze to bring forth colors that form images. Vy-Ro's, covered in blood, loudly calls orders from the edge of the
destroyed hover carriage. Braver boots rustle quickly outside, joined by
the clang of swords and the thud of dropping bodies. More thunderous
booms rattle the ground.

Dark, shadowy smoke billows into the air. Red and orange flames
travel the streets. White Braver uniforms are painted crimson.

Pain shackles her, burning her hands, her knees, her face, inside her
throat, and her stomach. She's on the ground of what remains of the
carriage, lying on her front amongst white-hot debris.

With all of her might, she pushes her palms against the ground and
rises to her hands and knees. Blood covers what remains of her tunic,
though she isn't sure if it's her own. The heat of the environment, and
the ache of landing on the ground, deny her the ability to pinpoint a
specific injury.

Vy-Ro unsheathes his sword and launches into the fray, tearing
through one Revolution fighter after another.

Clarity arrives through the haze. The Revolution attacked the carriage.

The world spins, her head pounds, and her knees tremble, as she forces
herself up and onto her feet. She isn't entirely stable, but she's standing.

Her exoskeleton appears to have protected her; she finds small chips and
fractures in it through the holes in her tunic, but they all seem superficial.

Every muscle in her body seizes when she discovers Rafael on the
carriage floor. His clothes are lightly torn and singed, as he was farther
from the blast, but there is far more blood on and around him. The
explosion has clearly torn through some part of his body, but Kyoko
can't see where his wounds are.

She only sees the blood pooling.

Kneeling next to him, she places a hand under his nose, and then
her ear to his chest.

He's alive.

As she prepares to lift him, footsteps clomp behind her. She turns and
unsheathes the tanto in a split second, keeping it held in front of her.

The light of the suns spills down on the broad shoulders of an
orange-skinned Mega clothed in sleeveless fabric armor. It reveals
massive biceps and the tightly packed muscles of her abdomen.

Her clothes are as worn as her expression—loaded eyes that have grown familiar to loss. Every inch of exposed skin is decorated by scars or healing wounds.

And she is armed to the teeth.

They hold eye contact for a tense few seconds, Kyoko on her knees with the tanto outstretched, the Mega standing still in the doorway.

"Do you know her?" the Mega asks, breaking the silence.

Kyoko keeps her eyes and position locked. "Do I know who?"

"The Librarian!" she barks. "The one they're looking for."

"Who are you?" Kyoko shouts back, refusing to offer any information to the stranger.

The Mega looks outside at the ongoing battle, then turns back to Kyoko with a frustrated and anxious expression. "My name is Ovida. I'm the General of the SunSide Revolutionary Forces, and I can help you find the other Librarian."

Kyoko pauses. Her mind reels from the explosion, but she forces it to focus long enough to respond. "If you think she killed anyone, I can assure you she's innocent."

"I figured out that much on my own, igni. Librarians don't stroll into foreign kingdoms and assassinate public officials."

"Then why are you looking for her?"

"Because if the Bravers are trying to pin this on her, there's a reason, and I need to find out what it is."

Ovida steps forward and Kyoko tightens her grip on the tanto's hilt. The Mega lifts her hands defensively.

"You won't be able to find her without our help. Come with me."

Kyoko takes a deep breath, pushing through the fogginess to assess her choices. She turns to Rafael. There's more blood around him now than there was before. "He needs salvers."

Ovida peers over Kyoko's shoulder. "The mari needs a burial at sea. He's not going to make it to salvers."

"I'll come with you on two conditions. First, we bring him with us. Second, when we find Unisa, no one touches her."

Ovida nods, steps forward, and hoists Rafael onto her shoulders. When she gets back to the shredded edge of the carriage, she turns back to Kyoko. "Welcome to the Revolution, igni."

CHAPTER 53

THE REVOLUTION

Theocratic-Monarchy SunSide
Date *22nd Day of Month 6, Year 1628 DG*

DARKNESS. VIBRANT CHATTER. SOFT BREEZES. Taste of blood. Scent of smoke.

The sensations become defined as Rafael's consciousness crawls back. He swallows painfully and tries to pry his eyelids apart, but light flashes into his pupils and he's forced to shut them again. A headache rages and a deep ringing pierces his ears.

This is a shitty way to wake up.

An unfamiliar voice nearby states, "Go get Kyoko. Her companion appears to be stirring."

Yes, I'm stirring. And it feels terrible.

He takes a deep breath and attempts to open his eyes again, this time much slower, allowing them to adjust. Pain ignites, then fades with the haze, and the environment focuses.

The room is inundated with Mega. Shades of red, blue, green, yellow, pink, orange, purple. Worn armor, torn and singed, revealing scars beneath.

Doruh and humans mix in as well, with far fewer numbers, though they're dressed the same and share the murals of battle scars.

The cavern is massive, clearly underground, with lanterns and torches illuminating the lair. His tunic has been removed and his bandaged body throbs and burns in more places than he can count.

A lemon-skinned Mega sits to his right with a tray of salver's tools and a wide leaf.

"Welcome to the SunSide Revolutionary Forces, human," she says. "Let me help you up."

She reaches forward and gently aids Rafael's transition into a seated position, leaning back on pillows against the cavern wall. "I have ale for your pain. We don't have access to much medicine, and Radiant healing treatments will take some time."

"I'd prefer carajillo," Rafael responds, "but ale will do."

The Mega nods and lifts a small mug of ale from under her cot.

Rafael finishes it in a single swig. "Is the Revolution not dissolved?"

"It was. However"—she gestures to the busy Mega around the massive cavern, looking over maps and sparring with weapons—"we are operational again."

Rafael points to the tray of tools. "You must be the Revolution's salver."

"One of them, yes."

"What's the leaf for?"

The Mega lifts it from her lap and begins to fan it at Rafael, bringing the cool breeze back to life. "Your body is exhibiting hyperthermia to fight off your infections. You were hit with a bit of shrapnel from our explosives."

Rafael's ears stand alert at the last two words. "*Your* explosives?"

The Mega's cheeks turn orange. "We inadvertently injured you in our attempt to acquire your custody. But not to worry, I've removed the shrapnel and bandaged your wounds. With adequate rest, hydration, and treatment, you'll feel much better in no more than a month. Give or take."

A chuckle erupts from Rafael and he shakes his head. "I do not intend to be here for a month. Give or take. The 'hydration' part of your treatment plan is all I need. Throw me into the ocean."

The Mega's smile dies. "That's not how I treat my patients."

"Have you ever treated mari before?"

The Mega hesitates. "Well...no, but—"

"Rafael!"

The familiar, silvery tone soothes Rafael's ears. Before he can register a face, Kyoko wraps herself around him. He winces as she presses on the burns and wounds around his shoulders.

Kyoko retreats. "Oh! I'm so sorry."

Rafael forces a smile. "No worries."

"I'll leave you two to speak," the Mega says. She leans forward and whispers to Rafael, "We'll discuss your treatment plan more when you're no longer hyperthermic."

Rafael nods politely.

"How do you feel?" Kyoko asks, brows furrowed with concern.

"Like I need a swim. What are we doing here?"

Kyoko exhales deeply. "The assassinations have brought the Revolution back into the fold. They're convinced the MegaFather orchestrated it, despite allegedly being one of the victims."

"What do you mean by 'allegedly'?"

"No one has seen him since last night. The proclamation of his survival was distributed by the Bravers this morning, but the Revolutionaries don't believe it..."

Rafael leans back further against the pillows. "Have you heard anything more about Uni and Alba?"

Kyoko shakes her head. "Unisa is likely alone. If Alba were with her, she wouldn't be hunted like this. The Revolution can help us find her."

"What if they've returned to the Library?" Rafael poses.

The igni scoffs. "There is no feasible way in which they simply walk through PeakHaven Pass undetected."

There aren't many options for a path forward. Kyoko is right, Rafael realizes; the priority is to find Unisa and return home safely. The Revolution holds the greatest opportunity for success.

"You need to rest for now," Kyoko insists.

"How long was I out?"

"It's just past sunsdown now, so five, maybe six, hours. We've been here in the Revolution's safe house" —she gestures overhead—"directly under the Castrum."

She points to wide openings around the cavern's perimeter. "There are underground tunnels, used to get to various important points throughout the city."

Kyoko's reconnaissance impresses him. "You've learned so much about their operations."

A solemn expression conquers her face. "I've learned about more than operations."

She speaks at length about the various Revolution warriors she's met and the stories they've shared with her about how they came to be in this battle. Devastating tales of the dead and forgotten. And the ones left behind to live for little more than vengeance. Those for whom seconds and minutes and hours no longer pass—for whom hope is a children's tale.

Those who carry the burdens of bloodlust. A ravenous yearning for retribution.

"It's harder to be a Librarian on an active mission than I thought," he admits. "Gatekeepers are blissfully ignorant. These stories are heartbreaking."

"Alba taught me that our job is to record, not to react. Once you advance from Gatekeeper to Recorder to Educator, and then to Vice and Ambassador, that's an ideal we have to remain loyal to."

"This is different," Rafael points out. "Thanks to whatever mess Unisa is in, we're involved."

"That's the entire reason we rescued you," echoes a booming voice.

A muscular, orange-skinned Mega approaches them and sits on the adjacent cot. "To persuade your friend to trust us."

"This is Ovida," Kyoko introduces. "General of the Revolutionary Forces."

"I'm trusting you to find her before the Bravers do," Rafael says to the General.

"I have no doubt we will, but you have to rest until we do. We're going to move you to a new location, another safe house. A smaller one under an inn that's owned by a former Revolutionary. We're hoping she'll take you in; until we find the other Librarian, you two are our most valuable assets."

"I really just need to be submerged, and I'll heal a lot quicker," Rafael insists. "Your salver mentioned a month or two, but it won't take that long underwater."

Ovida smiles. "Inns have bathtubs."

The mountain of a General leads the Librarians through cold, wet tunnels illuminated by small torches along the walls. She explains that the pixie who built these tunnels was only thirteen. A Radiance prodigy. Her mother, Zalona, owns the inn above the safe house and, if she agrees, will be caring for Rafael until he recovers.

"Almost there," Ovida tells Rafael as he leans on her. She supports all of his weight with ease.

They arrive at a wooden door and Ovida opens it to a well-lit basement with a table in the center and adjoining rooms at opposite ends. Seated at the table are three individuals. Two of them are unfamiliar, but appear to be twins.

The third is Unisa.

The three humans gasp in unison. There's a moment of stillness as silence enters the air, then Unisa's arms instantly wrap around Rafael.

He embraces Unisa back as she sobs into his shoulder. Despite the pain it causes him, a warm relief spreads throughout his body.

She's safe.

Rafael raises one arm and Kyoko enters the embrace, as well. They hug for eternity, silently bathing in incalculable joy. Nothing in this world, Rafael believes, feels like reuniting with old friends.

One of the twins stands nearby, watching them with tears in her eyes. The other, uninterested, studies a map.

Kyoko breaks from the embrace and looks around. Her brow furrows and she turns back to Unisa. "Where is Alba?"

Unisa's expression warps into a frown so quickly Rafael forgets what her smile looks like.

Kyoko repeats herself. "Where is Alba, Unisa?"

Unisa shakes her head and breaks into a loud sob. She moves her arms from Rafael to Kyoko.

The igni is frantic now, her volume growing to overpower Unisa's sobs. "Unisa. WHERE. IS. ALBA?"

Unisa hugs her tighter and whispers, "I'm sorry. I'm so sorry, Kyoko." They drop to their knees. Unisa tightens her grip further.

As Kyoko's tears hit the ground and she melts into a puddle of agony, her voice fades into a whisper. She repeats the same question over and over again, faintly.

"Where is she? Where is Alba, Unisa?"

"...Where is Alba?"

CHAPTER 54

TRUTHS REVEALED

Theocratic-Monarchy SunSide
Date *22nd Day of Month 6, Year 1628 DG*

UNISA FEEDS HER FRIENDS MORSELS of detail, but Kyoko demands mouthfuls. The igni doesn't appear satisfied until she can close her eyes and picture Alba's final, violent hour vividly.

A tormenting truth comes to light: only hours earlier, Kyoko and Rafael had been sitting in the back of a carriage, inches from Alba's killer. It compels Kyoko to request time alone to process, so Rafael escorts her to the bedroom as Unisa turns her attention to a fiery conversation across the table.

"I don't understand," Ovida growls with narrowed eyes, "why wouldn't you come to me?"

"Why *would* I come to you?" Zalona counters. "Unisa was scared and alone. She needed refuge and safety."

Ovida throws her arms in the air. "Have you looked outside, Zalona? The Ore Monger now has absolute power. Refuge and safety were assassinated last night."

She raises a powerful finger at Unisa. "She's clearly valuable after what she witnessed. You were going to let her fly back to the Library?"

"What was I supposed to do, Ovida? Drag a terrified human barely older than Zakia to your base for interrogation?"

"If that's what it takes to prevent what happened to us from happening to anyone else, then yes. Fucking drag her."

Zalona places her fingers gently on Ovida's. "I miss Zabeza, too, but we have an example to set for Zakia. She and the others will be home soon. We have to show her that violence cannot eradicate virtue. That injustice cannot butcher integrity."

Reluctantly, Ovida nods, and the bedroom door creaks open. Rafael winces and limps as he returns, so Unisa reaches to assist him. His embrace transports her back home to where they were safe—far from warfare and wounds and scars.

"We should find you a tub to heal," Unisa suggests, recalling memories of a bloody Rafael bathing in her apartment after an archery lesson gone awry.

Rafael's eyes transfix on the twins, catching Naina's attention.

She turns to him. "Staring tells me you either want to fight or fuck, and I won't fuck you. Lower the eyes before you lose them."

"You're the twins," he spouts plainly. "The falcon and the wolf."

A nervous glance shoots between the Doruh sisters.

"How did you know that?" Salessa inquires.

Rafael hesitates. "The TreeKeeper told me."

"She's real?" Unisa responds, eyes wide.

"She is. And Hay-Ro's claims have revealed more truths than even he intended."

"Hay-Ro's *what*?" Zalona says, leaning forward.

Rafael locks eyes with Unisa. "You haven't told them why you and Alba came to SunSide?"

She shakes her head. "I didn't know who to trust, Rafa."

"What letter?" Ovida demands.

Unisa inhales. "I uncovered a hidden letter in the Library, written by Hay-Ro. It claimed that many historical details of the MegaParents' life had been altered or outright fabricated to protect Red-Lo's legacy and besmirch Drof-Fa's. Including the details of her death, which he implied was not accidental."

Rafael continues, "Unisa and Alba were sent here to question the MegaFather and the Braver General about the validity of what was written, while Kyoko and I ventured to find the TreeKeeper, hoping she would provide insight."

"Isn't the TreeKeeper a tale told to misbehaving children to scare them?" Ovida asks.

"Evidently not," Rafael confirms. "We found her."

Rafael unburdens himself of the TreeKeeper's tale: Drof-Fa's new form, the ancient Sprites, Red-Lo's servitude, his biological inability to produce offspring, and the search for a power source strong enough to forge a changeling and offer it in place of an organic heir.

Rafael's words spread to every ear, and affect every heart. The knots of their lives have come untangled. Naina and Salessa learn that they're being hunted so that the Goddess can power the changeling. Zalona and Ovida know the truth behind their loved one's abduction and murder.

In a few short sentences, Rafael sheds piercing light over years of impenetrable darkness.

"We know everything he does," Rafael comments through the deep silence clenching the room. "Who he is. Who he serves. What he's done."

Unisa's mind flashes back to the conversation she had with Alba in MoonSide. *Knowledge empowers. As long as he knows more than us, he has power over us.*

"We know far more than he does," she replies. "We know his wife is still alive."

Power, control courses through her veins. "And he's lost the only eyewitness to eight assassinations."

"Nine," Ovida attempts to correct her.

Unisa shakes her head. "No, eight. When Alba and I were ambushed, Saila wasn't home. She's still alive."

Ovida's hands drop onto the table and she rises to her feet so quickly, her chair falls backwards. "Saila lives?!"

A moist shield envelops Zalona's eyes and she raises her arms to the Four. "The theocracy survives."

Unisa nods. "And he doesn't know her location. But I do."

"Then we'll send a messenger," Ovida suggests.

Her statement unearths a buried memory from the bedrock of Unisa's trauma. Alba's final words break free of her chained, damaged psyche and step into the light of her consciousness.

As soon as you're out of SunSide, send a letter to Saila. She's with her mother in Eloa, remember?

Unisa frantically recollects every word uttered in Alba's final moments. "Saila's in Eloa with her mother. I have to get her to come back to SunSide and challenge the MegaFather."

"She loved Alba," grows Kyoko's approaching voice.

Her eyes are swollen and red, but she holds her chin high. "When Saila finds out what's happened, she'll be back in Larso before we even have a plan developed."

"We?" Ovida asks. "Librarians don't get involved."

"Well I can't speak for every Librarian in this room—"

"Yes, you can, Ambassador," Rafael says with a reassuring smile.

Kyoko returns it, then turns to Unisa, who nods encouragingly. The igni continues, "We're not going anywhere until I have Vy-Ro's head."

"And I have Red-Lo's," Ovida joins in.

Naina smiles a wide-toothed grin, nearly salivating. "And I have the green pixie's."

"Unisa leaves for Eloa tonight," Ovida lays out. "The Revolutionary Forces will be ready for an assault on the Castrum by the time she gets back. Saila will lead the slaughter of the Braver organization, and the end of the Red-Lo Royal Dynasty."

"The team will be back from Lily Beach soon," Naina mentions. "The Ore Monger will have no ore left beyond what's here in Larso."

"Perhaps I should go to Eloa," Salessa suggests. "I can take your mentor's map for guidance. Falcon's fly faster."

Unisa ignores the sting of her comment. "I think she should hear about Alba from me. This is my mission."

"How are you going to get out of SunSide?" Zalona questions. "You're still wanted."

Ovida smiles. "Nivyan Hollow. She can take to the skies from there. The canopies will mask her ascent."

Kyoko nods. "Then it's settled. Unisa flies for Eloa. Tonight."

CHAPTER 55

GRIEF UNITES ALL

Theocratic-Monarchy SunSide
Date 22nd Day of Month 6, Year 1628 DG

SOLITUDE AND DISTRACTION ARE HARBORS from grief.

Kyoko finds both in the Bunker, after Zalona retires to the inn, Ovida to her base, the twins and Unisa to their cots, and Rafael to the tub.

The igni hovers over a map of the continent, tracking Unisa's flight path. It's a long way north. Eloa is a tiny village just beyond Ona's River that Unisa will have to pinpoint. It'll take longer than a day to get there and return with Saila—no more than two, if they're lucky.

Very lucky.

Conflicting emotions tear her heart apart: joy for the memories she has, sorrow for those she never will. There was so much left to say.

How will she tell Ana?

The bedroom door creaks open and Naina enters the main chamber, rubbing her fist into her eye. She doesn't notice Kyoko until she's standing across from her at the table.

"Oh, sorry," she mumbles. "Would you like to be alone?"

Yes.

"No, that's alright." She gestures to the seat next to her. "Can't sleep?"

Naina shakes her head. "Too excited."

Silence fills the air until Naina, shifting uncomfortably in her seat, asks, "Would you like…to talk about…your loss…or…"

"Please stop."

Naina exhales with relief. "Oh, thank the Twins." She eyes the map. "Planning the journey?"

Kyoko nods. "Among other things."

Her finger traces the various locations where the MegaFather stations his Bravers. "Trying to assess the strength of their forces. We have tens of thousands of Bravers to face. They've been recruiting, the last few days."

"We may not have time to wait for Saila to get back, then. The Castrum'll be too fortified to storm if we delay and allow his warriors to roll in."

Sinking pessimism arouses a dangerous thought in the back of Kyoko's mind: *the wolf may be right.*

The trapdoor leading directly up to the streets rattles open. Naina perks up at the sound, but quickly deflates when Ovida walks in, long fabrics slung over her shoulder.

Seeing her change in expression, Ovida remarks, "Happy to see you, too."

"Sorry. I was expecting Symin and the others. They're taking longer to return than I thought."

Ovida offers her a reassuring smile. "They can take care of themselves. Especially with Zakia there to protect them."

"Brought the disguises?" Kyoko gestures to the fabrics.

The General lays them out on the table. "Patient gowns. My salver is waiting in her carriage up on the street." She leans in, and her tone hardens. "Are you sure this is a good idea?"

"Rafael and I are going to see her off. We'll stay disguised and" — she pauses, struggling to articulate their hesitation to separate — "we'd like to stay together as long as possible."

"Friendly faces never hurt," echoes the angi's voice from the bedroom door. Unisa enters the main chamber, flanked by Rafael and

Salessa. The mari dries himself with a towel as they enter, his damp hair slicked back, dripping small droplets down his shoulders and chest.

The Librarians tie the gowns over their clothes and Unisa bids farewell to the twins.

"Take care," Salessa says with a warm smile.

"Fly fast, Feathers," Naina adds.

"Feathers?" Rafael raises an eyebrow.

Unisa takes a long pause, holding eye contact with Naina, then smiles and says, "It's grown on me."

An older vehicle from the pre-ore era, the carriage rolls smoothly against the polished surface of the ore roads. Unisa and Kyoko sit next to one another, with Rafael across.

"What if I went to the Library?" Unisa asks, breaking a long silence. "Instead of going to Eloa, what if I went back to the Prime and told him everything?"

"And start a war?" Kyoko responds. "Alba used her final moments to tell you to alert Saila. Not an army of Librarians, many of whom will end up dead."

A soft smile trembles onto Unisa's expression. "That's not all she used her final moments to say, Kyoko. She asked me to remind you, Ana, and Hassan how much she loved you. All three of you were in her final thoughts."

Her words agonize Kyoko. Turmoil bubbles in her chest, knowing she'll never have the opportunity to return those thoughts.

I hope you know...I loved you, too.

The carriage reaches the southern gate and a discussion ensues between the Revolution salver and the Bravers on patrol. Kyoko clutches the hilt of the tanto tightly, ready if the rear doors swing open. After a few disconcerting moments, the carriage moves again and begins to head toward the forest.

As the wheels roll forth over dirt, Rafael tells Unisa more about the journey to EverEmber, including his interactions with the Doruh Headwoman, the Radiance, and Joaquina's essence.

"I had to let her go."

Unisa reaches forward and takes his hand lovingly. "I'm so proud of you, Rafa."

The carriage comes to halt, and the lemon-skinned salver opens the rear door for the humans to exit. They embrace, Unisa and Kyoko under Rafael's wide armspan.

"I don't feel good about us separating again," Rafael comments.

"I won't be long," Unisa promises. "A day and a half—two at most."

"Map," Kyoko says, handing her a long, rolled paper.

Unisa takes it from her, then turns toward the sky and stretches her wings. With two flaps, she's in the air, and with a few more, she's over the canopy of the forest and gone into the night sky.

Kyoko and Rafael watch her silhouette dwindle until she disappears into the starry specks amongst the clouds. The igni swallows hard as the sky absorbs the Revolution's hope.

They step toward the carriage again, when a rustling amongst the trees startles them. Kyoko raises the tanto, Rafael his forearm fins, and the salver her glowing palms.

The louder the rustling gets, the faster Kyoko's heart pounds. It thrashes in her throat as she sees a red foot step into the clearing. A Mega comes through the trees, followed by a bright pink one behind him.

"Kruga! Symin!" the salver says, relief evident in her tone. She smiles and the illumination of her palms settles. "Where are the others?"

Kyoko doesn't know these Mega, but she recognizes in their expressions a common sorrow. That sorrow carries all five of them back to the Bunker. Gazes low, the ache in their swollen faces is unmistakable.

Kyoko and Rafael descend first, followed closely by Symin and Kruga. When they reach the bottom steps, they're met by excited embraces from Zalona and the twins.

And then the excitement dies when they notice the newcomers' expressions.

"What happened?" Naina asks. "Where is everyone?"

Silence.

Salessa approaches Symin and places her hands on either side of his face, forcing him to make eye contact. "Where is Zakia, Symin?"

Silence.

She demands harder. "Where. Is. Zakia?"

Symin reaches up and wraps his fingers around Salessa's, pulling them off of his face and holding them in front of him. He speaks only in whispers.

"She wanted me to tell you she's sorry, but she won't be able to make it back for that cup of chai, after all."

Salessa breaks down into tears as Naina wraps her arms around her. Zalona falls to her knees and Kruga comforts her in the same manner. Symin steps back until he hits a wall and can't back up any farther, where he breaks down, as well.

The room is quiet except for the echoing of heaves and sobs. Their pain resonates with Kyoko. They're not grieving the loss of what they had; they're grieving the loss of everything they could have had.

Though shades of skin, exoskeletons, and shifting abilities differentiate them, one thought is apparent to Kyoko in this moment: grief unites all.

CHAPTER 56

The Serpent's Tail

Theocratic-Monarchy *SunSide*
Date *23rd Day of Month 6, Year 1628 DG*

THE NIGHT IS SPENT IN mourning, and the morning is spent in the exchange of information.

Kruga and Symin recount the courage and sacrifice that Gina, Ray-Mi, and Zakia embodied in their final hours. Ovida comforts Zalona while briefing them on the events of the previous two nights, and the plan for the assault on the Castrum.

The Librarians contribute their own intelligence: Unisa's initial discovery and the subsequent journey.

"Zynima was taken from us in an effort to forge this changeling," Symin discerns.

"They want us for the same reason," Naina adds.

Symin's lips press into a hard line. "They can't have you."

"Did the TreeKeeper tell you anything about Red-Lo's weaknesses?" Kruga asks the Librarians. "Something that can be used against him."

Kyoko shakes her head. "The exact opposite, actually. She told us that with each passing generation, with each transfer of Red-Lo's essence into a new body, the Sprites imbue him with a bit of their own power."

Kruga looks down at the table and falls silent for a few long moments, before his thoughts make it to his tongue. "I think our grief may be inciting short-sightedness."

Symin frowns. "Explain."

"There are centuries of crimes for which Red-Lo has to answer. We all deserve justice. But what then? Red-Lo isn't the greatest threat here. He's a cog in a far larger mechanism. We should refocus on challenging the true threat."

"How would we do that?" Ovida questions. "He may be under the Sprites' influence, but Red-Lo is our most direct connection to them. I agree, we have to prepare for what's next, but there's no way of getting to the yolk without cracking the shell first."

"I understand," Kruga assures her. "Red-Lo is our first priority, but he isn't our last. Has anyone considered what will happen when the Ore Monger is deposed and the Sprites are denied their sacrifice? Are we so preoccupied with the serpent's tail that we haven't prepared for the fury of its fangs?"

A wave of silence washes over the Bunker. Kyoko realizes she hasn't yet considered the ancient ones; though, without knowledge of the scope of their abilities, it's nearly impossible to prepare.

"The Three Deaths come next," she says, gathering the group's attention. "You want to prepare for what comes after Red-Lo? It isn't the Sprites. They're going to send a beast of the soil, a beast of the sky, and a beast of the sea."

"We don't know when they'll come. How they'll come," Salessa contributes.

"Red-Lo will tell us," Rafael responds. "All answers lead back to him. Whether we want to prepare for the Sprites or their pets. It doesn't matter. We need Red-Lo in custody first."

Kruga nods, seemingly acknowledging the path ahead. "In that case, Symin and I have some information that will help in the battle to come. We believe there's a way for us to restore connection to the Radiance in Larso."

Symin's eyes sharply meet Kyoko's. "What we're about to tell you may be difficult to hear."

She nods, encouraging them to continue, though a daunting uneasiness radiates from them, expanding exponentially when they recount a tale of genocide against the igni on Lily Beach.

Ore is igni corpses.

Kyoko's fingers clench the edge of the table, her body's attempt to stave off the growing nausea. Her parents have moved to the settlements. Friends live there.

Kruga's tone breaks through her fog. "The high temperatures in the ore production polarize the igni cells, counteracting the Radiant energy in Mega."

"Low temperatures have the opposite effect," Symin adds, "amplifying Radiant energy. If we can place a fragment of supercooled ore or exoskeleton into the hands of every Revolution fighter, the assault will feel like crossing a road."

"No," Kyoko blurts out definitively. "I want justice, but we will not use dead igni."

Kruga's tone hardens. "We won't get another chance, Kyoko. Larso is ready to tear itself apart. If we don't do this now, they win."

"If we use their evil to beat them, they win."

Kruga turns to Rafael. "Surely you understand how important this is?"

"I understand that Kyoko has made her decision. We aren't going to sacrifice our morality."

Kruga opens his mouth to offer a rebuttal, but Symin interjects. "Can you synthesize it?"

The crimson Mega takes a step back, eyes wide, as if Symin has physically pushed him.

The pink nymph continues. "You know the biochemistry of the ore better than anyone. Can you synthesize the igni exoskeleton?"

Kruga chuckles incredulously. "Is that a joke? Of course not. It's organic matter, I can't create life."

"The Facilitator believes he can forge a changeling," Rafael points out. "It isn't out of the realm of possibility."

"It is for us. I could write an entire thesis on the reasons why it's possible for him, but not us."

"What reasons?" Rafael challenges. "Indulge me."

Kruga scoffs. "He has a lab full of leading biotechnology. Teams of chemists and geneticists at his fingertips. A kingdom full of loyalists ready and willing to donate what tissue samples he may need. But the biggest reason of all: he's a Mega trying to synthesize Mega life."

He gestures to Kyoko's exoskeleton. "Humans have proteins, DNA, lipids, and all manner of molecular structures I'm wildly unfamiliar with. The Radiance can theoretically help me replicate what already exists, but I can't pull molecules and cells out of air."

"Please, Kruga," Salessa pleads. "Take a second and think about it. What can be done to avoid using the existing ore?"

His expression softens and he stares intently at Kyoko's exoskeleton. "I need to start with the most basic components and work from there. High concentrations of magnesium and iron."

"Where do we find that?" Zalona asks.

Kruga sighs. "The best source would be a volcano, but we aren't near one, so a mid-ocean ridge. Divergent plate boundaries on the ocean floor—"

"Done," Rafael interrupts. "Anything you need from the ocean floor, I can get it."

"With your wounds?" Kruga's eyes narrow. "How much stone and mineral can you drag to the surface with those bandages?"

"Ovida and I can do it," Zalona volunteers instead.

Ovida nods. "What else do you need?"

Kruga's shoulders tense as he turns to the twins. "I'll need the kind of Radiant energy the Facilitator does."

Salessa turns to her sister, lines appearing on her forehead. "He'll have to drain us."

Naina recoils, then closes her eyes and nods.

"No, he won't," Rafael interjects. "I may be able to help."

Kruga raises an eyebrow. "With Radiant energy?"

Rafael nods. "I can access the Radiance. It's involuntary, but I've done it three times now. I can try to provide you with the energy you need."

Genuine gratitude and relief washes over the twins' expressions, while the Mega all look on with skepticism.

Kruga hesitantly agrees. "All I need beyond the stones and energy are live igni cells to copy." He faces Kyoko. "You wanted to do this ethically, right? Then I need a consensual donor of igni exoskeleton, blood, and tissue."

Kyoko's chest tightens as the request grasps her. She withdraws the tanto from its sheath and places her hand down on the table, hesitantly preparing to remove a finger and offer it to Kruga.

Rafael places his hand on the hilt of the tanto to stop her. "Can this be done painlessly?"

"Possibly," Symin chimes in, scratching his chin. "I'm a Siphon; I can pull Radiant energy from others who can access it. If you truly are able to, even amongst the ore, I can feed on your energy and sedate Kyoko while Kruga extracts what he needs."

Kruga shakes his head. "Symin, our plan cannot rest on an *alleged* connection to the Radiance."

Symin secures his gaze to Naina's and they smile softly while exchanging a knowing expression. "If Rafael can access the Radiance, it appears the world is opening up to new possibilities. Everything is changing."

He turns to the group. "And strength thrives in change."

CHAPTER 57

HUMAN RADIANCE

Theocratic-Monarchy SunSide
Date 23rd Day of Month 6, Year 1628 DG

SOFT MATS ON THE STONE floor cushion Rafael and Symin, who sit facing one another, legs crossed, knee-to-knee.

Zalona provided the mats, along with bandages and a numbing agent, before she and the General departed to complete their delegated task. Kyoko and Naina strategize the offensive strike on the Castrum, while Salessa and Kruga look on.

"Tell me about your Radiance," Symin instructs the mari. "How did you know you could exercise a skill no human has in a millennium?"

A glimpse of a smile appears on the corner of Rafael's mouth as he recalls the night he spoke with the Doruh Headwoman and relays the experience to Symin, who listens intently.

"Fascinating," the nymph responds. "Harnessing emotional energy to access the Radiance. And you were successful?"

"Unintentionally. I allowed the Radiance to carry me when I felt its pull. Soon after"—his memories drift back to Innkeeper's Ranch, and he shudders—"long-repressed emotions resurfaced."

"What did it feel like? When the Radiance carried you?"

"Hovering. Floating. Gusts of wind and energy on my skin. Then…"

Rafael sighs. Words escape him. How can he articulate the abyss?

"And then you entered the void," Symin speaks for him.

The mari's eyes widen. "How did you know that?"

Symin smiles. "We are all familiar with the void, a spiritual manifestation of the Radiance. New users find themselves there until they've achieved proficiency in drawing the energy out of it. The void is the source, a place to train and refuel."

"I don't know how to get there voluntarily," Rafael reminds him.

"Close your eyes. Reunite with the emotions that brought you there before."

Hesitantly, Rafael obliges.

His memories drift back to the night at the inn, when he and Kyoko played Joaquina's hand game, and the emotions return. The shock of seeing the bloody visions appear over Kyoko's skin. The guilt of his culpability in Joaquina's death.

Then, to the HearthBark, as the Vine Demon squeezed the life from Kyoko. He remembers the terror of nearly losing her, knowing yet another death would be on his hands.

He thinks back to Tusa, flooded with relief as he remembers Joaquina's essence finding her eternal peace, and then with love when she gives him permission to forgive himself.

"There it is," Symin says, smile simmering. "Incredible. Human Radiance. I can feel it."

He reaches forward and places pink fingertips on Rafael's face. A wind so powerful it might tear his limbs off, throws him backward. His arms flail as he tumbles through the air, left and right, backward and forward. He isn't just floating, he's flying amongst the clouds, headed for the stars.

The pressure fades and he lands gently. He's in the void, and he isn't alone.

"It's been so long," Symin comments, turning about and staring out into the darkness. His gray eyes have changed; here, they glow a magnificent red.

"How did you bring us here?" Rafael asks.

"I didn't, you did. Your emotion formed a trickle of energy along your skin. All I did was Siphon it and guide us here. It was easy—smooth. The Headwoman was right, this method is powerful."

"Now you can tell Kruga I wasn't lying."

A soft chuckle escapes the Mega. "Indeed. And now I can absorb what energy Kruga needs for the experiment directly from the source."

A red glow illuminates his fingertips, then travels to his palms and over his wrists and forearms. It crawls through his shoulders and chest and covers his entire body.

He turns to Rafael. "Human Radiance is indescribably potent. Ours flows through us like a trickling stream. But this…" He examines his glowing body. "This is a raging river of raw power."

A red beam erupts from his chest and hits Rafael, giving his body the same glow as Symin's. Despite the way it looks, it's cooling and gentle, like a balm.

Rafael closes his eyes and allows himself to tumble, fly, and land again. His eyelids separate and he's in the Bunker, facing Symin on the soft mats. His bandages are gone, and what were once open wounds are now sealed scars. All ache has vanished. He feels strong.

"I'm healed."

Symin nods. "The human Radiance is unaffected by ore." He raises his hand and the red glow emanates from his palm. "I have my access back, thanks to you. Healing you is my end of the transaction."

"Rafael!" Kyoko exclaims from the table, her expression bright. Kruga and the twins follow her line of sight to a healed Rafael.

"His service is complete," Symin says to Kyoko, gesturing for her to join them on the mat. "It's time for your donation."

Radiant power gallops through him like never before. It courses through his veins, covers his skin, flows through muscle, bleeds into every cell.

Kyoko lies flat on her back as Symin, Rafael, and Salessa hover over her with the vial of cleansing agent and bandages on hand.

"Are you ready?" The nymph asks.

She nods and taps her outer thigh. "Take it from here."

"Deep breaths. Relax." His left palm hovers over her chest and he feels the tension evaporate from her body. He grows envious of how fluidly she can calm herself.

His hand glides to her forehead and the Radiant energy sedates her. Red glow sprinkles her skin, and within seconds, she's snoring.

His right hand traces a square in the air above her body. A small shard of exoskeleton separates from the Librarian's outer thigh. It's precise, surgical. On the underside is the outer layer of Kyoko's gelatinous igni skin, and droplets of blood lay scattered across the outer rim of the shard.

The donated tissue hovers gently into a small bag in Rafael's hands, which he shuts tight and deposits into a box filled with ice. Salessa moves quickly to rub the cleansing agent onto the exposed wound and wrap the bandage around Kyoko's thigh.

Symin holds her, sedated, until the wrap is complete and Salessa signals that he can wake her. The glow fades and Kyoko's snoring ceases.

She yawns wide and slowly sits up, then looks down at the bandage on her thigh. "Did we get what we needed?"

Rafael nods and taps the box of ice. "We have the tissue and the energy. All we need now are the—"

The door to the tunnels creaks open. Ovida and Zalona haul a waist-high wooden cart behind them, filled to the brim with minerals and stones. The Mega stop to catch their breaths and wipe sweat from their foreheads.

Symin's gaze catches the frowns plastered on their expressions, and a weighty ball of tension forms in his chest. "What's wrong?"

A concerned glance simmers between them, before Ovida speaks. "The Revolution forces have identified a problem. We can't wait for Unisa to return with Saila."

Silence flows through the room, as smiles drop and listeners lean in closer.

Ovida continues. "After the destruction of Lily Beach, the Ore Monger has shut down all activity at the Panaerth processing center."

"Which means," Zalona clarifies, "every Braver stationed on Pan-aerth, and every one in the Fleet, is being recalled to Larso."

Worry lines stretch across Ovida's forehead. "Their numbers will soar."

Naina sinks back into a chair. "We're already outnumbered."

Ovida nods. "The ships will start to arrive at dawn tomorrow morning. After that, this war is over. They'll run right through us, Radiance or no Radiance."

"Then we attack tonight," Symin declares.

All eyes turn to him.

"The synthetic exoskeleton will be ready by sunsdown. We strike then. By the time the suns rise tomorrow, Larso must be ours. No matter how powerful she is, Saila will not make a difference if we're outnumbered fifty to one."

He addresses Ovida. "Prepare the Revolution forces. Tonight, we take Larso back."

CHAPTER 58

RESTORED

Theocratic-Monarchy *SunSide*
Date *23rd Day of Month 6, Year 1628 DG*

"HERE."

Kyoko points to a tower at the center of the Castrum, the top of which hosts the Theater. "That's where we'll find him. Alba called it his 'lair.'"

"After we've taken out this quadrant"—Naina hovers her fingers over the southwest quarter of the Castrum—"it'll lure the Facilitator into the open. He's too arrogant to stay hidden for long. I can come in from the north and"—she pauses—"take what's mine."

"Agreed," Kyoko responds, grateful for the wolf's assistance. Salessa and Zalona provide quality counsel, but Naina holds invaluable knowledge of battle strategy from her years in the Pit.

Having instructed the Revolution forces to prepare, Ovida returns to the Bunker and Kyoko enlightens her on their developed strategies.

The General assigns each of them to a unit of Revolutionaries, whom they'll join at the start of the strike. Salessa, to her evident relief, will remain in the Bunker with the map of the Castrum, guiding Naina and her team through the battle telepathically.

"If Kruga's experiment is successful in restoring the Radiance, I can guide the aerial," Zalona volunteers.

"And Rafael?" Kyoko asks. "Do you have archers?"

Ovida nods. "A unit of eighty. Can he join them?"

"He can lead them. He teaches wartime archery courses at the Library."

"Excellent. We can use a Librarian's leadersh—"

Kyoko shakes her head. "No Librarians, no tunics. We're just Revolutionaries today."

"I understand," Ovida assures her. "You and Rafael will both have our armor."

Kyoko exhales, relief settling her.

Stones are sorted.

With a wave of his hand, Symin organizes three hundred usable stones and minerals into vertical rows and columns, hovering in the air between Rafael, Kruga, and him.

Kruga examines the floating stones, each large enough to fill his palm, and explains the next steps to Symin.

"They have to be restructured, molecularly, to an identical size and shape, and then divided into ten fragments each. Can you do that?"

Symin looks down at his glowing palms, the energy pumping strength into every fiber of his form. "With this? I can do anything."

He swipes his hand quickly, releasing a pulse of energy. Like strings of red electricity, it jumps from one stone to the next, reshaping and resizing each until they're all identical.

The release sucks the breath from his lungs. He leans forward, hands on his knees, as he tries to regain control over the air in his body. Containing the mighty magic strains him; a small, crimson droplet leaves his nose and splatters below.

"Are you alright?" Rafael asks.

Symin straightens, breathes deeply, and wipes his nose clean. "I'm fine."

"If you need a break..." Kruga begins to offer.

Symin shakes his head. Again, he fills his cells with glowing energy and unleashes it through his fingertips, into the minerals. They cleave neatly and smoothly, as if a warm blade has passed through them.

The three hundred stones become three thousand.

The room tremors beneath his feet, dropping Symin to one knee. More droplets of blood escape his nostrils as he battles the haze of lightheadedness.

Kruga helps him back to his feet and holds him until his legs stabilize.

"What's next?" the pink nymph asks.

"Symin, you have to rest. Human Radiance might be too raw for a Mega body to contain."

Symin locks eyes with him. "This is our only option."

"We're going to need you for the battle ahead. If you tax yourself further—"

"Kruga," Symin interrupts with his volume raised slightly. "We don't have time for this. What's next?"

Kruga's hesitation is palpable when he gestures to Rafael to bring the ice box.

"The living tissue. The same way you assessed the composition of the stones, you have to familiarize yourself with the molecular design of Kyoko's exoskeleton. And then"—he picks a stone out of the air and places it into Symin's palm—"replicate and supercool it."

Symin's brows furrow.

"I told you this wasn't going to be easy," Kruga reminds him. "It may not even be possible."

"We'll make it possible."

He clenches his fist around the stone in his right hand, and calls forth the exoskeleton with his left. It levitates out of the ice box, and he allows the energy to penetrate it at its deepest levels.

Complicated. He applies more energy, and then more, and more again. A red glow bathes the entire room. His organs heat, as if he's digesting flames. His teeth clench involuntarily, and his eyes shut tight. Blood fills his nostrils.

The structure of the macromolecules become clear in his mind. He shifts the energy flow entirely, ripping it out of the shard and forcing it into the stone. Its temperature soars, burning through the flesh of his right palm, cratering him to the bone.

The stone begins to change.

He sustains the energy flow as the room spins. His knees waver, but Rafael and Kruga each grab a shoulder and hold him upright. They're speaking, but he can't hear them. The heat becomes too much and his legs give way. They help him lower to his hands and knees as he drops everything he's holding.

"Symin? Symin!"

A crowd has formed around him, but it's hard to see through the fog. Slowly, light arrives and the faces start to come into focus. Everyone has come to his aid.

"You did it, Sy," Kruga says, showing him the small fragment of frozen igni exoskeleton in his hand, formerly a stone.

Relief washes over him. He breathes deeply and moves from his hands and knees to a sitting position.

Kruga smiles. "I can feel the Radiance." He wraps his fingers around the synthetic exoskeleton. "I'll modify the remaining stones."

"We'll need more than three thousand," Ovida remarks.

Kruga raises an eyebrow. "The Revolution doesn't have three thousand fighters."

"Not yet. But I have an idea."

CHAPTER 59

ASSAULT ON THE CASTRUM

Theocratic-Monarchy *SunSide*
Date *23rd Day of Month 6, Year 1628 DG*

THE NATURAL ORDER OF LIFE is for a great end to give way to a new beginning. The suns drift beyond the horizon, bringing a great end to the day. When they return tomorrow, they'll find a SunSide that will remain in the grasp of those who hold it, or one whose new beginning has come to set it free.

Is your monologue done, Lessi? Naina asks, pulling the clay cup to her lips and blowing softly on the chai's surface.

This is a big moment in our lives, forgive me for being somewhat pensive.
Naina sips, taking in the vibrant flavors and gentle aromas.

How's the chai?

Not as good as yours.

Don't try to spare my feelings. That's city chai—better than what I can make in a small village.

You're too humble.

You're too relaxed. Is this a wise time to be drinking chai?

Naina pauses. She looks to the horizon from the small chai shop a road away from the Castrum, watching the fourth and final sun fall beyond. The time for the strike is near.

It is. I needed a 'great end' before the 'new beginning,' she mocks.

Salessa laughs. *Take care of yourself, Nain. Please. I love you.*

Gross.

She laughs again.

I love you, too, Lessi.

The final strands of orange, purple, and gold abandon the sky, bringing to life the lighting panels installed on the sides of buildings around the street, illuminating the ongoing chaos.

Nymph, pixie, and Doruh citizens chant obscenities at the Castrum from behind a Braver barricade. They point accusatory fingers at the dark ore towers and buildings within the complex. Some citizens are thrashed and hauled away by officers, while Braver and MegaFather loyalists attack others from behind.

Kruga was right. The city is ready to tear itself apart over the actions of one crazed faerie. The clashes will continue until there's nothing left but the MegaFather, his warriors, and his supporters.

Likely the monarch's goal.

A violet-skinned Mega with two large knives strapped to her hips takes a seat across the table from the wolf.

"The time has come," the Mega whispers, gesturing to the activated lighting panels. "That's our signal."

"On your command, Lieutenant," Naina responds. "Are the other units in place?"

The Mega nods. "I've just received word. The General is in place with her wave at the southern gate, the archers have taken to the roof-tops, and the aerial unit is prepared for takeoff when signaled."

Naina turns toward the Castrum where the Facilitator waits for her. After twelve long years, her moment has arrived. Excitement fills her.

"Is the wolf ready?" the Mega questions.

Naina growls and reveals a long-toothed grin. "Always."

The Lieutenant stands and turns toward the street behind them. Naina follows her gaze.

Revolutionaries wait everywhere. Not just on the street, but along the pavements, in the alleyways, over the rooftops, sitting on balconies, hovering about storefronts. Mega, Doruh, humans, dressed in the fabric and hide armor of the Revolutionary forces.

"You have the synthesized exoskeleton?" Naina questions to confirm.

The Lieutenant nods. "We all do."

She raises a fist into the air, and hundreds of eyes find it. The Doruh crouch, ready to launch into new forms. The Mega clench their fists around shards of exoskeleton. The humans tighten their grips on their weapons.

The Lieutenant turns toward the Braver barricade at the end of the road, protecting the Castrum, and drops her arm until it's parallel to the ground. Her fist points directly at the target ahead. A bellowing battle cry escapes her throat and tears into the air.

The ground shakes and rumbles as the wave of fighters passes on both sides of her. Mega use the Radiance to make giant leaps and strides forward. Igni and mari bound forth, weapons extended, their own battle cries echoing through the city. Elephants, bulls, rams, chimpanzees, snakes, and a vast cloud of angry hornets bound ahead, ready to take on the Bravers.

The Bravers recognize the rumble and stand in tight formation, shields extended, weapons drawn. The wave reaches them and mayhem ensues as fighters savagely rampage through the shields and barricades, pushing the fight into the empty streets closest to the Castrum.

The MegaFather's warriors are well-trained. The Revolutionary forces don't get far before swords and metal meet flesh and bone, painting the streets crimson.

A smile stretches across Naina's face. Her clothes tear as the wolf erupts. Her jaw becomes sore as her salivary glands pulse, begging for the taste of faerie flesh and blood.

She bounds forward quickly and enters the fray.

"Impenetrable."

Saith stands at the window wall, staring out into a city blanketed by nightfall. "The recalled warriors will be arriving by dawn. Larso will become impenetrable and the radical scum will be cleansed once and for all." He turns to meet the MegaFather's gaze. "You can make an appearance before your supporters once you've significantly healed from your life-threatening injuries."

Zar-Lo chuckles. "SunSide's new age will arrive on our shores by sunrise. Let the citizens believe in my *recovery*. It'll give me time to focus on the Sprites."

"Once our numbers have escalated, the twins will no longer be able to hide. The changeling will be—"

A violent energy provokes his skin, his bones, his muscles, his teeth. The power is unlike anything he's felt before.

"What's wrong?" Zar-Lo asks.

Saith looks down at his hands, palms throbbing with power. "I'm not entirely sure. I feel...a surge of Radiant energy."

"That"—Zar-Lo pauses—"doesn't sound like a problem."

"It isn't, as long as I'm the only one feeling it. The return of the Radiance in Larso could be catastrophic."

He turns quickly to look out at the city again, as an unmistakable stench suddenly fills his nostrils. The odor of canine.

"It's her." His voice is nearly a whisper. The energy grows and grows until Saith can feel it like a torch of pleasure and power held tight to his skin. "The wolf. She's coming to me."

He closes his eyes and uses the Radiance to search for another energy signature, but only finds the one.

"Wayward children always return home," Zar-Lo proclaims. "Where they belong."

Metal clinks metal, bodies and blood stain the roads.

Rafael and his unit of archers watch from the ledge of their designated rooftop. They wait on his word, full quivers on their backs and additional collapsible arrows around their waists.

"Alert the second wave," Rafael instructs the light-green Mega to his right.

The Mega nods and withdraws an arrow with a small explosive strapped to the head. "On your command, Lieutenant."

Rafael raises his arm to the stars. "Light it up."

The Mega draws the arrow back and aims high. A quick release and it's airborne, cutting over the Castrum. He balls his fist around a shard of synthetic exoskeleton.

"Now?"

"Not yet." The arrow continues to climb, moving over the main gates of the complex.

"We shouldn't delay, Lieutenant."

"Wait."

Farther and farther, it's now directly over the Castrum, close to the tower where Kyoko said the Theater is. It starts to slow as the air forces it to reach a peak.

Rafael grits his teeth. "Now."

The Mega jabs the air, and the explosive arrowhead detonates over the Castrum. A seething blaze expands out from the tip. The explosive produces a ball of flames so wide, the walls of the towers nearby turn black.

Bravers on the ground scurry about. Some cover their heads, others yell orders for the troops to get into defensive formations.

Rafael's gaze shifts to the south, to a stout, abandoned warehouse just beyond the complex's southern gate. The second wave huddles inside, awaiting the overhead blast.

Be safe, Kyoko.

The ground shudders from the explosion over the Castrum.

"Rafael's signal," Kyoko recognizes, staring out of a grimy warehouse window. "It's time."

Revolution fighters stand shoulder to shoulder, a shard of synthetic exoskeleton in their palms or pockets. Ovida faces them, an eager smile plastered on her expression, hope dangling before the warriors.

"Our moment has come. Seize it, claim it, conquer it. If you must, mark this kingdom with your blood, but never let them forget that we were here tonight. The stains of your bravery and selflessness will live on eternally. We will not let the suns rise on a SunSide under faerie supremacy. Either they will be decimated, or Larso will be. Do you understand?"

A simultaneous grunt of acknowledgement throttles the building.

Ovida turns and kicks the dusty doors of the warehouse off their rusted hinges. As the Revolution fighters charge past her, disrupting the stillness of the cold night, she declares resolutely, "FOR SUNSIDE!"

The fighters echo in one voice, "FOR SUNSIDE!" Arms and weapons extended, they exterminate the space between them and the patrolling Bravers. The unexpected attack overwhelms them, and the Revolution wave demolishes a number of Braver lines.

"Honor your word, General," Kyoko reminds her.

Ovida nods. "They can capture him, but they cannot kill him. Vy-Ro is yours."

Kyoko scans the southern gate beyond the warfare. Standing calmly before the ore walls, armed and ready, is the Braver General.

"Today is a day of retribution," she declares.

"Indeed, it is," Ovida agrees.

The General closes her eyes, channeling energy from the synthesized shard. With a forceful leap, she's launched into the air, landing mere feet from the front lines. A shockwave propels out from her, blasting Bravers into the air.

Kyoko withdraws the tanto.

"For Alba," she whispers, before charging forth into the violence.

Rafael watches the second wave of fighters empty out of the warehouse and into the streets. His concerns remain on Kyoko's safety, but he thrusts them away to focus on his own unit.

The main gate of the Castrum, just below the archers, is the complex's most heavily-guarded point. The Bravers remain mostly in impenetrable, defensive formations, but some are ordered to defend the north and south from the Revolution waves.

"It's working," he announces to the archers. The confidence of his tone masks the realization that the main gate alone is guarded with more Bravers than warriors in the entire Revolution.

Four rows of archers stand with him, twenty in each row. He raises his volume so they can all hear him, but not loud enough for the wind to carry his voice down to the Bravers.

"Remember our formations! Nock your arrows!"

All together, eighty archers and their Lieutenant reach into their quivers. The first row of twenty steps forward onto the ledge.

"Draw!"

The sound of stretching bowstrings as the arrows are drawn back and aimed.

Rafael's line of sight extends directly from the end of his arrowhead to the face of a blue-masked Legion Director.

Let the leadership fall first.

"Release!"

Fwip. Fwip. Fwip. Fwip…

Twenty arrows leave the rooftop and cut through the air at full acceleration, blades raining from the sky, a storm of doom and death.

The first row of archers moves aside, allowing the second row to step forth and release their arrows. The first row then steps back and nocks a new set of arrows, the second takes their place laterally, and the third steps forward to release theirs.

The formation continues in rapid succession as upwards of one hundred arrows are released every few seconds, twenty at a time. The rows rotate, over and over again, nocking arrows by the time their turn to step onto the ledge arrives again, and releasing them quickly to allow the next row to step forth.

They revolve with the fluid spin of a fatal top.

The Bravers that remain throw their shields up overhead, deflecting the hail of projectiles.

Rafael raises his fist into the air, and the rotation stops instantly. "Don't waste your arrows. We'll have other opportunities."

He tilts his head back and explores the landscape of the skies. The fourth and final wave of the Revolution appears overhead amongst the starlight.

A sea of fighters led by Zalona: Mega using the Radiance, angi humans, and Doruh who soar. Hawks, harpies, herons, falcons, and even a few doves, pigeons, and owls join the battle as the Bravers withdraw their own weapons and engage the onslaught.

The overhead shields break their tight formations and expose vulnerable areas between the Bravers. Rafael calls out to the archers again to resume their rows.

"Release!"

The rainfall of arrows darts over the side of the building again. The Bravers are much quicker this time to defend themselves, and far fewer arrows hit their targets.

The rotation continues until Rafael makes a startling observation. A collective of Directors breaks off from the mayhem and instructs their Legions to swarm the building upon which the archers stand. The Bravers rush in at the bottom level, a thousand strong.

His fist rises again, and the rotation pauses. "Arrows in, weapons out."

The archers hustle to get their arrows lodged back into their quivers. The faeries and humans withdraw swords and other weapons, while the nymphs and pixies channel the energy of the exoskeleton shards, and the Doruh shift.

Rafael withdraws a sword from the sheath on his hip. His heart thrums against his chest as the archers glare at the opening where the staircase exits onto the rooftop. They await the thousand-Braver barrage.

The odds are against them, but Rafael feels excitement, not fear. He was called to war a long time ago and he didn't answer.

Tonight, he does.

Rows of Bravers succumb to the wolf's mighty jaws and sharp claws.

She maneuvers dexterously through the crowd, dodging swords and spears, while tearing through Braver bodies. Hot blood flows like fuel through her veins, energizing her attacks.

A Braver approaches from behind and raises his sword over the wolf's head. Her fur stands on end and she kicks her hind legs, knocking him backward, then turns quickly and places a powerful paw on his chest, holding him down.

Her jaw opens wide and envelops his head, clenching shut while her teeth penetrate the neck. One forceful tug decapitates the warrior, and his skull shatters between her jaws and slides down her throat.

Enraged Bravers circle the wolf. She spins wildly, barking and baring her teeth, excited panic setting in. She dares them to come forth, and they oblige.

The circle implodes as Bravers from all sides rush at her with weapons extended. She clenches her jaw around the leg of the nearest one and violently jerks her head back and forth, up and down, side to side. The Braver's body whips around, slamming into others.

Naina uses her as a club until the head comes off and the torso becomes frayed. She opens her mouth and sends it flying into one side of the circle.

Her violence has aroused hesitation in the Bravers. They inch forward, but Naina barks and bites at them, taking large chunks of flesh out of their arms and legs.

Abruptly, they hold position and cease the advance.

She continues to spin and bark, entering the telepathic conversation again.

They've stopped.

What do you mean, Naina?

They're just standing around me, staring.

Perhaps you've scared them. Move forward to the gates.

The ore walls of the northern gate taunt her over Braver heads. With a daring leap, she takes to the air and lands feet before it. She craves entry into the Castrum, but uneasiness holds her paws to the ground.

Something's wrong, Lessi.

What's wrong?

I don't know.

She turns around and looks behind her. The avalanche of Bravers faces her. Staring. Smiling beneath their masks.

For the first time since she was an eight-year-old girl running through the woods with her sister, fear takes hold of her.

The ground rumbles with the opening of the gates. She faces them, and standing before her is the green-skinned, one-armed pixie.

A volcano of hatred hammers her heart against her chest. Heat erupts on her skin and the flames of vengeance rage in her gut.

I can feel that, Naina. What's happening?

He's right here. In front of me.

Who?

The Facilitator.

Naina barks and growls wildly. Her saliva runs onto the ground like a river.

The Facilitator doesn't move, doesn't flinch, doesn't cower. His expression is blank.

"Thank you for coming to me, my love," he says, coolly.

Naina's paws leave the ground, and her jaw widens to accept the pixie's head. She's inches from him when he blinks and she freezes in the air, paralyzed.

He approaches her, putting his face mere inches from her muzzle and raising a hand to gently caress the muscle under her fur.

"So much raw power." His slimy tone disgusts her. "I need you and your sister, pup. I need your bodies and your essences, and everything within them."

With a snap of his fingers, her lungs tighten. She battles to take a breath, and starts to lose consciousness. The last thing she sees before the world goes dark around her is a craven grin widening on his lips.

CHAPTER 60

DEATH AND DECIMATION

Theocratic-Monarchy *SunSide*
Date *23rd Day of Month 6, Year 1628 DG*

"DOME!" ECHOES KYOKO'S VOICE OVER the sounds of ore
swords and falling bodies.

The Revolutionary next to her, an aqua-shaded pixie, throws a fist
up into the air, generating an invisible barrier around them. Both she
and Kyoko are drenched in sweat, muck, and blood.

"I need more time," the pixie pants.

Kyoko inhales and exhales evenly, preparing for the next round.
She ignores the ache throbbing from every muscle, the rancid stench of
death and decimation singeing her nostrils, the sound of allies wailing
around her. "You have five seconds."

"I need to catch my breath, Kyoko."

The Librarian shuns her pleas. "Four. Three. Two. Drop!"

With an irritated grunt, the pixie lowers her fist and they launch
forward. The strategy has led them deep into the Braver lines, but a
significant journey to the southern gate remains.

Kyoko holds Vy-Ro's face at the front of her mind. She knows where he is, behind Braver barricades, a worm in the water.

She locks eyes with an advancing Braver and dodges his blade, tumbling forward and knocking him back. The igni presses her knees to his chest and shoves the tanto through his eyes. He goes limp as Kyoko pulls the ore sword from his hand and sheathes the tanto.

Two more approach, one with an axe, the other with a spear. She evades the point and grabs hold of the staff, lifting it to block the blade of the axe coming down on her. A quick kick to the torso gives her enough time to swipe her blade past his throat and then nestle it between the spear-wielder's ribs.

She conquers another three rows unscathed before a blade catches her bicep. Her exoskeleton defends her well; a strike that would've severed another's arm cuts minimally through her stone exterior. Spurts of blood drip down her arm; the split burns, but she pushes it to the back of her mind and drops the faerie, plunging her sword into his chest.

She stands, breathing deeply to catch her breath and pressing her fingers tight against her wound, but the respite is short-lived. Another advances, sword swiping wildly at her. She backs away and dodges, only for two more to knock her forward and pin her wrists down against the muddy ground.

Immobilized. Her fate draws near as the swordswoman steps over her and brings the sword down over her chest. Kyoko shuts her eyes, praying that the integrity of her exoskeleton isn't compromised.

Her prayer is unneeded. She feels the Bravers pinning her lift off, hears the scream as they're launched through the air. She opens her eyes, and the swordswoman lies next to her, the light gone from her face.

The General waves her bloody palm around, wildly tossing Bravers away from the Librarian, then helps her to her feet. She's split open in several places and is missing an ear, yet somehow smiles as she lifts a fist and domes them.

"He's not far now," Ovida informs her, pointing to the southern gate mere yards away. "I can clear your path."

She drops the dome and slams her fist into the mud at their feet. Another shockwave spreads quickly around them, tossing

Bravers like toys, making way for Kyoko to march forward to the Braver barricade.

Ovida drops onto one knee, strained from the release. "Go. Now."

"Are you alri—"

"Go, Kyoko!"

The Librarian nods and advances before the Braver lines can recover. A waist-high ore barricade stands between her and the Braver General.

She sees him, beyond the semicircular barrier, cutting down Revolutionaries attempting to cross into his path. Even those with access to the Radiance don't seem quick enough to use it before he dispatches them.

Rage intensifies as Kyoko recounts the details of Alba's final moments—the brutality with which Vy-Ro's team ended her; she vows to return it a hundredfold.

"Vy-Ro!" she bellows, leaping over the barricade and entering the semicircle with him.

He doesn't attack. He stares at her in clear confusion.

"Kyoko?" His tone betrays disbelief. "Did they abduct you from my carriage?" He scans the fabric armor covering her and his eyes widen. "Why are you wearing their armor?"

She doesn't answer his questions. Instead, she offers one of her own. "How could you, Vy-Ro? Alba, of all people?"

The wide-eyed incredulity leeches from his expression, replaced by patronizing acquiescence. He sheathes his weapons and raises his hand in mock surrender.

"Kyoko, listen to me. This is far more complicated and nuanced than you can understand. Your response is disproportionate. Joining with political radicals? Librarians cannot—"

"Am I wearing a fucking tunic?" she cuts him off. "This has nothing to do with the Library. You killed Alba." Her voice tremors, so she clears her throat to solidify it. "This is personal—not professional, not political."

Vy-Ro sighs and places his hands on the hilts of his weapons. "You *cannot* be serious, Kyoko. The first time I held a sword, you were still on your mother's breast. Walk away now, please."

She surprises herself. Knowing that Vy-Ro is accurate in the disparity of their experiences, she still isn't afraid. Alba thought of Kyoko in her final moments, and now Kyoko thinks of Alba in hers.

"There are only two options left for me, Vy-Ro. This ends with my head held high, or rotting in the mud. But it ends tonight."

Without another word, clutching the ore sword in one hand and the tanto in the other, she charges at the Braver General.

No, no, no...

The word repeats in Rafael's mind as he helplessly stands on the ledge, watching the Facilitator paralyze Naina at the northern gate and then disappear with her.

"Incoming!" an archer shouts. Rafael turns quickly and extends his sword in front of him again. There's little time to process before the sound of heavy footsteps echoes from the staircase.

"Hold positions!" he instructs. Four rows of twenty Revolution fighters surround the opening. The patter of the footsteps grows until every thump causes a tremor on the roof. He can hear it as if they're marching beside him.

They appear, flowing onto the rooftop like water from a faucet hitting the ground.

"Now!" Rafael commands, and the first row, those with access to the Radiance, grabs hold of Bravers and launches them off the roof. Braver screams echo into the night, only to grow duller and duller as they fall to their deaths. The plan works quite well for a time, as Bravers reach the rooftop and only make it a few feet before being thrown off.

But the well-trained warriors learn and adapt; they remain hidden on the top steps and launch daggers in unpredictable patterns, obscuring the use of the Radiance.

With the Revolutionaries perplexed, Bravers fill the rooftop again and engage the archers hand-to-hand. A deluge of mayhem and chaos surrounds them like fog as Bravers breach the initial line of Revolution fighters and move on to the ones behind.

Rafael joins the battle. His sword clangs against a Braver's and then he skillfully dodges multiple swings. Years of swimming against currents and waves, years of dodging the arrows of his students, have prepared the fluidity of his motions.

The Braver grows tired and Rafael takes advantage, pushing his sword into the faerie's neck and through the back of his head. He bathes in the victory until another approaches with a wide hammer.

Rafael begins to dodge again, finding it easier as the Braver takes time to swing the hefty weapon. In moments, Rafael has the sword buried deep into his abdomen, then kicks him off of the ledge to his death.

More Bravers approach. Not one or two, but ten, twenty, and thirty. They form a semicircle around him as he backs to the edge of the building.

They've inundated the area. A few Revolutionaries remain, locked in a battle for their lives. They might have the Radiance, but they don't have the numbers.

Rafael takes stock of his situation. Death behind him, death before him. This is war. This is the predicament he feared when he was fifteen—a situation Joaquina likely found herself in with a different opponent.

It found him, eventually. His fate. He ran from it then, but he cannot run from it now. Backward to the ground or forward through the swords, he's out of options.

He takes a deep breath and steps back until his heel is no longer supported by the rooftop. His fingers press tightly on the gems of Joaquina's bracelet. Her love courses from it and into his veins.

As he prepares himself for the inevitable, an unsettling breeze caresses the back of his neck. He watches as the Bravers' eyes widen, and their heads tilt back to watch something rise into the sky behind him. Rafael steps forward onto the ledge again and turns around.

They fill the night sky. Not a handful, not even a hundred. Thousands of nymphs and pixies hover like stars, glowing with Radiant energy. They fly erratically and chaotically as they join the battle. Clearly untrained, undeniably determined. Many drop down into the streets, charging the Castrum's main gates.

Symin and Kruga land on the rooftop next to Rafael, and the pink nymph claps his hands together powerfully. A blast of energy reverberates from his palms and knocks every Braver onto their back. Nymphs and pixies rain down from the skies and land on the rooftop, using the Radiance to exterminate the monarch's military with suffocation, explosion, and all manner of death and decimation.

"I see your journey to Nivyan Hollow was successful," Rafael says, his expression betraying his relief. "You came at the right time."

"I've instructed them to split up," Kruga adds. "A few hundred at each of the gates."

The word "gates" triggers Rafael's memory.

"Naina!"

Symin raises an eyebrow. "What about Naina?"

"He has her!"

Symin's eyes widen. "*Who* has her?"

"The Facilitator! She breached the northern gates and he—"

Rafael's sentence is cut short when Symin grabs Kruga's shoulder with one hand and makes a wide, circular motion with the other. As if they were apparitions, the two Mega fade away.

They've teleported out. Somewhere.

CHAPTER 61

FATHERHOOD

Theocratic-Monarchy *SunSide*
Date *23rd Day of Month 6, Year 1628 DG*

THE ROOFTOP FADES, THEY JOURNEY through the void, and the Bunker forms around them.

Teleporting is complex, and requires a significant amount of Radiant energy, but slivers of the human Radiance still remain in Symin's veins.

Salessa frantically searches the map of the Castrum, her eyes swollen, her cheeks red. She's startled when they appear in the Bunker without warning.

"Where is she?!" Symin questions, volume high, blood rising to his skin.

Salessa turns back to her panicked perusal. "I-I don't know."

Symins fist lands hard and rattles the wooden table.

Salessa jumps backward, moisture developing in her eyes.

"Can you hear her or not, Salessa?!"

Kruga places a hand on Symin's chest. "You're not helping. Calm the *fuck* down."

The younger nymph's words blanket Symin and he takes in Salessa's distress. Her expression starts to crumble into a mix of fear and hopelessness. The nymph realizes he isn't angry. Not at Salessa, not at anyone.

He's terrified.

He steps forward and gently takes Salessa's hand, leading her back to the wooden table. "I'm sorry, Salessa." He gestures to the map of the Castrum, lowering his volume, softening his tone. "Think. Where could she be?"

Salessa wipes her eyes and her expression hardens as she scans the many structures and starts speaking quickly.

"Six towers. Eight buildings. Last heard from her when he took her." Her eyes hectically trace the map until they widen with alarm. Her finger shoots down to a section of the ore walls behind the laboratory building. "What is this?"

"The walls," Kruga responds.

Salessa growls. "Why do they jut out like this?" Salessa traces her finger along the walls surrounding the Castrum, until she reaches a portion that extends a few yards out and then retreats in again, forming an apparently random alcove.

"He has her in the labs," Symin says. "Where he's developing the changeling."

Kruga shakes his head. "This isn't a public project. He can't use government labs."

"He needs access to his equipment and workers, doesn't he?" Salessa asks. "And this wall has clearly been shifted to accommodate *something*."

Kruga's expression ignites with realization. "He's not *in* the labs. He's under them." He places his hand on Symin's shoulder. "Take me to the alcove."

The nymph makes a wide circle with his arm, and as they begin to fade, Salessa grabs Symin's other shoulder. She joins them in the void of the Radiance, and then in the alcove behind the laboratory building, where she drops to her hands and knees and begins to dry heave.

Symin kneels next to her and rubs her back. "What are you doing?"

"She's my s-sister." Salessa coughs. "I just need a second."

"I found it," Kruga says, hands extended to the ground in the alcove. "There's hollow space here. A lot of it. And it extends under the labs."

Symin turns back to Salessa. "I know that was difficult for you, but we have to keep moving."

Salessa nods, and he helps her to her feet.

"Hold your breath and close your eyes this time."

She follows his instructions and they teleport into a wide chamber brimming with laboratory equipment. The tables and machinery seem to be made of ore, yet the walls are stone brick. There are no windows, only lighting panels that don't seem to be operating at full capacity, giving the room a dim sinisterness.

"Are you alright?" Symin asks Salessa.

She nods silently, focused on something ahead.

Beyond the many laboratory tables ahead of them, beyond the heavy equipment and machinery lining the walls, beyond the jars and vials and canisters of fluids and chemicals stored around the chamber, is a row of cots against the rear wall.

Four cots. The two on the ends are empty, while one is covered with a metal dome, forming a massive container, and the fourth cot is occupied by a skeletal figure.

Salessa steps toward it and Symin calls to her. "Where are you going?"

Silence. It's as if the figure calls to her. She gravitates past the ore tables, past the machines, past the glass containers, and the two Mega follow closely behind her, keeping their palms raised, ready to access the Radiance when needed.

Salessa clutches Symin for support when they reach the cot. The nymph realizes what Salessa noticed upon arrival in the chamber.

The skeletal figure is Naina.

She's unrecognizable. All life and energy has been drained from her. Her face is thin, shriveled skin stretched over bones. Her hair seems to be falling out, and her eyes have lost all glow.

She's unclothed. There are cuts and wounds all over her body, indicative of torture. Symin surmises the Facilitator wanted Salessa's location and Naina wouldn't give it to him. There are three ore cuffs around her body: one around each of her biceps, and one around her waist.

Symin's constitution quivers, as well. His darkest memories collect in the forefront of his mind; the corpses of his dearest friend and his daughter dance on the periphery of his consciousness.

"It's happened again," he whimpers.

"No," Kruga responds. He holds his palm out over Naina's body. "It's faint, but she still has a pulse."

"She's alive?" Salessa asks.

Kruga's gaze falters. "Barely."

Salessa places a hand on her head and kisses her forehead. "We're going to leave here together. I promise."

"How is he getting the energy out of her?" Symin asks.

Kruga taps the ore cuffs with his finger. "Similar technology to the lighting panels. Pulling and storing Radiant energy, without the additional step of converting it into light. He can place the same cuffs on the changeling and inject the stored energy into it."

"But he doesn't have me," Salessa says.

Kruga nods. "Naina holds an immeasurable amount of raw energy, but it still won't be enough to forge an essence. Only both of you, together, can do that."

He turns to the massive container next to Naina's cot. "The changeling must be in there. He's protecting it."

"Can we inject the stored energy in the cuffs back into Naina?" Symin asks.

Kruga hesitates. "I can try."

He points to a small machine on a table next to Naina's cot, with a series of dials and a sliding needle on the face. "The cuffs are controlled there. We'll have to play with the dials until it revers—"

A bright blue light swallows them and launches Kruga over the cots, slamming his body against the stone wall at the end of the chamber.

Symin turns to the source of the blast. Standing a few yards away, by a staircase leading up to the ground floor, is Saith.

"Get her out, now," he whispers to Salessa, who leaps over Naina's body and begins fiddling with the machine's dials.

Symin channels the human energy into his palms and releases a beam of red light at the Facilitator. It travels the distance of the chamber, but stops inches from his face, as if there's an invisible wall protecting him.

"You'll have to do much better than that," the Facilitator taunts him.

"I will."

The nymph forms a fist and brings it quickly down in front of him. The metal panels of the ceiling over Saith's head drop rapidly down on the pixie. Symin hears the crunch of bone. He teleports quickly to the other side of the room and digs through the damaged panels, but there's no body.

Symin's muscles stiffen involuntarily. His body lifts into the air and spins to face the smiling Facilitator.

"You have no idea who you're dealing with." He sniffs. "Nymph."

Arms pinned to his sides, barely breathing, Symin squeezes out what few words he can. "I could say the same about you."

"Enlighten me. Who am I dealing with?"

"A father. Whose daughter you abducted."

Saith chuckles. "I've abducted many daughters. And sons. And parents and brothers and sisters and wives and husbands. Your fatherhood is as irrelevant as mine. It will be your downfall."

Light engulfs the room again and Symin is released, dropping onto the hard stone floor. He coughs and gulps air as tears well up in his eyes. Saith raises his arm, blocking and absorbing a purple beam from Kruga, firing from across the room. Symin diverts Radiant energy into his knuckles, pushes up to his feet, and swings his arm around to connect his fist to Saith's face. The pixie is hit so hard, a shockwave of energy is released, blowing him backward into a stone wall.

Kruga teleports to Symin's side. "Is he down?"

"Not for long." He sees Salessa fiddling with the dials and knobs on the machine. "We have to buy her time and lure him to the surface."

Before Kruga can respond, one of the damaged metal panels lifts into the air and hurtles toward them. Symin performs a chopping motion and the panel splits in half, each shard moving around them. He turns and sees Saith hovering toward them.

"I'm irritated," the pixie announces.

Kruga places a hand on Symin's shoulder, but before either can make the teleportation circle, their bodies turn, back-to-back, and slam into one another. They're being held together, immobile below the neck.

"Eyes!" Symin yells. The younger nymph understands. They channel energy into their eyeballs and release a beam of concentrated energy at the Facilitator.

The machine is far beyond the scope of Salessa's technical knowledge. There are three dials, each with a semicircle drawn over the top, and a small arrow on the crest of the semicircle.

She kneels down next to the cot. "I need your help, Nain. You have to tell me when you feel the energy coming back in. Do you understand?"

There's a long, hesitant pause, then Naina's head slowly tilts up and back down again. It's as much of an acknowledgement as she can muster.

Salessa moves the first dial slowly toward the left. The more it turns, the louder Naina groans in pain. Salessa quickly moves it back to where it was, then further to the right, beyond the arrow on the semicircle. Naina's head slowly moves up and down.

"You're doing great," Salessa encourages her.

A whisper emerges from Naina's lips and Salessa puts her ear to Naina's mouth. "Right...arm."

Salessa understands. Each dial controls one of the cuffs. She continues to experiment until she's certain of the direction in which each dial needs to be turned.

After all three dials are turned correctly, color begins to fill Naina's face again, and a smile curls onto her lips.

CHAPTER 62

Vengeance

Theocratic-Monarchy SunSide
Date *23rd Day of Month 6, Year 1628 DG*

VY-RO'S THREAT COMES TO LIFE before Kyoko's eyes.

It becomes evident quite quickly that he has decades of experience over her. She twirls and dodges and evades, keeping him at the tip of her blade, attempting to strike when an opening presents itself, but the Braver General is unfazed.

He's opened a wound on her thigh, thrown a dagger through her shoulder, and knocked teeth out with spiked ore knuckles. Her exoskeleton defended her cheek, and it's the only reason so few attacks have wounded her.

His years of experience have made him adept at recovering quickly and continuing the battle, yet she successfully knocks his blade from his hand and jabs the tanto into his side. He hollers and she tries to repeat the motion, but he quickly grabs her wrist and pulls her forward, driving his knee into her ribs and knocking her onto her back.

Before she can get up, his fingers fly to the hilt of another throwing dagger. She catches a glimmer of starlight off of the metal and realizes what he's going for. By the time the dagger is launched, Kyoko is expecting it and picks it right out of the air.

Alba trained her how to do it; the mari would've easily done it herself.

As Kyoko holds the dagger and maintains steady eye contact with Vy-Ro, she realizes something. Something that could save her life.

Vy-Ro thinks he's unbeatable, but Alba truly was. The quantity of his experiences cannot outweigh the quality of hers. He needed twelve Bravers to defeat her, because he couldn't do it alone.

Without hesitation, Kyoko launches the dagger at his wound so hard that even part of the hilt digs into his side. He falters, but is quick to regain his footing and pull the throwing dagger out of his side, releasing it into the mud. He unsheathes another sword so quickly, Kyoko isn't sure where he pulled it from, and charges toward her.

She tightens her grip on the tanto, still dripping with his blood. This time, she keeps Alba's words in her mind. She remembers every lesson and brings it to the table.

Vy-Ro slashes the blade at her multiple times in quick succession, but she twists her body in a fluid motion that allows her to backhand the tanto directly into the side of Vy-Ro's neck. It's an evasion tactic Alba would use with her spine fins to divert the path of an opponent's blade.

Vy-Ro stumbles back and tears the tanto from his throat. He drops his sword and tries to contain the blood flowing from the wound. It sprays out as he drops to his knees and gurgles blood through his mouth and nose.

Kyoko moves quickly to dig her thumbs into his gray, pupil-less eyeballs, pushing them deeper into his skull. His hands fly up and wrap around her wrists. He tries to scream, but nothing comes out other than the blood gushing from his neck.

Kyoko pushes harder and harder until she punctures the eyeballs and blood runs down his face from the sockets.

His hands become limp and fall to his sides. Kyoko removes her fingers and the Braver General's corpse drops into the mud. The Librarian stumbles backward as the world spins and a lightheaded fog takes over.

She's lost blood. A lot of it. Her thigh, hip, and side throb with the ache of the clustered wounds mangling her exoskeleton. The muck and dirt become her resting place as she grows cold and nauseous. The smells and sounds penetrate her eyes and ears and nose. She's exhausted, physically and emotionally. This is war, and she isn't sure if she's going to survive it.

A vision approaches her and she accepts she must be dying. She sees Alba...nares in place of a nose, forearm and spine fins; the vision is definitely mari.

But when it speaks, it has a low-toned voice that doesn't belong to Alba. It is familiar, though, and it brings her comfort in what she believes to be her final moments.

"Kyoko," the mari voice says. "I've got you."

Warm arms wrap around her and hoist her up, carrying her from the battle. Before the world starts to go dark, she musters out what few words she's able to.

"Thank you, Rafa."

The Facilitator blocks Kruga's beam, but Symin's makes contact. The paralysis ends and the two Mega drop to their knees as the pixie is launched backward.

Symin gathers his wits long enough to place a hand on Kruga's shoulder and make a circle in the air with the other. He completes it and they're teleported into a wide courtyard, surrounded by stone columns and the night sky overhead.

"Where did you bring us?" Kruga asks, catching his breath.

"Somewhere within the Castrum," Symin pants, registering the faerie architecture.

Saith appears over Kruga's shoulder. The nymph's knuckles light up and he swings around, but it goes through the Facilitator's face, as if he's made of mist. The apparition disappears, and reappears next to Symin, who does the same.

"He's toying with us," Symin growls.

"I do enjoy playtime," says the pixie, appearing again in actuality. He uses the Radiance to slam them down, face-first, into the stone ground of the courtyard. Pain rattles Symin as blood pools out of his nose and onto the ground.

He rises to his knees but his surroundings start to blur. He blinks and tries to rise, but all he sees is Saith standing over him and smiling. The pixie raises his hand and his palm lights up, ready to blast Symin's life away.

Until something attacks him.

Symin has never seen anything like it. The creature has the head of a wolf, but stands on two legs. It's enormous, towering over the Facilitator. A mane of thick fur rings its neck and trails down its spine. Dagger-like teeth sit in a powerful muzzle. Tight skin stretches over thick blocks of muscle.

It's terrifying, but fascinating.

The bipedal wolf battles a startled and repulsed Saith. It dominates him until a beam from the pixie's eyes launches it across the courtyard. The creature whines in pain and growls loudly.

Then it shrinks back into Naina.

Symin musters energy to lift the stone columns around them. He launches them at Saith, who blocks the first six with ease, but the following come at wild angles. They collapse in on him, slamming into the ground and burying him under tons of broken stone.

He finds Salessa and Kruga helping Naina to her feet. She looks healthy and strong, and a wave of relief washes over him.

"It was more than just *my* energy in those cuffs," she explains. "Every ounce of Radiant energy from the abductions was injected into me."

"You have to leave," Symin says to her, urging her to escape.

"No," Naina protests. "I've been waiting twelve years for this."

"Naina, he could kill us all," Kruga pleads.

"I came here knowing that was an option."

"We can't run now," Salessa says, peering over Symin's shoulder.

A cyclone of stone rubble twirls over the columns. Massive blocks rise into the air and launch to the sides of the courtyard.

Saith hovers toward them, brushing dust from his clothes, wiping away a droplet of blood from a small cut on his forehead. "You'll suffer for that."

Naina pushes Salessa toward the side of the courtyard. "Sit down behind one of those columns. Don't make a sound."

"What are you going to do?"

Naina turns back to face the Facilitator. "Get my vengeance." The bipedal wolf erupts from her body and howls into the blanket of darkness over their heads.

The pixie grimaces. "What are you?"

She bounds at Saith, and he raises his hand to paralyze her. Successful at first, she's immobilized, but Symin can see her struggle against it until she overpowers it. She crawls forward, teeth bared, tugging at the ground like a shark battling a current.

Saith's eyes widen and it becomes evident he's never experienced this before.

Symin recognizes this as the only moment Saith's focus is lowered. He places a hand on Kruga's shoulder to command his attention, and when their gaze meets, a silent understanding transfers through a short nod.

This is it.

Kruga's eyes ignite purple and soar over the crawling Naina to blast the green pixie. He's knocked backward, dropping his hand and releasing Naina, who bounds forward again, closing the gap between them.

She reaches him, jaws wide, inches from claiming his head, when he sinks into the ground below him and vanishes.

Naina spins, growling and barking wildly, searching for the pixie's escape route. He appears again, rising out of the ground behind Kruga. The nymph doesn't have time to react. Saith grabs hold of the back of his neck and carries him through the air, slamming him against stone walls and columns.

Within seconds, Symin has heard every bone in Kruga's body shatter. He leaps forward and claps his hands together, releasing a blast directly at Saith, who drops Kruga's limp body to raise his forearm and block it.

Symin slams one foot on the ground. The stone of the courtyard ripples away from him like a wave. Saith closes his eyes and drops into the ground yet again, as the wave of stone crashes into the wall behind him.

The pink nymph searches frantically until an idea strikes. He closes his eyes and casts a web of Radiant energy out around him. The web is disrupted by the sudden appearance of unfamiliar energy behind him.

I got you.

Symin turns quickly and blasts beams from his eyes again. The pixie is pushed backward, smoke rising from him, until he opens his mouth wide and allows the energy from Symin's eyes to flow down his throat.

"Delicious," he says, swallowing. "That doesn't taste like any Radiance I've experienced before."

"It isn't," Symin admits, taking the moment to catch his breath.

"It tastes powerful. Perhaps I don't need the animals after all. Could you be the key, nymph?"

Before Symin can respond, a sharp bolt of lightning drops down into the courtyard and hits Saith, who cries out in pain and drops to his knees. Symin looks up to the skies and sees Zalona lowering down next to him.

She puts her arm around Symin's waist to help support him, but he shakes his head and warns her, "Keep your eyes on him, not me."

Saith hovers again. He is no longer smiling. He makes a wide sweeping motion, and a dark cloud appears in front of him. Massive daggers of ice erupt from the cloud and soar toward Symin and Zalona.

Symin slams the ground with both fists and a wall of stone pops up in front of them. The ice daggers shatter as they collide with it. Zalona steps up onto Symin's back and launches over the stone wall, kicking yellow blasts of energy at Saith.

Saith skillfully catches the energy in his palm and shoots it back out at the stone wall. It strikes their protective barrier and explodes. Symin crosses his forearms and is able to maintain his position, but Zalona is blown backward. Her body rolls along the ground and then she slowly gets back up to her feet, bleeding from hundreds of tiny cuts all over her face.

"Are you not exhausted, nymph?" Saith asks.

Symin doesn't respond, keeping his forearms crossed and gaze focused.

"Alright. We'll continue."

Saith's arm lifts overhead. Dark clouds form in the night sky and Symin steadies himself for whatever punishment will rain down on them. The clouds sit menacingly for a moment, before raging balls of flames descend from them like blazing hailstones. They come so quickly, there's little time to protect themselves.

Symin closes his eyes and ducks, awaiting the falling flames, but they don't come. He looks again and finds the embers extinguishing on an invisible barrier overhead.

Ovida enters the courtyard, both fists raised, drenched in blood. Her barrier not only protects Symin and Zalona, but Salessa on the side of the courtyard.

"Let's finish this, Sy," she says.

Symin relaxes his exhausted muscles, breathing a sigh of relief. His energy wanes and he questions the power he has left.

"What's the plan?" Zalona asks Ovida.

"I don't think we need one," the General responds.

Zalona and Symin follow her line of sight to the stone wall behind Saith. Naina crawls down toward the pixie from the top of the wall like a spider. She is slow and agile, and the ripples of her massive muscles shiver in the starlight. She keeps her growls in check, and the Facilitator remains unaware of her.

She drops down quickly from the wall and latches her jaws onto Saith's one remaining arm. Before he can retaliate, still caught off guard, Naina jerks her head back and tears his one remaining arm right out of his shoulder.

Blood paints the ground. Bellows of agony ring out into the night sky. Naina doesn't hesitate; she leaps forward for a second bite, this time at his head, but he's alert now. His eyes light up and blast her in the face at point-blank range. She's blown backward, whimpering as her body slams into multiple stone columns.

Saith's wounded shoulder begins to glow, and Symin realizes he's using the Radiance to contain the blood flow and heal himself.

Now armless, the pixie growls in Symin, Zalona, and Ovida's direction. "You'll all die."

His mouth opens wide and releases a high-pitched shriek. The soundwaves extend out forcefully, tearing the stone floor apart and pushing the Mega backward. They all cover their ears while trying to maintain enough balance to stay upright.

The sound waves enter Symin's ears like explosive needles and cause ruptures. Blood seeps out and down his cheeks. He clasps his hands on his ears harder to try and drown it out, to end it.

And it does end. Symin opens his eyes wearily, the courtyard spinning. Ovida and Zalona lay behind him, unconscious. Naina, back in her human form, slowly starts to stir on the other side, rubbing her head and rising to her knees.

He's the only one left in any real shape to fight. And yet, he feels inadequate to do that, his energy depleted.

Saith closes his eyes and another copy of him appears to his left. Then to his right. Then another to his left. More copies arrive in the courtyard until there is a line of twelve. They all stand, smiling, facing Symin.

The nymph looks down at his hands and tries to sense how much of the Radiance is left in him to fight.

Next to nothing.

He has enough human energy for one final action.

The twelve Saiths' eyes light up, and twenty-four beams of energy blast out at Symin. He closes his own eyes and uses what little Radiance is left in his body to perform his final Radiant action.

When he opens his eyes, he's in a verdant forest. It feels alive, like it's breathing around him. He is dressed in a white outfit made of light, airy material that covers him from the shoulders down.

An entity appears before him, startled. "No essence has ever arrived before their time. You're here seconds early. How?"

Symin's essence rises to its feet. "I used what little Radiant energy I had left to come. To buy time."

"Time for what?"

"A request—one which I humbly beg you to honor, TreeKeeper."

CHAPTER 63

WELCOME HOME

Theocratic-Monarchy *SunSide*
Date *23rd Day of Month 6, Year 1628 DG*

POUNDING SKULL, BURNING FACE, BLURRED vision, bloody knees. Naina is exhausted.

But no amount of pain compares to the erupting agony of watching Symin on his knees, with twelve Saiths' ignited eyes around him.

This is it. The final blow.

She sees how little fight Symin has left. He closes his eyes, and Naina closes hers, too. And then all of her pain melts away.

She opens her eyes to find herself in a forest of lush, colorful leaves and stunning trunks. She sits on a log near one massive tree in the center of the clearing. A white cloud of a dress winds around her.

No wounds, no injury, no pain. Her skin simply glows.

"Naina?" a familiar voice calls to her.

Salessa approaches, skin glowing identically, also wrapped in a cloud.

"What's happening, Lessi?"

Salessa shakes her head. "I have no idea." She places her hand on Naina's cheek. "Are you alright?"

Naina raises her hand and places it over Salessa's. "I'm fine, Lessi. Unless Saith killed us and this is the world beyond?"

"You're alive," another familiar voice reassures them.

Symin steps out of the hollow center of the massive tree, a resolute calm in his expression as he takes a seat on the log and invites the twins to join him.

"We're on the island of Tusa," he explains. "Where the TreeKeeper carries essences forth into the world beyond."

Naina raises an eyebrow. "We were just in the courtyard."

"Physically, we still are. Saith is moments from—" He hesitates and looks around, as if the words he's searching for will appear at his feet. "I'm not going to survive."

Naina's heart sinks into her stomach. "No. There has to be a way."

He shakes his head, and a sorrowful smile curls the edges of his mouth. "My journey is complete. That's certain and I can't change that. But it hasn't ended in defeat. I faced him. I can die knowing I never gave up. Even when I was afraid."

He kisses the twins on their foreheads. "Now, I get to say goodbye to each of you in a way I never got to do with Zynima."

Salessa speaks in a strained voice. "Symin, I think we can still win the fight."

Symin nods. "I know you can. And you will. You'll just have to do it without me. It's time for me to be with my child again."

Naina's throat tightens, but she forces words out—the only words she wants to say. "I'm sorry for what I said in Nivyan Hollow. That we couldn't trust you. I shouldn't have—"

Symin shakes his head. "You were right. I couldn't be trusted. Not because I would ever harm you, but because I was letting my emotions cloud my decisions."

He sighs deeply, and moisture develops on his bottom eyelid. "There's no way to explain the loss of a child to those who've never experienced it. It's unnatural; it's the death of hope. I lost it until the day I walked into a small chai shop in Evic."

Salessa meets his gaze and smiles softly. Tears threaten Naina's eyes and she quickly wipes them away. Together, they embrace Symin and hold one another for as long as they can.

The TreeKeeper appears from the center of the tree.

"Have they agreed to come?" Symin asks her. "Both of them?"

The TreeKeeper nods. "They have."

She gestures to an opening between two trees that is filled with a bright, pulsing light from which a figure with bright pink skin appears.

The young woman steps forward and approaches Symin. She appears younger than the twins—seventeen or eighteen. Her smile is bright and infectious.

Symin wraps his arms around her, and she whispers, "Welcome home, Daddy."

"I've missed you," he responds to her.

She leans back and takes in the lines on his face. "You've gotten so old."

Symin laughs and his pink cheeks burn red.

Zynima turns to the twins and Naina, recalling the torture Saith put her through, blurts out the first words that come to her. "You didn't deserve what he did to you. I know how it felt."

Zymina's smile fades and a profound sincerity washes over her. "Promise me something."

"Anything."

Zynima holds her gaze steadily. "Make him suffer."

Naina nods. "He will suffer. I promise."

Another form, royal purple skin glowing, appears out of the light between the trees. Salessa stares, blankly, mesmerized, until Zakia approaches and embraces her, loosening the falcon's tears.

"I'm sorry," Zakia says. She reaches up and wipes Salessa's cheeks. "I had to protect—"

Salessa nods. "I know. You don't have to explain." She releases a light sob.

Zakia moves a few loose strands of hair away from Salessa's face and wraps them behind her ear. She places her forehead against Salessa's and says, "Find someone to share your chai."

Symin puts a hand on Zakia's shoulder. "She's waiting for us." He gestures to the TreeKeeper, hovering impatiently by the golden light between the trees.

The three Mega say their final, tearful goodbyes to the Doruh twins before exiting the clearing, hand-in-hand, through the golden light.

As soon as they step through, the TreeKeeper turns to the twins. "Your welcome in my dominion is rescinded."

The pain shoots back into Naina's body, wounds open, knees bloody. The courtyard spins around her, but she manages to find Salessa sitting next to Rafael, Kyoko, and the salver cradling Kruga.

Time resumes. The beams reach Symin and he disintegrates into dust, a smile stretched across his lips. The many Saiths collapse into one again, grinning smugly.

Naina's rage erupts like a volcano in her chest. She shifts back into the bipedal wolf, charging with full force at Saith. She topples him over onto his back and tries to close her jaw around his head, but he blasts her in the face again and she is knocked backward.

She's unable to hold the lupine shape while exhausted. Her entire body aches, and the dizziness heightens.

Saith approaches her, and with every step, conveys his frustration.

Step. "I have killed…"

Step. "…so many animals."

Step. "And yet, *you*…"

Step. "…just won't stop."

Step. "I can't kill you…"

Step. "…but I can tear the Radiant energy from a bloody body."

He steps onto her hand and her bones crunch under his foot. She cries out in pain.

"You. Stupid. Bitch."

He winds his leg back, ready to swing it forth into Naina's face, when a powerful bellow resonates throughout the courtyard.

"SAITH!!"

He moves off of Naina's hand, and she cradles her bloody, mangled fingers.

Saila and Unisa descend from the sky and land in the courtyard. Unisa, dripping with sweat, stops short, falling to her knees to catch her breath, while Saila marches toward Saith.

"Saila! Daughter!" Saith pleads to her sense of family. "Look at what these brutes have done to your father."

"You killed Alba."

Saith's expression morphs from one of a broken, defenseless father to panicked prey. "Vy-Ro killed Alba."

Saila continues marching and shakes her head. "You killed Alba."

"Saila, stop right there."

"You killed Alba."

"I said stop!" He blinks, and a stone barrier rises from the ground ahead of her. She blows on it and the barrier turns to sand and flows away with the wind. "Saila, I'm warning you."

"You killed Alba."

"Saila, listen to me!" His voice has turned into little more than a frightened whimper. A ball of flames erupts from his mouth and grows as it approaches Saila, but she simply waves her hand at it, as if it were an irritating insect. The fireball changes direction, shooting up into the sky and dissipating.

She makes a fist and the Facilitator's body stiffens. He's paralyzed. She lowers her fist quickly and he's forced onto his knees. For the first time, Naina sees earnest terror in his expression.

Saila stands over the kneeling pixie. "You killed Alba, knowing what she meant to me." A tear flows down her cheek.

Through a clenched jaw, Saith squeezes out his final plea for survival. "You are a theocrat. A believer. Your spiritual doctrine prohibits you from taking a life, and preaches forgiveness. Honor your gods, prove your devotion. Spare me."

Saila looks to the horizon, from where the Four will soon rise. "The light of the Four dims at the loss of innocent life. You, your master, his dynasty, have dimmed their light for far too long now."

She takes a deep breath and gazes into her father's horrified eyes. "It's time for them to burn brighter than they have in a millennium. And that can only be achieved when you burn, too."

She breathes long, continuous flames that grow wider and hotter, engulfing Saith's body. He screams in agony. It echoes throughout the Castrum until he can scream no longer.

When the fire stops, Saith is gone. All that remains is ash.

Unisa steps forward and helps Naina to her feet. Saila turns and looks up at the highest tower in the Castrum.

"This ends now," she says. "Zar-Lo is up there." She begins to rise, but Unisa wraps her fingers around the pixie's wrist and gently tugs her back down to the ground.

"We can't kill him," Unisa says. "There's a lot I haven't explained to you, and I promise I will. But he may actually be a valuable resource for us in the future."

Saila hesitates. "He must face justice."

Unisa nods. "He will. But violence doesn't always mean justice. Certainly not today."

Naina's gaze lands on Kruga's broken body and she remembers his warning.

Red-Lo isn't the greatest threat here. He's a cog in a far larger mechanism.

"She's right," the wolf defends Unisa. "I can't believe I'm saying this, but Feathers is right. We'll need him for battles to come. Violence isn't the answer today."

"Let me talk to him," Unisa proposes.

Saila shakes her head. "Absolutely not."

"Please, Saila. Trust me. I can talk him into your custody."

There's a long hesitation before Saila nods.

CHAPTER 64

THE ORE MONGER

Theocratic-Monarchy SunSide
Date 23rd Day of Month 6, Year 1628 DG

"YOU HAVE FIVE MINUTES," SAILA reminds her. "Then I come in."

Unisa nods. "I understand."

The young human places a quivering hand on the Theater door, pushes it open, and steps into the chamber with a long inhale.

The eight hundred-year-old faerie monarch stands before a wall of glass, arms folded behind his back. Unisa wonders how much of the carnage is visible from this elevation. When she steps forth, his pointed, turquoise ears perk up, but he doesn't turn to face her.

"The day has come, Saila," he says, coolly. "You might try to take my life, but it won't be easy."

The MegaFather stands taller than Unisa imagined he would. But a towering presence doesn't equate to an intimidating one. As it does for the Prime, knowledge empowers the king who keeps his kingdom in the dark, not his stature.

Unisa reminds herself that, at the moment, she knows more than he does.

"I'm not Saila," she responds, matching his even tone.

He turns to her and raises an eyebrow. "You're not." He notices her wings and his eyes widen. "Our fugitive Librarian."

Unisa nods and a wide smile stretches across his lips.

"What will you tell the Prime about Alba's death?"

Unisa considers his question carefully, bouncing it around in her mind until she decides to answer honestly. "I'm not entirely sure."

"Fair." He saunters toward a stage-like platform in the center of the room. "And what is your name?"

"Unisa."

He takes a seat behind the ore desk and folds his hands tightly upon it. "Are you here to surrender, Unisa?"

Unisa takes a deep breath before she responds. "No. I've come to persuade *you* to surrender."

His finger rises to stroke his chin, as his eyes narrow. "Well, that is interesting. I can't imagine this was Saila's idea."

Unisa shakes her head. "It was mine."

He nods. "And what makes you think you can persuade me? Is it because we are so similar?"

Unisa's expression betrays her dismay. "We are not similar."

He leans forward and raises an eyebrow. "Aren't we, Unisa? I've spent my entire life protecting and preserving the history of my ancestors. My dynasty. As a Librarian, haven't you done the same?"

Unisa's heart sinks. *He's right.*

He rises to his feet and steps around the ore desk. "You may think I'm a monster. A demon. But I can assure you, Unisa, putting on a tunic every morning, you spread the same rot in this world that I do. We are both a chalice, holding the same poison, allowing the world to sip from us."

His heavy feet drop down from the platform, stepping closer to Unisa. "Tell me again how different we are."

Unisa steels herself and shoves his taunts to the back of her mind. "I can tell you what makes us different. I know where your wife is, and you don't."

The MegaFather scoffs. "I don't have a wife."

"Not anymore. But you did. Didn't you, Red-Lo?"

Neither the MegaFather's posture, nor his overall demeanor change at the mention of his name. He simply gazes upon the Librarian quizzically. "I believe you may have your history confused. Red-Lo was my ancestor."

Unisa doesn't let her gaze waver. She reaches into her pocket and pulls out a piece of paper, stepping forward until the gap between them is eliminated and she's staring up at the faerie. He calmly takes it from her.

"Hay-Ro sends his greetings."

As he reads the letter, Unisa walks toward the glass wall.

"You mustn't believe everything you read, Unisa," he says after he's finished.

Unisa, facing the MegaFather from the window, fails to restrain a chuckle. "I wish I had learned that a long, long time ago. I've believed everything I've read, everything I've been told, for my entire life. Ironically, that letter is now the *only* thing I believe."

She keeps her eyes locked on him as she utters her next words. "I know the truth, Red-Lo. Confess, and I'll tell you where Drof-Fa is."

The MegaFather's demeanor deteriorates radically. All smugness dries like a dewdrop in the desert. His eyes narrow and his jaw tightens.

"Do not say her name. She has long since died. Alone—somewhere I could never find her."

Unisa shakes her head. "She lives, Red-Lo. She was cursed with the same immortality with which you were blessed."

He shakes his head and grits his teeth. "Impossible."

"She told me everything. How you begged the Sprites to spare her. You're right, they hid her away from you. But they also made it so she could not die."

He steps aggressively toward her, rage in his eyes.

Unisa continues as he walks. "She told me about your agreement. Trading the essences of your offspring for the chance to live on, generation after generation, in their bodies."

He stops walking and his eyes widen. "How is this possible?"

"It's possible because I've learned not to believe everything I read—not to idolize powerful people, because they only want one thing: to keep their power."

"Tell me! How do you know?"

"Drof-Fa told me. You still have your connection to the Sprites, but she doesn't. She's connected to you."

The MegaFather steps backward, as if Unisa has physically pushed him. "No."

"Yes. Eight hundred years, Red-Lo. Every thought, every experience, she has lived with you." Unisa lowers her volume but hardens her tone. "Every single time you attempted to create new offspring, bringing someone into your bed who wasn't your wife, she was watching you."

He reaches the steps of the platform and falls backward onto them. "No, no, no."

Unisa walks toward him, her chin held high. "She watched you slaughter the igni and become the Ore Monger. Surrender your offspring to the Sprites. Terrorize the Doruh. Assassinate the Members of the Assembly *and* the Alphocracy of MoonSide."

"Take me to her," he begs in a whisper. "Where is she?"

She reaches him and maintains eye contact. "She doesn't want to see you. You disgust her." She scoffs. "You disgust me, too. Your life story resonated with me. Generations of Librarians hailed you as a hero. We taught the world about your bravery and sacrifice, while you tarnished Drof-Fa's legacy. How could you? You claim to love her. What kind of love is that?"

His volume erupts. "I have held the throne for centuries...for her!" His fist comes down and rattles the room. "I will annihilate you for questioning my love for her."

"Do it. I'm the only one who knows where she is. Kill me, and you'll truly never see her again."

His jaw falls and he sits quietly for so long, staring at the ground, Unisa thinks the suns might have risen while she was waiting for him to speak.

"Immortality is nothing but loneliness and exhaustion, Unisa. Consider how quickly the years start to flow in a lifetime, and imagine the blur that these past decades and centuries have been for me. I would change it if I could. I would save my child, and Drof-Fa, and I would die in a warm bed together, knowing our legacy was safe."

He raises his eyes and Unisa sees them moisten.

"Drof-Fa is the only reason my fingers have been so tightly wound around this kingdom, generation after generation. Had I let the Sprites raze it, her death would've been for nothing." He makes a final, desperate plea. "I've ached for her every day, Unisa. If she's alive, please, take me to her."

"Perhaps, one day, I will," Unisa says, dangling the carrot before the horse, "but for now, you have to surrender to Saila's custody."

The Ore Monger scoffs. "Why? Because you think I'll help you prepare for the Sprites and the Three Deaths? Unisa, you have no idea what they are capable of. The Sprites will build their kingdom atop our ashes. You think you're winning this competition, but you don't even know who you're competing with."

His warning rattles her heart against her chest. *What if he's right? What if the danger is too great?*

And then her thoughts unbury a young MoonSidian boy who, in the face of danger, became a lamb and fought back.

"Have you ever been to MoonSide, Red-Lo? I have. I saw children playing. Amongst brutal blades and wicked walls, children were laughing."

The MegaFather raises an eyebrow. "I'm not sure I understand your point."

"My point is that we enter this world imbued with resilience. Let the Sprites come; they also don't know who they're competing with."

Red-Lo shakes his head. "It won't end the way this conversation has. Words are not weapons that can be used against them. They will not yield for discourse. You will have to bathe your hands in blood to defeat them. Are you ready for that?"

Unisa hesitates. She heard it from Alba first, then Naina, and now from Red-Lo. Violence will one day inevitably be the solution.

But that day is not today.

"I can tell you another way in which we're different, Red-Lo. You've allowed the world to sip from you, knowing the poison you held. I just found out recently, but I'm willing to shatter myself if it means saving the world another taste. Can you say you would do the same?"

The MegaFather smiles and looks past her, at his kingdom beyond the window wall. "Bring Saila in. I'm ready for it all to end."

His smile fades and he meets Unisa's gaze. "If you'll take me to my wife."

CHAPTER 65

ONE WEEK LATER

Sovereign City-State *The Library*
Date *30th Day of Month 6, Year 1628 DG*

UNISA WAITS IN THE SMALL reception room outside of the Prime's door. The chairs, the desk, the fountain, the black door—it all looks the same, save for one missing piece.

Rafael isn't seated at the desk. And he never will be again. Whoever takes the seat will have quite a large tunic to fill.

This was the room in which it all began.

"Welcome home, Ambassador," comes the Prime's voice from the doorway to his office. The mari man with eyes that are cold and warm at the same time.

Unisa stands and quietly nods, light bouncing off of her yellow silk tunic. She enters the office and he closes the door behind her.

When she sees the chairs in front of his desk, she stops. A pang of sadness fills her heart, as memories of her last time in this office flood back. She exhales, pushing them away, and takes a seat.

"Quite a journey you've been on," the Prime states, sitting across the desk.

"It was certainly enlightening. I came here to apologize to you in person about" — she pauses — "the things I wrote in my letter."

The Prime exhales deeply. "I can't say I was pleased to read about the behavior you four displayed. Safety always comes first. This decision to record the civil unrest cost Alba her life; and it's a decision that's tied my hands, or I would've had thousands of armed Librarians storming the Pass and invading SunSide the day your letter arrived."

Unisa nods, trying to hold back a smile. *He bought it.*

"I don't fully understand why Alba would send for Rafael and Kyoko to join you. Couldn't the two of you have recorded the assassinations and come home?"

Unisa thinks as quickly as she can. "We were all recording in different parts of the city, Great Prime. We needed as many eyes as possible for the most accurate recording."

The Prime smiles. "Accuracy. That was the whole point of your journey to SunSide in the first place. So tell me: what did you learn about the accuracy of our records?" He leans in and Unisa knows what he wants to hear.

Alba's voice echoes in her ears. *Let him think he's won.*

She swallows hard, and the words burn her tongue on the way out. "I learned the truth, of course. That everything you've ever taught me is completely accurate. Our allies keep the peace in MoonSide against the radical scum. I feel closer to the ideal of the Fully Bonded now than I ever have before."

There's a long pause as the Prime's eyes narrow, and he gazes so hard at Unisa, she thinks he might be trying to look *through* her. But then a wicked smile widens on his face. "You *are* Fully Bonded, Ambassador. I am so very proud of you."

His pride sickens her, but she maintains composure.

"I'm lucky to have you, still. After Rafael, Kyoko, and Ana decided to leave the Library together, I felt very lonely."

He slides his hand out, leaving his palm open in invitation. She swallows the bile back down her throat as she hesitantly places her hand in his. "But you won't let me feel lonely, will you, Unisa?"

Unisa pulls her hand back before she vomits, then forces a coy smile. "As long as you're here, in this office, behind that desk, I will be here, Great Prime. I can promise you that."

"Thank you, Unisa. It warms my heart that you see the truth and have accepted your place here."

A genuine smile crosses Unisa's face as the Prime unwittingly sits across the desk from his eventual downfall.

She rises to her feet and prepares to head back out into the city, taking one last, long look at the leader, and accepting what so many have expressed to her: she will have to be comfortable with violence.

The Prime isn't a problem that can be solved without it.

FAITH, TRUST, AND UNITY

Theocratic-Monarchy *SunSide*
Date *30th Day of Month 6, Year 1628 DG*

THERE IS NO GREATER SYMBOL of SunSide's devotion to its theocracy than the Temple Complex. A stage was erected in the court-yard overnight, identical to the one upon which Sonali was executed.

Saila stands at the podium, waiting for the applause to die down. Using the Radiance, Saila projects her voice so that it echoes throughout the Complex, between the monuments and shrines, within the chapels and halls.

"There is so much to say. I'm a little lost as to where to begin. One week ago, the MegaFather, the Facilitator, and the Braver General staged a coup in an attempt to gain sole power over SunSide. They found success in eight assassinations, but by the grace of the Four, I survived."

The applause resumes, and Saila gestures for the crowd to settle down.

"In light of these difficult truths, it is apparent that heavy govern-mental changes are imperative. Until a suitable candidate for the throne is found, SunSide is a sole theocracy once again. In the coming months, the Assembly of the Radiance will be rejuvenated with new Members. We will hold fair and equal elections to fill the seven empty seats. The three remaining seats will be filled by the Chief Member and our two Ambassadors to MoonSide."

She gestures to the Doruh twins sitting behind her on the stage, who smile and wave to the cheering crowd.

Saila continues. "Per their counsel, we have developed a three-phase plan that will work to restore faith, trust, and unity between us and our sister kingdom. The details of this plan have not yet been outlined, but we do know the main objective of each phase."

She looks down at a piece of paper with Salessa's handwriting outlining the three phases, along with Naina's notes in the margins, and strikethroughs across some of Salessa's ideas.

"Phase One will work toward eradicating all signs of occupation, and Braver activity, within MoonSide. Phase Two will see the construction of two new cities within SunSide. The faerie settlements will be evacuated and demolished, and the land will be returned to the Doruh. The settlers will be relocated to the new cities within our own borders."

Saila ignores the jeers in the crowd, likely from some faeries and loyalists, and continues. "Phase Three will reinstate the Alphocracy and assist MoonSidians in holding fair elections to select their new Alphas."

She turns to Naina and Salessa, who smile at her encouragingly, then back to the crowd with a deep exhale. "The Doruh won their liberation and it is time to honor their freedom. They were here, fighting to liberate Larso alongside us. SunSide's soil has been blessed with Doruh blood. This is the very least we can do."

The crowd erupts again, and the twins stand to applaud her. Pride and hope build in her chest, bringing tears into her eyes. She prays that only good days are ahead—the days that Sonali and Alba used to believe were possible.

She turns to invite the twins to speak, but they're no longer clapping. They're staring down at a small piece of paper in Salessa's hands.

"What is it?" Saila asks.

"A child brought this note up to the stage and said it was for Lessi," Naina explains. "He said some large Doruh—half cat and half man— gave it to him and then left."

Saila holds her hand out for the note, and Salessa hands it to her:

Come find me, Salessa.
I'm waiting for you on Lover's Plateau.

Come find me.

GLOSSARY

Terms marked with (F) relate to fictional characters, settings, concepts, or items.

Terms marked with (NF) relate to non-fictional concepts or items.

The Academy of Librarians / "The Academy" (F) – institution of study and training for Student Librarians / comprises the first three floors of the Center above the atrium (the bottom level) / course difficulty increases as the students ascend the floors, with introductory courses taught on level one and advanced courses taught on level three

Adera (F) – both a gerontocratic village and the pixie for whom the village is named / Adera, the pixie, was the mother of the Twins, the Doruh deities / Adera, the village, is governed by an elderly Head-woman / pronounced *a-DAYR-a*

Aerthomni (F) – one of the two known continents of the All-Sphere / pronounced *air-THOM-nee*

The Agrarian Townlets (F) – federation of small towns governed by local farmers and those who cultivate the land

Alasa Belita, Alasa Nekita (F) – "Unlimited Skies. Unlimited Love." / official motto of the human city of PeakHaven / in the ancient Nysabaani language / pronounced *ah-LUSSA bay-LEETA, ah-LUSSA nay-KEETA*

Alba (F) – 38 years old / Ambassador Librarian / mari human / her uncle Alvaro is the Prime Librarian / Ana is her younger sister / has been Kyoko's mentor for six years / regarded by other Librarians as a paragon of the Library's teachings / arrived at the Library when she was 10 / shares common mari anatomy: fins on the forearms and down the spine, piscine nare slits in place of a human nose, webbed fingers, and internal organs that allow for breathing underwater

The All-Sphere (F) – planet on which the story is set / has two known continents: Aerthomni and Panaerth

The Alphocracy of Moonside (F) – government headed by twenty Alphas in MoonSide / formed immediately after the Doruh Uprisings in 784 DG / governed for nearly six hundred years / all twenty Alphas were assassinated in 1381 DG following SunSide's invasion of Moon-Side and the start of the military occupation by Tya-Lo the MegaMother

Alu Paratha (NF) – a flatbread made with whole wheat flour, boiled potatoes, spices & herbs common in the South Asian subcontinent / typical Doruh breakfast item, as the development of the fictional Doruh culture was influenced by the culture of the South Asian subcontinent

Ambassador Librarians / Ambassadors (F) – seventh rank of the Librarian hierarchy / uniform is yellow silk tunics / lead groups of Recorder and Vice Ambassador Librarians around the continent to witness historical events and record them for the Library's Catacombs

Amma / Headwoman of Adera (F) – village elder who governs Adera / Shifa's grandmother / animal form is a bison

Ana (F) – 29 years old / mari human / accomplished Nysabaani translator and researcher / Alba's younger sister / arrived at the Library when she was 1 / shares common mari anatomy: fins on the forearms and down the spine, piscine nare slits in place of a human nose, webbed fingers, and internal organs that allow for breathing underwater

Angi (F) – one of three human clans / possess wings whose feathers appear silver and polished, resembling steel / built the city of PeakHaven atop the highest mountains of the PeakHaven mountain range

/ governed by a Super-Montane Stratocracy: headed by the military / religion requires the angi to face a temple called the Holy Summit during prayer / pronounced *aan-jee*

***Ardev Ocean* (F)** – one of the All-Sphere's two known oceans / sits between the two continents / Lily Beach is in the waters of Ardev Ocean / pronounced *ar-DAYV*

***Arlun* (F)** – capital city of MoonSide / founded at the time of the Alphocracy's formation in 784 DG / connected to SunSide's capital city, Larso, by PeakHaven Pass / where Naina and Salessa lived with their parents until they were 8 years old / pronounced *ar-lin*

***Ashiyu* (NF)** – a Japanese public bath in which the feet are bathed / common in EverEmber, as the development of the fictional igni culture was influenced by Japanese culture

***The Assembly of the Radiance* (F)** – one-half of the SunSidian government / comprised of ten Members / govern as a theocracy, with the goal of establishing and enforcing the will of the Four over SunSide / created the monarchy to act as a liaison to the SunSidian citizenry, who felt SunSide's original sole theocracy had become disconnected from the general public / Members are greeted with four fingers placed over the center of the forehead / meet in a vast chamber called the Forum

***Ayuma Liyuna* (F)** – Doruh folk song sung by Adera's Headwoman / sung in Nysabaani / title translates to "the Mother of Shifts" / pronounced *aa-YOO-ma lee-YOO-na*

***Bibi Sands* (F)** – small island between the igni city EverEmber, and the mari city SeaBed / ownership of the island caused a territorial dispute between the two human cities called the War for Bibi Sands, which lasted from 1603 to 1622, after which EverEmber relinquished Bibi Sands to SeaBed / now under mari control / pronounced *bee-bee sands*

***Braver* (F)** – SunSidian warriors / originally the monarchy's royal guard, now the Braver organization is the principal military and law enforcement within SunSide / also used as occupying, oppressive force in MoonSide, maintaining the faerie settlements therein

Braver General (F) – head of the Braver organization / reports directly to the Facilitator / position currently held by Vy-Ro

The Bridge Tree (F) – spiritual location that connects this world to the world beyond / watched over by the TreeKeeper / girthy tree with so many branches and leaves, it would take a millennium to count / interconnected roots expand out to the other trees in the Forest of Essences / where essences arrive in order to be ushered into the world beyond by the TreeKeeper

The Bunker (F) – a track-proof safe house Zakia built when she was 10 using the Radiance, in 1618 / connects to the underground tunnels used by the SunSide Revolutionary Forces / built under Zalona's inn

The Caracal (F) – Doruh Headman whose village incurred massive damage, and whose villagers were traumatized, when igni and mari warriors used it as a battleground during the War for Bibi Sands / an elderly man who is tall, but quite frail / shifts into a caracal: a feline with a short face, long tufted ears, and a relatively short tail

Carajillo (NF) – a coffee drink to which a liquor is added, common in Spain and several Latin American countries / a typical mari drink, as the development of the fictional mari culture was influenced by Spanish culture

The Castrum (F) – complex of buildings and structures in Larso through which all SunSidian government functions operate / the monarchy's throne room, the MegaFather's Theater, the Assembly's Forum, the Head Salver's clinic, and all government administration lies within the Castrum / heavily protected by ore walls and gates, as well as thousands of Braver warriors

The Catacombs / The Library's Catacomb Network (F) – system of tunnels under the city connecting large chambers called "sections," in which the Library houses and catalogs the entirety of Aerthomni's written history / also connects all of the sections to the Center: the Library's hub for government and administration / the records and documents held within the Catacombs are the most valuable artifacts in existence / brightly-lit and tiled / can be confusing to navigate for newer Librarians and recent graduates of the Academy

The Center (F) – the Library's hub for government and administration / bottom level is the atrium / the Academy comprises the first three floors of the Center above the atrium / the top floor of the Center is a wide, open chamber filled with sturdy, metal desks and flimsy, wooden partitions between them / this is where the Supreme Librarians' and the Prime's offices are

CereCenters (F) – educational epicenters constructed and governed by the Library / there are a total of fifty-six CereCenters / Educator Librarians are sent to CereCenters for the academic season to teach human, Doruh, and Mega students about the continent's history, along with various other subjects / at the end of the academic season, the Educators return to the Library until the following season, during which they are assigned to a new CereCenter / the MegaFather has provided Bravers to the CereCenters for security and law enforcement, to aid in the Library's mission / the Prime seeks out impoverished villages to which he can offer economic and architectural rehabilitation in exchange for building the CereCenter / pronounced *seh-ra-sen-ters*

CereCenter Forty-Two (F) – a maze of claystone buildings nestled into a valley, this CereCenter rests between the Library and SunSide, just west of the Red-Lo River / where Hassan, an Educator Librarian and Alba's friend, is stationed for the current academic season

Chai (NF) – a popular tea throughout the South Asian subcontinent / *chai* is the full name of the beverage, and it should never be called "chai tea" / popular Doruh beverage, as the development of the fictional Doruh culture was influenced by the culture of the South Asian subcontinent

Chaitender (F) – one who serves chai at a chai house / Salessa's second job

Chiragh (F) – Doruh man in his early 20's / earns a living from chauffeuring passengers around the Library / animal form is a cheetah

Court Democracy (F) – form of government in which seven elected officials, known as the Court, each representing one of EverEmber's seven political jurisdictions, governs the city by the will of the majority / officials are given the title of Courtman or Courtwoman / this is the only human government that is not led by the military, as both SeaBed and PeakHaven are Stratocracies

Currency / Stones (F) – polished stones, etched with the MegaFather's portrait are used as currency / a circular blue stone, a triangular green stone, and a rectangular red stone / the currency is designed and manufactured on a mass scale in SunSide / the value of the currency soon overpowered all others, causing it to take over as the dominant form of payment across the continent

Directors / Legion Directors (F) - mid-level rank in the Braver hierarchy / officers report to the Legion Directors, while the Directors then report to the District Supervisors / uniform mask color is blue

The Dissolved Nations – once dominated by prosperous kings and queens, ministers, councilmen, and presidents / wealth driven into the hands of a fraction of the population leading to rampant poverty in all other classes / greed gave way to collapse and ruin / now empty land that others do not settle, as it is believed to be cursed / each nation in the region was named for the most common occupation of the residents there: Merchant, Bard, Cobbler, Courtesan, and Smith

District Supervisors / Supervisors (F) – upper-level rank in the Braver hierarchy / Legion Directors report to District Supervisors, who then report directly to the Braver General / uniform mask color is green

Diya / Husband / Son (F) – Doruh family who transport travelers through MoonSide / Diya and her husband are in their early 40's, their son is twelve or thirteen years old / their animal form is horse / Diya and Alba have a cordial, professional relationship

Doruh (F) – species of shapeshifters / shift into animals using energy from the Radiance / their animal forms are typically hereditary / Doruh twins, whether identical or fraternal, will always shift into the same animal form / have two essences: one human and one animal / originally were the human teri clan until the War of New Clans / the term "animal" is used as a slur to refer to this species / most Doruh worship the Twins / pronounced *doe-ROO*

Doruh Genesis (F) – current calendar era / began upon the creation of the Doruh species during the War of New Clans / noted as "DG"

The Doruh Uprisings / Doruh Liberation (F) – Liberation originally planned for 767 DG, but was stopped by the usurping of the SunSidian throne by Red-Lo, Drof-Fa, and the Faerie Empowerment Forces / this led to the Uprisings in 784 DG, which freed the Doruh and set up the Alphocracy / the Doruh were free until 1381 DG, when SunSide invaded MoonSide, assassinated the Alphas, and set up their military occupation

Drof-Fa (F) – faerie / General of the Faerie Empowerment Forces until 767 DG / MegaMother of SunSide from 767 DG until her mysterious death in 783 DG / wife of Red-Lo the MegaFather / pronounced *DRO-fa*

Dupatta (NF) – a long shawl-like scarf traditionally worn by women in the South Asian subcontinent to cover the head and shoulders / most commonly as part of the women's shalwar kameez outfit / common Doruh attire, as the development of the fictional Doruh culture was influenced by the culture of the South Asian Subcontinent

Educator Librarians / Educators (F) – fifth rank of the Librarian hierarchy / uniform is red linen tunics / teach courses at both the Academy and the CereCenters

Eloa (F) – small village on the northern coast of SunSide / where Saila grew up and where her mother, Saith's ex-wife, currently resides / pronounced *eh-lua*

Era of the Nysabaan (F) – original calendar era of recorded history / noted as "EN" / era during which ancient inhabitants of the All-Sphere, known as the Nysabaan, were the dominant species / Nysabaani was the dominant language / runs until 2165 EN, the year during which historical records indicate the extinction of the Sprite species, and evolutionary divergence of the human and Mega species / pronounced *NEE-sah-baan*

Essence (F) – soul

EverEmber (F) – one of the three human cities / governed by Court Democracy; only human city without a military-led government / populated by the igni human clan / comprised of three islands: Roba, Sila, and Tusa / Roba is the largest island, a hub of commerce, recreation, government, and residences of the upper class; also known as "The Mother" / Sila and Tusa are smaller islands known as "The Sisters"; Sila houses the lower and middle classes, while Tusa is nothing more than dense forest / at the center of Roba is Mt. Mother, the volcano around which the igni settled during the Teri Age / heat from the volcano rises into the air, then descends and covers the waters around the island, forming a natural defense, while towering ore walls surrounding the islands form an artificial one / the igni do not display any particular organization in religion or spirituality, yet they do "feed" their dead to Mt. Mother, so that their stone exoskeletons can be liquified and become part of the volcanic rock across Roba / EverEmber was engaged in the War for Bibi Sands with SeaBed for nineteen years until Courtman Tomohiro discovered Lily Beach; the latter was far larger, and far more geologically-equipped to handle the construction of the igni settlements that the Court once desired to build on Bibi Sands, so EverEmber ended the war and relinquished control of the smaller island to SeaBed

The Everlasting Journey (F) – both a journey taken by the MegaParents of SunSide and the autobiography of Red-Lo the MegaFather / a journey in search of immortality taken by Red-Lo the MegaFather and Drof-Fa the MegaMother in 783 DG, which leads to the latter's death under mysterious circumstance / this is considered a pivotal moment in SunSidian history, as Red-Lo's grief propelled him to focus on SunSide's technological and scientific revolutions / toward the end of his life, with the help of his Head Salver, Hay-Ro, he penned an autobiography and titled it after this event

Evic (F) – small village on the farthest edge of MoonSide, directly to the east of Red-Lo River / the entire village is a narrow strip, a string inhabited by little more than broken-down homes, destitute clay huts, and the warming fires of the hungry and impoverished / towering walls separate the Doruh residents from the prosperous faerie settlements on the other side / not on most maps due to its size / this is where Naina and Salessa settled after escaping Arlun at 8 years old / pronounced *EE-vik*

The Facilitator (F) – high-status position in the SunSidian monarchy / advisor and confidant of the monarch, responsibilities include: general monarchy administration, provide counsel to the monarch, ensure the enforcement of domestic and foreign policy and decree, communicate the monarch's wishes to to other members of government, maintain strict loyalty to the monarch, advise on all political and economic matters, administer justice, safeguard the monarch by any means necessary, etc. / position currently held by Saith

Faeries (F) – one of the three Mega clans / like the humans, said to have evolved from the Sprites toward the end of the Era of the Nysabaan / originally possessed the ability, as the other clans do, to access and harness the energy of the Radiance, though that ability dwindled as the faerie reliance on technology increased and they used the Radiance less and less / present-day faeries can no longer access the Radiance at all / share the common physical traits of all Mega: pointed ears and solid-gray eyes with no pupils or irises / led the Mega campaign to enslave the Doruh after their creation in 1 DG / prevented Doruh Liberation in 767 DG by usurping the SunSidian throne / invaded MoonSide in 1381 DG and assassinated the Alphas / created the Braver organization and used it to set up a military occupation in SunSide / built settlements in MoonSide in 1422 after capturing land that belonged to MoonSidians and driving them from their homes / drove most of the nymphs and pixies out of Larso and into Nivyan Hollow / introduced the ore to SunSide, and later to the entire continent, severing any remaining nymphs and pixies in Larso from the Radiance / most faeries are followers of the Four, the dominant Mega religion / faerie familial naming conventions hyphenate a family name to the first name (e.g. Red-Lo and Zar-Lo; Hay-Ro and Vy-Ro)

Faerie Empowerment Forces (F) - warriors who provoked the battle for the SunSidian throne in 767 DG / led by Red-Lo and General Drof-Fa / after acquisition of the throne, become the SunSidian Royal Army, predecessors to the Braver organization / started by Zif-Lo, father of Red-Lo

The Final Act (F) – document written and signed by Members of the Assembly of the Radiance during the early days of their incumbency / should they perish prior to the end of their term, theocratic law states that their Final Act will be read before the Assembly and the MegaParent(s), and acted upon swiftly / a Final Act can be nullified by a majority vote amongst the remaining Members, by a criminal conviction of the late Member during their lifetime, or by any other circumstance that dilutes their spiritual status in the eyes of the Four

The Forum (F) – vast chamber in the Castrum where the Members of the Assembly of the Radiance hold their sessions / a magnificent stage rests on one end of the chamber, tall windows line the walls, and polished stone, embedded with gems, covers the floor

The Four (F) – the four suns, deities of the dominant Mega religion / the Four are Ona, Lona, Throna, and Frona; this is the order in which they rise from the horizon, as well as how they are ordered in size and age / Ona is the oldest and the strongest while Frona is the youngest and weakest / Ona and Frona are typically referred to with feminine pronouns, while Lona and Throna are typically referred to with masculine, though there is no certainty of gender from scripture / they are praised often with the phrase "Glory to the Four!" / statues, monuments, and shrines to the Four are featured in designated areas all around the vast compound of the Temple Complex in Larso

Frona (F) – Frona is the youngest and weakest of the Four, deities of the dominant Mega religion / she is the last to rise from the horizon, after Ona, Lona, and Throna / she is typically referred to with feminine pronouns, though there is no certainty of gender from scripture / pronounced *FROE-nah*

The Future is Forever! (F) – official motto of SunSide

Fully Bonded (F) – an ideal that the Prime commands all Librarians to strive toward / the Fully Bonded individual is one who: abandons victimhood and fosters accountability, is introspective, listen to the teachings of the Prime and learns from it, respects and safeguards knowledge, truth, and history, thirsts for more knowledge, obeys commands and rules decreed by the Prime and the Supremes, devotes their life to collecting and protecting the information in the Catacombs, inherently trusts the Prime and Supremes to know what is best for them, and above all else, believe in the Prime's mercy and wisdom

Fully Broken (F) – an ideal that the Prime warns all Librarians to avoid / the Fully Broken individual is one who: embraces victimhood and lacks accountability, lacks self-awareness, disobeys the Prime, the Supremes, and their commands, lacks respect for knowledge, truth, and history, lacks a devotion to protect the information in the Catacombs, doesn't trust the Prime and Supremes entirely to know what is best, doesn't believe in the Prime's mercy and wisdom / the Fully Broken are promptly arrested and taken for rehabilitation or exile

Gatekeeper Librarians / Gatekeepers (F) – third rank of the Librarian hierarchy / uniform is gold cotton tunics / oversee the intake and out-take of records, documents, and artifacts from their assigned sections within the CataCombs

Gerontocracy (NF) – a form of government led by elders

The Gerontocratic Villages (F) – federation of small villages governed by local elders

Gina (F) – mid-50's / chartreuse skin / shares common Mega features: pointed ears and solid-gray eyes with no pupils or irises / former Co-General of the SunSide Revolutionary Forces / joined Symin's group of warriors after the Siege of the Castrum / pronounced *JEE-na*

Guardleaf Grove (F) – one of the farming villages within the Agrarian Townlets

Hassan (F) – 42 years old / Educator Librarian / angi human / shares trait common to the angi: wings that look like steel in color and texture / religious; prays facing the Holy Summit / fluent in Nysabaani / stationed at CereCenter Forty-Two for the current academic season / has been good friends with Alba for many years

Hay-Ro (F) – faerie / originally a salver in Larso, joined the Faerie Empowerment Forces as a warrior / became Head Salver during Red-Lo's and Drof-Fa's reign as MegaParents / assisted Red-Lo later in life in writing his autobiography / had a strong friendship with Drof-Fa, but Red-Lo regarded him with disfavor / ancestor of Vy-Ro, current Braver General / pronounced *HAY-roe*

Head Salver (F) – high-status position in the SunSidian government / healer of the monarch, the royal family, the Members of the Assembly of the Radiance, other high-status government officials, and others authorized by the monarch or Members / responsibilities also include: providing monarchy and theocracy with guidance on advisable and feasible domestic healing policies / position currently held by Saimiza / formerly held by Hay-Ro

Headwoman (NF) – female chief or leader of a tribe or village

Headwoman of Adera / Amma (F) – village elder who governs Adera / Shifa's grandmother / animal form is a bison

The HearthBark (F) – dense forest at the south of the continent / some describe it as a maze, or a prison if a traveler gets lost / said to be inhabited by *Reyu Paleyu*, a Vine Demon

Hof-Lo the Unflinching (F) – faerie / MegaFather and thirty-third member of the Red-Lo Royal Dynasty / known for the construction of the settlements in MoonSide in 1422 DG

The Holy Summit (F) – sacred angi temple constructed on a mountaintop in the PeakHaven mountain range / the angi face the Summit during their daily prayers

Hover Chariots (F) – vehicle used in local transportation around Larso / oval in shape, with two rows of seats / bottom half is metal, painted white, and the top is made of treated, protective glass / hovers over the ground as a magnetized ore plate affixed to the bottom pushes against the ore embedded in the roads

Igni (F) – one of the three human clans / possess stone exoskeletons / built the city of EverEmber on three islands surrounding the volcano, Mt. Mother / governed by Court Democracy / seven members to the elected Court / do not display any particular organization in religion or spirituality, yet they do "feed" their dead to Mt. Mother, so that their stone exoskeletons can be liquified and become part of the volcanic rock across Roba / engaged in the War for Bibi Sands with the mari for nineteen years until Courtman Tomohiro discovered Lily Beach; the latter was far larger, and far more geologically-equipped to handle the construction of the igni settlements that the Court once desired to build on Bibi Sands, so EverEmber ended the war and relinquished control of the smaller island to SeaBed / pronounced *ig-nee*

Innkeeper's Ranch (F) – one of the farming villages within the Agrarian Townlets

Joaquina (F) – 17 years old at the time of her death / mari human / Rafael's sister / olive-toned skin, taller than Rafael, golden-brown eyes, chestnut hair cut just under her earlobes / was self-conscious about the sharpness of her forearm fins; Rafael called her "blade-arms" / agricultural prodigy / gave her bracelet to Rafael before she died / shares common mari anatomy: fins on the forearms and down the spine, piscine nare slits in place of a human nose, webbed fingers, and internal organs that allow for breathing underwater

Kanako / Yala (F) – 32 years old / igni human / Kyoko's sister / Natsu-mi's mother / came to the Library with Kyoko when she was 16 and Kyoko was 12 / shares common igni anatomy: stone exoskeleton

Koal (F) – Recorder Librarian / Unisa and Maksi's direct supervisor / nymph

Kura (F) – igni human / owner of Kura's Kitchen, a dining stall in the Library's marketplace

Kurti / Kurta (NF) – a kurta is a loose collarless shirt or tunic worn in many regions of South Asia / a kurti is a short hip-length kurta worn traditionally by young women and girls / common Doruh attire, as the development of the fictional Doruh culture was influenced by the culture of the South Asian Subcontinent

Kruga (F) – 35 years old / crimson skin / shares common Mega features: pointed ears and solid-gray eyes with no pupils or irises / formerly a scientist who worked in the MegaFather's laboratories / formerly a member of the SunSide Revolutionary Forces, after the murder of his fiancee, Zynima / joined Symin's group of warriors after the Siege of the Castrum / strong bond with Symin after their shared grief; his late fiancee was Symin's daughter / pronounced *KROO-ga*

Kyoko (F) – 28 years old / Vice Ambassador Librarian / igni human / her sister is Kanako, with whom she came to the Library when she was 12 / has been Alba's Vice and protege for six years / shares common igni anatomy: stone exoskeleton

Larso (F) – capital city of SunSide / originally known by Nysabaani name *Afuna Ji'Una*, as described in ancient texts from the Era of the Nysabaan / after the Doruh Uprisings in 784 DG, the city plunged into chaos and violence between the faeries and the other two Mega clans, the nymphs and the pixies, who stood behind the Doruh during the

Uprisings / this lasted until 790 DG, when the majority of the nymphs and pixies were driven out of Larso, into Nivyan Hollow, as a result of their support for the Doruh / with the nymph and pixie communities in Larso mostly emptied, Red-Lo razed them and built the Temple Complex he had promised the Assembly / over the following years, those nymphs, pixies, and Doruh who remained, along with some humans and progressive faeries, slowly started to band together and form the underground SunSide Revolutionary Forces / connected to Moon-Side's capital city, Arlun, by PeakHaven Pass / where the Castrum is / pronounced *lar-soe*

Larso University (F) – educational institution in the middle districts of Larso / classrooms are packed with faeries whose parents have either paid handsomely to educate them or have leveraged friendships and status to enroll their children / non-faeries are offered *generous* sums of money to attend classes by wealthy faeries to whom they'll be indebted for the remainder of their lives / offer a wide range of courses of study, including biochemistry.

Legion Directors / Directors (F) – mid-level rank in the Braver hierarchy / Officers report to the Legion Directors, while the Directors then report to the District Supervisors / uniform mask color is blue

Lexona (F) – Salessa's ex-girlfriend / Naina's references "the Lexona situation," in which Salessa trusted her too quickly, leaving the twins vulnerable to Lexona's betrayal / pronounced *LEXA-na*

The Library (F) – sovereign city-state in the northwestern corner of the continent / built with the sole purpose of housing and cataloging the entirety of Aerthomni's written history / this history is preserved in a system of tunnels under the city called the Catacomb Network, which connects various parts of the city and large chambers called, "sections" / for ease of transportation, also has a Stream Network and Loop Network built into the city's infrastructure / Stream Network is interconnected canals, intricately woven under bridges, around buildings, and through tunnels for those who wish to travel by water / Loop Network is a framework of multicolored hoops that direct and manage the airborne traffic throughout the Library / many of the Library's citizens desire to become Librarians: the Library's primary military, law enforcement, government officials, and healers / individuals find themselves in the Library in one of four ways: (a) born in the Library, (b) accepted by the Library under refugee or exiled status, (c) accepted by the Library for the youth education program and assigned to a Librarian for care and upbringing, or (d) accepted by the Library to train as a Librarian after displaying a high level of skill or intellect in a particular field / has strong political ties and allyship with SunSide / governed by the six Supreme Librarians and the one Prime Librarian / protected by golden gates, and surrounded by a nearly impenetrable forest

Librarians (F) - the Library's primary military, law enforcement, government officials, and healers / devote their lives to the history recorded and preserved in the Catacombs, as well as the wisdom and teachings of the Prime / the various ranks dutifully collect, defend, or manage the information, but their focus remains the same regardless of where in the Library's hierarchy they fall: protect the history, protect the Catacombs, protect the city / Librarians are extensively trained in combat and weapons skills, and have some level of fluency in speaking and understanding Nysabaani / the ranks in ascending order are: Student, Scribe, Gatekeeper, Recorder, Educator, Vice Ambassador, Ambassador, Supreme, Prime / each Librarian rank is associated with a different color tunic as a uniform, and performs a specified function or duty / the only Librarians with a duty or function that differs from that of their colleagues are the Prime's Gatekeeper, who acts as a personal and professional assistant to the Prime, and the Librarians who guard the gates

Lily Beach (F) – island situated on Ardev Ocean between the two known continents / EverEmber's Courtman Tomohiro discovered the island during the War for Bibi Sands / realizing it has greater potential for development and construction, he urged the Court to end the war and relinquish Bibi Sands to the mari / Lily Beach now hosts EverEmber's newly built luxury settlements

Lona (F) – Lona is the second sun and deity of the Four / considered oldest and strongest after Ona in the Mega religion / typically referred to with masculine pronounce, though there is no certainty of gender from scripture / pronounced *LOE-nah*

The Loops / The Library's Loop Network (F) – a framework of multi-colored hoops that direct and manage the airborne traffic throughout the Library / the Stream and the Loop reach the outer neighborhoods of the Library / the last exit of each is only a few minutes' walk from the Library's southern gates

Maksi (F) – late 20's / Uni's coworker / carrot-colored skin / shares common Mega features: pointed ears and solid-gray eyes with no pupils or irises / likes writing poetry and vegetable stew in a corn bowl / dislikes breaking the rules / pronounced *max-ee*

Mari (F) – one of the three human clans / possess anatomy that assist in sub-oceanic travel and existence: fins on their forearms and down the spine, piscine nare slits in place of a human nose, webbed fingers, and internal organs that allow for breathing underwater / built the city of SeaBed at the bottom of Ardev Ocean / the city consists of domed communities with interconnected walkways as well as tubes through which mari can swim from one community to the next if they are in a hurry / the domes allow for their vast agricultural production / governed by Sub-Oceanic Stratocracy: an underwater government led by their military / the military requires all soldiers to name an Undersoldier, one who will replace the soldier in battle should the primary soldier perish / no organized religion or spirituality amongst the mari / engaged in the War for Bibi Sands with the igni for nineteen years until the igni discovered Lily Beach and ended the war / SeaBed now controls Bibi Sands / pronounced *ma-ree*

Mega (F) – humanoid species, said to have evolved from the now-extinct Sprites toward the end of the Era of the Nysabaan / divided into three clans based on internal anatomical variances and differing levels of connectivity to the Radiance: the pixies, the nymphs, and the faeries / common traits amongst all Mega: pointed ears and solid-gray eyes with no pupils or irises / skin colors occur from all over the color spectrum / pixies tend to have the strongest connection to the Radiance, with nymphs having a less connection; present-day faeries have lost their connection to the Radiance as their dependence on technology has grown / spread out across Aerthomni, though the highest concentration of Mega in one place is in SunSide / *Mega* is both the singular and the plural / pronounced *may-ga*

MegaParents / *MegaMother* / *MegaFather* / *SunSidian Monarchy (F)* – one-half of the SunSidian government / ruling monarch(s) of SunSide / referred to as "Father" or "Mother" / greeted with a circled fingers placed over the center of the forehead / monarchy created by theocratic law to act as a liaison to the SunSidian citizenry, who felt SunSide's original sole theocracy had become disconnected from the general public

Mohuway (F) – a term of endearment for children in Nysabaani / pronounced *moe-hoo-way*

Monarchy (NF) – a form of government in which an individual, a monarch, is head of state for life or until abdication

MoonSide (F) – capital city is Arlun / largest state on the continent after SunSide, directly west of PeakHaven Mountains / encompasses all land between the PeakHaven Mountains and Red-Lo River / originally settled by a community of Sprites who evolved into the teri human clan / inhabited by the teri through the Teri Age, though their numbers dwindled as human exploration led the teri to PeakHaven, SeaBed and EverEmber / SunSide invaded MoonSide during the War of New Clans and turned the remaining teri humans into the Doruh, marking the beginning of the new calendar era, Doruh Genesis (DG) / many Doruh captured and removed from MoonSide; brought back to SunSide and enslaved until the Doruh Uprisings in 784 DG / Alphocracy of twenty Alphas formed to govern MoonSide until the next SunSidian invasion in 1381 DG by Tya-Lo the MegaMother, when they were assassinated / following this invasion, SunSide's new Braver forces remained in MoonSide to set up military occupation on captured land, driving many of the Doruh out of MoonSide and into the remainder of the continent /

in 1422 DG, more Doruh were driven from MoonSide, as their land was further captured and faerie settlements built by Hof-Lo the Unflinching

Mosto (NF) – a type of grape juice beverage made from pressed grapes, common in parts of Spain / a typical mari drink, as the development of the fictional mari culture was influenced by Spanish culture

Mt. Mother (F) – the volcano around which the igni settled during the Teri Age / located in the igni human city of EverEmber, on the island known as Roba / heat from the volcano rises into the air, then descends and covers the waters around the island, forming a natural defense, while towering ore walls surrounding the islands form an artificial one / the igni do not display any particular organization in religion or spirituality, yet they do "feed" their dead to Mt. Mother, so that their stone exoskeletons can be liquified and become part of the volcanic rock across Roba

Naina (F) – 20 years old / Salessa's twin sister / Doruh / animal form is a wolf / black hair cut just above shoulders / professional cage fighter in Evic's underground fighting ring known as the Pit / heals quickly, but covered in scars / parents were murdered when Naina and Salessa were 8, by SunSide's Facilitator / they ran from Arlun until they found a small, inconspicuous village called Evic, where they settled / have been hiding from the Facilitator, who is searching for them, since / pronounced *NAN-na*

Natsumi (F) – 2 years old / igni human / Yala's daughter / Kyoko's niece

Neha (F) – young Doruh in Roxie's class / pronounced *NAY-ha*

Nivyan Hollow (F) – large forest forming the southern border of Moon-Side / paths run through the forest from Larso to the docks / where the nymphs and pixies were driven out to, as a result of their complicity in the Doruh Uprisings / powerful epicenter of Radiant energy / pronounced *nih-VY-in*

Nusta. Ista. Hosta. (F) – "Knowledge. History. Truth." / official motto of the Library / in the ancient Nysabaani language / pronounced *NOO-sta. EE-sta. HAU-sta.*

Nymph (F) – one of the three Mega clans / like the humans, said to have evolved from the Sprites toward the end of the Era of the Nysabaan / can access and harness the energy of the Radiance, though they tend to have a weaker connection than the pixies do / share the common physical traits of all Mega: pointed ears and solid-gray eyes with no pupils or irises / many nymphs supported Doruh Liberation and fought alongside them in the Uprisings / were driven from Larso, into Nivyan Hollow, as a result / some nymphs are followers of the Four, the dominant Mega religion / nymph familial naming conventions build names within families around a common vowel (e.g. Symin, Syma, Zynima, Nypa)

Nypa (F) – early forties / Symin's younger sister / nymph / pregnant with third child, with wife Rona

Nysabaan (F) – name for the ancient inhabitants of Aerthomni and Pan-aerth during the Era of the Nysabaan (EN) / largely made up of Sprites, ancestors of the Mega, and the ancient humans, ancestors of the four human clans and the Doruh / spoke an ancient language called Nysabaani

Nysabaani (F) – ancient language that was the *lingua franca* during the Era of the Nysabaan (EN) / modern-day Librarians are taught to understand, translate, and converse in Nysabaani during their training / some national mottos are written in Nysabaani

Occupied Territory (NF) – a political territory placed under the authority of a hostile military

Officers (F) – low-level rank in the Braver hierarchy / report to the Legion Directors / uniform mask color is red

Ona (F) – the oldest and strongest of the Four, deities of the dominant Mega religion / she is the first to rise from the horizon, before Lona,

Throna, and Frona / she is typically referred to with feminine pronouns, though there is no certainty of gender from scripture / pronounced *OE-nah*

Ora (F) – retired Librarian / Unisa's assigned mother / pixie / celadon-colored skin

O'raha (F) – group of devotees formed in 21 DG, after the Twins had a shared vision that they would one day be resurrected / the O'raha continued to keep oral records of future visions the Twins had, passing them down through the generations / eventually disbanded after losing sight of the purpose of the group and becoming extremists

Ore (F) – mysterious black stone or mineral discovered by the SunSidian monarch / revealed in 1621 DG during the Siege of the Castrum / SunSide initially manufactured ore weapons and armor, later including it in roads, buildings, and Larso's infrastructure / the MegaFather also began to distribute the ore to political allies / interrupts the Mega connection to the Radiance, though the size of the ore, the distance from it, and the strength of the Mega's connection to the Radiance all play a role in how each individual is affected by it / the MegaFather used it so much, he earned the nickname—later a slur—"The Ore Monger"

Ovida (F) – former Co-General of the SunSide Revolutionary Forces / orange skin / shares common Mega features: pointed ears and solid-gray eyes with no pupils or irises / widow of Zabeza, Symin's closest friend / disbanded the Revolution after the Siege of the Castrum and opted not to join Symin's group in their continued efforts / Zakia's sister-in-law / pronounced *oe-vee-dah*

Panaerth (F) – one of the two known continents of the All-Sphere / pronounced *pahn-AIRTH*

PeakHaven (F) – one of the three human cities / governed by Super-Montane Stratocracy: headed by the military / populated by the angi human clan / built atop the highest mountain of the PeakHaven mountain range / built a temple called the Holy Summit / settled during the human exploration of the Teri Age / remained neutral during the War for Bibi Sands

PeakHaven Pass (F) – built through the narrowest part of the PeakHaven mountain range / connects Arlun and Larso, the respective capital cities of MoonSide and SunSide.

Picana (F) – MegaMother during the time of Red-Lo's and Drof-Fa's usurping of the throne / said to have been the most just of all MegaParents, fighting for equity amongst the clans and species of SunSide's citizenry / planned to liberate the Doruh before the regicide in 767 DG / pronounced *pee-KAH-nah*

The Pit (F) – Evic's underground fighting ring where Naina makes her living

Pixie (F) – one of the three Mega clans / like the humans, said to have evolved from the Sprites toward the end of the Era of the Nysabaan / can access and harness the energy of the Radiance/ tend to have the strongest connection to the Radiance of all Mega clans / share the common physical traits of all Mega: pointed ears and solid-gray eyes with no pupils or irises / many pixies supported Doruh Liberation and fought alongside them in the Uprisings / were driven from Larso, into Nivyan Hollow, as a result / most pixies are followers of the Four, the dominant Mega religion / pixie familial naming conventions build names within families around a common initial phoneme (e.g. Saith, Saila, Saimiza; Zakia, Zabeza, Zalona)

The Prime (F) – ninth and top rank of the Librarian hierarchy / political, social, and spiritual leader of the Library / uniform is black silk tunic / title currently held by a mari man: Alvaro, Alba's and Ana's uncle / late fifties / shares common mari anatomy: fins on the forearms and down the spine, piscine nare slits in place of a human nose, webbed fingers, and internal organs that allow for breathing underwater / his most unique feature is his eyes; they are somehow warm and cold at the same time

The Radiance (F) – energy fields emitted from organic matter / Mega possess the ability to access and harness the energy for any purpose (dependent on the strength of the Mega's connection to the Radiance and their personal skill level) / in present continuity, faeries have lost their ability to access the Radiance, while the nymphs and pixies have retained it / Pixies tend to have the strongest connection to the Radiance, of all three clans / ore blocks the nymphs' and pixies' abilities to connect to the Radiance / Doruh cannot actively harness the Radiance, but do use Radiant energy when shifting / humans have no connection to the Radiance in present continuity, though they were able to access and harness the Radiance prior to 1 DG, when the human teri clan was transformed into the first generation of Doruh

Radiance-Return (F) – the Mega religion dictates that the Four use energy from the Radiance to build essences prior to life / after death, the essences become energy again and return to the Radiance

Rafael (F) – 23 years old / Prime's Gatekeeper / mari human / arrived at the Library 8 years prior, immediately after his exile from the underwater city of SeaBed / wears a bracelet that originally belonged to his sister, who gave it to him prior to her death / skilled archer and agriculturalist / his sister, Joaquina, was 2 years older than him / shares common mari anatomy: fins on the forearms and down the spine, piscine nare slits in place of a human nose, webbed fingers, and internal organs that allow for breathing underwater

Ray-Mi (F) – late forties / faerie / cornflower-blue skin / many piercings: one ring in each nostril, three on each eyebrow, one on each nipple, five on each side of his body along his ribs, and more / Legion Director in the Braver fleet before he defected and joined the Revolution / owns a sailboat / loves a good myth / pronounced *ray-mee*

Recorder Librarians / Recorders (F) – fourth rank of the Librarian hierarchy / uniform is purple cotton tunics / duties include: accompany Ambassadors on missions to record historical events for the Catacombs, supervise Gatekeepers, record testimonies, managing the intake of those entering the Library, etc.

Red-Lo (F) – faerie / leader of the Faerie Empowerment Forces until 767 DG, when he usurps the SunSidian throne from MegaMother Picana and becomes the MegaFather / started the Red-Lo Royal Dynasty / MegaFather from 767 DG until his death in 809 DG / husband of Drof-Fa / widowed in 783 DG, during the Everlasting Journey / faced the Doruh Uprisings of 784 DG, eventually freeing the species from enslavement after the nymphs and pixies rose up to join the Doruh cause / dealt with unrest in the kingdom until 790 DG when he led a campaign to drive the nymphs and pixies out of Larso as a result of their support of the Doruh / in 792 DG, he followed through on the promise he made to the Assembly in 767 DG, to build the Temple Complex in Larso, using land when nymph and pixie communities once stood / ancestor of current MegaFather Zar-Lo

Red-Lo River (F) – named after Red-Lo the MegaFather / forms the western border of MoonSide

Red-Lo Royal Dynasty (F) – current SunSidian dynasty / started in 767 DG with Red-Lo the MegaFather after the regicide of MegaMother Picana / current MegaFather is forty-sixth member of the Dynasty

Reyu Paleyu / The Vine Demon (F) – mythical demon said to inhabit the HearthBark / body of a lion, with thick, green vines forming a mane around its head and down the spine, as well as forming patterns and designs along its sides and back pronounced *ray-yoo pa-lay-yoo*

Roba (F) – largest island of the igni human city EverEmber / a hub of commerce, recreation, government, and residences of the upper class; also known as "The Mother" / at the center of Roba is Mt. Mother, the volcano around which the igni settled during the Teri Age / heat from the volcano rises into the air, then descends and covers the waters around the island, forming a natural defense, while towering ore walls surrounding the islands form an artificial one / the igni do not display any particular organization in religion or spirituality, yet they do "feed" their dead to Mt. Mother, so that their stone exoskeletons can be liquified and become part of the volcanic rock across Roba / intricate network of streets and roads and lanes / sprawling black stone architecture weaves around projections of volcanic rock erupting from the ground / lanterns depicting popular igni figures, both historical and fictional, hang in doorways / pronounced *ROE-bah*

Rona (F) – early forties / nymph / her wife, Nypa, is pregnant with their third child / Symin's sister-in-law

Roxie (F) – Educator Librarian / nymph / teaches at the Academy / azure skin

Ryokan (NF) – a type of traditional Japanese inn / common in EverEmber, as the development of the fictional igni culture was influenced by Japanese culture

Saila (F) – 35 years old / Theocrat; Member of the Assembly of the Radiance / pixie / green skin, inherited from her father, Saith the Facilitator / powerful connection to the Radiance, also inherited from her father / was sent to live with Saith at the age of 15 due to her mother's illness / nearly six feet tall / one of Alba's closest friends / pronounced *SY-la*

Saimiza (F) – elderly / Head Salver / pixie / Saith's aunt / Saila's great-aunt / passed her green skin and powerful connection to the Radiance on to both Saith and Saila / pronounce *sy-MEE-za*

Saith (F) – late fifties / Facilitator / pixie / lost one arm years prior while protecting the MegaFather; now receives treatment for buildups of Radiant energy that can no longer be expressed through his missing limb / Saila's father / Saimiza's nephew / inherited his green skin and powerful connection to the Radiance from his aunt / pronounced *sy-th* (like "scythe")

Salessa (F) – 20 years old / Naina's twin sister / Doruh / light brown eyes / mid-length hair, dyed auburn / teaches at the village schools and orphanages during the daytime, then works the evening and night shifts at Sultana's Chai Palace / parents were murdered when Naina and Salessa were 8, by SunSide's Facilitator / they ran from Arlun until they found a small, inconspicuous village called Evic, where they settled / have been hiding from the Facilitator, who is searching for them, since / pronounced *sa-LESS-sa*

Salvers (F) – healers

Sangria (NF) – alcoholic beverage originating in Spain and Portugal / sangria traditionally consists of red wine and chopped fruit, often with other ingredients / a typical mari drink, as the development of the fictional mari culture was influenced by Spanish culture

Sari (NF) – a garment consisting of a length of cotton or silk elaborately draped around the body, traditionally worn by women from South Asia / common Doruh attire, as the development of the fictional Doruh culture was influenced by the culture of the South Asian Subcontinent

Scribe Librarians / Scribes (F) – second rank of the Librarian hierarchy / recent graduates of the Academy; initial rank out of training / uniform is pink cotton / duties primarily revolve around assisting Gatekeepers, be that with copying, filing, general tasks, etc.

SeaBed (F) – one of the three human cities / governed by a Sub-Oceanic Stratocracy: headed by the military / populated by the mari human clan / at the bottom of Ardev Ocean / the city consists of domed communities with interconnected walkways as well as tubes through which mari can swim from one community to the next if they are in a hurry / the domes allow for their vast agricultural production / the military requires all soldiers to name an Undersoldier, one who will replace the soldier in battle should the primary soldier perish / no organized religion or spirituality amongst the mari / engaged in the War for Bibi Sands with the igni for nineteen years until the igni discovered Lily Beach and ended the war / SeaBed now controls Bibi Sands

Shalwar Kameez (NF) – shalwars are trousers, common in the South Asia subcontinent, which are atypically wide at the waist but which narrow to a cuffed bottom / the kameez is a long shirt or tunic that often accompanies the shalwar / common Doruh attire, as the development of the fictional Doruh culture was influenced by the culture of the South Asian Subcontinent

Shersa (F) – theocrat / Member of the Assembly of the Radiance at the time of Red-Lo's usurping of the throne in 767 DG

Shifa (F) – granddaughter of Adera's Headwoman / animal form is a bison

Siege of the Castrum (F) – In 1621 DG, with the help of collaborators within the SunSidian government, the SunSide Revolutionary Forces were able to infiltrate the Bravers ranks / the vulnerability of the Bravers and the intelligence gathered during infiltration allowed the Revolution to to besiege the Castrum / the Bravers emerged wielding ore weapons and armor, severing the Mega of the Revolution from the Radiance / after the failure of the Siege, and the loss of the Radiance in Larso, Ovida disbanded the Revolution / Symin and his group opted to continue the fight by attempting to find ways to rid the MegaFather of the ore / those efforts continued for years until they realized they must destroy the ore processing center on Panaerth, for which they would need Doruh assistance

Sila (F) – Sila and Tusa are smaller islands known as "The Sisters"; Sila houses the lower and middle classes, while Tusa is nothing more than dense forest / pronounced *SILL-a*

Siphon (F) – a Mega who can feed off the Radiant energy of others in close proximity

Sonali (F) – Doruh / animal form is a bald-faced hornet / executed for aiding the Revolution during the Siege of the Castrum / buried in the Northern Hills of MoonSide with her father

Sonali's Mother (F) – Doruh / widow / looked after Saila after her move to Larso in the times when Saith was absent

Sovereign City-State (NF) – an independent city with its own sovereignty

Sprites (F) – extinct beings who, toward the end of the Era of the Nysa-baan, evolved into the Mega / not much else is known about them

Stratocracy (NF) – government led by the military

The Stream / The Library's Stream Network (F) – interconnected canals, intricately woven under bridges, around buildings, and through tunnels for those who wish to travel by water / the Stream and the Loop reach the outer neighborhoods of the Library / the last exit of each is only a few minutes' walk from the Library's southern gates

Stones / Currency (F) – polished stones, etched with the MegaFather's portrait are used as currency / a circular blue stone, a triangular green stone, and a rectangular red stone / the currency is designed and manufactured on a mass scale in SunSide / the value of the currency soon overpowered all others, causing it to take over as the dominant form of payment across the continent

Student Librarians / Students (F) - first rank of the Librarian hierarchy / study and train at the Academy / uniform is white cotton

Suikawari (NF) – traditional Japanese game that involves splitting a watermelon with a stick while blindfolded / common in EverEmber, as the development of the fictional igni culture was influenced by Japanese culture

Supreme Librarians / Supremes (F) – eighth rank of the Librarian hierarchy / uniform is blue silk / six Supremes / responsible for lawmaking, governance, and general administration along with the Prime / also responsible for managing the mission assignments of the Ambassadors

Sultana (F) – owner of Sultana's Chai Palace / Salessa's boss / not fond of Naina

Sultana's Chai Palace (F) – where Salessa works as a chaitender for the evening and night shifts

SunSide (F) – capital city is Larso / largest kingdom and political entity on the continent / governed by a Theocratic-Monarchy in which ten theocrats and a monarch rule together, with the theocracy holding slightly more power / encompasses all land to the east of the PeakHaven mountain range / southern border is formed by Nivyan Hollow / most of the kingdom, outside of the capital city, is comprised of smaller villages and the Library's CereCenters / originally settled by a community of Sprites who evolved into the Mega / these Mega further split into the faeries, nymphs, and pixies during the Teri Age / SunSide invaded MoonSide during the War of New Clans and turned the remaining teri humans into the Doruh, marking the beginning of the new calendar era, Doruh Genesis (DG) / many Doruh captured and removed from MoonSide; brought back to SunSide and enslaved until the Doruh Uprisings in 784 DG / after Doruh liberation, the capital plunged into chaos / this lasted until 790 DG, when the majority of the nymphs and pixies were driven out of Larso, into Nivyan Hollow, as a result of their support for the Doruh / with the nymph and pixie communities in Larso mostly emptied, Red-Lo razed them and built the Temple Complex he had promised the Assembly / over the following years, those nymphs, pixies, and Doruh who remained, along with some humans and progressive faeries, slowly started to band together and form the underground SunSide Revolutionary Forces in 793 DG / SunSide invades MoonSide again in 1381 DG, assassinating the MoonSidian Alphocracy and forming the Braver organization to set up a military occupation / in 1422 DG, more Doruh were driven from MoonSide, as their land was further captured and faerie settlements built

SunSide Revolutionary Forces (F) – formed in 793 DG after Red-Lo drove the nymphs and pixies out of Larso / disbanded in 1621 DG after the failed Siege of the Castrum

Supervisors / District Supervisors (F) – upper-level rank in the Braver hierarchy / Legion Directors ("Directors") report to District Supervisors (Supervisors), who then report directly to the Braver General / uniform mask color is green

Syma (F) – Symin's and Nypa's mother / Mega / elderly / pumpkin-colored skin

Symin (F) – early fifties / lost his daughter, Zynima, in 1613 / pink-skin / beard / nymph / shares common Mega features: pointed ears and solid-gray eyes with no pupils or irises / joined the Revolution until its disbanding in 1621, then set out with a group of warriors to continue the fight by attempting to find ways to rid the MegaFather of the ore / those efforts continued for years until they realized they must destroy the ore processing center on Panaerth, for which they would need Doruh assistance / is a Siphon / pronounced *SY-min* (like "Simon")

Tanto (NF) – a type of Japanese short sword / common in EverEmber's military, as the development of the fictional igni culture was influenced by Japanese culture

Tapas (NF) – an appetizer or snack in Spanish cuisine / tapas can be combined to make a full meal / a typical mari dish, as the development of the fictional mari culture was influenced by Spanish culture

Teri (F) – ancient human clan / direct evolution of the ancient humans who lived during the Era of the Nysabaan / their numbers dwindled as human exploration led the teri to PeakHaven, SeaBed and EverEmber, evolving further into the angi, mari, and igni clans, respectively / SunSide invaded MoonSide during the War of New Clans and turned the remaining teri humans into the Doruh, marking the beginning of the new calendar era, Doruh Genesis (DG) / pronounced *teh-ree* (like "Terry")

Teri Age (F) – calendar era between the Era of the Nysabaan (EN) and Doruh Genesis (DG) / noted as "TA" / era during which humans and Mega were the dominant species / era during which Nysabaani is no longer the dominant language / era during which human exploration begins, leading to the splintering of the teri clan into the angi, mari, and igni; the remaining teri humans settle in MoonSide / runs until 2579 TA, the year prior to the invasion of MoonSide during the War of New Clans, which marked the creation of the Doruh species from the remaining teri humans

Temple Complex (F) – idea for massive complex of shrines and temples, devoted to the Four, originally presented to the MegaParents by the Members of the theocracy / generations of MegaParents denied the motion on the grounds of economic impracticality / as he usurps the throne in 767 DG, Red-Lo promises to build it as his first royal act as MegaFather / due to personal turmoil, followed by the Everlasting Journey, the Doruh Uprisings, and further unrest, it isn't actually built for another twenty-five years, until 792 DG / no greater symbol of Sun-Side's devotion to its theocracy exists than the Temple Complex / tall buildings house chapels, feast halls, council chambers and classrooms / towering statues, monuments, and shrines to the Four are featured in designated areas all around the vast compound / the outer rim is guarded by gates and pylons, and an ablution river runs around the center courtyard / the Complex now stands as a long-enduring token of partnership between the two halves of the government

The Theater (F) – rests at the top of the highest tower in the Castrum / the MegaFather's favorite room. and the one in which he spends most of his time / the floor is polished stone, with shimmering gems embedded into it / along the south wall is a line of portraits / across from the portraits is a wall made entirely of treated, protective glass, floor to ceiling / the Facilitator and the MegaFather often stand at the window wall, gazing upon the citizens, monitoring the city.

Theocracy (NF) – a system of government in which religious leaders rule in the name of a god or gods.

Theocratic-Monarchy (F) – SunSide's unique system of government, in which two halves rule together / SunSide's original government was a sole theocracy / over time, the citizenry began to feel that, in its servitude to the Four, the theocracy had become disconnected from the general public / the throne was installed as a liaison between the citizens and the Assembly / while much of the monarch's power is similar and equal to that of the Members of the Assembly, the theocracy holds slightly more power, as theocratic law allows them the ability to abolish the monarchy with a unanimous vote amongst the Members

Throna (F) – Throna is the third sun and deity of the Four / considered the youngest and weakest after Frona in the Mega religion / typically referred to with masculine pronounce, though there is no certainty of gender from scripture / pronounced *THROE-nah*

Tomohiro (F) – a Courtman of EverEmber / igni / one of seven elected officials, known as the Court / during the War for Bibi Sands, discovered the island Lily Beach / realizing it has greater potential for development and construction, he urged the Court to end the war and relinquish Bibi Sands to the mari / Lily Beach now hosts EverEmber's newly built luxury settlements

The TreeKeeper (F) – a myth told to children about a grotesque, deformed figure who carries essences to the World Beyond, but will refuse to do so if the essence was a misbehaving child in its youth

Tusa (F) – Sila and Tusa are smaller islands known as "The Sisters" / nothing more than dense forest, an untouched look at EverEmber from before human exploration / popular with explorers and archaeologists / pronounced *TOO-sa*

The Twins (F) – deities of the Doruh religion / a brother and a sister who were the first naturally-conceived Doruh / born to Adera, a pixie, and her human lover, Anhum, who was originally a member of the teri human clan and was later transformed into the first generation of Doruh during the War of New Clans / the Twins are prophesied to be resurrected one day to prevent catastrophe / the time of their resurrection is said to be identified by the birth of two sets of Doruh twins who will shift into four different animals / genetically, all Doruh twins must shift into the same animal, so the varying animal forms of two sets of twins will signal the return of the Twins

Tya-Lo (F) – faerie / MegaMother and thirty-first member of the Red-Lo Royal Dynasty / known for the invasion of MoonSide in 1380 DG, and the assassination of the Alphocracy in 1381 DG / pronounced *tie-a*

Undersoldier (F) – requirement of the mari military / all soldiers must name an Undersoldier, one who will replace them in battle should they perish

Unisa (F) – 23 years old / Gatekeeper Librarian in the Catacomb section *Witness* / angi human / shares common angi anatomy: wings that look like steel in color and texture / accepted for the Library's youth education program at the age of four / raised by an adopted mother, a pixie named Ora / pronounced *oo-NEE-sa*

Uzair (F) – Doruh chauffeur manager / the Library has an agreement with his caravan for transport on official missions

Vice Ambassador Librarians / Vice Ambassadors (F) – sixth rank of the Librarian hierarchy / uniform is green linen tunics / assist Ambassador Librarians in preparation of, during, and after their missions to witness historical events and record them for the Library's Catacombs

The Vine Demon/ Reyu Paleyu (F) – mythical demon said to inhabit the HearthBark / body of a lion, with thick, green vines forming a mane around its head and down the spine, as well as forming patterns and designs along its sides and back pronounced *ray-yoo pa-lay-yoo*

Vy-Ro (F) – faerie / Braver General / long mustache and puce-colored skin / descendent of Hay-Ro / pronounced *VY-roe*

The War of New Clans (F) – SunSide invaded MoonSide during the War of New Clans and turned the remaining teri humans into the Doruh, marking the beginning of the new calendar era, Doruh Genesis (DG) / many Doruh captured and removed from MoonSide; brought back to SunSide and enslaved until the Doruh Uprisings in 784 DG

The War for Bibi Sands (F) – referred to as "the War" / started in 1603 and ended in 1622 / the igni and mari clans engaged in a territorial dispute over ownership of the island Bibi Sands / the war ended when the Courtman Tomohiro discovered a larger, more desirable island and relinquished Bibi Sands to the mari

Witness (F) – section of the Library's Catacomb Network in which primary historical records and eyewitness testimonies to historical events are stored / Unisa is the Gatekeeper assigned to this section

The World Beyond (F) – final resting place of the essences of this world

Xo-Rah (F) – faerie / a theocrat of the Assembly / pronounced *ZOR-ah*

Yala / Kanako (F) – 32 years old / igni human / Kyoko's sister / Natsumi's mother / came to the Library with Kyoko when she was 16 and Kyoko was 12

Zabeza (F) – pixie / Symin's closest friend / Zakia's older brother / Zalona's son / Ovida's husband / abducted and murdered in 1612 / pronounced *za-BEE-za*

Zakia (F) – 20 years old / pixie / Zabeza's sister / Zalona's daughter / prodigy of harnessing the energy of the Radiance / royal purple skin / joined Symin's group at the age of thirteen, after the Siege of the Castrum / was four years old when her brother was murdered / pronounced *za-KEE-ah*

Zalona (F) – early sixties / pixie / Zakia's and Zabeza's mother / owns an inn in Larso, under which is the Bunker / pronounced *za-LOE-na*

Zar-Lo (F) – faerie / current MegaFather and forty-sixth member of the Red-Lo Royal Dynasty / discovered the mysterious metallic substance known as ore / despite its Radiant energy-dampening properties, Zar-Lo manufactured ore weapons and armor, later including it in roads, buildings, and Larso's infrastructure / earned the nickname — later a slur — "The Ore Monger"

Zynima (F) – nymph / Symin's daughter / Kruga's fiance / spent time on the ocean and discovered a flower to use as a cure for seasickness / abducted and murdered in 1613 / nineteen years old at the time of her death / worked in the MegaFather's laboratories with Kruga / pronounced *zy-NEE-ma*

ACKNOWLEDGEMENTS

THE WORK OF FICTION YOU'RE holding in your hands wouldn't have been possible without contribution from everyone named in this section. Writing a book is more than just storytelling. It is an accomplishment that takes development, refinement, and, above all, encouragement. The individuals named here provided one or more of all of these. I give gratitude...

To my wife, Seenu. Not an hour or a minute or a moment passes without my thinking of how lucky I am to have you. Each day that the sun rises, my love for you grows. This has been the case since May 1, 2018. Your unbreakable support and boundless love is the anchor of my devotion to you. Never forget: you are the ember that gives warmth to my heart and light to my soul.

To my parents. Raising a child is possibly the hardest job in this world, particularly a child as hard-headed and unpredictable as myself. But there hasn't been a day since my birth that I haven't felt loved and encouraged and supported. By all accounts, you've mastered parenting. I love you so much.

To my brother and sister-in-law, Bilal and Anusha. One of the integral themes of this novel is the love amongst siblings. I could never have weaved a word of it without having had the experience myself. Thank you for the inspiration, thank you for never giving up on me, and thank you for two of the greatest gifts I, and this world, have ever received.

To Ayaan and Aleeza. One day, when you're old enough (in shaa Allah), Chachu will let you read his first book. The hope is, by then, you have a packed bookshelf and a love of literature. Chachu loves you both so much.

To both my maternal and paternal grandparents. The roots of our family tree, and the ones who taught me the true meaning of bravery. None of my characters could have taken their fictional journeys, had I not known of your courageous, real ones. I, and generations of descendants after me, owe everything to you and your decisions.

To the many aunts, uncles, cousins, and other extended family members who've had such a central role in my upbringing, and the shaping of my worldview. I'm lucky to have been raised as a swimmer treading in an ocean of love.

To Daniel Tilley. Raging wildfires begin with the smallest sparks. My publishing dreams were only realized after you sparked my passion for writing once again. I am forever indebted to you. A talented critique partner and photographer, a humble mentor and person, and above all, the very best kind of friend. Thank you for everything, Daniel.

To my readers: Noelle Riley, Rose Thomson, and Rebecca Coffindaffer. The story could've never been whittled down to its core without you. Thank you for all of your time and efforts!

To the consultants of my world-building: Gee Rothvoss, Maseeha Seedat, Ryota Ochi, and 凌危贊 of Shiranui Editorial. There's a significant kind of hesitation when building fictional cultures based on some of the richest and most beautiful cultures in the real-world. I was desperate to capture so many aspects of Japanese and Spanish tradition and society as authentically, and with as much dignity, as possible. I hope I succeeded. Thanks to all of you, I hope the wonderful people of Japan and Spain can feel proud of the igni and mari characters we see in the book.

To my cartographer: Alexandra. Thank you so very much for bringing the All-Sphere to the page!

To my very first friend on Bookstagram, and in the indie publishing world: Katrina N. Lewis. I don't think I have the words to genuinely express all you've done for me. You gave me confidence when I needed it, you gave me guidance in crafting Unisa's experience as a Black woman who grew up away from her culture and home, and you supported me when I was just some random guy popping into your DMs with a thousand questions about publishing. And you never made me feel rejected. Your grace, your patience, and your friendship are unmatched. Thank you, Katrina, for everything.

To my developmental editor, mentor, and very good friend: LJ Stanton. It truly feels as though fate was at work the day I happened to come across a Reddit post from a young woman who had posted about publishing her debut novel. I had started writing my own debut novel just a few days before I came across her post. *Something* took hold of my hand and forced me to message her with thousands of questions, and not only did she respond to each one, but she encouraged me to start my own author instagram account for marketing. Every connection, every conversation, and every ounce of support I've received since has been thanks to LJ. There hasn't been a day that's gone by in *three years*, that I've encountered a writing, editing, or publishing problem, and haven't thought "What would LJ advise me to do?" LJ has never failed to make me feel like I can do anything. She is a light in this world, and truly one of the most talented storytellers I've ever known. Thank you, LJ, for being one of my dearest friends, for the endless guidance, and for never letting me forget that anything is possible.

To my copy editor and friend: Rebecca Scharpf at Scrollwork Edits. If anyone reads through this novel and realizes how polished and meticulous the editing is, you can thank Rebecca for that. I certainly do. Rebecca's professionalism and glaring expertise is like nothing I've seen before in the publishing world, and I mean that for both independent and traditionally-published books. She is an editing master and extraordinaire, and to put it frankly, your book would be lucky to be touched by her. Mine was. Thank you, Rebecca, for applying your mastery of the written word to my humble little tale, and launching it to heights I never knew it was capable of.

To my friend and editor: Emmie Hamilton. It is difficult, or nearly impossible, not to fall in love with Emmie Hamilton's inspired story-telling. I first reached out to Emmie on the day of her debut novel's release. As I did with so many, I bombarded her with questions regarding independent publishing, and was met with the most open-hearted, graceful, and generous responses I'd ever received. Not only is Emmie a master at crafting a story (read her books, please), but she is, sincerely, one of the most genuine and warm people I've ever had the pleasure of speaking to. We've connected through a lot of humor and a few unfortunate typos over the years, and one thing has remained true through all of it: Emmie Hamilton's brilliance is not only a blessing to the writing community, but to this world. Thank you, Emmie, for every word and DM and voice message we've exchanged over the past three years. This book would've never made it to release, and I never would've become a published author, without you.

And finally, last, but most certainly not least, to the two greatest book besties I could have ever asked for: Ciara Hartford and Essie Rowley. I think, for the first time in my life, I'm speechless. How does one put into words what is meaningful about his friendship with two people who are the lighthouses that guide his ship to shore when he finds himself adrift? How many times throughout this writing and publishing journey have I found myself in emotional turmoil, only for the two of you to reach into the depths and bring me back? How do I qualify or quantify or verbalize that if I can raise the flag of being a published author, it is only because I'm hoisted on your shoulders?

In the early days of my Author Instagram, I somehow came across a single piece of art that, unbeknownst to me at the time, would change my life. It spoke to me, and I knew at that moment, whoever drew it, was the artist I would want to design my book's cover. Not because my book was worthy (to this day, I know it isn't), but because I knew that I had found the most talented artist I had ever seen. That was Ciara Hartford, and I will forever be indebted to her for agreeing to be my cover designer, because what followed has become one of the dearest friendships I've ever known. Thank you for agreeing to do, not only this cover, but the covers for all of my books moving forward.

Shortly after, I again happened across a post about a book called *People Like Us*; it was a short summer romance story from a new-ish writing account. This wasn't the typical genre that I read, but something was driving me to it, telling me that it was special. And that, "something," was right. Every word that Essie Rowley carefully places onto the page, from *People Like Us*, to *I'm Telling the Truth*, to *Papercut*, and beyond, is filled with her indelible and unique style. She may not write fantasy, but everything Essie writes is magic. Beyond her storytelling talents, Essie is the kind of friend and person that brings light to everyone who has the good fortune to interact with her. She is kind and humble and selfless, and we are all better, just for being alive in the world at the same time as Essie Rowley.

Ciara and Essie, thank you for reminding me that while so much can be done alone, none of it is worth it without the friends who keep you going. You both kept me going when I needed you most. Writing, editing, and publishing aside, you both have become two of the greatest friends I could've ever asked for, and I cannot wait to continue supporting you, in any and all endeavors, for many years to come.

ABOUT THE AUTHOR

ZAID HASAN IS AN AUTHOR who enjoys crafting epic Science Fantasy stories. He's written many books throughout his life, none of which you've read because they're buried in a box somewhere in his storage unit.

In 2021, however, Zaid started to outline a story that he felt could be worthy of publication one day, and that epic tale became his debut novel: The Ore Monger.

Outside of storytelling, Zaid is a happily-married husband, a Muslim, a devoted cat dad, a loving uncle, a tattoo enthusiast, a comic book collector (DC Comics), and an obnoxiously proud New Yorker.

Follow Zaid Hasan's projects on his website and his instagram. Or reach out to him at his official email address below, he would love to hear from you.

www.hasanfantasy.com
instagram.com/hasanfantasy
contact@hasanfantasy.com

OTHER WORKS BY INDIE AUTHORS

Ciara Hartford @the_zephi
The House of Starling
The House of Amfithere

Essie Rowley @essierowley
People Like Us
I'm Telling The Truth
Papercut

Katrina N. Lewis @authorknl
Heavy is the Head: Love & War
Heavy is the Head: Kingdom Come

Emmie Hamilton @authoremmiehamilton
Chosen to Fall
Fated to Burn
Destined to Rise
When Stars Become Shadows

LJ Stanton @stanton.lj
The Dying Sun
The Pantheon Prophet

Rebecca Scharpf @scrollworkedits
Dark Wolf
Gray Blizzard
Lost Pup
Young warrior
Black Night
Bleak War
Lone Commander

Roger Sandri @roger_sandri_wordslinger
The Den of Stone

www.ingramcontent.com/pod-product-compliance
Lightning Source LLC
Chambersburg PA
CBHW021835010726
47493CB00005B/1411